VERMILION SUNRISE

A Novel

for CARL —
May your life always
be full of BOOKS and ADVENTURE!

Lydia P. Brownlow

Lydia P. Brownlow

ISBN: 978-1-960146-33-5 (hard cover)
        978-1-960146-34-2 (soft cover)

Edited by: Melisa Graham

Warren publishing

Published by Warren Publishing
Charlotte, NC
www.warrenpublishing.net
Printed in the United States

for Austin and Luke

CHAPTER 1

Leigh closed her eyes against the nausea, but it didn't help. She huddled in the corner of the cramped shower, and her stomach somersaulted in revolt.

The peach-colored slime that encased her body was cold; the water spraying her feet, even colder. She tore off the thin scarf wrapped around her hair and crawled closer to the spray, letting the water wash over her head and down her back. The droplets thrummed against her skin like little pickaxes, and the nausea won.

She threw up.

Twice.

The watery yellow vomit sloshed down the drain along with the slime from her body. She shivered. Her stomach muscles spasmed—this time with no tangible result. She was empty.

The shower water stopped. Retreating to the corner, Leigh bent her legs and wrapped her arms around them. Through the transparent stall, she could see the central object in the small room: an empty cryosleep pod, its tubes and wires connected to spigots and outlets in the wall. Near the ceiling, a timer counted down in large red numbers:

05:49:38

05:49:37

05:49:36

Leigh rubbed her eyes. Pain seared through her forehead to the base of her neck. She wanted to lie down and curl into a ball. She wanted to wish it all away—the pain, the nausea, the room, everything.

But wishes were useless.

She tried to stand. Dizziness drove her to her knees, so she crawled out of the shower and into the cryorecovery room. She sat up, panting from the effort. Water ran off her skin and pooled on the bare white floor. Leigh blinked, her eyes struggling to focus in the bright artificial light. She squeezed the excess water from her hair, and the puddle beneath her expanded.

Her body still looked seventeen, but she felt like a newborn baby emerging from the womb, not knowing where she was or what to do next.

Someone was talking in the background. Her ears were clogged, filled with a dull, pulsing sound. She pinched her nose, closed her mouth, and exhaled. Her right ear cleared. She tried again, and the left one cleared as well.

The background voice echoed in the small room: "… arriving in the Epsilon Eridani system. The cryosleep pod has protected you from radiation and allowed you to travel unharmed. You are all teenagers. People under the age of twenty are the only ones who can physically handle the stress of cryosleep, and young children were not considered for the mission.

"Cryosleep is not sleep; it's a state of torpor like a hibernating bear. After thirteen years in hibernation, your body will need time to adjust. Stand up slowly when you are ready, then make your way to the other side of the room. This message will repeat at three-minute intervals until you move the red-and-black switch to the off position."

The disembodied voice paused, but the throbbing in Leigh's head grew. She'd been traveling in cryosleep? For thirteen years?

Impossible.

She needed to get home, to see her mom, to apologize for not finishing the planting.

Leigh reached up around her neck and clutched at … nothing. Her necklace! Where was her necklace?

She held out her arms and looked at her naked body. No jewelry. Nothing but bare skin covered with a pink rash. She ran her hands down her legs, wiping away water and feeling the bumpiness. The rash didn't hurt, but it was getting worse, darkening from pink to red.

A door slid open, and a woman walked into the room with a bundle rolled up under one arm. She wore a faded blue shirt and dingy red overalls patched with garish orange material. Even in that outfit, the woman was imposing—powerfully built with dark eyes that examined Leigh as if she were a lab specimen.

Leigh's headache intensified as she tried to stand. Her legs shook.

"Don't get up," said the stranger. "You're having a bad reaction to the cryosleep withdrawal." She put down her bundle and flipped the red-and-black switch as instructed in the video. "We'll be landing in less than six hours. You need to be ready." The woman walked over to the far wall, popped open a drawer, and reached into it. A large screen embedded in the wall glowed white, then displayed a single image: an alien planet covered in water.

Leigh tried to speak, but nothing happened. Her lips pursed like a fish, opening and closing, emitting no sound. It was as if her brain had forgotten how to turn thoughts into words.

"The cryosleep takes a while to wear off," said the stranger. "Your muscles will be stiff, your thoughts slow. You'll have trouble talking. That's normal."

This was *not* normal. Leigh stared at the screen, her attention drawn to the image of the watery planet, the blueness of its surface streaked with white-gray clouds—a bright, shining sphere surrounded by the blackness of space.

"You've had a long journey," said the stranger, "but it's almost over." She swiped her hand across the screen. The planet rotated, and Leigh could see one large land mass and hundreds of islands, though most of the surface was blue.

The woman walked back toward Leigh, crouched down, and handed her a chamois cloth. "You'll be landing on one of the islands," she said.

Leigh needed to escape, to get away from this woman and what she was saying. She tried to scoot sideways, but all that did was make things worse; now she was in the corner. She tried again to speak, and nothing happened. Trapped and voiceless, Leigh was out of options. She took the proffered cloth and dried her face, keeping an eye on the stranger in front of her.

The woman wasn't very old, early twenties at the most, yet she exuded the quiet confidence of someone at ease with her place in the world. Her black hair was pulled back, held away from her face by a lime-green bandana. Her expression remained serious, the way someone looks when they have a job to do and are determined to do it well.

With no warning, the woman reached out and grabbed Leigh's arm, her fingers pressing hard. Leigh flinched, then managed to hold steady as the woman twisted her arm one way and another, studying it from different angles. The stranger's flawless brown skin accentuated the almost translucent whiteness of her own; it drew attention to the raised red blotches covering Leigh's naked body.

"Does this rash itch?" the woman asked.

Leigh shook her head.

"Looks inflamed but feels cool to the touch. That's good." She released her grip. "Sorry, you must be a bit confused."

Leigh stared mutely. "A bit confused" didn't begin to cover it.

"I'm not supposed to be here," said the stranger, "but you need help. You're sick." She grabbed the cloth and dried Leigh's hair. "I don't know how much of the announcement you heard, and I'm sure you don't remember leaving Earth. The cryosleep steals those memories. The cryo's not perfect, but it got you here, barely aging at all ... only five days for every Earth year."

The woman finished drying Leigh's hair and sat back, twisting the cloth in her hands. "You traveled on the *Khepri*—the fastest starship ever created—going almost eighty percent the speed of light, from Earth's solar system to this one. It's explained in the video." She gestured toward the screen, where the alien planet still shone amid the darkness of the universe. "Watch the video as soon as you feel up to it. Or ask the colonists already on the surface. They can tell you."

Leigh continued to stare, her disbelief warring with something worse: fear. Fear she was hearing the truth. Once again, she reached for her necklace, and once again it wasn't there. She placed her hands around her neck and mimed that something was missing.

But the woman misunderstood. "Hey!" she said. "No one is trying to kill you." The stranger grabbed Leigh's hands. "Don't you get it? You're part of humanity's first settlement in another solar system. You *volunteered* to be a colonist."

That wasn't true.

Leigh broke free and swung her fist, aiming to strike the woman's face or neck, but the stranger moved quickly, stepping back. Leigh tried to stand, to get in a defensive posture, to use those self-defense lessons she'd never wanted to take. But dizziness swamped her, and she crumpled onto the floor.

"Don't be an idiot," the woman said. "I'm trying to help. You need to feel better before we land, and I don't have much time."

Leigh put her palms on her temples and pressed hard, trying to soothe her headache so she could think. She had fought against being shipped off to boarding school in another state; there was no way she'd volunteered to leave behind the entire planet, to abandon everything and everyone she knew. But this was not a dream. Even in her nightmares, Leigh never left home.

"The planet's habitable," continued the stranger. "No spacesuits. No domes or special habitats. And you're the third landing party to arrive on the island. So ... that's good news. Already people there to help." She rummaged in the pockets of her overalls. "Also good—the colony's on a stable part of the planet. No volcanoes. No quakes. ... Ah, here we go."

She withdrew a handful of items from her hip pocket, shook a small bottle of bubbly green liquid, and handed it to Leigh. "This should do it." The woman dumped the other items back in her pocket and unrolled a thin mat onto the floor. "Go ahead, drink it. I have to get back to the flight deck. You're on a shuttle now, not the *Khepri*, and the shuttle won't land itself."

Leigh grasped the small bottle of green liquid. She watched the bubbles settle to the bottom, then rise and pop one at a time. Something was wrong, very wrong, and she wasn't well enough to figure it out.

Should she drink the green liquid? The stranger was lying to her, but maybe not about that. Did she believe the woman at all?

As if in response to the unspoken questions, the stranger unhitched a strap of her overalls and fished out something from a hidden pocket behind the bib. It was a small russet-colored rock.

"This is from the surface." She held out the rock, offering it to Leigh for inspection. "It's beautiful down there."

Leigh reached again for her missing necklace, wanting to show her own rock, to explain why, of all the things the woman had said, this was the one she understood. But the necklace wasn't there.

She looked up into the stranger's eyes and saw no hint of deception. The small rock—unremarkable in its dull reddish-brown color and its uneven shape—lay cradled in the woman's palm as if it were a precious gem. Everything else might have been a lie, but her reverence for the ugly rock rang with the truth.

Leigh had made decisions based on less.

She unscrewed the cap, raised the bottle to her lips, and gulped the green liquid. The concoction slid down her throat like jalapeño juice—liquid fire. She sputtered, then coughed, surprised to hear herself capable of making sound.

She tried to speak, but words would still not come.

"Lie down on the mat," said the stranger. "I've got to get back to flying this thing, but first I'll grab you some clothes."

Leigh lay down as the empty bottle slipped from her hands. Then everything went dark.

CHAPTER 2

Hours later, Leigh prepared for landing. The pilot in the overalls was nowhere to be seen. But that green liquid—whatever it was—had made a difference. Leigh's headache was gone, her thoughts cloudy but clearing. The rash remained only on her stomach, and that was now covered with clothing.

The rest of her skin looked normal, but it felt like she'd been rubbed with sandpaper, scoured until the nerve receptors were closer to the surface. Her lightweight shirt and pants were soft and comfortable, but she was aware of every fiber touching her skin. Even the stagnant air in the small room tingled against her face.

As instructed by the informational video, Leigh grabbed her meager belongings: four vials of nutrient-dense liquid meals and a dark-blue drawstring backpack with three keepsakes from home. She dropped two of the vials into her bag and slid the others into the large pocket on the side of her pants. The vials contained a chalky-white liquid. Fingers crossed it would taste better than the bottle of muddy brown "rehydration meal." Although she'd managed to drink every drop of the salty sludge, it was not something she'd like to rely upon for survival.

Survival.

She was about to land on an alien planet and try to survive.

She could not believe it.

The timer on the wall reached 00:05:00 and flashed a brilliant orange. Leigh sat down in the seat provided for landing, strapped in, and held the drawstring bag tightly on her lap. So far, everything was happening the way the video had said it would. That should've been reassuring; instead, it made her feel at the mercy of forces she did not understand.

Her seat shook. For a moment, she wished the room had a window so she could see what was happening. Then a loud roar penetrated the floor, followed by a heavy thump. As the shaking increased, Leigh decided it was better not to see anything. She clung to her bag, closed her eyes, and focused on breathing—the one thing she could control.

***

A few minutes later, the shuttle landed. By the time Leigh extricated herself from the safety straps and stood up, the door to the cryorecovery room slid open. Looping the bag over her shoulders, Leigh followed exit lights down a dimly lit hallway and stepped into a nearby airlock. Six more colonists crowded into the small vestibule with her. No one spoke, though several opened their mouths as if to try. One girl stared straight ahead; other colonists glanced at those nearby. Leigh could hear the nervous breathing of the boy in front of her.

A loud buzzer sounded, and the door behind them clicked into the locked position. Yellow lights flashed overhead. The sour taste of bile rose in Leigh's throat. She swallowed it down, closed her eyes, and flattened her palm against the wall of the airlock. These were her first minutes with her shipmates. Not a good time to be throwing up or passing out.

It *was* time to act fine-thank-you-very-much on the outside while her stomach churned and her brain fought against what was happening. External calm masking internal turmoil—Leigh could do it. She'd had plenty of practice with that particular skill.

Swallowing once more, she opened her eyes and took her hand off the wall. A second buzzer sounded, and the lights flashed red. She held her breath as the shuttle's outer door slowly grated its way into a slot in the hull. It clunked loudly, stuck for a moment … then began moving again. The rattling noise echoed in the airlock, and Leigh wondered why anyone would build a state-of-the-art spaceship, then outfit its shuttlecraft with a crappy door.

No time for distractions.

The door stopped moving, and she shuffled toward the exit, the second person to climb down the ladder. The rungs were slippery. Leigh held the railings with both hands, mentally counting each rung as she descended.

… eleven,

twelve,

thirteen,

fourteen.

At fifteen, she stepped off the ladder and took her first footsteps on the planet. Her legs moved sluggishly, but her feet stepped firmly on the rocky surface.

She was standing on an alien world.

Nearby, a girl with short curly hair gulped lungfuls of air and looked around in bug-eyed wonder. The girl was not, in fact, slumped on the ground, turning blue with oxygen deprivation. Leigh unclenched her fists.

She took a small breath.

And another.

Inhaling a little more deeply, she moved away from the shuttle as more colonists exited the airlock. The nitrogen and carbon monoxide percentages in this atmosphere were lower than on Earth, with the oxygen and argon higher. Her lungs didn't notice. The air felt normal. Hot and humid, but normal.

The same could *not* be said for the gravity. The increase was slight but noticeable. Leigh walked with the awkwardness of a triathlete transitioning from the bike to the run. She stumbled, blinking in the sunlight, her legs adjusting, but her eyes unprepared for the onslaught of blue—sea and sky in every direction.

They had landed on an enormous plateau atop a cliff overlooking the water. Leigh scanned the dark-blue expanse, presumably the "large ocean of nondrinkable salt water" mentioned in the video. She saw no sign of land except for the island she stood upon—an unsurprising view on a planet 89 percent covered by water, but the sight still made her head swim.

Juxtaposed with the midnight blue of the ocean, the sky was pale, a light blue flecked with wispy white clouds, reminiscent of a winter sky over the Texas prairie. The planet's star, Epsilon Eridani, sat low on the horizon. It shone brightly, much like the Earth's sun.

But it was not the Sun.

This was not Earth.

And there was no sign of the colony she was supposed to be joining. Not much sign of life at all.

The dusty landing plateau was covered with russet-brown dirt, rocks, and little else. Tall dark-purple grass sprouted here and there and lined the plateau's edges along with a mix of shorter, oddly shaped plants. Some had fronds like a seven-fingered hand with a hole in the middle; others had small thick leaves the shape of perfect squares. But the plants were green, the square-leaf plants a deeper green than she'd ever seen. And though the tall grass was purple, it looked like grass.

She bent down to get a closer look, and the curly-haired girl walked by, grinning and emitting a sound that might have been a laugh. Leigh froze, fearful she'd been recognized, but the girl moved on, grinning at other colonists the same way. No need to be paranoid.

They were strangers here.

The cryosleep had erased their recent memories, including memories of volunteering for the mission, memories of meeting one another when preparing to leave Earth. And yet ... the cryosleep had not touched memories further in the past. Leigh's family had often made the news, usually not in a good way. The peak of their notoriety had been years ago, and the details of *those* memories were certainly intact.

She pulled her hair back and tied it in a knot, then reconsidered and let it hang loose. People might remember those times; they might remember the name Leigh Crawford, but she looked different now—older, her cheeks thinner, her hair longer and its natural brown. It was unlikely anyone would recognize her face.

Being strangers could have its advantages. If she used a different name, no one would know anything about her.

She shook off thoughts of the past—the present was enough!—and studied the coastline. Beach and cliffs stretched in both directions, while mountains loomed in the distance. No telling how far they needed to go for the "two sources of fresh drinking water, which should be treated every eight days to be safe."

Safe! Hard to know what that word meant anymore.

Hands trembling, Leigh pushed a strand of hair out of her eyes, then fastened shut the pocket where she'd stashed two vials of the liquid meals. Adjusting the straps on her bag, she listened to the shuttle's door grind its way into the closed and locked position. All twenty members of her landing party had disembarked.

She made a quick count—six girls, including her, and fourteen boys. Some stayed near the shuttle; others wandered toward the edge of the plateau for a better view of the beach below. Everyone walked cautiously, getting a feel for the higher gravity.

"Get back!" shouted a deep voice from behind the shuttle. "Get away from the cliff!"

Rocks crumbled. The colonists near the edge ran for safety—all except the small redheaded boy farthest away. With no time to run, he bent his knees and launched himself toward safer ground.

Part of the cliffside gave way, and a sea of dust swallowed the young boy in midair. Several colonists cried out. Leigh stood silently, her cryosleep-riddled brain unable to translate emotions into words, her thoughts as murky as the dark swirls of alien dirt in front of her.

A gust of wind blew across the plateau. She shut her eyes and held up her hands to block the dust. The wind slowly subsided, as did the sounds of the rockslide. An eerie hush enveloped the plateau as the airborne dirt settled on Leigh's skin.

When she opened her eyes, a hazy mist hung in the air, and she could see the boy's body on the ground. He lay facedown with his feet dangling over empty air. His hands moved, fingers clawing at the soil and rocks.

Leigh gasped in relief, her first sound since disembarking.

She ran toward the boy, then stopped as the noise of crumbling dirt returned. She couldn't see where it was happening, but she could hear it.

"Can you move?" Leigh shouted at the boy. She could speak!

The boy nodded but otherwise stayed immobile as an avalanche of rocks hit the beach below. The ground reverberated. Dust boiled up, once again clogging the air, and he disappeared from view.

"Don't stand up!" yelled Leigh. "Crawl this way." She walked into the dust cloud. Her heart pounded. It wasn't bravery that kept her moving; it was fear—fear that she didn't have the courage to help, fear that her first act on the planet would be something to be ashamed of. "Over here!" she called.

Her eyes watered. Squinting, she could see the young boy's outline on the ground. He crawled slowly, but he was moving. "I'm here!" she yelled and took a few more steps in his direction.

He collided with her legs.

Leigh helped the boy to his feet and led him away from the edge. Her hands still shook. But her heart no longer felt like it was shaking too.

As they emerged from the dust, she let go of the boy's arm. Other than torn pants and a bloody nose, the young redhead was unharmed.

Unbelievable.

But then, everything about the past six hours had been unbelievable.

The boy wiped the grime from his face and shook dirt from his hair. Leigh did the same. Together, they walked farther from the edge, and the boy whispered, "Thanks."

Leigh nodded, but her attention was no longer on him; it was on the rest of the colonists, all of whom faced the shuttlecraft, its gleaming white metal dominating the plateau. They were staring at the person beside it. Not the pilot—the woman in overalls was nowhere in sight. Instead, a broad-shouldered boy with black skin, wearing tan pants and no shirt, stood there silently, unsmiling, arms crossed over his chest.

As Leigh and the young redhead joined their shipmates, the silent boy moved toward them. He was average height but seemed bigger, as if he demanded more space than a normal person ... and was accustomed to getting it. He walked past the front of the shuttle and positioned himself about ten meters away, next to the landing gear.

From that distance, she could see a raised scar on one of his shoulders and a streak of gray in his otherwise black hair.

The boy uncrossed his arms and addressed the group.

"Good afternoon," he announced. "Welcome to Marjol."

No one responded. Whatever was going on, it wasn't a welcome. The boy was looking at them the way Leigh's mother looked at the chickens before taking their eggs.

"Please listen," he continued. "We're glad you're here, but do not come closer. For the next eight days, we need you to quarantine on the beach to make sure you're not carrying any diseases. Last time there was a landing party, we didn't do this, and we were sick for weeks."

The boy's speech had a lilting, lyrical quality to it, while his enunciation was deliberate and clear. His voice was pleasant. But he stood there like a prison guard, and his words were not what she wanted to hear. A quarantine?

"If you use that path," he pointed to a cleared spot in the tall grass, "it'll take you down to the beach where you'll find empty cabins. We have provided supplies and instructions. Stay there until we're sure it's safe for you to join the rest of us."

Beside Leigh, the young redhead wiped blood from his nose and called out, "What's your name?"

"Olumayokun."

"I'm Nick."

"Greetings, Nick. Glad you're all right."

Nick opened his mouth as if to say more, then closed it. He looked to be only twelve or thirteen. His pale cheeks reddened as he gawked at Olumayokun—his elder by at least four years and an imposing thirty kilograms heavier.

Leigh heard whispering among her shipmates, but no one spoke up. The thought of introducing herself made her nauseous. She reached for her necklace—which still wasn't there—and put her hands in her pockets to keep them still.

"Olumayokun," she said, shouting louder than intended.

"Please, call me Olu."

"Olu, we weren't told about a quarantine. Why should we trust you? What reassurance can you give us?"

"I'm not lying to you," he said, staring at her, then scanning the group. "But we're on our own here. I can't give you 'reassurance' about anything."

Before she could reply, a second boy appeared from behind the shuttle. He joined Olu next to the landing gear, and the whispering in the crowd abated.

The second boy wore tattered pants and a ragged, sleeveless blue shirt. At first glance, he looked like a beach bum—skin tanned from exposure, bare feet, and thick blond hair falling to his shoulders. But his deep-set eyes surveyed them with intensity, and he stood before them like a general inspecting his troops.

Leigh took a step back.

The boy gazed her direction, then surprised her with a wide smile. "We're sorry to do this," he said, slowly making eye contact with each colonist. "I know you're confused and tired, maybe a bit angry, or even a lot angry. It'll get better. After the quarantine, I promise we'll welcome you in a more friendly way."

His posture relaxed, and again he smiled. Many of the colonists smiled in return, but Leigh wasn't falling for the good cop/bad cop routine. Whether it was done with a scowl or a smile, the result was the same: they were being isolated.

"As Olu told you," the boy continued, "there are cabins a short way down the beach. Near the cabins, you'll see a path. It goes to a spring for drinking water. The ocean water between here and there is safe for swimming as long as you stay close to shore. But don't swim too far past the cabins. There's often a nasty rip current out there."

He received a glare from Olu but kept talking. "For the calmest water, swim close to here, down below, at the end of the path. You'll see. Anyway, the beach cabins have everything you need, including plenty of Foobrew, your liquid meals. It shouldn't be too bad."

Leigh stood silently while many in the crowd muttered to each other.

Olu took a step forward and called out, "Trust us. Please. If no one gets sick, the quarantine will only last a week."

They quieted down, but nobody moved until a voice said, "We'll do it. Come on everyone!"

She wasn't sure who'd spoken, but the rest of the newcomers headed toward the path in the tall grass. Olu grabbed his friend's arm and said tersely, "Lex, time to go," as he tugged him toward the far side of the shuttle. Everyone disappeared in one direction or the other.

Leigh stood there, alone on the plateau. She wiped the sweat from her forehead and dug her right foot into the ground. Ten centimeters deep, the alien soil remained dark and sandy. A heaviness settled in her chest that had nothing to do with the gravity.

There must have been a mistake.

She'd never wanted to leave Earth.

And yet, here she was—ninety-nine trillion kilometers from home. Part of humanity's initial settlement in a distant solar system, a colonization effort undertaken by teenagers because no one else could survive the cryosleep.

She dug her foot deeper into the ground, then rubbed her face with her hands. Her body hummed with nervous energy. She wanted to scream at someone ... anyone.

She took a deep breath instead.

And another.

One step at a time.

First, the quarantine.

Then, figure out how to get home.

She resituated her bag so that it sat lower on her back. Taking one last look at the shuttle, Leigh squared her shoulders and followed her shipmates into the tall purple grass.

⁂

The descent from the plateau turned out to be less menacing than it first appeared. Only three or four stories tall, the cliffside had an easy hidden trail down to a wide beach. Although they could see the quarantine cabins in the distance, no one headed that direction. Leigh was in no rush to do exactly what those on the plateau had told them to do, and it looked like her shipmates felt the same way.

The sun was low in the sky but hot. Wiping sweat from her brow, Leigh noticed its metallic scent. She was sweating off the dregs of the cryodrugs. Drugs given to her so she could sleep for thirteen years and travel to another solar system. She could not imagine a single reason to do such a thing.

Disbelief.

Denial.

Even fear was taking a backseat to those two emotions. This could not be happening, and yet here she was.

Using the bottom of her shirt, she wiped the perspiration from her face and neck, then began to explore the beach. Though the sand near the ocean was soft, the shoreline was littered with rocks and tufts of dark-purple grass. Leigh wandered slowly, stopping here and there to examine patches of the alien grass while she listened to her shipmates' conversations.

The video had said the colonists shared two characteristics: each person was under twenty years of age, and each had volunteered to colonize this new world. Leigh was relieved to discover they all had something else in common: everyone spoke English.

During the few wakeful hours on the shuttle, she'd wondered about language barriers. She'd wondered about a lot of things! Why had they sent colonists before fixing the cryosleep? How much memory loss had she suffered?

Stop.

She needed to focus on the quarantine, and that meant getting to know her landing party. Leigh searched for the young redhead and a chance to speak with him. Too late. Nick was already calling to the group.

"Gather up," said Nick. "Let's talk."

"About what?" said the curly-haired girl.

"About a plan. I have no idea what we should do. Do you?"

The girl shrugged.

"Gather up!" Nick called again.

Most of the colonists congregated quickly, but a tall lanky boy stood apart—feet in the water, arms akimbo, peering at the ocean, not the shore. When a large wave doused the boy's legs almost up to his waist, he laughed, then ambled over to join the group. Leigh watched him squeeze the water out of his pants as the discussion continued. He was about her age, but the easy way he was handling things made him seem older.

"Looks like the cabins aren't far," said Nick, "maybe half a kilometer. Let's check them out."

"Hold on," said one of the guys. "Why should we take orders from you?"

"Yeah, mate," said another, "I reckon we can think for ourselves."

"I don't know," said the first. "You don't look like much of a thinker."

The two colonists pushed people out of the way and faced off. Before they could do more than growl at each other, the tall lanky boy stepped between them. Gone was the easygoing attitude he'd shown when soaked by the wave. "Hey," he barked, "cool off. Argue about it at the cabins. Let's get there before the Sun goes down."

"It's not the Sun," said Nick. "It's Epsilon Eridani."

The lanky boy laughed. "You're right. Hard to believe, isn't it? I'm Cliff." He extended his hand to Nick. "Glad you introduced yourself up there. We all should've done it."

Nick and Cliff clasped hands, but their friendliness was not contagious. Other colonists shoved their way to the center of the pack, one of them elbowing Leigh in the process. It was time to speak up. Time not to be Leigh Crawford. It was time to be someone new.

"I'm Lorelei," said Leigh, her new name sounding awkward. "I agree with Nick. We should go check out the cabins." A few people groaned, but she continued. "We're the third group to land. Why not listen to those already here? We have no reason to think they're lying."

"No reason to think they aren't," said Cliff.

Murmurs of support for both positions rippled through the small crowd. Cliff arched his brow as if to say, *you know I'm right*.

Leigh almost laughed. She was used to being the suspicious one, not arguing against it. Being Lorelei was already making her a different person. She climbed onto a rock to see everyone better. "Can't hurt to go look," she said, gesturing toward the cabins. "I hate the quarantine, but maybe it's smart."

"Who knows," said Cliff. "You may be right." He jumped up on the rock next to her. Pointing at one of the older boys, he asked, "What's your name?"

"Shinichiro. Everyone calls me Shin."

"And you?"

"Sammi," said the curly-haired girl. "It's Samantha, but I never liked that name, and it's also my second cousin's name, and I never really liked her, and I guess that doesn't matter anymore, but everyone calls me Sammi."

A few colonists snickered at Sammi's rambling introduction, but Leigh appreciated it. Her own seemed smooth in comparison.

"Here's my suggestion," said Cliff. "Sammi, you take the girls to the first cabin. Shin and Nick, split the boys and each take one of the other cabins. Let's see what's what."

Given purpose, people divided up and headed down the beach. Leigh and Cliff lingered on the rock.

"Well done," she said.

"You were right. Might as well check it out."

"And you were right. No way to know who's a friend, who's an enemy."

"Me included," he said with a shrug.

Leigh managed a small grin.

She and Cliff jumped down from the rock to follow the others, then halted mid-stride as a rumbling noise grabbed their attention. All twenty new arrivals looked up at the plateau, where the shuttlecraft was taking off en route to the space station orbiting the planet.

The shuttle moved out over the ocean, a metallic imitation of a giant seagull. The roar grew louder as more engines ignited while the ship hovered several hundred meters above the dark-blue waves. The nose tilted up, and the spacecraft shot skyward. For a moment, the crashing waves and the engine echoes blended in a chorus of nature and machine; then only the waves remained.

Most of the group resumed the trek toward the cabins, but Leigh and Cliff continued staring upward as the shuttle left them far behind. Soon all they could see was a glowing ion trail against the backdrop of an alien sky.

"I guess we're stuck here," said Cliff.

Leigh was silent.

Up there was the spacecraft that had brought them to this solar system. Eventually, that ship would be heading back to Earth. When it did, she planned to be on it.

CHAPTER 3

While the new landing party stood on the beach and watched the shuttle depart, Lex ran along the thin trail that led from the plateau to the top of the cliffs behind the beach cabins. The tall grass brushed against his legs, and the sea breeze blew against his face. He lengthened his stride. After a long day of waiting around, the physical activity felt good.

In his periphery, Lex could see the shuttle hovering over the ocean, not far off the coast. The pulsating rumble of the ship's engines drowned out other noise. He couldn't hear his own feet hitting the ground, much less anything else.

Picking up the pace, Lex paid no attention to the fancy spacecraft. Six months ago, he'd been fascinated when a shuttle had dropped him on the planet. Three months after that, he'd watched in awe as the second landing party's craft arrived. But today, he no longer cared about spaceships, only about the colonists they brought. His duty was to the people on the planet, including the four he was running to find.

At a clump of plants covered with black thorns and broad purple leaves, Lex turned right and headed toward the ocean. Unlike the landing plateau, these clifftops were covered with spiky bushes and gnarled shrubs. By necessity, he slowed to a walk and picked his way through the vegetation, aiming for a spot near the edge of the cliff covered in dense, tall bushes.

Michele must have seen him coming. She extricated herself from a hiding spot in the plants and crouched low as she walked toward him. For the first ten meters, her head stayed no higher than the shrubs, then she stood up and walked normally. Even in the prickly groundcover, she moved with the grace of a mountain lion.

"What're you doing here?" she asked.

"Nice to see you too," said Lex.

"What's wrong?"

"I don't know," he admitted, "but it's not going exactly as planned."

Michele grinned. "When do things ever go as planned?"

Surprised into a laugh, Lex took a step closer.

"Ah," she said, "stay where you are. This far from the edge, they can't see you from down at the cabins."

"They're not at the quarantine cabins. That's what I came to tell you. The landing party left the plateau, then stood around *forever* on Sunset Beach. They're finally heading to the cabins, but slowly."

"We've been waiting all day. Another fifteen or twenty minutes won't matter."

"Marko needs to be off that cliff by dark," said Lex. "You know I'm right."

Michele put her hands on her hips. "What I *know* is that you ran all the way over here because you're worried." She gave an exaggerated sigh. "Marko's fine. Nestled safely in the little cave with a rope tied around him, a canteen slung over his shoulder, and a monocular in his hand."

"I'm not worried," said Lex, "just wanted to give you guys an update."

He feigned nonchalance, but it was a futile effort. He and Michele had been friends since their first few hours on the planet. They'd been through more in the past 192 days than most people shared their whole lives. She'd known he was running over to check on Marko before Lex had admitted it to himself.

"There's three of us," said Michele, "at the other end of the rope, ready to haul up Marko as soon as he gives the signal."

"He thinks he's going to be able to hear them."

"He might. And he'll definitely be able to see what they're up to." Michele took a step forward. She was tall enough to look Lex straight in the eyes. "He'll be fine," she said.

Lex nodded. The younger boy had volunteered for the dangerous duty, and Lex had been proud of him for doing so. Proud, and a little worried.

"Okay," said Lex. "I'd better go."

"You leave Olu by himself?" asked Michele.

"Told him I'd be right back."

"Bet he loved that."

"He didn't say anything." Lex offered a guilty grin.

"Let me guess," said Michele, grinning in return, "he gave you one of those looks—the kind that says, 'You're disappointing me.'"

She was right. But if there was one thing he wasn't going to do, it was stand here with Michele and discuss Olu. The two of them were his best friends. That hadn't changed when Olu and Michele became a couple, and it hadn't changed when they'd broken up. Lex wasn't going to pick sides, and Michele knew it.

"Sorry," she said. "This quarantine's stressing me out."

"We'll feel better about it tomorr—"

Lex paused, interrupted by the sound of voices from down below, not clear enough to distinguish words but loud enough to confirm the new colonists had reached the beach cabins.

"See you soon," said Michele, heading back toward the hiding spot in the bushes. Two steps later, she turned around. "You know, if anything goes wrong, I'm gonna rappel down the cliff and grab Marko myself."

Of course she would.

"You're right," he replied. "I should've known."

Michele flashed him a quick smile, crouched low, and moved away.

Lex delayed a moment before heading back. He bent down and carefully put his face next to one of the spiky plants, breathing in its sweet scent—an aroma richer than honeysuckle and laced with the tang of the salty air. In a world of sumptuous smells, it was one of his favorites.

Michele was right. He'd been stupid to run over. But Marko was the closest thing he'd ever had to a little brother—to any sibling. It was not the first time Lex had been stupid on Marko's behalf, and it probably wouldn't be the last.

**

The run back to the barren plateau helped Lex's equilibrium return. As expected, Olu was waiting for him near the entrance to the wide, well-worn path that led to Homesite.

"All good?" asked Olu.

"All good," said Lex.

He and Olu continued along the path through chest-high lavender grass. As the trail angled to the left, the grass grew thinner, and they entered a patch of dark-green vegetation with stalks like giant sunflowers. Topped by fluffy seedballs, the plants reached well over the boys' heads.

Lex and Olu stepped off the path, threaded their way through the towering stalks, and stopped at a long, flat rock. Olu retrieved the yellow shirt he'd left behind, and both boys sat down to wait at the designated meeting spot.

Lex made a mental note to add the rock's location to their checklist. As the colony's leaders, he, Olu, and Ada had been compiling a list of things to tell the new colonists. A couple of days ago, they'd put that work on hold and focused on the quarantine. Now it was time to get back to everything else, including the checklist.

He climbed up on the flat rock and peered through the tops of the tall thick plants.

"You just saw them," said Olu. "Am I right?"

"Yeah."

"It may be a while."

"I know." Lex wiped sweat from his face. He glanced skyward. The shuttle was long gone. "Ever wish you could go back?" he asked.

"Go back?"

"To Earth."

Olu stood up and put on his shirt.

"My bad, sorry." Lex resumed his seat on the rock.

"Hey," said Olu, "the past few days have been rough."

"Can't believe that kid, Nick. He almost went off the cliff."

"But he didn't."

Lex stretched his arms and rolled his shoulders. Despite the run, his muscles were tight. He wasn't used to sitting around all day.

He thought of Marko, wedged in a small cave about twenty meters up the cliff behind the beach cabins. What was he seeing? What was he hearing?

Although it'd been six months since his own arrival, Lex clearly remembered those initial hours, back when he'd noticed the difference in gravity. No one had greeted them. As the first landing party, they'd been on their own.

Of course, no one had quarantined them either.

"No," said Olu.

"No?"

"I don't wish I could go back. Why? Do you?"

"It's not like we have a choice."

"That's not an answer."

Lex stood up and paced around the rock, winding his way through the thick green stalks. He never should have brought it up. They'd all agreed not to talk about Earth.

"You *know* I don't want to go back," said Lex. "It's just, sometimes I wish we knew what was going on there."

Olu didn't comment. He didn't need to. This was an old argument.

They'd been provided with enough supplies, but the techs had never worked. With no way of communicating off-world, Olu felt a burden to create a colony that could exist without help. Lex assumed help would arrive sooner or later. Then again, Olu had lived through the drought and devastation in West Africa, when help was always too little, too late. Lex had only seen the images. Maybe their differences were as simple as that.

In practice, it didn't really matter. They greeted a new landing party every ninety-six days and, otherwise, figured out everything on their own. No help from Earth needed.

Lex refocused on the planet in front of him instead of the planet he'd left behind. The past few days had been crazy. He'd mediated arguments about whether to impose the quarantine, how to do it, and for how long; then he'd helped set the plan in motion. The chaos had affected him more than he'd thought.

One thing was for sure: he was off his game today. Fortunately, the people he'd most irritated were the ones most likely to forgive him. He stopped circling the rock and sat down.

"Think Ada will be pissed?" asked Lex, but he smiled as he said it.

The tactic worked. Olu chuckled in response.

"Seriously," said Lex, "we mostly stuck to the plan."

"Except for the part where you ran off by yourself—"

"I wasn't there long."

"—breaking our most important rule ... never going anywhere alone."

"I'm safe now," said Lex.

"You can guess what Ada will say to that."

"Yeah."

"And before that," said Olu, "there was the part where you spoke to the landing party—"

"Yeah."

"—and rambled on and on about stuff we carefully wrote down for them."

"Hmm."

"I think," said Olu, "you didn't like the answer I gave that girl."

"They looked scared."

"Of course they're scared."

"I mean," said Lex, "more scared than we were."

"Maybe," said Olu.

"I felt bad for them."

"It all worked out. They were on the plateau longer than we wanted, but they never came close."

"And no one died."

"Exactly."

Lex stood up and stretched again. He wouldn't relax until the others reported back. Having Marko spy was a good plan, but you never knew what might happen. Olu's earlier statement had simply been the truth—here on Marjol, there were no reassurances.

Lex had felt the urge to reassure them anyway. Something about the way that girl had asked her questions. She'd reminded him of Earth.

He jumped back up on the rock and rubbed his lower back. No time to think about the past. People here counted on him. People here liked him. Memories of Earth were nothing but trouble.

He had learned that lesson the hard way—they all had. Their third night on the planet, the stormy weather had ceased, the clouds had disappeared, and all three moons had shone in the night sky. They'd built a fire and gathered round it, the twenty of them staring at more stars than they'd ever seen on Earth. As they told stories and shared laughter, the oppressive weight of the unknown had started to lift. Until they made a mistake ... he couldn't remember who'd suggested it, but one at a time, each person revealed something they missed from Earth, something they couldn't believe they'd never see again.

Lex had told them about playing cards with his grandparents, sitting at their old wooden table, the one with his name carved into the underside, right next to his father's. It had been hard to talk and even harder to listen. By the time Rose had spoken about her dog, they'd all been broken by the weight of their cumulative losses. That night, the weather was clear, but storms churned inside everyone's hearts, and sleep remained elusive.

The next morning, they'd all agreed: Earth was behind them. Talking about it did more harm than good. They had a colony to establish, a new world to explore, and no help to do it. Their odds of survival were low; dwelling on the past would only make them lower.

A gust of wind blew through the tall plants. Lex pushed his hair out of his face. From his perch on the flat rock, he looked down at Olu, who stood quietly, content with how the day had unfolded. Olu's ability to prioritize the big picture, to always see the forest for the trees, made him a great leader. It was a trait Lex tried to emulate ... usually. Sometimes, a single tree was most important, or even a leaf.

The sound of voices carried across the plateau, and Lex could make out four familiar profiles in the distance.

"Is that them?" asked Olu.

"Yep."

"Must've gone well if they're making all that noise."

"True enough." He heaved a sigh of relief, happy to think of taking the good news back to Homesite, where everyone else was waiting to hear what had happened with the third landing party.

Olu remained standing next to the large rock while Lex lay down on its flat surface. He laced his fingers together and stretched his arms above his head, allowing himself to relax. Bits of evening sunshine warmed his face as it filtered through the tall plants. High above, two thin clouds floated slowly across the bright blue sky.

He smiled. It'd been a long day, but everyone was where they needed to be. With luck, none of the newcomers would get sick; with luck, they'd soon be part of the colony.

With luck, they'd come to love the planet as much as he did.

CHAPTER 4

Leigh stood inside one of the quarantine cabins, dug her fingernails into her palms, and vowed not to cry. She looked at the walls made of large russet-brown bricks, the same color as the sand outside. In spite of what the pilot had said, there was no way she had volunteered for this. Her mother would never have approved.

An ache pulsed behind her eyes. She had no memory of saying goodbye. No memory of wanting to leave. She'd traveled to another solar system and didn't remember agreeing to do it. How was that possible?

Leigh choked back what threatened to become a sob and forced herself to focus on the cabin. It had three rooms—boring but functional. The largest room had round tables with four chairs each, cabinets lining two of the walls, and additional chairs folded up against some of the cabinets.

The two smaller rooms were bedrooms, each with five bunk beds and nothing else. She stepped into the first bedroom and realized the other girls had already staked out the five lower bunks. The pain behind her eyes intensified.

A loud crash sounded from the front of the cabin. She rushed back to the common area, where Sammi and another girl laughed over a pile of fallen chairs.

"Do you want help?" Leigh asked.

"Sure," said the other girl, "though you won't believe how light these chairs are. I have no idea what they're made of. I'm Zalfaa, by the way."

"Lorelei," said Leigh, congratulating herself on a smoother introduction this time. "Nice to meet you, Zalfaa."

The three girls moved the chairs to an empty corner, then Zalfaa and Sammi left to see what was going on outside. Leigh headed back to the bunkroom. As she'd noticed her first time through, each of the lower beds had a bag on it, and each girl had placed a personal item on the pillow to claim her spot.

Five bunk beds and six girls was awkward. Should she grab a top bunk, possibly irritating her lower bunkmate, or should she sleep in the other bedroom, either gratifying or annoying the others? Undecided, Leigh wandered from bed to bed. Each one had a mattress, more like a futon really, covered with a duvet. She pushed on a pillow; it was comfortably firm, and the pillowcase was silky smooth—oddly luxurious accoutrements.

The lower bed against the far wall had a harmonica on it, and the closest bed held a colorful woven bracelet. The items on the other three lower bunks were an interesting mix: a smooth royal-blue stone with streaks of white; a small battered teddy bear that had once been orange; and a Batman LEGO keychain, devoid of keys.

Leigh pulled the dark-blue drawstring bag off her back and looked inside at the three things she'd brought from Earth: her family's lucky hat, one of her mom's embroidered handkerchiefs, and the multipurpose tool Grampy had given her when she turned eleven. He'd handed it over, unwrapped, and said, "Don't be one of those kids who can't fix their own stuff." For six years, she'd taken it everywhere. No surprise she'd packed it.

The surprise was her missing necklace. She wasn't wearing it; she hadn't packed it. That made no sense.

She heard footsteps: Zalfaa. Clutching her bag, Leigh regretted the indecisiveness that had left her standing in the middle of the room. She waited for the subtle yet knowing smirk that accompanied such situations, but it didn't come. Zalfaa walked over to the Batman LEGO keychain, patted the top bed, and said, "You can bunk with me. I don't move much, so it probably won't be uncomfortable for you." She offered a hesitant smile. "Plus, I'm smaller than you. I can take the top bunk if you want the bottom."

"Oh, no." Leigh made her way to that side of the room. "The top works great for me. Thanks."

"You sure? We could try to move one of the bunks from the other room."

"I'm good."

Leigh placed her bag on the top bunk, started to open it, then hesitated—reluctant to claim a spot in a place she did not want to be.

"Lorelei?" asked Zalfaa.

Leigh paused, almost failing to respond to her new name. "Uh, yeah."

"You okay?" asked the other girl.

"Yeah, fine."

"Listen," said Zalfaa in a low voice, "We're all scared. I know I am. I think the others are too, but they're covering it up."

"You're probably right," replied Leigh, cheeks heating. She contemplated saying more, but … what?

"Okay," said Zalfaa. "I'll leave you to it."

As her new bunkmate left the room, Leigh felt the familiar pang of knowing she'd bungled a well-intentioned conversation. She'd fallen right back into old habits—letting uncertainty and suspicions get the best of her.

Good thing she didn't plan to stay here long.

Reopening her bag, Leigh reached for her mom's handkerchief. Her fingers traced the embroidered bluebonnets along the edges. She carefully folded the handkerchief into a shape called the bouquet, and her mind flooded with memories from years ago, when her father had taught her the pattern.

How many of her memories had been lost to the cryosleep? Days? Weeks? Months?

She didn't know what Earth date it was, and she couldn't remember anything after one morning—the morning she and her mom had planted wildflower seeds and cactus plants around her dad's stone memorial on the ranch. Closing her eyes, Leigh could still smell the clay and dirt of the Texas ground as they'd dug it up for planting.

Enough!

Daydreaming wasn't going to get her anywhere.

She reached into her bag and pulled out the other two objects from home. Grasping her hair in a loose ponytail, she shoved it through the hole in the back of the baseball cap and fit the hat snugly on her head. She slid the multipurpose tool into the biggest pocket of her pants and removed one of the two liquid meals from there, adding it to those stashed in her bag, then she placed the folded handkerchief on top of her bed.

On the bunk below, the Batman LEGO keychain had fallen off Zalfaa's pillow. Leigh put it back. The little Bruce Wayne stared at her.

"Be glad you have the Batmask," she said to the figure.

She reached up to the top bunk and gave the folded handkerchief one last pat for good luck. It was time to see what she could learn from her shipmates.

***

A few hours later, Leigh sat by a campfire on the beach, kicked off her shoes, and tried not to be discouraged. Her shipmates didn't know any more than she did.

It was dark now, but there'd been time before nightfall to get a look around. Not a difficult task in a spot surrounded by empty beach, but it'd given them a chance to find the freshwater spring and to investigate the cabins. There were more than enough supplies to get them through the quarantine, with one crucial exception: no techs. Her plans for escape would have to wait.

Nonetheless, the search for techs had turned up useful odds and ends, including a bunch of matches. A stack of hefty driftwood sat inside one of the cabins, and a short walk along the beach had produced an armload of smaller sticks, which had led to the campfire. It didn't make up for the lack of techs, but it'd been a good chance to observe everyone.

The guys were full of false bravado. Or maybe some of it was genuine; they didn't mind the lack of running water, and several had already been for a swim in the alien ocean. Nevertheless, all fourteen of them had moved into one cabin together. It was likely that fear, as much as camaraderie, had played a role in that decision.

One of the older colonists, Milo, had brought a foldable frisbee. It seemed an odd choice for a special object from Earth, but a half dozen people had been entertained by it for the past hour. Leigh tugged her baseball cap a little tighter. She wasn't going to second-guess anyone's choice of objects from home.

The campfire was dying down, and those who'd been playing with the frisbee grabbed buckets of ocean water to ensure it died out completely. With the heat of the fire gone, Leigh could feel the drop in temperature that accompanied Epsilon Eridani's disappearance from view. Three moons occupied the night sky, an obvious reminder of the alienness surrounding them.

She turned her face toward the sea breeze and thought about the two guys who'd met them on the plateau. Their desire for a quarantine made sense, especially if the colony had faced an epidemic. But she could see no good reason for being stranded without any way to communicate.

Zalfaa hypothesized that techs were in limited supply. Leigh didn't buy it. Why not leave at least one comm, a pad or wrist-strap—a way to call for help, something. No, the decision to leave no techs whatsoever was a decision to keep them isolated in every possible way. Why?

She slipped her shoes back on. Sitting next to her, Cliff stifled a yawn. "Can't believe it's only been a few hours since we landed," he said.

"A lot's happened."

"Understatement."

"Did you mean what you said to Nick," she asked, "that we all should've introduced ourselves to those guys on the plateau?"

"Absolutely," said Cliff. "Would've made them see us as individuals, not just some nameless landing party."

"Hmm, that's smart."

"Not really, since I didn't think of it until it was too late!"

They both laughed.

His face reminded Leigh of her grandfather. Superficially, there was no resemblance. Cliff's youthful face evinced a mixed heritage from both sides of the Pacific Ocean, whereas her grandfather's craggy face was old and white with sun-worn scars across his nose. But the boy's dark eyes laughed the same way as Grampy's blue ones.

"We've only been here a few hours," she said, "and I'm ready for the quarantine to be over."

"Seven more days to go, I'm afraid."

"They said a week. You think that's the eight-day week the video talked about?"

"I think that's what he said—the first guy, Olu."

"He didn't tell us much. Neither did the so-called informational video."

Cliff laughed.

"I'm serious," said Leigh.

"Oh, trust me," said Cliff. "I thought we'd know a whole lot more by now."

"Like, which island did we land on? How many people are on the space station orbiting the planet? Will they join us? Can we get up there? Are they in touch with Earth? How can we contact home? Can we eat anything beside the liquid meals?"

"Or even what's in the liquid meals?"

"Yeah, and I'm just getting started …"

"Slow down," said Cliff. "We'll go crazy asking questions when we don't have any way to get the answers."

"I know, I know," said Leigh. "Wait out the quarantine and then get the answers."

"Could be worse," said Cliff. "I mean, if we were on Earth, it'd feel more like summer camp than a quarantine."

"I never went to summer camp."

"Me neither," he laughed. "I was always working. But I don't know …" He shrugged. "Sitting around the fire, especially when Eliana played her harmonica, that's what I always imagined summer camp would feel like."

"You sound optimistic."

"Guilty as charged," he replied. "Trying to be optimistic, but not naïve."

"Small difference sometimes."

"An important difference."

"One not everyone is making."

"True," agreed Cliff, "but don't worry. Everyone's coping in their own way." With that, he left to go talk to Noah and Matt, the two Australians, whose coping strategy was on full display: boisterous storytelling and blatant flirtation with several of the girls.

Leigh didn't want to cope; she wanted to leave.

Brushing sand from her pants, she stood up and looked into the sky. Thousands of stars stared back at her, and she had no idea which one might lead the way toward home.

* * *

Several hours later, lying on her top bunk, she could hear the quiet breathing of the five girls below. None of them remembered volunteering to be a colonist, yet they weren't obsessed with the memory loss. Maybe that's why her cabinmates were asleep and she was not.

Leigh rolled over on her side, careful to limit her movements so as not to disturb the sleeping Zalfaa down below. The nearest wall held the room's one window, and a salty breeze blew in from outside. With three moons in the sky, the alien night was not completely dark. She closed her eyes and listened to the waves, hoping the rhythmic sounds would lull her to sleep.

The whole situation felt like a nightmare. Except that it didn't. The five girls lying on the lower bunks were kind and smart. The boys, even the loud ones, seemed competent and resourceful. Not to mention, some of them were rather good-looking. Almost as good-looking as the two who'd greeted them on the plateau.

Argh! Leigh opened her eyes and rubbed her temples. She needed to get her act together.

She needed to get some rest.

Counting sheep—or anything else—had never worked. Instead, she practiced a calming exercise by envisioning the cabinets in the outer room, one section at a time.

In the cabinet closest to the door, a large crate with a handwritten note that said "Foobrew" was stuffed with little vials, each sealed tight with its own screw-off cap—hundreds, maybe thousands, of individual liquid meals.

The bigger cabinets held a lot of supplies, including bowls, spoons, a couple of knives, and six large buckets. No water bottles were provided, but the cabinets held dozens of old-school canteens with detachable shoulder straps, plus plenty of footwear, towels, bedding, drawstring bags, notebooks, pens, and rope in two sizes. One cabinet held five lanterns, all of which appeared to be in working order, though they couldn't determine the power sources.

The smaller cabinets held medical supplies and clothes. The clothing was plentiful but boring: yellow and blue shirts, tan pants, red sweatshirts, and green jackets. They'd laughed at the paltry choice in shirt color since there was no choice in anything else, except for boxer shorts in a variety of colors and patterns. Those were probably meant for the guys, but she hadn't been the only one who'd grabbed a few pairs for herself.

Leigh sighed, rolled onto her back, and stared at the ceiling. The visualization exercise was not helping.

She tried another tactic: mental calculations. Each "day" on the planet was 24.9 Earth-hours long, and she was in the third landing party, with a new one arriving every 96 Marjol days ... or 99.6 Earth days ... her mind focused on the numbers as she added together the journey from Earth and the time for the first two landing parties to reach the surface. Assuming some hours in stasis before departure and a few more as her pod was moved from the spaceship to the shuttle ... she'd spent 5,000 Earth days in cryosleep.

Math was usually reassuring. This was not.

Tears spilled slowly from Leigh's eyes as she allowed the reality of her situation to sink in. She lay in a quarantined cabin on a planet circling a star that was not the Sun.

She might never see Earth again.

Her chest tightened at the thought, but she couldn't ignore the facts any longer. Even if she found a way home, decades would've passed while she was gone.

Decades.

That math she didn't have to do herself. The shipboard video had calculated the Lorentz factor for them. It'd taken a little over thirteen years at roughly 80 percent the speed of light for the journey here. During that time, on Earth, almost twenty-two years would have gone by. The exact numbers were seared in her memory: twenty-one years and 310 days from launch to arrival at the space station orbiting the planet.

If Leigh reentered cryosleep for the journey home, she'd still be seventeen years old when she returned. Meanwhile, life on Earth would have aged over four decades. Her classmates would be in their early sixties.

Her mom. Her grandparents. She couldn't think about it.

She pulled the blanket around her shoulders and turned toward the window. One of the alien moons was full. Its bright round orb hung low in the sky, easily visible from the top bunk. The view grew blurry as her eyes flooded with tears.

She had to face reality.

And her reality sucked.

She was here, and she was never going home.

As much as Leigh didn't want to believe it, something must have happened that made her think leaving Earth was a good idea.

She clutched the blanket tighter, not giving up, not completely. Her chest hurt with physical pain—a smothering heaviness, a heartache akin to grief—because she longed desperately to know how and why she'd come here. And oh, what she'd give to talk to her mom … to see her grandparents.

If she couldn't go back, there had to be a way to contact Earth. To reach out to those she'd left behind and let them know she was all right. To ask them why she'd left in the first place.

She pulled the blanket up over her face and dried her tears. Answers to such questions would have to wait. First things first: get through the quarantine.

It'd be important to make friends. Both the quarantine and whatever awaited them afterward would be easier if everyone in her landing party got along.

She almost started crying again. For years, people had been urging her to make friends as if her life depended on it. And now, maybe it did.

Not good.

Not good at all.

What else could she do?

Stay healthy.

Whatever illness Olu was afraid of, she didn't want to get it.

She laughed quietly, her emotions riding ups and downs faster than she could keep up with. Grampy would be entertained. After years of teasing him about his "quadruple cure," it was the first thing she'd thought of: plenty of water, fresh air, exercise, and sleep. Her grandfather was convinced those four things would prevent 99 percent of the world's ills.

Couldn't hurt to give it a try.

Plenty of sleep. Hmm.

Maybe three out of four would be enough? Leigh rolled onto her stomach and rearranged her pillow. A strong breeze blew across her back. She listened to the pounding of the waves and tried to ignore everything else.

CHAPTER 5

Leigh woke up covered in sweat. She wiped her hand across her forehead. No fever. No metallic scent. Just sweat. The roots of her hair were damp, as was the pillow.

She sat up and unstuck her sweaty shirt from her body. Once again, she was thankful for the breeze coming through the window. The top bunk had its advantages.

She debated getting a fresh shirt, but it wasn't worth the risk of waking her cabinmates, so she lay back down. The waves were softer now, a dull sound in the distance. The full moon was still visible through the window.

"Hey!" a voice shouted outside the cabin. "Hey!"

Leigh sat up and listened for more. All she heard were waves and wind.

She began to lie back down, and the voice came again: "Hey, mate! Stop!"

Before she could second-guess herself, Leigh's feet were on the ground. She tripped over an errant shoe, but it didn't take long to get outside and see what was going on.

Waist-deep in the water, two boys wrestled with each other.

As she considered what to do, the door to the cabin opened, and Eliana stepped out. A dark brunette with warm olive-brown skin, Eliana was one of the quietest members of their landing party. She'd also been one of the most sought-after girls by those flirting at the evening campfire.

Like Leigh, Eliana was wearing boxer shorts and a yellow shirt … but her clothes weren't stuck to her body with sweat. And she'd grabbed extra layers.

"Here." Eliana handed her a sweatshirt and a pair of pants.

"Thanks."

"Who is it?" Eliana asked. "Even with all this moonlight, I can't tell."

"I think one of them's Cliff."

"Should we go over there?"

The two grappling boys fell into the waves. Leigh tensed. Maybe this was her first test at making friends. "Let's go," she said.

They jogged over as the boys stood up in the surf, Cliff flailing his arms to keep the other boy away from him.

"Back off, Noah!" said Cliff.

"Break it up, you two," yelled Leigh, but neither boy looked her direction.

"It's not safe," shouted Cliff.

"Calm down, mate," said Noah. "You're not dying. Let's get out of the water."

"It's not a fight," said Eliana, and she waded out to join the boys.

"Leave me alone!" Cliff shouted at Noah.

"Please, let me help." Eliana reached for Cliff's arm.

"Don't!" gasped Cliff. "Too hot."

"Look at me," she said. "There's a breeze on the shore. It will help you cool off. Your chest hurts?"

Cliff nodded.

"Trust me," said Eliana, waves lapping at her knees. "Let's go to the beach. I'll show you how much better that is."

Eliana guided Cliff out of the water, Noah following a short distance behind. Leigh gripped the edges of her sweatshirt—trying not to add to Cliff's anxiety, worried about unraveling herself—as the four of them huddled on the moonlit beach.

"*Ataque de pânico*," said Eliana. "That's what we call this in Brazil. It helps to name it."

"Cliff said he had to get out," replied Noah. "He was suffocating."

"I was," Cliff said bitterly. "I am."

"Keep breathing," said Eliana. "I know it's hard. Breathe in through your nose for one … two … three … four. Now out through your mouth, one … two … three … four. Slowly, from down low."

At Noah's suggestion, the four of them started walking the beach at a steady pace. Cliff was wringing his hands, but otherwise doing as instructed. Eliana's soft voice kept up a gentle cadence. They paced and they breathed.

Leigh's insides clenched; her stomach burned as if she'd eaten glass shards for dinner. She wanted to be useful—to help Cliff—but in truth, the pacing and breathing were helping her too.

A few minutes later, Noah dashed toward the tall grass.

"I need to stop walking," said Cliff.

"For a moment," agreed Eliana, "but keep breathing." She took off her sweatshirt, used it to dry off best she could, then handed it to Cliff so he could do the same.

"Here, mate," said Noah, returning to place a small rock in Cliff's hand. "Focus on this. We don't have fancy names for it back home, but there's nothin' fancy 'bout a panic attack."

Cliff tried to smile; it looked more like a grimace.

"What's the rock feel like?" asked Noah.

"Bumpy," said Cliff. "Little pits on one side, and a long crack down the edge."

"Tell us more," said Eliana. "You're doing great."

"No more walking."

"That's fine, but keep talking about the rock."

Cliff described the contours of the small rock in detail, then did it all over again a second time. Bit by bit, his voice regained its sturdiness.

"Be right back," said Noah. "Lorelei and I have something to find," and he tugged her toward the ocean.

***

A minute later, they were ankle-deep in the water. It was a pleasant temperature, but Leigh stopped to roll up her pants to keep them dry.

"What're we doing?" she asked.

"Lookin' for the smoothest rock we can find," said Noah, wading out a little farther. "Ever have a panic attack?"

"No."

"Me neither. But my cousin, Harry, he lived with us awhile. He has 'em. I never should've touched Cliff—I know better. That made it worse."

"You did the best you could."

"Nah, mostly I was goin' troppo because here we are on this planet with three moons, and that's heaps amazing, but I don't remember asking to come here, and then there's Cliff, walkin' straight out into the ocean like a newly hatched sea turtle. It really set me off."

Leigh laughed appreciatively at Noah's honesty as she ran her fingers through the wet sand.

"Got one." She held up a flat rock.

"Perfect."

Noah took the rock and washed it in the waves. "My cousin," he said, "wears a chain around his neck strung with two pieces of metal—one carved up and one smooth. He makes up stories about his amulets, says they're ancient symbols of power and balance. But really they're something to touch, to focus on … to keep the panic at bay."

"Noah." Leigh grabbed his arm.

"Not a good time for a swim, if you know what I mean," he said with a roguish grin. It dawned on her that Noah was out on the beach in nothing but soaking wet boxer shorts, his white skin practically glowing in the starlight, while the rest of them were fully dressed. Leigh's face flushed in embarrassment as she ignored his well-muscled body and concentrated on why she had grabbed his arm in the first place.

"Noah," said Leigh. "Uh, no, I wanted to say … I'm sorry."

"For?"

"For assuming you and Cliff were fighting."

"No worries," said Noah with another grin. "Quite reasonable on your part. I'm not one to run from a fight."

"I imagine not."

Noah laughed. He returned the rock to Leigh and ruffled his short, untamed hair. She'd pegged him as a flirt and a troublemaker. The flirt part was accurate, but maybe she'd misjudged the rest.

"Ouff!" said Leigh, stubbing her toe on something in the sand. She reached down and pulled up a fist-sized metal object.

"That's not a rock," said Noah.

She handed the small flat rock back to him and turned the new larger object over in her hands. It was wedge shaped, one side a smooth metallic white and the other jagged with bits of silver metal sticking out. If she'd stepped on it the wrong way, the metal could've easily punctured her bare foot.

"It's the same color as our shuttle," said Noah.

Leigh's mind reeled with the ramifications.

Noah reached for the metal object and rinsed it in the waves. He examined it carefully in the moonlight, turning his back toward the beach. Consciously or not, Noah was shielding the object from Cliff and Eliana's view.

"There's probably a logical explanation," he said. "Something other than the crash of our shuttle."

"Hmm."

"We saw the shuttle fly off," said Noah. "If it'd blown up, we'd have seen it. Heard it."

"Maybe."

"Likely."

They both stared at the wedge-shaped object. A larger wave washed in, cresting almost to Leigh's waist, but she barely noticed. Once again, words failed her. She could speak but had no idea what to say.

Noah broke the silence.

"Let's keep this to ourselves," he said, "at least during quarantine. If the shuttle crashed, people will worry we're the last landing party."

She looked at him. "There are supposed to be five more landing parties. We're number three out of eight."

"Exactly."

"We should show this to everyone."

"Even Cliff?" Noah placed the heavy object in her hand.

"If someone hid this from me," she said. "I'd be mad. Wouldn't you?"

He nodded. "Let's compromise. Wait and see how tomorrow goes. Can't hurt to wait one day."

"Okay."

If the shuttle had wrecked, it wasn't like they could do anything about it. She took off her sweatshirt and wrapped it around the metal object. Noah's argument made sense, but she didn't feel good about it.

* * *

By the time she and Noah rejoined the others, Cliff's panic attack had fully subsided. Leigh clutched her sweatshirt, and Noah handed over the smooth rock.

"Thanks," said Cliff.

"Contrast can help," Noah replied. "Keep the two rocks around, just in case."

"You mean for the next time?"

"Hey," said Eliana, "believe me, we're all a bit panicked. Don't worry about it."

They began walking back, moving closer to the water and squishing their bare feet into the wet sand. Leigh kept a tight hold on her balled-up sweatshirt, but no one else seemed to notice. She tried not to think about what the metal wedge might mean. Noah was right: that was a question for another time.

As they neared the cabins, Cliff said, "Thanks. Never felt like that before."

"You've never gone to another planet before," said Eliana.

"Or have you?" Noah added.

They laughed.

"Let's blame the full moon," said Leigh.

"Only one is full," said Noah, "but that works for me."

"Think all three are ever full at the same time?" asked Eliana.

"That'd be somethin'."

Everyone looked skyward, but Cliff held up a hand to block the view. "If you squint," he said, moving his hand a little higher, "and cover two of the moons, it almost looks like home."

"Where're you from?" asked Noah.

"America."

"Reckoned that."

"North of San Diego," said Cliff. "A town called Encinitas."

"You surf?"

"I did."

"Same," said Eliana.

"Sweet," replied Noah. "Grew up ridin' waves myself. We'll have to make us some boards."

Unbelievable. Leigh had been not only dumped on an alien planet but also stuck with a bunch of surfers. And the surfer colonists were staring at her.

"What?" she said.

"Do you surf?" asked Noah.

"No," she said indignantly. "I'm pretty sure that wasn't a requirement."

"Guess not," he winked at the others. "I wasn't thinkin' about requirements. I was thinkin' about fun. This beach is no Maroubra, but we'll teach you how to catch some waves."

"We have other stuff to worry about first," said Leigh. But Cliff was laughing, so maybe Noah had the right approach. "Fine," she relented. "You make a surfboard, and you can teach me."

"Give me time." Noah grinned. "Give me time. But I reckon right now we could all use some sleep."

"That's for sure," said Eliana, and Cliff echoed the sentiment.

As the girls headed silently back to their cabin, Leigh couldn't decide what had been the most surprising—Cliff's panic attack, the metal object, or the surfing talk. She hadn't handled any of it as well as she would've liked, but she hadn't embarrassed herself either. That would have to do.

Back in the cabin, the two girls moved quietly so as not to wake up anyone else. They draped their wet clothes over a table and grabbed fresh ones from the cabinets. Leigh stashed the metal wedge behind a pile of jackets.

She brushed the sand out of her hair and headed toward the bunkroom.

"Lorelei," whispered Eliana.

"Yeah?"

"I promised Cliff we wouldn't tell anyone."

"No problem," said Leigh. And she meant it.

Even so, she held back a sigh. Here for less than a day, and already she had more secrets.

CHAPTER 6

Lex wandered the barren area of the plateau and mulled over what he'd seen. He stopped several meters from the edge of the cliff and looked out at the ocean.

He and Olu had arrived on the plateau a few hours ago, shortly after nightfall, and received a brief update. Lex was pleased to hear the new colonists had enjoyed an evening campfire and surprised to learn they'd divided into two cabins. His own landing party had bunked together for the first three months—splitting up only after the arrival of the second group and the ensuing epidemic.

Naturally, each landing party would have its own way of doing things. That was the biggest argument against quarantine. Better to have a new landing party feel part of the colony than develop its own separate identity. By necessity, that concern had given way to the larger one of survival. Such was the reality on Marjol, and they all knew it.

Lex looked up. The cluster of stars they called the Jellyfish hadn't moved much. The night was young. Gazing at the Jellyfish, he wondered how many stars he was seeing—hundreds, maybe thousands, denser in the middle and then less so in the ethereal edges. He ran his hands over his face and through his hair and gazed down the beach. Thanks to the moons and their reflection off the water, he could see the outlines of the three cabins in the distance. Darkness was a good sign. If anyone were sick, they'd have a lantern on.

He wondered what had caused the fight in the waves. No one could've been badly hurt, or they wouldn't have spent all that time walking the beach. Still, Lex wished he'd brought a monocular so he could be sure.

He walked over to the large boulder where he and Olu were camping out. Wrapped in a blanket with his face turned toward the rock, the other boy stirred.

"Everything's good?" asked Olu.

"Yeah," said Lex.

"My turn?"

"Not yet."

Olu pulled his blanket over his chin and went back to sleep. No use waking him until the Jellyfish moved directly overhead. The quarantine plan was for the two of them to pull night duty on the plateau, return to Homesite for some sleep each morning, and join their work groups in the afternoons. It'd be a long week; might as well let Olu sleep when he could.

Lex sat down and listened to the waves hitting the shore below. Unlike his landing party's first night on Marjol, the sky was clear, and the stars were bright—an auspicious welcome. One of the two smaller moons was full, and he could make out the familiar craters on its surface.

He leaned against the boulder. The quarantine was in place. Seven days to go.

***

Midmorning, Lex was sound asleep in his bed at Homesite but soon found himself running back to the plateau. Mia had come to get him and Olu because of some emergency or, as Mia had called it, a "semi-emergency." Whatever that meant.

When they reached the plateau, there was no obvious sign of an emergency—full blown, semi, or any other kind. Nothing more than Ada and Shane staring through monoculars. The two stood side by side, talking quietly, the contrast in their silhouettes a reminder of how small Ada was. Shane—average in height and build—dwarfed her.

From a distance, an uninformed observer would assume Shane was in charge. Upon drawing closer, that assumption would change. The observer would notice the surety of Ada's stance, the confidence in her demeanor. Ada had glossy face-framing black hair and eyes just as dark, which gave her a look of intensity, but her smile was warm and genuine. It was this combination of grit and compassion that made her a great leader.

"What's up?" asked Lex.

"Here," said Ada, handing him a monocular, "see for yourself."

Lex worked to adjust the lens while Olu shaded his eyes and peered down the beach into the distance.

"Haven't seen one of those in a while," said Olu.

"One of what?" asked Lex. He saw nothing remarkable—merely a handful of new colonists wading by the beach cabins.

"Glitterblob," answered Ada, and Lex swung his focus farther offshore.

"Ridiculous name," said Olu.

"Don't blame me," Ada said. "You named it before I was here."

"It wasn't me, it was our landing party," said Lex, "but the name fits. And it's better than GASM—Giant-Ass Sea Monster—which was the only other idea."

"I don't know," said Ada. "I kind of like GASM."

"I voted for it," said Olu.

Lex ignored them. He had found the glitterblob. Even through the monocular, it was impossible to tell what kind of creature it was, other than large and iridescent. Its overall shape was hard to determine since much of it stayed underwater, but what they could see looked like a gelatinous mass. A rainbow of colors reflected off its sparkling outer layer, which was at least a hundred times the size of a human. No one knew whether the glitterblobs moved under their own propulsion or floated with the sea; no one knew whether they were animal or plant or something else.

"It's far from shore," said Lex.

"Not the glitterblob," said Olu. "Someone's out there."

Lex lowered the monocular to get the big picture. Sure enough, some idiot was swimming out toward the glitterblob—a male idiot from the looks of it. The creature would likely disappear long before he got there. The problem was the rip current.

Lex looked through the monocular once again, focusing on the errant swimmer. Yes, definitely male, and yes, definitely being pulled out by the current.

"Who wants to go with me?" he asked.

"No one's going anywhere," said Olu. "Mia, thanks for getting us. It's good to know what's going on. But Lex and I are going back to sleep."

"Very funny," said Lex.

"We set up the quarantine for a reason."

"What about him?" Shane pointed at the swimmer.

"Exactly," replied Lex.

"Look!" said Mia.

Lex watched as three figures emerged from one of the cabins and ran down the beach in the direction of the swimmer. He put an eye back up to the monocular.

"What are they carrying?" asked Ada.

"Looks like rope," said Lex, "and wait, the girl in the baseball cap picked up a piece of driftwood."

"I hope they don't do anything stupid."

"Here, you can watch." He handed her the monocular and debated whether to run down to the beach.

"I don't need this," said Shane, giving the other monocular to Olu.

"Don't you think we should help?" asked Lex.

"*Merde*," Ada replied. "We can't. There's nothing we can do. And if we try, we risk the whole colony. That's the point of the quarantine."

"We have to try," said Lex hopelessly.

Olu grabbed him by the shoulder and pointed. "Look. They are trying."

The three members of the rescue party had walked down the beach past the rip current. They waded into the calmer waters while trying to get the attention of the one in danger.

The misguided boy was being pulled quickly away from shore. But the swimmer was smarter than Lex had expected. Instead of pitting his brute strength against the ocean's, he was alternately floating and swimming parallel to the shore, trying to escape the grip of the rip current without exhausting himself.

Meanwhile, the three would-be rescuers were also proving their mettle. They were staying well away from the current and had tied a piece of driftwood to each end of the long rope. As Lex and the others looked on from afar, the rescue was slowly but safely enacted—the troublemaker pulled in toward shore.

Eventually, the four of them emerged from the water. Lex watched the girl in the baseball cap separate from the group. She carefully wrapped up the driftwood-rope contraption and walked it into a cabin while the other two berated the misdoer. Naturally, Lex couldn't hear the conversation, but their body language made it obvious what was going on.

The scolding didn't last long, however. In a few short moments, the rest of the third landing party came running down the beach to join them.

The baseball cap girl emerged from the cabin and stood by herself, now empty-handed. She turned and looked up toward the plateau.

"I'm going back to bed," said Lex.

"Same," said Olu.

"Sorry to wake you," said Ada.

"All good."

Lex and Olu didn't speak while they crossed the plateau, but as soon as they entered the tall grass, Olu remarked, "That was interesting."

"Really?" said Lex. "I don't know why they woke us up if we weren't going to do anything."

"Don't play dumb."

Lex stopped walking. "Ada," he said, rubbing his eyes. "Ada needed you to back her up on not doing anything, on sticking to the quarantine."

"Us," said Olu. "She needed us. But your dramatics were useful. It's good for everyone to see we consider the options."

"It wasn't dramatics," said Lex impatiently. "It's important to try. The *trying* is important."

"I get it. You know I get it."

Lex nodded.

Olu clapped him on the back. "The thing is ... inaction is sometimes the hardest action to take."

"Yep." Lex started to say more, but really there was nothing more to say. The boys continued down the path to Homesite, and he changed the topic. "You know," said Lex, "some of the new colonists seem really water savvy."

"Oh no you don't," laughed Olu. "They get to choose their work groups, same as the rest of us."

"I'm just saying—"

"No recruiting."

Lex laughed, and the two friends jostled each other the rest of the way back to Homesite.

CHAPTER 7

Noah's rip current escapade had been a sobering experience for the third landing party. It was one thing to be told there was a dangerous current ... quite another to watch someone be swept out to sea.

But at least they'd been *warned* about the rip. No one had mentioned gigantic sea monsters.

Searching for more clues about the planet, Leigh, Eliana, and Cliff gathered the information sheets from the cabins. They painstakingly compared notes to see if they'd missed any details the first time through.

They hadn't. Judging by the handwriting, three different people had written the notes, but the text was verbatim from one cabin to the next.

"That was a waste of time," said Leigh.

"Nah," said Cliff, "now we know."

"Well, thanks for helping me."

"*De nada*," said Eliana. "We're all in this together."

They left one stack of notes in the unoccupied cabin and walked out into the sunshine. Leigh stared across the ocean at a horizon filled with nothing but water. It was a calm, clear day with gentle waves, but all she could think about was what might be lurking below the surface—what creatures swam or writhed or wriggled in the alien sea.

"Come on," said Cliff. "Let's see what everyone's doing."

"Probably trying to find some shade," said Eliana. "It's hot."

Sure enough, they found the rest of their landing party lounging in the one shady spot beside the first cabin. A few colonists tossed the frisbee back and forth; everyone else sat on the sand. Having been told to stay put made going somewhere all the more desirable. Yet they weren't rebellious enough to return to the landing plateau and walk inland.

Their earlier high spirits had been replaced by ennui and restlessness—never a good combination. Leigh was tempted to retrieve the metal wedge from where she'd hidden it; that would interrupt the inertia. But more and more she agreed with Noah. Adding another layer to everyone's uncertainty wouldn't help.

"What's up?" Cliff asked the group.

"Trying to figure out what to do," said Nick.

"We could walk past the plateau," said Noah. "Not go up the path, stay on the beach."

"Head toward the mountains?" suggested Leigh.

"No," said Shin. "Too far away."

That's why she had said *toward* the mountains, but Leigh didn't push it. The mountain range dominated the distant landscape, stretching as far across the center of the island as they could see. The weather was tropical, but these were not the lush, welcoming mountains of somewhere like Hawaii; instead, the barren peaks rose unevenly against the sky, bleak and uninviting.

"How about that way," suggested Noah, pointing down the beach in the other direction. "Let's see what's on the other side of that big rock."

"I'd be up for that," said Shin.

"Me too," said Eliana

In fact, everyone agreed with the proposal. It was a good compromise between their desires and their fears.

The big rock was only about a kilometer and a half away, but the shoreline altered considerably in that distance. Halfway there, the wide beach narrowed into a thin strip of gravelly sand. By the time they reached the big rock, the colonists were ankle-deep in water, and the beach had changed to a rocky ledge. Fortunately, the water remained shallow, and they navigated easily around the rock.

A delightful surprise awaited them on the other side—a small inlet with a sandy beach and placid water. At Eliana's suggestion, they took a break in the peaceful surroundings.

Recalling Cliff's words from the night before, Leigh squinted and scanned the inlet, trying to ignore the purpleness of the plants and the darkness of the sand and rock. No matter how tightly she squeezed her eyes, it didn't look like home.

She watched Cliff for signs of another panic attack, but he seemed relaxed. Of course, that's how he'd seemed the day before. And it wasn't just Cliff. All twenty of them were walking around with a layer of anxiety right below the surface.

At Matt and Noah's prompting, they resumed the journey, and it didn't take long to reach the tip of the island. "Tip" was a bit of a misnomer, since it would've been impossible to pick one spot marking the island's end. Instead, it was a mixture of rugged ledges, towering cliffs, and rock formations jutting out of the sea in all directions. There was no way to walk around the end of the island, and judging from the rocks and waves, there was no way to swim it either.

The nuggets of dark rock dotting the deep blue ocean were objectively beautiful, but the sight made Leigh feel trapped. The landscape held forth against them on one side while forty strangers barred them on the other.

"What's that?" Noah pointed at one of the rocky protuberances.

"What's what?" she replied.

"Something shiny. Like metal." Noah waded out toward the rock. Had he already forgotten the rip current?

"I see it," said Cliff and Matt, and the two boys followed Noah into the choppy waves.

Fortunately, the ledge extended offshore. Noah made it to the craggy rock in chest-deep water. He rounded the corner of the rock and disappeared from view; however, his ensuing "Mates, have a look!" could be heard loud and clear over the surf.

"Let's go," said Eliana.

She and Leigh swam out to join the others. On the far side of the rock, Matt, Cliff, and Eliana were tall enough to stand with their heads out of the water. Noah bounced on his toes up and down, and Leigh treaded water. All five of them stared at what was wedged into the rock.

Cylindrical in shape, the object had been smashed on one side. Wires and dark-silver shards of metal stuck out from the damaged frame. It was at least ten meters in length. Scorch marks scarred the outer covering in several spots, but otherwise it was the same shiny white as the shuttle that'd brought them to the planet. The same shiny white as the piece of metal Leigh had stubbed her toe on the night before.

"White with silver spikes," said Noah, looking directly at her.

She swam backward a few strokes, attempting to see the top end of the cylinder, but the angle at which it was trapped in the rock made such a view impossible.

A few more colonists swam up behind her.

"What is it?" asked one.

"Looks like a piece of a spaceship," said Noah.

"Our shuttle?" said Cliff.

"Dunno." Noah moved closer to the rock and looked up into the center of the object. The bottom of the cylinder was several meters above his head.

"Careful," said Eliana.

Noah put his hands on the rock's rough surface. He pulled himself up, but his fingers slipped, and he splashed back into the water. A few more attempts ended the same way.

"Let me give you a boost," said Matt.

"Try me," said Eliana. "Push me up there." She put one foot on a groove in the rock and another in Matt's hands.

Noah moved behind them. "I'll catch you if you fall."

"I think the water will be softer," Eliana joked.

"Careful," said Cliff. "If that thing comes crashing down, you'll all be crushed."

He was right, but there was no need to worry. The rock was too slippery and the water too deep. Eliana didn't make it any closer to the cylinder than Noah had.

Leigh swam farther away, once again attempting to get a better view. The new vantage point didn't help, but she heard calls from back on shore. Swimming around the rock, she saw colonists waving at her to return. Zalfaa pointed at a spot on the beach where they'd stood a short while ago. It was now covered with water.

"Tide's coming in!" she shouted.

Leigh swam back to those huddled underneath the cylinder. They were swimming, not standing, and even Noah agreed it was time to leave. They swam into shore, and all twenty of them headed down the beach back toward the cabins.

Those who'd seen the cylinder described it to the others. The consensus was that it must be a piece of a wrecked shuttle, possibly the one they'd ridden in.

The tide continued to rise, and the colonists waded up to their waists through spots that'd been knee-deep not long ago. As others discussed the wreckage, Leigh thought about the pilot who'd helped her. Was she still alive? Were there other shuttles and other pilots who could bring the rest of the landing parties?

She wondered if Cliff were fingering his bumpy and smooth rocks. She missed her necklace.

Once they returned to the wider beach, Leigh steered the conversation onto something else. She walked with those at the edge of the waves, comparing notes about beaches they'd walked on Earth, assiduously avoiding more talk about wrecked shuttle parts.

Other colonists were farther from the water, throwing back and forth the foldable frisbee that had once again made an appearance out of Milo's pocket.

As they neared the cabins, Sammi sprinted to intercept the frisbee as Noah tossed it to Milo, but she didn't quite get there in time. Milo laughed and tossed the frisbee on to Matt, who snagged it out of the air in what was admittedly an impressive catch, despite the showboating.

"Heads up!" shouted Matt as he tossed it in Sammi and Milo's direction. The two of them went for the frisbee, and although Milo's reach was longer, Sammi picked the better angle. In the end, neither of them got a hand on the disc, which went skittering into the tall purple grass as Milo and Sammi crashed onto the ground alongside it.

They were laughing as it happened—then suddenly they were screaming. Noah and Matt ran over, but as they reached down to help, the boys drew back and started rubbing their arms.

"Get the med kit," shouted Noah.

Leigh took off for the cabins; Cliff joined her. They raced there and back, stopping only to grab the medical supplies.

By the time they returned, the four who'd been injured had moved into the water. Noah and Matt were farther out. As they swam into shore, Leigh could see their arms had patches that were swelling and blistering. Matt had blisters erupting on his forehead too.

Those who'd fallen into the plants were nearby, waist-deep in the water. Sammi's right side was covered in rash and blisters, but Milo looked the worst. The side of his face was bruised and puffy, and his left eye was swollen shut. It looked like he'd gone three rounds with a prize fighter, not fallen into a shrub.

Leigh's bunkmate, Zalfaa, was helping Milo rinse his face. And it was Zalfaa who reached for the med kit.

"What happened?" asked Leigh.

"Sap in the leaves," replied Zalfaa, "a thick milky-white sap."

"It ate right through my clothes," said Sammi.

Noah waded toward them. "Everyone should take a look at the bushes," he said. "Learn what to avoid. The short ones with the thick leaves."

Zalfaa dug through the med kit and pulled out several items. "I have some medical training," she said. "Anyone else?"

"A little," replied Eliana.

"Red Cross water safety," said Cliff.

"That works," said Zalfaa. "Cliff, you and Eliana watch how I treat Sammi's arm, then do the same to Matt and Noah." They nodded. "Milo, I need you to keep dunking your face in the water, but don't rub at it too hard. Shin, can you help him? I'll get to him after Sammi."

"Lorelei, each of them gets an antihist—one of the antihistamine tablets." Zalfaa handed the pills to Leigh. "And can someone go get towels and more fresh water?"

Two people took off running for the cabins.

"Now," said Zalfaa, opening a tube of ointment. "This should help."

***

That night, Leigh found herself once again staring into the darkness and listening to her cabinmates breathing down below. She couldn't help but wonder how the other girls did it—millions, no make that trillions, of kilometers from home, and yet her roommates had fallen asleep quickly. Mind-boggling.

What else was out there? Who knew what plants might carry even greater dangers? What creatures lived in the ocean? Or on the beach? They had no idea what was on this planet.

She didn't want to think about the shuttle wreckage, or whatever it was. At his lowest point today, Milo had asked, "What are we doing here?" Leigh had no good answers.

CHAPTER 8

Hours later, Leigh was still awake. She gave up on sleep, pulled back the duvet, and slid down from the top bunk. Zalfaa didn't move. Leigh picked up her shoes and headed to the cabin's main room. She grabbed a sweatshirt from the cabinets, debated taking pants but decided boxer shorts would be enough.

The sound of the waves grew louder as she stepped outside and stood on the beach, alone with the three moons, one almost a perfect circle and the others shimmering more than half full in the night sky. The rockiness of the hills behind her cast tangled shadows amid the reflected light. She wondered if there were ever nights that were truly dark.

Leigh tilted her head back and gazed up at the stars.

Same galaxy, different view.

Perhaps other planets were being colonized too. That hadn't been part of the briefing, but it might be true. She wondered where they could be. She wondered where Earth was, out there in the vast beyond.

Knowing her thoughts would lead to homesickness, Leigh returned her attention to the shoreline. She meandered along the beach toward the plateau where they'd taken their first steps on the planet. At the base of the cliff, she headed up the path toward the landing spot. It was littered with pebbles, but it was easy trekking.

Halfway up, she paused, reconsidering. The shuttle's video had told them to head a kilometer inland. The handwritten note in the cabin said to stay on the beach during the quarantine. What could it hurt to split the difference?

She pushed up her sleeves and headed toward the plateau.

***

At the top of the path, Leigh discovered she was not alone in the moonlight.

Two boys, both familiar faces, sat about ten meters away, leaning their backs against a tall smooth boulder.

"Don't come any closer," said Olu. "The quarantine is not a joke."

Leigh felt like a child who'd snuck out of the house and been caught by her parents.

Olu's blond friend, the one she'd heard him refer to as Lex, stood up. "Is someone sick?" he asked.

"No," she said defensively.

"Do you need help?"

"No."

"Then why are you here?"

"I couldn't sleep," said Leigh.

Silence.

"I couldn't sleep," she repeated, "so I was looking at the stars and the moons and the waves and wandering around."

"That's a lame excuse."

"But it's true."

Olu said, "You have to stay on the beach ... stick with the quarantine."

"What's your name?" the other one asked.

"What's yours?" she countered. After all, he had never introduced himself.

"Alexius," he said. "I'm Alexius. Everyone calls me Lex."

"Lorelei," she said, the name almost coming out easily this time.

Lex stared at her across the distance. Finally, he said, "Nice to officially meet you, Lorelei."

"Same."

"How's it gone so far?"

She almost laughed. He'd asked the question as if they were having a normal conversation, not standing ten meters apart on an alien planet in the middle of the night.

"Fine I guess, given the circumstances," said Leigh.

"Don't worry," said Lex. "It takes a while to get used to being here."

"Are you used to it?" she asked.

"Mostly," he said. "But there are surprises. Like a few weeks ago when Aegir showed up in the sky."

"Aegir?"

"The neighboring planet," said Lex, "over that way, down low."

She looked in the direction his finger was pointing, and sure enough, a ball of light hovered over the horizon, much smaller than any of the moons but brighter and larger than the stars.

"Go ahead," said Olu, "give her one of Ada's astronomy lessons."

Lex grinned, his smile apparent in the moonlight even with the distance between them.

"Who's Ada?" she asked.

"Ada," said Lex, "is the glue that holds us all together. She came with the second landing party."

"She's one of the leaders of the colony," said Olu, "along with me and Lex."

"The three of you run things? Like, you tell people what to do?"

"That's not how I would describe it," said Lex.

"Back to your earlier question," said Olu, "Ada knows a lot about astronomy."

"Ada knows a lot about a lot of things," said Lex. "Including astronomy. I loved looking at the stars as a kid, but I never learned much beyond our solar system. Did you?"

"Me?" said Leigh. "All I know is what I learned on the shuttle. We're circling Epsilon Eridani, an orange star, and we're on the second planet out. They used solar sails to get us to the system, to a space station orbiting the planet, and a more traditional shuttle to get us to the surface. That's all I know. I guess you know a lot more from the database."

There was silence as Lex and Olu shared a look between them, but neither responded.

"I can wait and learn it later," she said. "Obviously, we noticed you didn't leave us techs at the beach."

"There aren't any," said Lex.

"Aren't any?"

"Techs," he said. "There aren't any, at least none that work."

Leigh tried to let that sink in.

"Let's sit down," said Lex.

He started to sit, then refrained when Leigh said, "No thanks, I'm good."

She wasn't. Her legs trembled, and her stomach churned as if she'd eaten rotten fish. But the boys didn't need to know that. She felt faint with the realization that all her questions had no answers, that all the promises for more information were empty ones. But she had to keep it together. By confronting Olu and Lex, Leigh had unwittingly become a spokesperson for her landing party. She didn't want to let them down.

She shifted her feet and forced herself to stand taller.

"There are techs here," said Olu, from the comfort of the ground. "Pads, comms, goggles, holodiscs, all with a stash of solar batteries. But none of it works. Hasn't since we arrived."

"Maybe," said Leigh, "when you let us join you, we can fix them."

"If you can," said Olu, "I'll be thrilled."

From the ten-meter distance, she couldn't tell if he was being serious or sarcastic. But she was buoyed by the possibility: broken techs could be fixed. It was better than no techs at all.

"Let me tell you what we do know," said Lex.

"From Ada?" asked Leigh, determined to prove she could follow the conversation even as she absorbed the shock of what they had to tell her.

"Mostly Ada, but others too. Epsilon Eridani is a star that scientists have been studying for centuries. It's a lot like Earth's sun, though much younger, and an orange star instead of a yellow one."

"The video said we might know Epsilon Eridani as Rán," said Leigh.

"That's what most of us call it," said Lex. "According to Ada, Rán was one of the first stars to be given an official name in addition to a scientific designation. And let's face it, Epsilon Eridani is a mouthful."

"So," said Leigh, her mind racing, "the star's named Rán. After the Norse god?"

Lex laughed.

"Unbelievable," said Olu.

"Don't mind him," said Lex. "He's in denial that so many people know Norse mythology."

It was a petty thing to be worried about ninety-nine trillion kilometers from home, but she made no comment.

"Anyway," continued Lex, "yes, the sun is Rán, a goddess of the ocean; the planet we see in the night sky these days is Aegir, her husband. They were named a long time ago, back when Aegir was also called Epsilon Eridani b and no one knew Marjol existed, let alone thought about living here."

"You don't call them that because we're on practically a waterworld?"

"No."

"And Marjol? Is that one of Rán and Aegir's daughters?"

"Good guess, but no."

Leigh was annoyed at herself for being distracted by this chitchat. "How long is the quarantine?" she asked.

"Only six more days."

"If no one gets sick," qualified Olu.

"Obviously," said Lex.

"You use the eight-day week," she said.

"We do," said Olu.

"It may not seem like it," said Lex, "but we're sorry you have to stay at the beach cabins. We feel bad, but if you'd been here last time, you'd get it."

"What happened?" Leigh asked. "You said people got sick."

The look that passed between the two boys made her feel even more like an outsider. It was clearly Olu's decision whether she got to hear the story, and yet it was Lex who began to tell it.

He leaned back against the boulder. "Don't you want to sit down?"

"No, I'm good."

Lex sat next to Olu and crossed his legs. He looked up at the sky, then back at her. "Lorelei, I think you should sit down."

A tiredness had crept into his voice, especially when he said her name. Leigh relented and sat, awkwardly listening from ten meters away.

Lex pushed his hair away from his face and began the tale: "Just like you, we landed on the plateau. And just like you, we didn't know anything about this planet except for what we'd learned through the video ... which wasn't much. I was kinda pissed we'd been sent to this island instead of the large continent we'd seen on the map. But it was no use worrying about that. We had pouring rain and terrible storms the first few days. We had to deal with what was in front of us."

He grabbed a handful of dirt and sand and paused to watch it sift through his fingers. Olu kept his eyes on Leigh.

"The weather got better," continued Lex, "and we started to explore. We were alone, but we'd been told to expect more landing parties—twenty new colonists every three months. As I'm sure you heard, each day here is a little under twenty-five Earth-hours long. The orbit of our planet around Rán is 384 of those days, which is why the video encouraged us to use a calendar with eight-day weeks, four weeks—thirty-two days—per month, keeping twelve months per year.

"The point is, we'd been told when the next group would arrive, so we counted down to that date. We were here first but wanted to make the next landing party feel welcome."

"Really," muttered Leigh, immediately regretting it. The quarantine bothered her, but this was no time to let emotions take over.

"Listen to the story," said Olu.

Lex ignored them both. "Unlike your landing party," he continued, "which arrived much later in the day than we expected, the second landing party arrived right on schedule. Midmorning, ninety-six days after we did. The stormy season was over, and the weather was perfect the day they came. I thought Marjol had given them a better welcome than we got.

"But I was wrong. That night, one of them got sick."

"Dhruv," said Olu.

Lex moved his feet around in the sand, and Leigh noticed both boys were barefoot. Olu's feet sat unmoving while Lex's toes dug into the sandy topsoil.

"Yeah," said Lex, "Dhruv. He was feverish, congested, nauseous, and dizzy. We used the meds, but in less than twenty-five hours, he got a rash, and five more people got sick. Some illness came with them on the shuttle.

"Within three days, all twenty of them were ill, though Dhruv and Ada, the first two who got it, had started to recover—their fevers broke, they didn't have chills, and their breathing was easier. By the end of the week, almost all of them were better, though not healthy.

"Then," said Lex, "things went from bad to worse. Two from our landing party got sick. And it didn't stop until everyone had it. For whatever reason, the second round was worse. Way worse. We couldn't stop throwing up. The fevers were higher. The rash lasted longer. Everything. A handful of us nearly died."

Lex paused.

"One of us did," said Olu.

"Rina," said Lex, his voice quiet, barely carrying across the distance between them. He cleared his throat and dug his toes farther into the sand. When he resumed talking, his voice was once again easier to hear. "Rina," he repeated. "She died. I don't know why she's the one who didn't make it."

"That's awful," said Leigh.

"Yeah," he said, "it was. It is. Those weeks were terrible. We all suffered. But the worst ... the worst by far ... was losing Rina."

All three of them fell silent while Leigh debated what to say. She searched for words that would help but knew there weren't any, so she settled for the only ones she had: "I'm sorry."

"Thanks," Lex replied.

Olu simply nodded.

She understood their position. Lex and Olu were protecting the thirty-seven other people who'd gone through the epidemic with them and survived. She couldn't blame them.

But they needed to understand that she had her own nineteen people to protect.

"When you're sure we haven't brought an epidemic," said Leigh, "there are twenty of us ready to join you."

"We know," said Olu.

She refrained from asking more questions. The two boys had shared more than she would've expected, and she'd shared nothing in return.

Leigh stood up and looked at them once more in the moonlight. Lex leaned against the boulder, his toes gently stirring the sand. Olu sat, unmoving, staring at her.

"Don't go wandering again," said Lex, who accompanied the warning with a grin.

She instinctively smiled in return.

"He's serious," said Olu.

"I know." She turned and headed toward the beach, wondering what it would be like when the quarantine was lifted.

CHAPTER 9

A few hours later, Lex felt Olu nudge him awake.

"Already?" asked Lex.

"Red sky rising," said Olu.

"You're in a good mood for so little sleep."

"No complaints."

Lex laughed. Since when did Olu complain?

He stood up, shook himself awake, and raked his fingers through his hair. The refreshing scent of early-morning sea air blew across the plateau. Daylight was on its way. Though the stars had disappeared, all three moons still watched over them from up high. After six months, Lex hadn't lost his sense of awe at the sight. He hoped he never did.

The two friends stretched their legs and walked past the spot where Lorelei had stood a few hours ago.

"You think she'll tell the others about last night?" asked Lex.

"Would you?"

"Two days after landing? No, probably not."

"There's your answer."

They gazed at the dark ocean stretching in front of them, the final beams of moonlight gracing distant waves. Behind them, the star they called Rán rose in the sky, its fiery color never more apparent than during this transitional moment between night and day. An orange-red glow spread across the island, soon reaching the two boys on the plateau.

As true daylight sprawled across their corner of the planet, the boys turned their backs on the ocean. They traversed the plateau, stopping at the entrance to a well-worn path amid tall vegetation.

"What if," said Olu, "when we arrived, we'd been tossed into a surprise quarantine. Who would've gone exploring, gone asking questions?"

"I don't know," said Lex.

"Really? Because I'm guessing it would've been you."

Lex thought there was an equally good chance it would've been Olu and Michele, but he kept his mouth shut. That topic was a sleeping bear he didn't poke. Fortunately, sounds of those taking the next shift could be heard in the bushes, obviating the need for him to respond.

"You're awake," said Ada as she came into view.

"What'd you expect?" said Lex.

"Nothing less," she replied.

"Three from Maps. That's gutsy," teased Lex. "You keep stealing people from Rose's work group and she'll make you pay, you know."

"Don't start," laughed Ada. "You're the ones who won't let anyone help with the night shifts, so don't hassle me about the day shifts."

"Just an observation," said Lex.

Luisa and João, who'd arrived with Ada, grinned at the exchange. Lex gave them a wink. He wanted to ensure they knew the leadership remained on good terms despite the bumps along the way the past few days.

"We had a visitor," said Olu. "One girl. Nothing to worry about. She kept her distance."

"One of the rescuers from yesterday," said Lex.

"Anyone sick?" asked Ada.

"No."

"What about injuries?"

"She didn't say anything."

"Good."

"I knew they'd come looking for us," said Olu.

"Surprised it was this soon."

Lex stretched his arms and gave an exaggerated yawn.

"Get some sleep," said Ada. "We'll talk more later."

"You know where to find us," said Olu.

Lex gave the morning shift a wave before heading down the path with Olu. When they were a few steps away, Ada said, "Next time, we're doing night shifts differently."

"We can hear you," said Lex over his shoulder.

"That's the idea," replied Ada.

Even Olu laughed.

***

The day went smoothly. No more "semi-emergencies" occurred, so Lex slept through the whole morning. He spent the afternoon working in Boats with Michele and the rest of the crew. Then he and Olu took over for the night shift, and no one showed up in the middle of the night.

First thing the next morning, however, the twenty-five-hour respite from chaos ended as Lex felt Olu shake him awake more harshly than usual.

"Get up," said Olu. "She's back."

Lex stumbled to his feet and wished, not for the first time, that their supplies contained coffee. He grabbed his canteen and splashed a handful of water on his face. A low glow ebbed in the sky, but true daybreak was yet to come.

By the time he turned around, Lorelei stood in the same spot as the other night. She wore a faded black and red baseball cap with a fancy L on the front, and she was fully dressed, pants instead of boxer shorts this time. Not that he was looking at her legs.

"I waited till first light," she said. "We need your help."

He took a step in her direction. Olu put a hand on his arm to keep him from going farther.

"Is someone sick?" asked Olu.

"No. Not sick." She visibly took a deep breath, and then words poured out of her. "People are hurt. From falling into a plant. It happened two days ago. Everyone was getting better at first, and those who just touched the plant are fine, but the two who fell on it are worse."

"How so?"

"Milo—he's the worst—his face and neck are swollen. He can't see out of one eye, and it's starting to affect the other one. Sammi's better, but only because it hasn't reached her face. Not yet. Everyone else is acting like they'll be fine and arguing about other things, but Zalfaa and I are worried Milo's going blind."

"Blind?"

"You told me that last time around, people got sick the first night they were here. This morning starts day four for us. I did the math. It's been a minimum of 122 hours since coming out of cryosleep. And no one is sick, not like that. But Milo and Sammi need help, and I thought you might know what to do, so here I am."

She crossed her arms and stared at them.

"What's everyone arguing about?" asked Lex.

"What?"

"You said everyone is arguing. About what?"

"Dumb stuff, mostly," said Lorelei. "And a discovery we made."

"Discovery?"

"Trapped in a rock. Looks like a piece of a wrecked shuttle. A metal cylinder."

"Near the cabins?"

"No, near the tip of the island."

"You found this yesterday?" asked Olu.

"The day before."

"Same day as the injuries."

"Yes."

"You didn't tell us about either when you were here before," said Olu.

"No," she said slowly. "I didn't." She squeezed her arms more tightly across her chest. "We went back yesterday, some of us. At low tide. To try to remove the cylinder from the rock. We couldn't do it. But I can tell you that it looks a lot like this." She reached in her sweatshirt pocket, pulled out an object the size of her fist, and threw it toward Olu. It hit the sand a few meters in front of him.

The object looked man-made, and the side they could see was coated in the same glimmering white as the shuttle that had brought them to the planet's surface. Lex resisted the urge to pick it up. He didn't want to be the first to cross the boundaries of the quarantine.

"Does anyone else know you're here?" asked Olu.

"No." She looked down at her feet.

"Don't be afraid," said Lex.

"I'm not."

"Don't be stupid," said Olu.

Lex wasn't sure whether the comment was directed at him or Lorelei.

"Let's sit down," Olu continued. "We have more people arriving soon. We'll wait for them, then decide what to do."

They all sat. Lex stared at the metal object. Could it really be part of a wrecked shuttle? He looked back at Lorelei. The early morning sun put a blush of color on her face.

Holy crap!

He knew who she was. In the sunlight, with her hair pulled back, it clicked.

Lex stole another glance. Yep, she was Leigh Crawford. Older, her hair a different color, but it was her.

His first instinct was to reveal the lie. But he hesitated. After all, Lex didn't know her personally, only through media. Would anyone else recognize her? He doubted it. The story had gone international, but only in Texas did they care so much about the ex-governor's daughter.

Lex had lived in the Lone Star State one year—the worst year of this girl's life. It'd been the worst year of his life too, but his misery hadn't been public.

He looked at her again. Sitting on the plateau with her hands wrapped in the folds of her sweatshirt, she looked scared, but the set of her shoulders showed determination mixed with the fear.

Alone, she'd come to ask for help—not for herself but for others.

Lorelei.

A good name. He wondered why she'd chosen it.

Whatever the reason, Lex could respect the choice. He would sit here and call her Lorelei, and he would see what Olu and Ada wanted to do about her plea for help.

***

Later that morning, Lex once again sat with his back against the boulder on the plateau. He turned over the wedge of metallic debris in his hands and ran his fingers across the smooth surface on one side. He stashed the chunk of metal in his bag.

Olu and Ada had gone with Lorelei to gather the new arrivals. They'd been gone longer than expected when he heard voices on the beach below. He walked to the trailhead and received the hand signal from Ada that meant all was going well.

As they headed up the path, Lex's doubts about ending the quarantine diminished. The colonist walking next to Ada had to be Milo, and he looked worse than Lex had imagined. One eye was swollen shut, and the other was half open. A hideous bubbling rash spread down his neck and arms. The boy held his body stiffly, as if bending at the waist would further aggravate his discomfort. He was flanked on either side by Ada and another small girl. They each held one of Milo's arms, and he walked hesitantly, relying on the girls to guide him.

With her free hand, Ada once again gave Lex the signal that all was going according to plan. He waved back.

Ada was the most organized person on the planet, but she could also be the most demanding. If she thought things were going well, that was a good sign.

Although she grew up in France, Ada spoke flawless English. Lex liked to tease her that her English was too perfect; even with a slight French accent, she was better spoken than he was. Ada always laughed it off. He supposed she was used to being good at everything.

Olu brought up the rear of the group, talking quietly to Lorelei and a boy whose name Lex didn't know, but whom he recognized as one of the rescuers from the rip current incident. After the past hour, it was likely both Ada and Olu had everyone's names memorized. Olu would have made it a priority, and Ada would have done it without trying.

"Let me introduce you to Milo," said Ada, "and this is Zalfaa."

"I'm Lex. Sorry you've had a rough time. We'll get you to Homesite and see what we can do."

"For Sammi too," said Zalfaa, gesturing toward a girl whose arm was in a sling and whose neck was covered in the same lumpy rash as Milo's face.

"We'll take care of everyone," Lex assured her. "Let's back up a little to make some space."

Ada leaned close to Lex and whispered one word: "Noah."

Lex nodded to show he'd heard her, then raised his voice: "Greetings! My name is Alexius. Please call me Lex."

The group quieted down. The frizzy-haired miscreant who'd created such a stir the morning of the glitterblob was easy to pick out. Noah was one of the few whose posture was relaxed, not tense. The only one who was smiling.

Lex's job was to get an instinctive feel of the situation before deciding whether to continue to Homesite. He wondered whether Olu or Ada knew how little he relished the task. Yes, he'd been able to stop some fights before they began, and yes, he'd known when Gwen needed to change work groups. But that had been the luck of being in the right place at the right time, plus some common sense.

Those same instincts told Lex these people weren't hiding anything that Lorelei hadn't already told them. Sure, it was a gamble to take the newcomers to Homesite after only two and a half days of quarantine. But it'd be a different kind of gamble to send them back to the beach cabins.

"Let me show you the way," said Lex, and he turned to lead them through the tall purple grass to their new home.

CHAPTER 10

Leigh trudged inland, a nagging worry hovering in the back of her mind—what if someone in her landing party got sick? What if they infected the whole colony? It would be her fault.

Earlier, Lex had looked at her strangely. Did he think she didn't understand the risk? Did he feel differently now that he'd seen Milo and Sammi for himself? It didn't matter. She didn't care what Lex thought.

She *did* care that they didn't have much farther to walk. Her stomach hurt. Her legs ached. She had thought the increased gravity was no longer affecting her, but maybe she was wrong.

The path turned once more, and Leigh stopped thinking about gravity. She gaped at the colony's homesite. The buildings were the same size and construction as the quarantine cabins and built in a familiar row—five cabins this time, two more than on the beach. But the similarities ended there.

More than a kilometer inland, these cabins were surrounded by vegetation, even something resembling short trees, but mostly clumps of shrubs and tall grass. In front of the cabins at each end of the row was a large cleared area. The nearest clearing had three fire pits and a bunch of flat rocks. It was a big area—another cabin could've fit in it. The other cleared area was barren except for a wide, shallow, stone-circled pit in the middle. Scrubby trees and bushes grew between the two clearings, but not thickly enough to block the view.

Physically, the landscape looked nothing like the beachfront area of the past few days. Even so, the biggest difference was the intangible one. This site felt permanent, as if people actually lived here. The ground was scuffed with well-worn pathways between the cabins and from the cabins to the clearings. Sticks lay in small piles beside the fire pits, a torn yellow shirt on top of the closest one. A round table sat on the far side of the clearing, a handful of spoons on top of it and a pair of sand-caked shoes discarded below.

Sweat trickled down Leigh's neck and pooled around her collar bone. The humidity felt thicker here. The sea breeze blew more faintly inland, and the scent of human life mixed with the saltiness in the air.

"Welcome to Homesite," said Olu.

"Home sweet home," said Ada.

The moniker was surprisingly apt. Beside the center cabin was a water catchment system: wide cones of thick tarp feeding into hand-carved wooden pipes that emptied into a giant barrel-like container. The front of the building was decorated with a garden—alien plants and grasses lining both sides of a rock-bordered walkway in front of the cabin's door.

Farther down the row of buildings, the next cabin was painted with a kaleidoscope of colors. Splotches of red, orange, yellow, and pink were punctuated here and there with bits of glistening brown and black. The colors covered all but the top corner of the building's front, the one unpainted patch a dull, unfinished scar on an otherwise brilliantly breathtaking façade.

In contrast, the other building next to center—the cabin Leigh thought of as number two—retained its original sandy color, with one exception. Someone had decorated the front by chipping away at the external layer to create a beautiful, almost geometric design.

As they walked closer, Leigh saw that the chipped decorations extended past the front of the cabin and partway down the building's side. It was subtle, intricate work. The bottom color was only a shade darker than the surface, but shifting shadows in the carved lines made the design appear almost alive. Mesmerized by the décor, Leigh missed the first part of Olu's announcement.

"The three work groups are out doing their jobs," he was saying, "but Food will be back by midafternoon to start preparing dinner, and the others will be back before we sit down and eat. By tonight, you will have met everyone. In the meantime, four of us are here to help, to take care of Milo and Sammi, and answer any questions that come up."

Four?

"This is Rose." Olu gestured to a girl with an angular face, black skin, and a multilayered braid of thick hair running down her back. "Unlike Ada, who arrived in the second landing party, Rose has been with us since the start. That means she lives in Floraville, the center cabin, with eight other girls who came on the first shuttle. We decided, since there are only six girls this time around, that you could join Rose in here."

"Who lives in the other buildings?" asked Nick.

"The rest of the girls live there." Olu pointed at the painted building. "And this one," he said, "is the first cabin we ever lived in." They all turned toward the building with the geometric carvings.

"It's got all the boys," said Olu, "and is full with eighteen. So we're giving you a new building. Right next to ours." And he pointed to the first one in the row.

Noah took a step in that direction and made a show of inspecting the five cabins. Several of the other boys followed suit.

As Olu watched the newcomers' theatrics, his expression didn't change. He did, however, glance over at Lex, who crossed his arms but otherwise didn't move.

Noah pivoted toward the cabin at the far end of the row. "I reckon we might want the other empty one."

"Yeah, why not that one down there?" asked Shin.

"Come on, guys," said Cliff. "The first one'll be fine."

Olu stood, unmoving, but Lex stepped into the mix … literally. He pushed several of the boys aside and stood directly in front of Noah. "We agreed," said Lex, "to answer all questions. Even stupid ones."

Noah gave him an exaggerated smirk and a brief eye roll.

Ignoring both gestures, Lex said, "Two reasons why you're in this cabin. First, we have a system, and it's working. We'd appreciate it if you didn't screw it up. Second, we use the fifth cabin when someone is sick and we need to take care of 'em." He leaned closer to Noah. "You sick and didn't tell us?"

"Never been healthier," Noah replied.

"That's good."

The two boys stared, their faces centimeters from one another, their eyes unblinking. No one made a sound.

Lex said, "Let me show you the cabin."

"Appreciate it," said Noah.

And that was that.

As the boys departed, Cliff shared a quick grin with Leigh. She smiled back, attempting an expression that would mask the feeling in her gut. She'd put all this in motion, and while it had garnered them the help they needed, she didn't know if it'd been worth the cost.

Lex led the boys into the cabin while the other two leaders, Olu and Ada, exchanged a few words with Zalfaa, then guided Milo away from the group. Zalfaa walked over to where Leigh was standing.

"They're going to take care of Milo," said Zalfaa, "then come and get Sammi."

"You think Milo will be all right?" asked Leigh.

"This was his best chance."

"Sounds like he needs to stay out of the sun."

"Should've kept him inside yesterday," said Zalfaa, "but I thought the salt water might help."

"You didn't know," said Leigh. "It's their fault. They didn't even mention the plant in the notes."

"It's nobody's fault."

"Ada didn't seem overly worried."

Zalfaa put a hand on Leigh's arm. "Can you imagine what they've been through? I'm guessing it takes a lot to get that girl worked up."

"Hey!" yelled Sammi. "You coming?"

"Right behind you," said Zalfaa.

Leigh took one last look in Milo's direction, then joined the other girls as they followed the stern and silent Rose through the alien garden and into their new cabin.

***

During dinner that night, Leigh stared at one of the cookfires as she finished her meal of seaweed and fish. Only a handful of hours had passed, but she could already laugh at how intimidated she'd been by Rose.

That morning, Rose had led them into the cabin without a word, and Leigh's muscles had been taut. But once the girl graced them with a big smile, everything changed. In an engaging British accent, Rose provided the greeting to Marjol that Leigh had been waiting for. She would have loved such a greeting a few days earlier, with any accent! But better late than never.

Rose had empathized with the difficulty of accepting the decision to be a colonist, especially when they couldn't remember making that choice. She provided practical tips, like how to alter the shirts for a variety of looks and fit, and how to keep sand out of the bed even when it was everywhere else. Rose answered their questions without guile, even the dumb ones about bathroom habits and the dumber ones about the boys.

She'd taken them on a thin downhill path to a nearby spring and given Sammi and Eliana squishy objects. In fairness, the objects looked more like dark pieces of poop than anything else, but Rose said the substance grew in the shallow coves and functioned like a sponge. They filled buckets with clean spring water, and Sammi used one sponge to clean her injuries. Eliana joyfully scrubbed her face with the other one before handing it to someone else. When it was Leigh's turn, she rolled up her sleeves and washed her arms. The sponge was heavier than it looked, but it worked well; the sand and salt rinsed off easily.

While at the spring, Rose had asked about Olu and Lex's initial greeting on the plateau. She'd been horrified at Nick's close call but had otherwise laughed at Sammi's version of those events. According to Rose, Olu and Lex had been nervous about the whole thing, and

Olu had planned to be the only one to talk. It was oddly reassuring to know the two of them hadn't been as composed as they'd appeared.

The girls had also talked to Rose about the cylinder in the rock.

"Could you tell how long it'd been there—days, weeks, longer?" she'd asked.

"No idea," said Sammi, "but it was still shiny white ... except for the scorch marks, obviously."

"I don't think it's moved since landing there," said Eliana. "Didn't look like it to me, at least."

Rose had nodded somberly, then shifted the mood by jumping to her feet. She'd led them back up the hill and left them alone to settle into the empty bunkroom that was their new home. The six of them had chosen the exact same spots as they'd had on the beach. Leigh had taken the top bunk above Zalfaa without a second thought.

"Water?" asked Cliff, interrupting Leigh's thoughts and offering a canteen as he sat down beside her with his dinner.

"Thanks."

"The quarantine's over," said Cliff. "I thought you'd be happy."

"Oh, I am. Just tired."

"Know what you mean. First time I've been relaxed since we landed."

Leigh nodded.

Cliff took a few bites of his meal, then pulled out his two rocks. "Don't worry, I'm not getting rid of these anytime soon."

He stuffed the rocks back into the pocket that fastened shut. Leigh appreciated that feature of their pants. She kept her multi-tool there. It served the same purpose as Cliff's rocks, more than she wanted to admit.

"Of course," he continued, "I'm still worried about Milo."

"Same here."

"And I have a lot of questions."

"Yeah," said Leigh, "like where does all this firewood come from?"

"And what about the wrecked shuttle pieces?"

"Hmm."

"And the broken techs." He finished chewing another mouthful of food. "Can't decide which is worse: no database or no comms."

"No database," said Leigh. "With that, we could fix the comms."

"I'm not giving up. Other people couldn't get the techs to work, but maybe we can."

"You sound like Eliana."

"Yeah, she already convinced Olu and Ada to let us take a stab at it."

"As your daily work?" asked Leigh.

"No," said Cliff, "during downtime, after dinner."

"You still have to join one of the three work groups?"

"Oh yes."

"Picked a group yet?"

"Either Boats or Maps," said Cliff. "Not Food."

"Really? You seem to be enjoying your dinner as much as I did." She showed him her empty bowl. "I mean, what they call fish isn't much like fish, but at least it's not Foobrew."

"Totally agree," he said after finishing another mouthful. "But I'm not a good cook. Catching fish, gathering seaweed ... I don't know." He shrugged. "Food's a clever group. I mean, cooking grates out of metal shelving. Nice! Not sure I'd be much help."

"But you think you can fix the pads and comms that no one else has been able to fix for months."

"That's different."

"Just teasing," she said. "I'm doing Maps."

"That's what Eliana's doing."

"You should join us. Rose leads the group. We'll get to explore. Learn to identify dangerous plants. Know our way around. It'll be fun."

Cliff gave her a look as if her version of fun might not be the same as his, but before she could convince him, Rose interrupted their conversation. The collegial Rose of earlier was gone, replaced once again by the stern, no-nonsense girl of Leigh's first impression.

"Lorelei," said Rose, "finish up. The leadership is having a special meeting tonight because of you. We need to go."

"Is she in trouble?" asked Cliff.

"Not for you to worry about," replied Rose.

Cliff stood up as if to come with them.

"I'm good," Leigh assured him. But oh, how she appreciated the offer.

Rose grabbed the bowl out of Leigh's hands, gave it to Cliff, and said, "Can you wash that for us?"

"Thanks," added Leigh. She followed Rose away from the dinner area and toward the painted cabin. She had to do this alone. That way, if her plan backfired, the leadership would hold it against her personally, not against her entire landing party.

She flexed her fingers, took a deep breath, and walked through the door.

CHAPTER 11

Lex paused a minute before entering the girls' cabin affectionately known as Jackson Pollock. As was often the case after dinner, several residents were painting the outside of the building, adding to the colorful splashes, blots, and drips that were slowly transforming their home into a work of art. Given that every drop of color and every means of applying it had to be crafted from raw materials, it was a time-consuming task. It was also awesome.

He stepped into the cabin and closed the door behind him, surprised how cool the floor felt on his bare feet, but not surprised he was the last to arrive. It was difficult to be late on a planet with no clocks, yet somehow Ada and Olu always interpreted "after dinner" to be a few minutes earlier than he did. And naturally, Rose and Lorelei had arrived as quickly as possible after washing their bowls.

"Greetings." Lex grabbed an empty chair, turned it around, and slid it between his legs. He leaned over the back of the chair.

"Nice of you to join us," said Ada.

"Happy to be here," replied Lex, concluding the ritual.

"Let's get started," said Olu, a sign he was taking the meeting seriously since "What's new?" was his typical opening salvo. Lex was used to Olu's formal way of talking, but he became wary when his friend turned it up a notch.

"Rose," said Ada, "why don't you begin."

"If you want."

"You're Maps leader," said Olu. "We want your opinion."

"Because," said Ada, "the issue began with Lorelei asking to join Maps and do interviews, which brought up the questions about our leadership and our rules."

Lex glanced at Lorelei to see if she appreciated the diplomacy at work, but he could read nothing but wariness on her face.

"Before we get to all that," said Rose, "I'd like to go back a little further. To talk about how the leadership and the work groups got started."

Lex hadn't seen that coming. Even Olu lifted an eyebrow in response, and almost nothing surprised Olu.

"Go ahead," said Ada.

Rose looked more carefully at Lorelei, as if willing her to envision a past of which she had not been a part. "You have to understand," she said, "what it was like that first fortnight, what it was like to be the first landing party. Every morning, we turned to Olu. We never elected him; we didn't have to. He was our gaffer—our leader. We all knew it.

"We kept trying to get the techs to work," continued Rose, "waiting to hear from someone, to learn something, but Olu helped us move on from that. He suggested work groups; we never questioned it. We were building something here, learning our way around, making this place our own. And we worked hard. Every day. Except for the rare occasion Olu declared a day off work—a Freedom Day."

Rose leaned back, shifting her body in conjunction with the inevitable shift in tone.

"I've heard you know what happened next," she said. "Three months passed, Ada's landing party arrived, and we all got sick." She looked down at the table, then back up. "One of us died; thirty-nine of us didn't.

"That's when Ada became one of our leaders. She was the one we looked to when so many of us were close to dying, and Olu was," she hesitated, "not much better."

Rose glanced at Ada, who'd folded her hands together on top of the table. Ada showed no sign of surprise that Rose was sharing these thoughts. Did she know Rose planned to discuss this? Had Ada encouraged her to do so?

Lex had no clue. There were always layers upon layers when dealing with girls.

"During the epidemic," continued Rose, "Ada made sure the water catchment system was looked after, she set up shifts to care for those who were sick, and she started regular meals that weren't liquid. Let me tell you, daily solid food tasted brilliant, even when there wasn't much of it.

"Finally, the worst of the epidemic ended, and the whole colony met together. As usual, Olu and Ada were a step ahead of the rest of us. They formalized the work groups. Michele had always led Boats; we made her the official leader. I was asked to lead Maps. And Dhruv was asked to lead Food. Everyone else divided up as they wished, and most people are still working in the groups they chose a couple of months ago.

"The leadership began meeting after dinner every night, then switched to every other. We became a real colony. We formalized our rules, like not going anywhere alone and not talking about Earth." Rose paused.

Lex noticed she'd omitted the most controversial rule, the temporary one—no sexual relations. There'd already been plenty of argument about it earlier. He understood their outrage, but the newcomers had never seen friends almost die because they'd had a miscarriage.

"Let me stop," Rose said to Lorelei, "and see if you have any questions."

"Now?"

"Before we talk about the interviews."

"Um, no," said Lorelei. "Wait ... I ... well, I have a lot of questions, but just one for now."

"Ask."

"Why is Lex here?"

He stared at her.

"I mean," she continued, "I know he's part of this ... uh, this unelected triumvirate who rule the place, but why? Your story talked about the leaders being Olu and Ada."

Lex reined in his indignation.

Rose and Ada both started to speak, but Olu put out his hand and said, "Let me answer that one."

"Actually," said Lex, "let me."

Olu nodded.

"First," said Lex, "none of us 'rule' ... we 'lead.' There's a difference. Second, I'm here because Olu and Ada want me here. If that changes, I'll be happy to let someone else take my place."

He and Lorelei regarded each other for a long moment. Lex was telling her the truth but couldn't tell if she believed him. He was tired of this meeting already.

"Let's get back on track," said Ada, "and talk about the proposed interviews. Lorelei wants to do them as an addition to the history I'm writing of our colony, correct?"

"Yes," said Rose. "She wants to interview each colonist about their time on Earth. Learn everyone's story of their lives before becoming colonists. We're the first settlers—"

Her words were interrupted by a crashing noise and shouting outside the cabin. Lex bolted out the door.

Over by the cook fires, two boys were throwing punches, and a whole lot of people were doing nothing but watching. Lex ran over, wrapped his arms around Declan, and pulled him back from the fight. His adversary—who was almost twice Declan's size—advanced toward them, but Noah stepped in and pulled the larger boy away.

Some of the onlookers scattered; others hovered nearby. Lex could feel the tension in Declan's muscles as he glared at the other combatant.

"That's enough, Matt," said Noah.

Matt—not the newcomer Lex had foreseen as a threat.

He heard the door to Jackson Pollack close as Ada and Olu joined the scene. Colonists were gathered behind either Matt or Declan, ready to take on the other faction if Lex and Noah let go. Two groups willing to fight each other was an annoyance. More troubling was the rest of the tableau. The colonists were divided by landing party.

Ada marched over in front of Declan, who'd arrived with her three months ago, as had many of those standing next to him. A few members of the first landing party flanked them as well.

"Declan," said Ada. "What's going on?"

Lex allowed Declan to shake himself free.

Olu approached the other group. Noah loosened his hold on Matt but did not let go. Nobody spoke.

"Declan," repeated Ada. "What's going on?"

It was a good question. Declan was a big talker, and he could get under people's skin, but he was no fighter ... though he was a lot scrappier than Lex had thought. Both Matt's and Declan's faces showed signs of having received more than one punch.

Lex resisted the urge to give them each a few more.

"Speak up," Ada said to Declan.

"I started it," said Matt. He stepped forward as Noah released his arm. "But I'm not sorry. I'm not letting some bogan tell me what to do."

Declan's face colored as he glared at Matt. "I was just remindin' our two new friends from Down Under that they have to follow the rules same as everyone else. Rules apply to cabbage-headed eejits too."

"No one," said Matt, "tells me who I can talk to."

"You were doin' more than talkin' to her," said Declan.

Ah-ha.

"You do have a lot of rules," said Noah.

"No," said Ada. "Only a few. Help your work group. Don't go off alone. Don't talk about Earth. And don't have sex until we can deal with the results. No, I don't know when that will be. Yes, I know you don't like it. But those are the rules. Same ones we talked about earlier. They're for everyone's safety, one way or another."

Matt took a half step forward. He towered over the diminutive Ada, but he was mistaken if he thought that would intimidate her. Lex felt the adrenaline kicking through his veins, making it harder not to punch Matt's smug face.

Someone walked up behind Lex and placed a hand on his shoulder. He turned, ready to throw the first punch, but it was Michele—

whether she meant to provide Ada further backup or to keep Lex from doing something stupid, he wasn't sure.

For a moment, no one moved.

Then Ada took a step even closer to Matt and Noah, her face composed but her hands clenched. "In case you haven't noticed," she said, "we're battling for survival. It may not seem like it when you're hanging out with your pals after dinner, but trust me, we're in a war. Every day is a battle. Every. Day. The rules are in place to give us a chance to win."

No one responded. Matt frowned at Ada, Declan scowled at Matt, Noah clapped Matt on the shoulder, and the silence dragged out.

"Are we done here?" asked Ada.

"Almost," said Olu. He walked over to the water catchment barrel, which had been knocked on its side during the fight. There was a pool of water on the ground. Olu righted the container—not a barrel really, but a scooped-out burl cut from a tree found many kilometers away. He made a show of checking it for cracks, then turned back to face everyone.

"We haven't had much rain lately," said Olu, "and we need all the fresh water we can get. Declan, I suggest you and Matt make some trips to the spring to replace what you spilled."

Suggest, as if it were an option.

"I'll do it right away," said Declan.

"Same," said Matt. "Sorry about the water."

He did not apologize for punching Declan, but it was a step in the right direction.

"No worries," said Noah. "I'll help too."

"Me too," added others standing near him.

"Same," said some of Declan's supporters.

All in all, about a dozen people headed toward the spring. Lex was glad to see Dhruv went with them. He had stood beside Declan during the face-off. Nevertheless, as Food leader, Dhruv would be more worried about the water than anything else.

***

A few minutes later, Lex reentered Jackson Pollock. Once again, he was the last to arrive.

"That's not over," he said.

"Maybe not," said Olu.

"Let's finish this discussion first," said Ada. "Rose, why don't you pick up where you left off."

"No," said Lex. His adrenaline was still pumping, and their calm attitude was not helping. He turned another chair around and sat down. "No more nice talk. We're all being polite in here, but you saw what's going on. They've been here less than a day and they're already stirring up trouble." He looked at Lorelei. "The only reason they're here at all is because you challenged the quarantine."

"We had to," she said.

"That's not the point."

"What is your point?" asked Ada.

"Discussion time is over. Let's make some decisions."

"I'm for that," said Olu. "But let's make them wisely."

"Fine," said Lex. "Problem number one: Milo and Sammi. Sunlight makes the rash worse; frequent cleaning makes it better. Put them on the double-antibiotics, keep them inside, keep ... uh, what's her name? The healer girl?"

"Zalfaa?" suggested Lorelei.

"Yeah, sorry, Zalfaa. Let her stay with them for a couple of days. They can all join work groups when everyone's healthy. The Food work group comes back to Homesite midday. If your friends want to do something useful, they can help prepare meals. Problem solved."

"And if Milo or Sammi gets worse?" asked Lorelei.

"Here on Marjol," said Lex, "we deal with what happens, not what might happen."

Lorelei gripped the edge of the table and met his gaze with a steely glare, but he didn't care. She was part of the problem. It was one thing to ask for help, one thing to lie about your name, but it was another to constantly cause drama. He was over it.

"Meanwhile," he said, "you've already cut short the quarantine, and now you want to do interviews—have us all talk about the past."

"Let's slow down," said Ada. "Rose brought the interview question to us because she thought Lorelei's idea was useful. And I agree."

"But what you said outside is true," argued Lex. "We're fighting for our survival. And we won't get anywhere looking backward. It does no good to make people homesick when they can't go home, when many aren't sure why they left. You were just arguing for this rule a few minutes ago."

"I'm not saying we give it up," said Ada, "but rather make an exception—for the interviews. I'm aware the rules aren't perfect, any of them. Telling people not to talk about Earth doesn't mean no one ever mentions it in a private conversation, and it doesn't mean people don't think about it."

It was the same with sex, and they all knew it.

"I remember," said Rose, "when we first decided not to talk about Earth. We'd sat around reminiscing about what we missed most. That was stupid. These interviews would be different."

"Olu," said Ada, "what do you think?'"

Olu didn't speak immediately. When he did, it was not what Lex expected.

"I cannot tell," Olu said directly to Lorelei, "if you're one of those people who thrive on stirring up trouble, or if you're someone who'll help make our colony better."

He paused, and no one uttered a word.

"I think perhaps you are both," said Olu. "We're creating history every day. I'm proud of that, and I hope everyone is proud of that. We need to focus on what's in front of us, not behind us.

"However, ignoring the past never ends well. I believe there'll be a point in the future when we'll want the information, when some of it might be useful. At the same time, there's a lot going on, and I don't know if this is worth the risk."

"Every day is a risk," said Ada.

"That is true."

They sat quietly for a moment. Lex felt his heart rate slow. He was finally coming down from breaking up the fight. And he was starting to see a solution.

"If we're considering this," he said, "let's be sure these interviews are what we think they are: fact-finding, not 'pour your heart out' conversations."

"I agree," said Rose.

"That would be essential," said Olu.

"Here's what I propose," Lex replied. "What if Lorelei interviews me? I'll be her guinea pig. We'll know what it's really like. Then we can decide yes or no."

"I like it." Ada nodded slowly.

"A reasonable plan," agreed Olu.

"It's settled," said Lex.

"You haven't asked me," said Lorelei.

He stared at her. He was annoyed, but damn, she was right. "Well?" he said. "What do you think?"

"That's a fair solution," she replied.

"Why don't you interview him tomorrow night," Ada said to Lorelei. "You can do it right after our normal Friday leadership meeting."

"Works for me," said Lex.

"I'll be there," Lorelei replied.

"Good plan," said Olu. "Thanks for bringing this to our attention, Rose."

Rose nodded. As she and Lorelei got up and walked toward the door, Lex pulled out the wedge-shaped hunk of metal.

"Now," he said to Ada and Olu, "what do you want to talk about next—spaceship parts falling from the sky or new colonists wanting to have sex?"

It was too many problems to be dealing with at once, but none of the problems could wait.

CHAPTER 12

The next morning, Leigh officially joined the Maps work group. She looked around at the dozen colonists on Sunrise Beach who were waiting for Rose. None of them had been involved in last night's fight. Maps might be a good choice for more than one reason.

It was her fifth day on the planet after her fourth night of not enough sleep. Reaching down, Leigh stretched and touched her toes, then placed her palms flat on the sand and held the position for a slow count to ten. She could feel a tug on the scar tissue under her shoulder blade, but it was a muted twinge, nothing too painful.

Rose arrived. "Good morning," she called. "We have lots to do today."

Leigh straightened up and pulled her ponytail tightly through her baseball cap.

"Nothing is a secret on Marjol," said Rose to the group, "so you probably know that Maggie, Luisa, João, and Ada aren't working with us today. They're part of the squad over on the other side of the island … trying to dislodge the cylinder from the rocks.

"The rest of us will teach the newbies all they need to know and then put them to work. We'll divide into three small groups. Once your group goes out searching, if you find anything that looks like a piece of a shuttle, bring it back, but chart where you found it. If it can't be moved, sketch it and map the spot.

"Shane and Mia, grab your groups and head off. Lorelei, Eliana, and Cliff, you're with me."

Leigh dutifully followed Rose as they separated from the larger group. For several hours, Rose taught them how to catalogue the vegetation. They learned to identify the poisonous plant with the milky-white sap, which grew amidst the tall grass that was purple-and-green striped. The grasses had many subtle differences—numerous textures, blade widths, and colors depending on how much sand was in the soil and whether the grass was ever shaded.

After the botany lessons, Rose taught them how to recognize the limits of high tide and how to calculate distance with ropes. She was a stern but fair taskmaster. As they grew more proficient, Rose's manner eased up a bit, but it was always clear she was the boss.

When Rose was satisfied that all three of them had the knack of standard practices, they hiked down the beach toward the tip of the island, mirroring the walk Leigh's landing party had taken three days ago on the opposite side. The coastline remained sandier for quite a while on this side, but eventually, it too turned to ledge, and the rocks became darker and more jagged.

"What do we do now?" asked Eliana.

"Wade into the water around that bend," said Rose. "I've never been past here. But that's why you joined Maps, right? To see what's not yet been seen." She headed into the knee-deep water. "Oh," Rose looked back over her shoulder. "One more thing. I hear you're all bloody good swimmers. I'm not! I'm counting on you to be sure I don't drown."

"Remind me again," said Cliff, "whose idea was it to join Maps?" But he laughed as he said it.

Leigh laughed in return. It felt good to have something useful to do and friends to do it with.

"Hurry up!" said Rose. So they did, wading into the water and following Rose into the unknown.

***

The rocks near the tip on the sunrise side were layered and relatively easy to climb. No metal debris turned up, but at the end of the workday, Leigh made a discovery: an entrance to a cave. It was big—

almost as tall as Cliff. Even so, with the mouth of the cave tucked between rocky ledges, she'd almost missed it.

They ventured a handful of meters into the opening, but Rose turned them around before they could go farther. No reason to explore without a lantern. Leigh and Eliana measured the opening, and Cliff noted its location on their hand-drawn map.

"Time to go home," said Rose. "See how Rán's getting low? That's our deadline for heading back. If we're late, Dhruv and the rest of Food won't be done before nightfall."

"Does Boats return the same time as us?" asked Cliff.

"In theory," said Rose. "Sometimes Michele gets carried away and forgets, but Lex tends to remind her."

Lex.

Leigh was interviewing him after dinner.

She'd stayed up late writing and rewriting the questions until her hand cramped so much she had to stop. She was as ready as she could be.

They hiked back along the coastline. As before, they didn't need to do any swimming, though they waded at knee level for about a hundred meters. The waves were stronger than they'd been earlier, with a few cresting above their waists. Rose quieted during that part of the journey, but soon the four explorers were out of the water and back on the beach.

They had less than a kilometer to go when they turned uphill onto the trail that led from Sunrise Beach to Homesite. Leigh's feet began to drag, and she had to push herself to keep up with the others. The vegetation was a good distraction. After a day of Rose's teaching, Leigh could identify almost everything. She was able to tell when the landscape shifted to more dirt and less sand simply by noticing what was growing on the side of the path.

Near the top of the hill, a scorching scent interrupted her thoughts. The cook fires smelled different. Rose took off in a sprint, and Leigh chased after her. Upon entering Homesite, she skittered to a halt.

One cookfire blazed out of control, as did several nearby bushes. Smoke was starting to pollute the air, and three people were on the ground, injured. Leigh recognized Shin and Dhruv as two of the injured colonists. She couldn't remember the name of the raven-haired girl who was sitting up, holding her head in her hands.

Olu was shouting orders, organizing a water brigade from the spring to Homesite, directing others to tend the wounded. For a fleeting moment, Leigh wondered why they didn't use the water barrel, then she noticed the barrel on its side. An odd combination of fire and flood ravaged the dinnertime spot.

Her first instinct was to ask Olu how to help, but another voice called out.

"Lorelei!" said Zalfaa. "Over here!"

She raced toward Zalfaa, who was bent over Shin. Leigh took one look at him and hoped she didn't throw up. Shin's left side and chest were badly burned. The pupils of his eyes were dilated and darting back and forth.

"You're doing a great job of holding still," Zalfaa said to Shin as Leigh knelt down next to her.

"What can I do?" Leigh asked. Chaos erupted around them as more bushes caught fire and more voices and bodies joined the scene.

The escalation agitated Shin, but Zalfaa's voice soothed him. "That's just Boats returning. More people to help. And look—Lorelei is here to help you."

"Me too," said Lex, kneeling on Shin's other side. "What happened?"

"Short version," said Zalfaa, "Shin fell into a cookfire. His breathing is normal, no head injury, nothing major broken. We have to treat the burns. I think we're looking at a combination of first- and second-degree burns, but I won't know for sure until we get his clothes off."

Leigh expected Shin to react to that statement, but he lay listless with his eyes closed.

"We need to move him away from the fire," said Zalfaa. "See if you can get him in a cabin. Lie him down, feet elevated, head flat. Unless he starts throwing up, then turn him on his side and come get me right away. Got it?"

Leigh and Lex nodded.

"Lorelei," said Zalfaa, "get the filled canteens. Use water and wet towels to clean any skin that's burned. You can mix a little soap with some of the water if an area looks dirty. Once you've cleaned his wounds, you need to keep them free from sand and dust."

"Won't be easy," Leigh said.

"It's critical."

"We got this," said Lex.

"One of you come get me when he's cleaned up," said Zalfaa. "Keep any burned skin uncovered until I can see how bad it is." She rubbed her eyes with the back of her hand. "On second thought, let me see it before you start cleaning. I want to be sure none of these are third degree."

"Where'll you be?" asked Lex.

"Helping the others." Zalfaa stood up and headed into the smoke.

Amid the cacophony, Leigh willed her stomach to keep its contents. She focused on Shin's undamaged face.

"Lorelei, you okay?" said Lex.

"Fine."

"We got this," he repeated. "Shin, I'm going to lift you up and carry you to your cabin. It's the closest one, and I'll go as fast as possible, but this'll probably hurt like hell. Hang in there. We'll take care of you. Got that?"

Shin nodded but didn't open his eyes.

"Lorelei's going to run ahead," said Lex, "and move a mattress out to the big room, near the window, so we'll have plenty of light."

She took her cue and ran for the cabin.

**

Leigh had no previous experience caring for burns, or any other trauma that wasn't her own, but she was determined to be useful. As they stripped cloth away from Shin's body and uncovered the extent of the damage, her stomach tightened with worry. She willed her hands to stop shaking so that Shin wouldn't feel her concern.

Lex's hands were calm. His step-by-step explanations were clear. By the time Shin lay in nothing but his underwear, Leigh felt steadier despite the red and darkened skin covering much of Shin's left side.

"Do you have water?" asked Lex. "Zalfaa mentioned canteens."

"We keep a stash in our bunkroom," said Leigh. "I'll grab them and be right back."

"And find Zalfaa," he called as she headed out the door.

The air was filled with smoke, but the flames had been extinguished. A couple of Leigh's cabinmates circled the buildings, searching out any smoldering grass amid the blackened vegetation.

"You okay?" asked Eliana as Leigh ran by.

"Yeah," she said, "You?"

"All good."

"Do me a favor?"

"Sure."

"Find Zalfaa and send her to Shin's cabin?"

"Got it."

Leigh grabbed a handful of canteens and ran back to the two boys, slowing her footsteps as she opened the cabin door. No need to let Shin think that a quick pace was necessary for his recovery. She walked across the floor, proud of herself for not gasping at his damaged body.

Pathetic! It was time to toughen up.

Zalfaa joined them in less than a minute and verified no third-degree burns. She gave concise instructions before heading back outside, and they got to work. Shin's left hand, arm, and shoulder had suffered the worst of the burns and were, therefore, the most difficult to clean. Some of those burns were already starting to blister. Leigh and Lex washed one area at a time, moving methodically and being careful to use clean water.

Lex spoke to Shin in low tones throughout the process. Shin rarely flinched or moved, but Leigh couldn't decide if that was good or bad. He seemed to know they were there, but he kept his eyes closed and didn't speak.

Zalfaa returned with medicine and aloe ointment for the burns. She stood back and examined him from a few steps away.

"What is it?" asked Lex.

"I think the burns cover less than twenty percent of his body," she said, "but not by much."

"Is that important?"

"Less chance of shock," said Zalfaa. "Shin, how're you doing?"

"Had better days," he replied.

"What's bothering you most?"

"Hand."

"Several fingers are broken. You must've tried to break your fall, put out your left hand and landed on it."

"Don't remember."

"I want to treat the burns first," said Zalfaa. "Let the skin start to heal before splinting the fingers. Make sense?"

"Yes."

"The good news ... your hand is not blistering. If that's true tomorrow, it shouldn't be long until we can do more for those fingers."

"Okay."

Leigh's shoulders relaxed as she heard Shin speak. He was more alert than she'd thought. But he closed his eyes again as Zalfaa and Lex walked outside.

She was impressed—with Shin's stoicism, Lex's steadiness, Zalfaa's expertise. Olu and Ada's leadership. The two of them had taken control and averted disaster. Equally impressive was their willingness to listen. They'd wanted Shin moved to the empty cabin so that all the injured were in one place. But Zalfaa had advised against it, and they'd deferred to her judgment. Leigh questioned less and less why Olu and Ada were the de facto leaders of the planet.

She reached out and gently held Shin's undamaged arm, first to feel his pulse, then to let him know she was there. His heart rate was elevated, but not as much as she would've expected. Leigh had been seriously injured before, and she hadn't been anywhere close to this calm. Then again, she'd been alone. Shin was not.

"We're going to take care of you," she said. "It's good people here. They know what to do."

"I know," he whispered.

"You can trust them. And me. We won't leave you."

"Thanks."

Leigh squeezed his arm, then let go so she could dampen a towel and grab the ointment. She hoped the painkillers were starting to help. The next part of the process wasn't going to be easy, but if Shin was ready then she was too.

CHAPTER 13

Long after nightfall, Leigh sat on the floor and watched a sleeping Shin. She'd recently run to her cabin for some clean clothes. Now Lex was doing the same.

They'd lightly bandaged the blistered areas on Shin's upper arm. The rest of his burnt skin glistened with aloe. Zalfaa was due back any moment. A lantern sat nearby but far enough away for Shin to sleep.

He mumbled something, and Leigh scooted closer to check on him. Shin's pulse was steady, he didn't feel feverish, and his breathing was normal. She sighed in relief.

With her adrenaline waning, she stayed put next to Shin, looking at him and thinking about what she'd learned from her cabinmates. The way Sammi told the tale, she laid the burden on Dhruv, but Leigh had long ago learned to hear biased stories and pull out the basic facts.

It had started while Shin was tending a cookfire, waiting for fish to be brought over. Gwen had approached with a bottle of isopropyl rubbing alcohol in her hands and offered to give him a backrub after dinner. Shin had demurred, but Gwen hadn't left him alone. Instead, she'd opened the bottle of rubbing alcohol and tempted him to smell it, claiming to have enhanced it with a fragrant leaf she'd found that morning. Leigh was certain flirting had been going on from both sides by that point. Which was when Dhruv had arrived with the fish.

Their three stories varied, though their actions were not in dispute. Dhruv moved the grate off the fire pit, loaded the fish per normal, then stood up and physically pulled Gwen away. In the process, she dropped the rubbing alcohol into the fire, Shin attacked Dhruv, and the cookfire flamed up.

Leigh didn't know the details of the altercation, and she supposed it didn't matter. Gwen wacked her head on the ground, and Shin fell into the fire. Dhruv yanked him out, but by then Shin was enraged and his shirt was in flames. He swung at an off-balanced Dhruv, who fell on the edge of the fire pit and hurt his arm. Shin ran for the water barrel but knocked it over. Fortunately, somebody yelled, "Stop, drop, roll," and Shin did. That put out the flames, but he'd already been injured, and he'd already rolled into a bush, which had then begun to burn.

Given the alcohol-infused cookfire, Shin's actions, and the dry weather, the fire had spread rapidly—a result of bad luck and bad behavior. Never a good combination.

The door to the cabin opened. Leigh looked up expectantly, yet it wasn't Zalfaa; it was Lex. His face was in the shadows, but she recognized his shape in the doorway.

She stood up as he drew near.

"How's Shin?" he asked.

"Good," she whispered. "Sleeping better than I would've expected."

"Excellent." He gestured for her to sit with him, far enough away not to disturb Shin.

As they leaned back against the wall, Lex moved next to her, shoulder to shoulder. This way they could whisper more easily and not disturb their patient.

With the lantern nearby, Leigh could see Lex's face. He'd washed off the smoke and dirt, but his eyes were bloodshot. He looked even wearier than she felt.

"Everything okay out there?" she asked.

"I guess. The cabins are fine. The only major damage to Homesite is the loss of the water barrel, cracked right down the middle. And we can solve that."

"But?"

"How'd you know there's a *but*?"

"There's always a *but*."

"True enough." He rubbed at some grime on his pants, which only served to spread the dirt over a larger area. "So much for my clean pants," he joked.

She smiled.

Lex stopped messing with his pants and let his arms drop to his sides, one of his hands resting in the gap between his legs and Leigh's. He flexed his fingers, and she could feel the motion carry up his arm and into the shoulder that rested against hers. He heaved a sigh, and she could feel that too.

"The *but*," he said, "is that we have three seriously injured people—five total if you include Milo and Sammi—and everyone's angry at each other."

"How are Dhruv and Gwen? I thought they weren't badly hurt."

"I don't know. At first, it seemed Gwen had nothing more than a small bump on the head, but now she's scaring me. Zalfaa says it's a concussion, which would explain Gwen's confusion. Gotta tell you though, I've never seen a concussion this bad. People are worried. Ada, Zalfaa, and Eliana are still with her."

"Is she able to sleep?" asked Leigh.

"She shouldn't sleep for long, not until she can have a normal conversation."

"She's not talking?"

"Gwen responds, but what she says doesn't make much sense."

"And Dhruv?"

"Dhruv has a broken arm from landing on it wrong. They set it and put it in a splint. My advice—don't ask Matt about it."

"Matt?"

"Yeah, he—well, 'repositioned' is the word Matt used to describe holding Dhruv's arm, but Zalfaa says it wasn't that bad. Just that Matt's probably never seen a broken bone before in his life."

"Good job, Matt."

"Olu's with Dhruv now," said Lex, "but Matt was the one who first took care of him. He didn't hesitate to help, even though he and Dhruv have been at odds since Matt's fight with Declan last night."

"A silver lining."

"Yes."

Shin winced audibly in his sleep, but he didn't move or awaken. They watched as his breathing returned to normal.

"Guess we're not doing your interview tonight," said Leigh.

"Hah, yeah, guess not."

"Seems trivial with all that's happened."

"I don't know," said Lex. "I'm looking forward to it."

"Maybe tomorrow."

"No, it'll have to be Sunday. Saturdays after dinner I help Marko."

"With what?"

"Come by our cabin tomorrow night and find out."

"If I'm not taking care of Shin."

"Bring Shin," said Lex. "If he can do it, it'll be important for him to get up and around."

"It's a plan."

They sat in companionable silence. The warmth radiating from Lex's shoulder soothed her. The lantern glowed softly across the room, and Shin slept soundly not too far away.

She could go back to her cabin. Lex had returned, and many of the boys sleeping in the nearby bunkrooms had offered to take shifts. Even so, now that she was quiescent, Leigh was too tired and too comfortable to move.

She said quietly, "Thank goodness for Zalfaa. I know she doesn't know how to help Milo's rash, but she knew what to do tonight."

"Did you know she had medical training?"

"I didn't realize how much. I'm surprised they didn't put her in the original landing party."

Lex slowly turned his head toward her. "That's a conversation I just had with Olu. It's interesting how much the two of you think alike."

"Me and Olu?"

"Oh yes," said Lex.

"Olu wouldn't be thrilled to hear you say that," said Leigh, drawing her legs up and encircling them with her arms. "I think I've been on his troublemaker list since day one, or at least day two, ever since our middle-of-the-night chat."

Lex laughed, quietly so as not to disturb Shin, but it was a real laugh. "Truth is," he said, "that was the first time I noticed how similar you two are." Leigh started to protest, but Lex kept talking. "When we were at the boulder, and you were so resistant to sitting down, it made me think of Olu. He would've done the same thing, would've found a way to show he was not a pushover."

"And that's a bad thing?" said Leigh, consciously keeping her voice low. "I thought Olu was your friend."

"Best friend I've ever had," said Lex. "It's not a critique. Olu doesn't want to appear weak. He can have trouble compromising when he knows he's right. He's insanely competent but doesn't always realize it, and he questions everything."

"And you think I'm like that?" she asked, unsure whether to hope for a yes or a no.

"I think—"

The door opened. A worn-out Zalfaa walked in and sat down cross-legged on the floor, face-to-face with Lex and Leigh. "Good news," she said. "Gwen is stabilizing."

"Very good news," said Leigh, as she tried not to wonder what Lex had been going to say.

Lex leaned toward Zalfaa, his shoulder no longer touching Leigh's. "You were incredible tonight," he said to the other girl. "You look exhausted. I hope you get some sleep after you check on Shin."

Leigh tamped down an unexpected spike of jealousy. Ridiculous! She agreed wholeheartedly with everything Lex had said, and she was glad he'd said it.

"How's Shin doing?" asked Zalfaa, and Leigh realized the question was directed at her.

"Okay," she said. "His arm isn't oozing much, and he's hardly moved. Honestly, I'm surprised Shin can sleep. It's got to be painful."

"No doubt," said Zalfaa, "and the painkillers aren't strong."

"Ibuprofen and acetaminophen, right?" asked Lex.

Zalfaa sighed. "Yes, most times that's all anyone would need, but it'd be nice to have something stronger the next few days."

"Just as well not to have anything like that on the planet," said Lex.

"Maybe you're right. It's an interesting assortment of medicines."

"What do you mean?" asked Leigh.

"Two mild pain relievers," said Zalfaa, "but nothing for any serious trauma. Some diphenhydramine, which is an antihistamine. Four kinds of antibiotics: a cephalosporin, a penicillin, clindamycin, and a sulfa drug. A bunch of epineph-injectors and atro-pens, various ointments, and that's it other than basic first aid supplies."

"I've seen the list of what medicine to use for what illness, but it wasn't what I'd call thorough," said Lex.

"I don't understand why we don't have more emergency supplies— portable IVs with fluid bags, inflatable casts, insta-ice, all that stuff. I assume the database has detailed information," said Zalfaa, "but that doesn't help us."

"Hopefully, we won't need any medical stuff after this," said Leigh.

"I'm all for that," said Zalfaa, "but ..."

"Yeah," said Lex, "it's not realistic."

"More than that ..." said Zalfaa, her voice trailing off again.

"What is it?" asked Leigh.

"I'm concerned about the supplies," admitted Zalfaa. "They seem plentiful now, but they're finite. We didn't bring additional meds with us, and I assume that'll be true for future landing parties."

"Who knows," said Lex.

"So how is it okay that Gwen had her hands on the isopropyl alcohol?"

"Because now we've lost a bottle for no reason," added Leigh.

Both girls looked to Lex, who raised his hands in supplication. "I don't have any answers. No one's ever bothered the supplies before."

"Is it a big deal we lost that bottle?" Leigh asked Zalfaa.

"Any loss is a big deal," she said with uncharacteristic vehemence. "If I had to pick one thing to lose, a bottle of isopropyl alcohol is a good one. We can use it as a disinfectant, but it's not critical. Plus, we have a lot and should use it diluted. But it's not a plaything."

"And obviously flammable," said Lex.

"Honestly, I'm surprised at how much damage it did. But then I don't know the chemical properties of the plant Gwen mixed in there."

"Which," added Leigh, "probably ruined the alcohol in the first place."

"Who knows?"

"I'll give the medical supplies some thought," said Lex, "and talk to Ada and Olu about it."

"Thanks." Zalfaa got to her feet. "Time to check on the patient." Leigh and Lex stood up too. "I can do it myself," Zalfaa assured them.

"I'll come with you," said Lex. "You can give me final instructions. I'm pulling out two more mattresses; Marko and I will camp here for the night."

"Good plan. Time for all of us to get some sleep."

Leigh could see no reason to stick around. "See you shortly," she said to Zalfaa. "Goodnight, Lex."

"Night," he said, "sleep well."

Leigh stretched her arms and yawned. She imagined it'd be the first night on Marjol when falling asleep was no trouble at all.

CHAPTER 14

Leigh slept straight through sunrise. By the time she opened her eyes, her roommates were already gone. She understood their desire to get up and get moving. The light of day often brought a new perspective on things that had happened at night.

She threw on some clothes and stumbled out the front door of the cabin. Morning wasn't as far gone as she'd thought. Most of the colony was milling around Homesite, and only the Boats work group had gathered to make plans.

Leigh watched Michele organize her crew. No building boats today. They'd be hiking along the sunset coast toward the Crooked Teeth, the mountain range that stretched from one side of the island to the other. Michele was looking for a specific grove of thick, squatty trees, hoping to find another large burl to use as a water barrel. It was a long hike, so they were taking extra supplies in case Boats ended up camping overnight.

Lex was missing from his work group. Leigh assumed he was still sleeping on a mattress next to Shin. Not that it concerned her. Michele had plenty of help without him.

On the other side of Homesite, Olu stood next to the remnants of some burned shrubs. Like Leigh, he was watching Boats get organized, albeit from a distance. A second look revealed more. Olu wasn't watching the group; he was watching its leader.

She couldn't blame him. The Boats leader was one of the most striking human beings she'd ever seen. Tall and athletic, Michele was an imposing yet graceful figure with bronze-brown skin, prominent cheekbones, and wide-set eyes that took in everything.

She had short, thick dark hair. The weather was impossibly humid, and the only means of cutting hair were the same knives used for gutting fish. Yet Michele's hair was stylish.

She was the only colonist who wore earrings. Leigh hadn't brought jewelry with her, but others had. Dhruv wore a thick engraved metal band around his left wrist; Eliana had a necklace with a silver cross; and Janie wore her colorful friendship bracelet. A handful of colonists had brought a ring with them from Earth. But only Michele had earrings. Each was a silver stud in the shape of a whale.

According to Sammi, the whale earrings had something to do with Michele's Māori ancestry. Skepticism was a good filter through which to hear Sammi's gossip, yet Michele was the only Kiwi on the planet, so maybe the rumor about her earrings was true.

Leigh glanced once more at Olu. He had banished sex, but even Olu couldn't banish his own feelings. She was, however, surprised to see those feelings etched clearly on his face. She was even more surprised when Olu walked her direction.

"Lorelei," he said, "I heard you were a big help last night. Thank you."

"Actually," she said, "Zalfaa and Lex did most of the work."

Olu frowned. "A simple 'you're welcome' would be better than failing to accept my thanks."

Her stomach clenched. She never seemed to get it right with Olu.

"Let me try again," said Leigh. "You're welcome."

"Your throat hurt?" he asked.

"What?"

"You keep touching your throat. Does it hurt? From last night's smoke?"

"No ... I'm fine." It was a reflex, still reaching for her necklace. Her necklace that was gone. "How's Shin?" she asked.

"Sleeping. He woke several hours ago in pain, but more ibuprofen and aloe did the trick. Lex said Shin slept soundly afterward."

"Is Lex still with him?"

"No, Cliff and Marko. Lex is in Q-cabin."

"Q-cabin?"

"The quarantine cabin, the last one. Where Dhruv and Gwen are. Milo too."

"Oh," she said. "Nice of him to check on the others."

Olu raised his brow. "Lex is talking to Dhruv. It's too soon to deal with Gwen or Shin; they're too sick. Dhruv's doing better."

"That's good news," said Leigh, but Olu continued as if she hadn't spoken.

"We have to find a way for these things not to happen," he said. "We must get along. We must. People from all landing parties need to be friends, equals. Shin and Dhruv need to figure that out."

"And Gwen needs to draw less attention to herself."

Olu shrugged. "Gwen is Gwen."

Leigh hadn't expected such a comment from him. More proof she didn't really know these people. As she tried to come up with a reasonable response, Rose stepped out of Q-cabin and headed their direction.

"Better?" asked Olu.

"Better," said Rose. "I think Gwen's head feels like a squirrel that's been used as a cricket ball, but she's talking sense again. As much sense as usual."

"Be nice."

"Bloody hell, Olu. You know she's always chatting up the guys, right? This wasn't a one-time thing."

"I know."

Rose looked him straight in the face. "We had a long night of it, but that's no excuse. Don't go holding the girls to a lower standard than the lads. That'll lead to even more trouble than we saw last night."

"You're right." Olu rubbed his eyes with his fingertips as if to clear his vision. "I just want everyone to get along."

"He means," Rose said to Leigh, "that things have been rough since your landing party moved to Homesite."

"Hey," said Leigh.

"Nothing personal."

"Not fair," said Olu. "We're all adjusting. It's no one person's fault."

"Tell that to Dhruv," said Rose.

"I believe," said Olu, "that's exactly what Lex is doing."

"We're off!" called Michele, and they watched as the Boats work group departed from Homesite.

"I should go look in on Shin," said Olu. He nodded in the girls' direction. "Ladies, see you later," and with that he turned and walked quickly away.

Rose intertwined her fingers, stretched her arms over her head, and said, "Boys!"

Leigh grinned. "Does he always talk like that?"

"Olu?" said Rose. "He tones it down once you get to know him, but yeah, he's polite and formal and ..." she paused.

"Full of himself," suggested Leigh.

Rose laughed. "Maybe a little," she agreed. "Mostly I think it's the way he grew up. You get used to it."

Leigh sighed and rubbed her eyes. She couldn't imagine getting used to anything about this place.

"How're you doing?" asked Rose.

"Fine."

"For real? You look as awake as I feel. And that's not very awake."

"All good. What's the plan?"

"In a little while, we're going to go check out that cave you found. Right now, a bath! Boats is bathing in the ocean. For the rest of us, there are extra buckets and soap by the spring. Our group has first dibs before Food."

"Sounds great. My hair smells like smoke."

"Don't get me started," said Rose, pulling on her long braid. "Maps boys are at the spring now. We're next, soon as they're done."

"It's kind of funny," said Leigh, "how everything is divided up into girls and boys. I mean, we did the same thing on the beach. Girls in one cabin, boys in another. Girls take one chore; boys take another."

"You want to go bathe with the lads? Be my guest. I'm sure they wouldn't mind."

"Very funny."

"You're the one who brought it up."

"I'm just saying it's interesting how we separate everything by gender. After years of complaining about it, when we get to make the rules, we do the same thing."

"We all share the outhouse."

"You're mocking me."

"A little," said Rose. "I get what you're saying, and it didn't start that way. Not at all. But you've got to admit, it's a funny thing to bring up after some girl/boy drama almost burnt the place down."

"Olu can outlaw sex," said Leigh, "but he can't outlaw sexual attraction."

"Whoa, girl," laughed Rose. "I get it. I do. But they're not Olu's rules. I mean, we all agreed. Of course … I know more than a few people who break that rule."

Rose paused, but Leigh wasn't about to ask.

"Things changed after the second landing party arrived," said Rose, "and not just because we all got sick."

"Because Rina died."

"Lots of reasons. I'm not surprised things are changing again. Some stuff needs to change."

"Because eventually, we have to populate the planet."

"I guess you're right," laughed Rose.

More laughter could be heard coming up the hill—the Maps boys returning from their turn at the spring.

"Brilliant!" said Rose. "Bath time."

* * *

Later that morning, Leigh stepped into the cave she'd discovered the previous day. Her lantern lit the way through the darkness as the entryway narrowed. Rose crowded behind her, both girls slightly hunched to keep from bumping their heads, arms tucked near their bodies in the thin crevice. Leigh was beginning to worry about claustrophobia when the passageway turned and widened, then opened into a huge cavern. She and Rose stood up straight, lanterns held high, barely able to see the rocky ceiling several body lengths above them. They gaped at the sight.

Rose turned toward the cave's entrance and called, "Come on in!"

Ada had joined today's exploration. Leigh could hear her and Eliana and Cliff walking through the passageway to join them.

"It's cold in here," said Cliff.

"It's enormous," said Ada.

Leigh moved her lantern in a slow, wide circle. The shape of the cavern seemed to change as different parts of the rock were bathed in light while others were left in darkness. Several tunnels led away from the cavern. Along the rocky walls, some spots were smooth, others rough. The only constant was the lack of vegetation or any other sign of life.

"We're the first humans to ever see it," whispered Eliana.

"Seeing what's not yet been seen," said Leigh.

"Told you," said Rose.

Cliff laughed, and his laughter echoed in the stony chamber.

"Time to get to work," said Rose.

For several hours, the five of them mapped the central cavern and started to explore its network of tunnels. Given the uneven terrain, they had trouble measuring the cavern's size with any degree of accuracy, or at least enough accuracy for Rose; nevertheless, they all agreed it was almost twenty-nine meters across in its widest spot.

Six tunnels led away from the cavern. The widest one was easily accessible and extended an astonishing 46.6 meters almost perpendicular to the coast. The rest of the tunnels were shorter and smaller but relatively easy to access, though crawling was necessary.

The smallest of the tunnels proved to be the most difficult because it began a meter and a half up the cavern wall. Eliana made a valiant attempt, but she failed to fit both the top half of her body and a lantern into the opening, so she didn't see anything.

They regrouped and tried a new approach. Rose and Ada positioned lanterns to illuminate the opening. Meanwhile, Cliff and Lorelei held Eliana and guided the front of her into the tunnel. With a measuring rope between her teeth and a lantern held in front of her, Eliana looked like a figurehead on the bow of a ship. But it worked. Once she was in, Cliff held Eliana's legs while she called back information and Leigh wrote it down.

After they gathered the data, Cliff helped Eliana exit the tunnel, and the five of them collapsed on the cavern floor. The normally impeccable Eliana was a mess of cave dirt and slime, but she flashed a triumphant grin: "Mission accomplished!"

"Even without a flashlight," said Cliff.

"No use wishing for what we don't have."

"Exactly," said Ada.

Leigh drank some water from her canteen and looked at the bulky lanterns. No one had figured out their power source, but at least they worked. Too bad the same could not be said for the techs, though she remained hopeful Cliff and Eliana could fix them.

"Think there are more caves?" asked Cliff.

"It's possible," said Rose. "We found three small ones on the sunset side, also in dark rock. But nothing like this. You neophytes join us and find a giant cavern right away."

"Wonder what the rest of Marjol looks like."

"That reminds me," said Leigh. "Why Marjol? I thought the shuttle video called it Epsilon Eridani something."

"Epsilon Eridani e," said Ada, and they laughed appreciatively at her perfect memory. "It was the fourth planet discovered in this solar system. That's why it has the e designation. The star is 'A,' first planet discovered is 'b,' and so on."

"All the same," said Rose, "Epsilon Eridani e is not what I want to call my home."

"I'm glad you renamed it before I arrived," said Ada.

"The first landing party picked the name?" asked Cliff.

"We had a vote," said Rose, "a kind of contest ... Lex's idea. Each person could suggest a name, and we'd vote on it. Marjol was the unanimous choice."

"Unanimous?"

"Marko came up with it. Have you met Marko?"

"Think so."

"Marko's the youngest from our landing party." said Rose. "Only fourteen. Pale white skin—well, it's a bit darker now, but not much. Slight, wiry build. Quiet. Dark dark-brown hair that he wears back in a ponytail. Works in Food."

"I know who he is," said Cliff.

"He realized all our names started with one of six letters and he put them together."

"All twenty of you?" asked Leigh.

"M, Marko," said Eliana, "A, Ahaana; R, Rose; J, Jamaar; O, Olu. Like that?"

"Jamaar was in the second landing party with me," said Ada. "But yes, that's the idea."

"I can say it in my sleep," bragged Rose. She quickly recited: "Mary, Maggie, Michele, Myrah, Mak, Marko, Michael; Ahaana, Alexius; Rina, Rose, Raj; Jasmine, João, Jason, Javier; Olumayokun; Luisa, Laney, Lars."

"Are you trying to impress us?" asked Cliff.

"Think it'll take more than that!"

Ada laughed at them both. Leigh smiled to see the easy rapport Cliff had already established. Even with his own anxieties, Cliff had a knack for getting others to relax.

Ada stood up.

"You going?" asked Rose, as Cliff too got to his feet.

"Yes," said Ada. "Time for me and Cliff to check on the injured."

"We can come too," offered Eliana.

"No. You three stay here and finish the job."

"Leave me one of your lanterns as a backup," said Rose.

Cliff turned off his lantern and set it down next to her. "See you at dinner."

As he and Ada exited the tunnel, Leigh looked up at the cavern's roof. Most of it was swathed in darkness. With only three of them, it felt larger, spookier. For a few hours, she'd been busy enough to forget everything except the task in front of her—to put aside worries about those who were injured, about shuttle debris washing up on shore. Busy enough not to dwell on being stranded ninety-nine trillion kilometers from Earth.

Eliana reached over and turned on the lantern Cliff had left behind. The light bathed the girls in illumination and cleared away some of the darkness above.

"Two more tunnels to measure," said Rose, "and then we can do the outside work."

Leigh checked her pocket to be sure her multi-tool was there. She saw Eliana reach up and clasp the cross she wore around her neck.

It was time to get busy again.

CHAPTER 15

At the end of the workday, Rose, Eliana, and Leigh lugged the lanterns and other equipment up the path to Homesite. They were the last to return. Even Michele's crew was back. Boats had found the trees and hacked off a new burl. After rolling it halfway, they left it behind and jogged home, opting to retrieve the burl in the morning so they could join the rest of the colony at night.

Many of the physical scars from the fire were visible, but the charred remains of the brush had been cleared away. Someone had spread a blanket over the worst of the scorch marks and turned that area into a dinner spot. The smell of grilled fish permeated the air. Homesite was once again a welcoming place.

Leigh gratefully accepted a bowl of fish and seaweed and went to see Shin. He was sitting with Cliff and Milo at a table in their cabin. Shin's mobility was impaired, and the burns on his arm continued to ooze. He moved carefully, as if he would prefer not to move at all, and he barely said a word. Neither did Milo. Though the rash had stopped spreading, one of Milo's eyes remained closed, and half his face was so swollen he couldn't move it.

Cliff carried the conversation. Leigh thought back to the first night on the planet, when Cliff had needed assistance. Now he was the one doing the propping up. Cliff did both with grace. It was a good lesson to remember.

Shin stirred his food while Leigh gulped hers down. Cliff's and Milo's bowls were already empty.

"Did Cliff tell you about the cavern?" she said between mouthfuls.

"Sounds enormous," Milo replied.

"Felt enormous."

"I put Eliana on my shoulders," said Cliff, "and the top of her head wasn't even halfway to the roof."

"Do you think I could switch to Maps?" asked Shin.

"Uh, isn't that up to Rose?" said Cliff.

Shin stared at his bowl.

"You want to switch," said Leigh, "or you think Dhruv will want you to switch?"

"Both," admitted Shin.

"Why don't you focus on healing," said Cliff.

"And getting out of this cabin." Leigh collected their bowls and spoons. "I'm going to wash these while Cliff helps you get ready to walk around. You too, Milo."

Milo gave her a half-grin. Shin's countenance told her he didn't think much of the idea, but she didn't care.

"I cut the left sleeve off a shirt," Cliff said to Shin. "Let's give it a try."

"When I get back," said Leigh, "we'll walk next door and see what Marko is up to."

"Marko?" asked Shin.

"Yeah, he and Lex are working on something tonight."

"Probably Little Italy."

"What's that?"

"It's where they live," said Cliff, as he and the other two boys shared a look that indicated Leigh was clueless.

Fine. They could believe whatever they wanted so long as it got Shin out of the cabin. She knew all too well that sulking around and hiding didn't help wounds heal any faster—especially not the ones no one else could see.

* * *

Shin had been right about Little Italy. Marko and Lex were the artists chipping away at the outside of the cabin.

Each part of the design involved tiny, intricate scraping and sculpting. Marko used two objects that looked like they came from a dentist's office: a metal stylus and a sgraffito tool. He said they were used when making ceramics. Leigh was fascinated by Marko's work and intrigued that two of the things he'd brought from Earth were pottery tools.

Lex used something more familiar: a Swiss Army knife. Studying their art, Leigh could tell they'd worked separately on different parts of the building's front but were now combining styles as they chipped at the side.

The boys were mismatched, with the younger, slightly built, dark-haired Marko working next to the broad-shouldered, blond-haired Lex. She wondered what had sparked their interest in the project. Who'd been the first to suggest it? How had that conversation started? It was another reminder that months of living had gone on before her landing party had arrived.

They remained outsiders, but the barriers to their acceptance had softened, and injured or not, she and her landing party needed to mingle and find a way to fit in. Isolation often felt like a good idea initially, but it rarely worked in the long run.

As they watched the two artists, Rán drifted toward the horizon. Lanterns were turned on, highlighting the intricacy of the artwork. Other people stopped by—to chat and watch or to see how Shin and Milo were doing. Eventually, Milo left to talk with Sammi, while Zalfaa brought over a sling for Shin's damaged arm. With his forearm cradled in the sling, the pain in Shin's eyes lessened. He even smiled when thanking her.

Then Dhruv joined them. Leigh felt her jaw clench as he approached, but her worry was for naught. Shin and Dhruv apologized to each other, and though their words were stilted, the emotions behind the words seemed genuine.

During the apologies, Leigh turned to look at Lex. He winked. "Bring Shin," he'd said. Hmm. He'd manipulated the whole thing.

Neither Dhruv nor Zalfaa hung around long, but Shin was still talking about them after they left. "Dhruv says people are getting superstitious about Fridays. That's when the worst things happen."

"Give me a break," said Lex.

"And next Friday is Friday the thirteenth," added Shin.

"There's a Friday the thirteenth every month!"

"It's an artificial calendar," said Leigh.

"All calendars are artificial," said Lex.

"And this one's not very original."

"What do you mean?"

"The days of the week. With an eight-day week, you came up with Monday through Sunday, and tacked Freeday on the end. Not too original.

"Freeday is short for Freedom Day," she told Cliff and Shin.

"That true?" asked Cliff.

"I guess." Lex stopped his work on the wall. Marko, although listening to the conversation, was not diverted from his art. "Early on," said Lex, "we didn't keep track, not by weeks. We counted thirty-two-day blocks, one month at a time, so we'd know when the next landing party would arrive, but that was it.

"We worked almost every day. Whenever we took a day off, Michele jokingly called it 'Freedom Day,'" said Lex, making quotation marks with his fingers while holding the opened knife. "The name stuck. When Ada wrote out a Marjol calendar, she labeled the eighth day Bonus Day, but we told her, that's not Bonus, that's Freedom. She wrote down Freeday, and we've been saying it ever since." He shrugged.

That's how the world worked. When people were part of the evolution of things, it all seemed natural. When someone entered from the outside, it was different. Leigh vowed to do a better job of educating the next landing party.

The past twenty-five hours were catching up to her, and she was ready to leave. However, one look at Shin told her they needed to hang around a little longer. He stood awkwardly, but his face had lost its sallowness and regained some of its natural warmth.

"What are the *months*?" asked Shin.

"Good question," said Cliff. "All I know is there are twelve, like on Earth, but the names are different. We're in Virgil now, right?"

Marko smiled even as he concentrated on the wall. Lex, who hadn't yet returned to his carving, continued fielding their questions.

"Yep," said Lex, with one of his disarming grins, "you arrived on the first day of Virgil, year one."

"So," said Cliff, "I'm guessing the other months are something like Dante, Beatrice, Aeneas ..." He stopped as he noticed their stares. "Epic travelers, like us."

Leigh suggested: "Or Virgil, Homer, Horace, Euripides ..."

"Yeah," said Cliff, "ancient writers."

Lex shook his head. His eyes lit up as he smiled, his light-brown eyes and blond hair both glinting in the lamplight.

"What's with the ancient stuff?" said Shin. "Think about it. Here we are in space. Emphasis on *space*. Virgil, Ed, Roger, Michael, Judy, Ellison ..." Shin's voice faded as Lex's expression went from bemused to perplexed.

"Early astronauts who died for the cause," said Shin. "I thought it was obvious."

"You're all thinking way too hard," said Lex.

Marko spoke up: "Why don't you tell them?"

"Don't want to ruin the fun."

"Give us a hint," said Cliff.

"Fine." Lex closed the Swiss Army knife and tossed it back and forth between his hands. "One hint: next month is Turk."

"What?" cried Shin. "You named the months from *The Godfather*?"

Lex laughed; it was Cliff and Leigh's turn to say, "What?"

"Virgil. Turk," said Shin. "Virgil 'The Turk' Sollozzo. He's one of the bad guys in *The Godfather*—you know, the classic movie."

"There are good guys?" said Lex.

"*The Godfather*?" asked Leigh.

"Mafia names!" said Cliff.

"That would be so dark," muttered Marko.

They all looked at Marko, then Leigh turned to Lex. "No more hints," she said, "tell us."

"Shin had the right idea," said Lex, "but wrong classic. Ever see the *Ocean's Eleven* movies? Not the super ancient or the holo. The best ones, the trilogy, made around year 2000."

Leigh was totally confused.

"Virgil and Turk, the brothers," said Shin. "Never would've thought of that. But wait, there are twelve months, not eleven."

"We used *Ocean's Twelve*," said Lex.

"So … one month is Tess."

"True enough." Lex smiled. "Glad someone knows their classics." He opened up his knife, drew twelve lines in the dirt, and pointed to them as he explained the months. "Tess is month number two. The year starts with Danny, then Tess, Rusty, Frank, Basher, and Livingston. This month is Virgil, then Turk, followed by Saul.

"On Linus 1 the next landing party arrives, and the year wraps up with Reuben and Yen. By the time Danny 1 rolls around to start the new year, you'll be longtime residents, and we'll be welcoming the fifth landing party."

"I'll educate them about the calendar right off," said Leigh. They laughed, but she wasn't joking.

"I love it," repeated Shin.

"Your idea?" Cliff asked.

"Me?" said Lex. "No. All my buddy, Marko."

"Awesome," said Shin.

"It's entertaining," admitted Leigh, "and I've never even heard of the movie."

"Same," said Cliff.

"I'll fill you in sometime," Shin told them.

"No rush," said Leigh. "But I wish Marko had named the days of the week too—they'd be way more interesting."

She was rewarded with laughter from Shin and Cliff, a small smile from Marko, and a big grin from Lex. Then the two mismatched boys went back to their art while the others headed for some much-needed sleep.

Leigh rubbed her eyes. Her brain was foggy, but not so foggy she failed to note the improvement in Shin's mood. It'd been an evening well spent.

CHAPTER 16

Twenty-five hours later, Leigh was immersed in her interview with Lex. They sat at one of the round tables in Little Italy's common room, an empty chair between them.

Lex was from Minnesota. He didn't identify a town, and she didn't ask. The more Leigh made it clear no one had to share information they wanted to keep private, the more likely Lex would approve this venture.

The first part of the interview went smoothly. Although he'd said to avoid "pour your heart out" questions, Lex had been giving some rather heartfelt responses. He'd loved his early years in Minnesota, including his school, his friends, and his family. His father's parents had lived two hours away in a cabin near a lake, and Lex had spent many holidays and weekends there. He'd always loved being outdoors, whether swimming in a pond, fishing in a stream, or tromping through the woods in the middle of winter.

Having grown up in Texas, Leigh thought Minnesota winters must be brutally cold, but Lex made them sound magical.

The magic had stopped abruptly when Lex was thirteen. His parents announced their divorce, the cause of which he never understood, and he was forced to move out of state with his mother. A few months later, his mom was diagnosed with an aggressive form of cancer, a rare kind for which there was no cure. An aunt moved in to help care for his mom and, ostensibly, for Lex as well. In reality, he was left to his own devices.

He rarely saw his father, whom he blamed for everything—not only the divorce but also the cancer. He knew that was unfair, but he didn't care. His father became the enemy.

Life, therefore, was almost unbearable when Lex's mom died and he was forced to move back to Minnesota. Desperate to help, his grandparents bought the house next door. While Lex officially lived with his father, much of his "at home" time was spent with his grandparents.

"Did you still go out to the cabin by the lake?" asked Leigh, for he had spoken fondly of it early in the interview.

"No," said Lex. "Grams and Gramps sold the cabin in order to buy the house next door."

"Quite a sacrifice."

"Yeah, and I didn't repay them well."

Leigh waited for him to say more. When he didn't, she said, "You sound like you're close to your grandparents."

"Very."

"Do you think they supported your decision to come here?"

Lex shifted in his chair. He stretched his legs and studied his feet as he mulled over her question.

As usual, he was sitting with the chair turned around backward, and he wore no shoes, having discarded them once Boats finished for the day. Uncharacteristically, he was wearing a red sweatshirt. The evening breeze was cool, but Leigh had gotten used to seeing him in a blue shirt with the sleeves cut off. She'd never imagined he wore anything else.

Lex still hadn't answered her question, so she tried another angle. "Do you think your father approved of your decision to come here?"

"He must have, right?"

"Sorry. I'm not phrasing it well." She tried again. "Because we're underage, our parents had to agree. But there are many ways to agree. I've wondered if my mom thought it was a good idea. Did she encourage me, or did she give in because I wanted it? Know what I mean?"

"Yes." Lex sat straighter in the chair. "How did we learn about coming here? Who brought up the possibility? I have no memory of that."

"Had you ever been to space before?"

"Been to space?"

"An orbit vacation, anything like that?"

He laughed. "No, definitely not. Been in an airplane once."

Ugh. What a faux pas! Orbit vacations were expensive. She'd need a different way to ask about space travel. Assuming, of course, she got to ask anyone else these questions.

"You been to space?" asked Lex.

"I have now," she joked, trying to get off the topic. "But I have no memory of ever talking about, much less planning, to do anything like this."

"I understand why they set it up that way. Helping us not dwell on the separation."

"The cryosleep meds took those memories."

"They could've sent us with letters or videos," said Lex, "messages we left for ourselves, something. Although, for most people, it might be good they didn't. It's probably easier this way."

"But not for you?"

"Leaves me with lots of questions."

"Same," said Leigh.

"And maybe we did record messages to ourselves ... explanations lost to us because the techs don't work."

"Could be."

"I figure," he said, "that I must've really wanted this. We all must have."

Leigh nodded.

"So I'm not surprised," he continued, "that my grandparents would've supported my decision. My grandmother." He paused and smiled. "Ah, you would like Grams. She's always backed anything I wanted to do. And Gramps, well, he encourages adventures."

"This one's pretty extreme."

"True enough," said Lex. "Also true—I was headed down a bad path back on Earth. Nothing awful. But nothing good. My father had no idea what to do with me. He may've thought this was my chance to find something worthwhile, to escape the path I was on."

"He'd be proud to see you as one of the leaders."

"Surprised," said Lex, "very surprised. But then, you're also surprised. What was it you called us—the ruling triumvirate?"

"Well, you are."

"Not by choice, not for me."

"Maybe not," she said, "but Olu and Ada count on you. I see that."

"Really?"

"You do the tasks no one else will."

That had gotten his attention. Lex stared at her. His light-brown eyes seemed a darker hue than usual, maybe because of the evening light, or the red sweatshirt, or maybe because he was looking at her so intently.

"For example?" he asked.

She shrugged, attempting to convey it was obvious. "Setting up Shin and Dhruv so they'd apologize to each other, finding girls willing to befriend Gwen, telling Olu when he's wrong, doing this interview. Lots of stuff."

"I can be ruthless." He leaned over the chair, looking anything but ruthless. "Ada and Olu are the leaders. But they're idealists. They want everyone to agree, to like each other. I'm the realist. And you're right about one thing—for the messy stuff, I'm your guy."

"You let the others keep their idealism."

"Hmm."

"You protect them."

"In a way," Lex admitted. He got out of his chair and moved to the one immediately beside her. "Let's get back on track. You're supposed to be asking me about Earth."

"Sorry." Leigh could feel her cheeks blushing. She looked down and scanned her notes. "Two more questions. And you don't have to answer them."

Lex grinned broadly, his eyes alight with a hint of mischief. "I thought that was true for all your questions."

"Yes, of course." She looked down at the notepad again and calmed her skittering pulse, all too aware that Lex was now sitting next to her, no more empty chair between them. Raising her head back up, she asked, "Do you want to share a favorite memory from Earth?"

"That's easy." he said. "Times when I was a kid out at the lake. All those are favorites."

"Anything more recent?"

"No." His smile faded, and she regretted asking him.

"Last question," said Leigh. "We've established that like me, like everyone else as far as I know, you don't remember volunteering to come here. So what is your last memory from Earth? What's the last thing you remember happening?"

Lex looked off in the distance, then turned back in her direction. "I'm going to skip that one."

"Okay." She scribbled a few useless notes, buying time to think of something else to ask, wondering at her disappointment. Lex's nonanswer felt like a betrayal, which made no sense. He didn't have to tell her anything.

She shook her head. They were ending on a bad note, and she couldn't think of a way to fix it.

"All done?" he asked.

"All done," she agreed reluctantly.

"Great," said Lex, "because I have some questions of my own."

"What do you mean?"

"Before I decide what to recommend to Ada and Olu, I have some questions."

"For me?"

Lex stood up. "Let's take a walk."

"Aren't we supposed to talk here?"

"Your interview of me is over, correct?"

"Yes."

"My interview of you is starting. No one said where that had to take place. In fact, no one said it had to be just you and me, so I've asked Cliff to join us."

Leigh held back a groan as she wondered, not for the first time, what she'd gotten herself into.

***

Cliff was waiting for them outside Little Italy; he was carrying a lantern and a blanket. Leigh took her notebook back to Floraville, stuffed it under her pillow, and grabbed a sweatshirt.

Lex led them to the landing plateau. They sat on the blanket, enjoying the salt-laden air, and leaned against the same boulder where she'd found Lex and Olu during quarantine.

At first, it was unclear what Lex hoped to gain from the conversation. He and Cliff sat on either side of her. They talked to each other, and Leigh listened. She didn't bother trying to figure it out. There were always layers upon layers when dealing with boys.

She listened as both boys expressed dismay that no one had been able to dislodge the long metal cylinder from the rock. But she noticed neither of them were ready to give up. As they switched to happier topics, Cliff recounted seeing Shin and Dhruv chatting after dinner. And Lex told a funny story about rolling the new burl back to Homesite, complete with an imitation of Michele shouting at Noah to slow down.

Leigh leaned against the boulder, gazed at the alien ocean, and watched the evening sunshine sparkle on the water. The reflected light changed from silver to amber as the waves flattened into thin, uneven layers like icing on a cake.

Rán sank slowly into the horizon, and she listened to the rhythm of the boys' voices back and forth. Her thoughts calmed and her mind wandered.

"Hey," said Leigh.

"Hey yourself," said Cliff. "Thought you'd gone to sleep."

"Lex," she said, "why'd you tell me about Aegir when I came by Tuesday night?"

"Tuesday night?" asked Cliff.

"Her first visit," said Lex.

"You never mentioned it," Cliff said.

"She doesn't trust anyone," replied Lex.

"What's Aegir?"

"I trust you, Cliff," said Leigh. "You were my first friend here."

"Same," he replied.

"Do you trust me," Lex asked, "enough to tell me something?"

"Is this the start of your interview?" she said.

"Suppose so."

"What's the question?"

"Wait," said Cliff, "what's Aegir?"

"Sorry." Lex pointed to a spot above the horizon. "Aegir's the nearest planet. When full darkness comes, you can see it over there, larger than any of the stars. I told Lorelei about it on Tuesday night. Don't remember why. We were just talking."

"During the quarantine?"

"He and Olu were here," said Leigh, "at this rock. I sat way over there."

"That's how you knew where to find them," said Cliff.

"Should've told you."

"Can we get back to my question?" asked Lex.

"What question?" said Leigh.

"What's the real reason you want to do these interviews?"

They all stopped talking. Leigh stretched out her legs and put her hands in her lap.

She said, "I'm trying to create a backstory to our arrival on the planet. To add to our history. If the colonization succeeds, people will be born here who've never seen Earth. They should have an idea about where we came from. I want to help with that."

"Bullshit," said Lex.

Cliff smothered a laugh.

"You don't believe me?" she said.

"Too boring of a reason to go to all that trouble," said Lex.

"Not boring to me."

"I'm not saying your answer is a lie," said Lex, "but it's incomplete. You're trying to figure out something, something else. And I won't approve the interviews until I know what it is."

Leigh drew her knees up and wrapped her arms around them.

"Listen," he said. "I don't have to tell Olu or Ada or anyone else. I asked Cliff to be here because you seem to trust him." Lex sat up and turned her direction. "You said it yourself earlier: I protect the others. I need to know what's going on."

Leigh hugged her legs tighter. With Lex's eyes upon her, she stared at the ocean. There wasn't much to see. Clouds had moved in, hiding two of the moons, and the third was only a fuzzy glow in the sky. She watched the clouds, unwilling to look at Lex, unsure whether she was more afraid of telling him the truth or telling him a lie.

Eventually, he leaned back against the boulder. Then he surprised her.

"The last thing I remember from Earth," said Lex, "is a fight with my father. He didn't want me going camping with some friends, said I'd be smokin' and drinkin' and end up in trouble. I told him it was my life and to stay out of it. He grabbed me, actually grabbed my arm, and held me in place. The man had never laid a hand on me before in my life."

Lex stood up, walked a few steps away, and looked at the sky.

"Then what?" asked Cliff.

"Then my father said the last words I remember. 'Alexius,' he said, 'I'd do anything to make your life better.' I tore my arm away and said something awful, basically that he'd already ruined his own life and my mom's and that I wouldn't let him ruin mine. I stormed out the door.

"And that's it. After that, I don't know what happened. That's my last memory from Earth."

"That's rough," said Cliff.

"That's life," said Lex.

Leigh closed her eyes. She listened to the waves breaking on the shore below and willed herself to return the same level of trust.

"You're right," she said, "I have other reasons for the interviews, things I'm trying to figure out. First, why were we the ones chosen? And second, why did we agree to leave?"

"No one has those answers," said Lex.

"Not alone," she admitted. "But maybe we each know a little, maybe we each know enough to piece together some answers."

"Why do you care?" he asked.

"What?"

"Why do you need those answers?"

"Aren't you curious?" said Leigh.

"I'm more curious about what's in front of me, not what I left behind."

She took a deep breath. Now that she'd decided to be honest, she'd tell them all of it.

"There's more," said Leigh.

"More?"

"One more question: Are we it? Because surely, we're not the only colony out here. Are there more on other planets?"

"Who cares," said Cliff.

"Or are they here?" said Lex. "Other colonies, here on Marjol. I've wondered about that."

"You think there are?" asked Cliff.

"Why would we be the only one?" replied Leigh. "If you were going to go to all the trouble to ship us out here, wouldn't you pick more than one landing spot?"

Cliff turned on the lantern. Leigh shielded her eyes, adjusting to the sudden light. A few meters away, Lex stared at the ocean, but Cliff looked right at her.

"Doesn't something feel wrong?" said Leigh. "Like the shuttle video lied to us."

"Lied to us?" said Cliff.

"By omission. There's so little we know."

"Enough." Lex turned to look at them. "The first weeks are stressful. It takes a while to get used to being here. Trying to figure out what to do next."

"That's just it," said Leigh. "Why no guidance? No training? We're just kids."

"We were told all this," said Cliff. "The cryosleep kills everyone over twenty. Who else could they send?"

"Why not wait till they fix the cryosleep?" she said.

"I don't know," admitted Cliff. "Maybe they didn't think they could."

"The video said they planned to send ships with adults as soon as possible. Sounds like you're agreeing that's a lie."

"I'm agreeing we need to fix the techs to get some answers."

"Let's not argue," intervened Lex. "Obviously we'd have more info if the techs worked, but they don't." He bent over and picked up a rock. The lantern lit his face unevenly, shadows adding to his pensive expression. "Even if your interviews could provide these answers, I'm not sure what we'd gain." Lex tossed the rock up and down in his palm as the others stood to join him. "We're here. Why or how we got here, what does it matter? Whether we're the only colony or not, what does it matter?"

"Don't you want to know?" asked Leigh. "Simply to know the truth."

Lex stopped tossing the rock. He walked over to her and opened his hand, dropping the rock onto the ground. It hit with a soft thunk, but she didn't look down. Lex was staring at her.

"Truth," he said, "is a curious thing. Not everyone's truth is the same."

She managed to meet his eyes but had no other response, having already said more than she'd planned.

"I think we should go back," said Cliff.

"Let's go." Lex turned away from her. "I got what I came for."

They headed back to the cabins. Emotions had been stirred, and the three of them barely spoke as they moved inland. Leigh watched the shifting light as the lantern swung back and forth with Cliff's arm.

When they reached the edge of Homesite, Lex said, "Cliff, give us a minute?"

"No problem," he replied, and Cliff and his lantern moved away from them.

Leigh stood motionless as Lex turned toward her. Cliff's footsteps faded. She could hear voices laughing and talking near the cabins, but they seemed far away, as if she and Lex were standing in their own bubble of silence.

In the darkness, his face was barely visible, but his presence filled her senses. Only centimeters away, she could feel his breath on her cheek and smell the salty brine on his skin.

"Lorelei," he whispered.

"Yes."

"Thanks."

"For what?"

"For telling me the truth."

She stood mute, words failing her.

Lex took a step back, breaking the invisible bubble around them. "See you tomorrow," he said.

"Yeah, see you tomorrow."

He headed toward his cabin as she walked toward hers, carefully picking her footing in the dark. Leigh had no idea whether he'd approve the interviews. Either way, she could not regret the night's conversations.

CHAPTER 17

The next afternoon, Lex swam in the ocean and kept his thoughts on the waves. It was Freeday—a time for having fun.

When the edge of a big wave was two body lengths away, he put more muscle into his arm strokes and looked toward shore. The swell reached his feet. Lex kicked harder, extended his arms, and lifted his head. The wave thrust him forward; for a moment, he felt a part of the sea, unified with its power and mystery.

Then the ocean spit him out, tumbling Lex onto the shore. His already bruised shoulder hit hard. He wiped sand from his arms and picked himself off the ground.

"Nice wipeout!" yelled Cliff, who, along with Marko and Eliana, had already called it quits for the day.

Lex waved at the three of them, up near the beach cabins. He almost laughed at how small Marko looked next to Eliana and Cliff. Both were tall, lean, and strong, their bodies made for ocean swimming. Eliana had grown up on the beaches of Brazil, and Cliff had been raised in Southern California. Lex supposed it wasn't surprising they'd been surfers back on Earth.

He walked toward them. It was nice hanging around the new arrivals, who regularly forgot, or maybe ignored, the rule about not discussing Earth. They didn't think anything about relating a previous experience if it fit the conversation. No doubt Marko was enjoying that too; he'd always thought the rule was stupid.

"That was fun." Lex took a seat on the sand.

"Unique style you have," said Marko.

"Timing the waves is the hard part," said Eliana, "and you got the hang of that no problem."

Cliff stretched his arms over his head. "I wish Freeday were every day," he said. "Bodysurfing in the waves. Day after day of beach life. Think you can talk Olu and Ada into that?"

"I'd be covered in bruises," Lex joked. "Layers of bruises."

But Marko took the question seriously. "Trust me," he said, "you don't really want that. I know I don't."

"Me neither," said Eliana, answering Marko's seriousness with her own. "I need more than being here. I need a reason to be here."

"True enough," said Lex.

Marko lay down on his back while Cliff and Eliana whispered something to each other.

Lex looked out at the three swimmers still in the water: Michele, Noah, and Lorelei. Everyone who'd gone bodysurfing was a strong swimmer, but those three were practically sprouting fins and scales. They were well past the break point, bobbing in the waves, talking and laughing. It did his heart good to see Michele with kindred spirits. She too was benefitting from new friends.

It'd been Noah's idea to walk down to the beach by the cabins and ride the surf. Apparently, he, Eliana, and Cliff had discovered their common ground of surfing during the quarantine. There seemed to be more to that story, but Lex didn't know what. Even a shortened quarantine had given the third landing party their own secrets.

Noah had accused Lex of looking like the walking stereotype of a surfer dude, but that was laughable. Until arriving on Marjol, he'd never been in an ocean, much less surfed. There was general agreement that Marjol's water was saltier than Earth's; Lex had no way to compare. And part of him was still not at home in the waves.

Noah, on the other hand, was one with the sea. No surprise he'd joined Boats. Lex might look like a surfer dude … Noah was one. No wonder he was talking about making a surfboard.

The oceanside breeze picked up a notch. Lex leaned back, rested his elbows in the sand, and closed his eyes. His face was suffused with the warmth of Rán's late afternoon rays.

A week ago, he'd been in the same spot—on the sunset side near the three beach cabins. That Freeday had been full of work, gathering driftwood and setting up for the third landing party. At the time, his biggest worry had been reestablishing unity between the colonists who'd been in favor of the quarantine and those who'd been against it.

A week ago, life on Marjol had been simple. He'd enjoyed his work in Boats. And he'd done what was needed to support Olu and Ada.

Simple.

A week later, not so simple.

Lorelei had him thinking about the planet he'd left behind. The fights and injuries had him worrying about everyone's health. The washed-up shuttle debris had him wondering whether anyone else would arrive. Plus, he had no good answer to Lorelei's question about why he was one of the leaders.

Nope, not so simple at all.

Cliff and Marko laughed at something Eliana said.

Lex sat up, opened his eyes, and searched the waves for the remaining swimmers. There they were—spread out from one another close to the break point. He could see all three scanning the horizon for a perfect wave.

Noah was the first to grab one and ride it in, bodysurfing with one arm in front of him and the other held behind, steering his way through the wave with an impressive combination of elegance and power.

"Sweet as!" shouted Noah, bursting from the surf.

The Aussie waited at the water's edge as Michele and Lorelei found their way to shore, each leaving the ocean with a wide grin. Lorelei wiped something off her cheek, Michele ran her hands through her hair, and the three bodysurfers headed toward those waiting on the beach.

As they approached, Lex consciously calmed his quickened pulse. Why could Lorelei never do anything the normal way? Months ago, the girls had decided to wear black bras and cutoff shorts as bathing suits. It was a sexy but practical look, and the boys had adjusted to it. In fact, Lex found he no longer noticed what the girls were wearing. He supposed if they'd been a nudist colony, he would've adjusted to that too.

But here was Lorelei wearing a cutoff blue T-shirt and a pair of black panties as if that were a normal thing to wear at the beach. This, he was having trouble adjusting to.

"Hey, mate," Noah said as he grabbed a towel and rubbed his hair. "Reckoned you'd be a natural."

"Can't think when I've had more fun on a Freeday," said Lex.

"Wait till Noah makes us a surfboard," said Eliana. "Then you'll see what fun is."

"I can wait," said Lex.

"Not me," said Michele. "I'd love to learn."

"Same," said Marko.

"No worries," said Noah. "I'll find a way."

"Soon would be good," teased Eliana. "Then I can show you what real surfing looks like."

"I was on a board before I could walk," bragged Noah.

"She was born on Santa Catarina," said Cliff. "My money's on the Brazilian."

The convivial banter continued as they walked up the beach toward the plateau. Lex glanced at Lorelei, who'd been quiet since leaving the water. She often wore her faded baseball cap, but she'd left it behind for swimming and braided her long brown hair in some intricate fashion. Her cheeks were infused with color; he suspected it was as much from the exhilaration of the bodysurfing as from the sun. She caught his eye, and he smiled but looked away. He didn't want her to think he was staring.

Standing on the edge of Homesite last night, he'd wanted to kiss her. Proof positive he was batshit crazy! There was a 50 percent chance she would've slapped him and a 95 percent chance she would've lectured him about breaking his own rules. He thought there was a 1 percent chance she would've kissed him back. Okay, maybe a .5 percent chance.

He knew he was being stupid. Even so, he smiled thinking about the .5 percent.

The bodysurfers split up as they reached Sunset Beach, the stretch of sand at the foot of the plateau where everyone hung out on Freedays. It was late afternoon, and a handful of people had already returned to Homesite. The bulk of the colony, however, was still at the beach.

Lex walked over to Olu, who was standing at the water's edge. The waves were gentle by the plateau, but trouble could arise in an instant. Olu was the self-appointed lifeguard.

"How was the bodysurfing?" Olu asked.

"Excellent. You should try it."

"Maybe next time."

"You go swim," suggested Lex. "I'll keep an eye out."

"No, I'm good. But thanks."

"You okay?"

"All good."

The two of them watched as Michele, Lorelei, and Noah joined the dozen or so people in the water.

"I think Michele's found others who're part fish like her," said Lex.

"Good."

Lex shifted to safer ground. "All the injured colonists are improving."

"Let's hope for no new injuries this week."

"It's been a good day today."

"True."

"Who rigged up that tent-like thing for Shin, Milo, and Sammi?" asked Lex.

"Matt," said Olu, "with help from Noah. Those two have quite an array of talents. Some are even useful."

Lex left the comment alone.

It was a welcome distraction when Ada walked over.

"Success!" she said.

"With what?" asked Lex.

"With this," laughed Ada, sweeping her arms in a wide gesture. "Our colony."

"Oh, that!" Lex laughed along with her.

"Look around you, Olu," said Ada, still smiling but with more weight in her words. "I know it seems like a lot of people, and I know this week hasn't been easy. But look—you wanted unity. I think we've got it."

"You may be right," acknowledged Olu.

"Of course I'm right," she said, "so stop standing over here and scowling. Go swim. Have some fun. Otherwise, everyone will think you're disappointed in them."

"I hate it when you're bossy."

"He means," said Lex, "we hate it when you're right all the time."

Ada laughed again, and Olu finally smiled.

"All right," he said, "I get the message."

"I'll stay here," said Lex.

Olu nodded, then he walked toward a handful of colonists who were standing knee-deep in the water.

"He okay?" asked Ada.

"Adjusting to the larger group," said Lex.

"Aren't we all."

"And worrying about the wrecked shuttle."

"We agreed not to call it that until we know more."

"Fine," laughed Lex. "He's worrying about chunks of metal falling from the sky that might be pieces of a destroyed shuttle or something even more mysterious."

Ada narrowed her eyes in response. "Please, Lex, don't say it that way to anyone else. No need for everyone to know how worried we are."

"True enough," said Lex, but he thought Ada was mistaken if she believed the other colonists weren't just as worried as they were. Everyone operated under the understanding that the first landing party was the starting point, the beginning. Seven more landing parties of teenagers were due to arrive in three-month intervals, followed at some point by adults and equipment and help. That's what they'd been told.

What changed if it wasn't true? If no one else was coming?

He didn't want to think about it. He wanted to dislodge the cylinder from the rock and prove it wasn't from the same shuttle that had brought the third landing party. Or to find other debris that proved the same thing.

"Ada," he said, "I know Rose wants to start clearing a path to the mountains. Can you convince her to delay that? Or to spare some of Maps to keep looking for shuttle debris—sorry, for pieces of random metal?"

Ada rolled her eyes but managed to laugh. "Don't worry. Rose and I already talked about it."

"And?"

"Rose is leading the search herself."

"Excellent."

"We all want the same answers," said Ada.

Lex looked out at the colonists in the water and wondered if that were true.

**

No one cooked on Freedays. Foobrew for dinner was a fair trade for the ability to give everyone the day off. The small fire pits sat empty, but the large one, the big pit in front of Q-cabin, did not. Freeday was bonfire night.

Lex usually helped start those festivities. This evening, however, he was busy doctoring Shin's burns. In the hours immediately after the fire, Zalfaa had taught Lex and Lorelei about burn care. The next morning, she'd done the same with Cliff. As a result, Shin trusted only four people to help him—Zalfaa and the three she had trained.

They'd set up a burn care area in Q-cabin, which made it easier to doctor Shin out of sight of prying eyes. After three days, he was healing well. The biggest worry was the oozing from the burns on his shoulder, and even that had improved. Shin was using fewer pain meds, and his left hand had healed enough to splint the broken fingers. Progress.

"You up to joining us at the bonfire?" asked Lex.

"Feeling pretty good," said Shin.

"Tired?"

"Took a long nap today."

"Good. Now let's be extra careful wrapping your shoulder."

"Because you know Zalfaa will rewrap it if it's not good enough," said Shin.

Lex laughed. It was true, so true. But it was also good to hear Shin joking around.

Once Lex had finished bandaging the oozing spots, he helped the injured boy into a fresh one-sleeved shirt. Shin repositioned his left arm in the sling, and the boys stepped out of Q-cabin to join the rest of the colony at the bonfire.

Lex stood at the edge of the gathering, pleased to see Shin maneuver his way into the heart of the group. Even better, Dhruv and Cliff made a place for him to sit between them.

Not far away, four girls—Eliana, Ada, Zalfaa, and Lorelei—sat with Gwen. Ada was telling a story, gesturing and entertaining the others. Every so often, Lex could hear the slight lilt of her voice carry across the fire, her French accent more pronounced when storytelling.

Ada finished her tale, and the girls erupted in laughter, then Lorelei and Zalfaa left to go check on Shin. Michele threw another log on the fire and moved into the spot they'd vacated. The happy hum of conversation continued.

Olu stood on the opposite side of the fire, talking with Noah and Matt, ensuring they'd met everyone. He brought João over for introductions, then waved Mary and Jasmine to join them.

With everything going on, Lex thought he'd slipped into the crowd unnoticed. He was wrong. After Zalfaa inspected Shin's bandage, she signaled him a thumbs up, and Lorelei gave him a quick smile.

He returned both the thumbs up and the smile, then scanned the area: no Marko.

The fire's warmth faded as Lex walked over to Little Italy. As expected, Marko was there, a chair and lantern set up so the light shone where he was chipping and sculpting.

"Hey, Marko," said Lex.

"Hey."

"How's it going?"

"I'll be right there."

"I'm not harassing you."

"But you think I should go to the bonfire."

"We miss you."

"I've been with people all day." Marko stopped his work and wiped off his tools with his shirt. "Don't you ever want to be alone?"

"Yeah," admitted Lex. "And the bigger our little colony gets, the more I think we'll feel that way."

"But you were checking on me."

"Guilty."

Marko put his tools in one of the drawstring bags and looped it over his back. "I'm ready for a break anyway," he said and turned off the lantern.

Zalfaa and Lorelei had moved to the edge of the crowd and waved over Lex and Marko as they approached the bonfire. A new sound began: a chorus of voices, punctuated regularly with metallic clinks. Cliff, Shin, and Dhruv were learning a song from Declan and Shane. The metallic sounds occurred at regular intervals—Shin and Dhruv using their uninjured arms to clink canteens before drinking from them.

"An Irish drinking song," said Zalfaa.

"Should we worry about what they're drinking?" joked Lex.

"I think it's called friendship," said Marko.

Lex gave Marko an appreciative grip on the shoulder. Someone tossed a few logs on the fire, and more voices joined the rowdy singing. Lorelei spoke, but the song drowned out her words. She stepped closer.

"I thought those two might end up hating each other," she said.

"Dhruv and Shin?" asked Lex.

She nodded.

"No way. It's not like they're in love with Gwen."

"You're the relationship expert?" said Marko.

"Very funny."

"Yes, it is." Marko gave him a lopsided grin.

"It's a fact," said Lex. "Two guys acting stupid because they're in love with the same girl, they might end up enemies. But two guys manipulated and made to look stupid by the same girl, well, they'll become friends."

"So cynical!" said Zalfaa.

The four of them laughed and returned their attention to the singing. Several other colonists started clinking canteens in time with the music, and a handful of girls joined the boys in song.

Lex leaned over and whispered in Lorelei's ear, "Your interviews are a go."

She grinned broadly in reply, her eyes crinkling along the edges.

"You can start a week from tomorrow," he said. "Ada will give you details in a few days."

"Awesome!" she shouted over the music, and it was his turn to answer with a grin.

He didn't know if the interviews would do any good, but as he'd told Olu and Ada, he didn't think they'd do any harm.

Lorelei gave him another smile before she and Zalfaa threaded their way through the crowd to the other side of the bonfire. He appreciated her enthusiasm, though he wasn't at all convinced the interviews would provide the answers she was looking for. He wasn't even sure she was asking the right questions.

But those were worries for another day. This evening, Lex wanted to keep things simple. He looked up at the sky, so much clearer than the night before. The stars tumbled overhead, millions of brilliant points of light. He gazed at their beauty, letting the view overwhelm him—no room for worries about spaceships falling from the sky or Texas girls who asked too many questions.

More voices joined the singing; more canteens joined the clanking. Lex switched his attention away from the cosmos and back to those around him.

As befit a good drinking song, the words were easy to learn, and the tune was easy to sing. Before long, fifty-nine voices were raised in a raucous rendition of a silly Irish song—a song brought from a lush emerald isle on one planet to a smaller, sandier island elsewhere in the galaxy.

The bonfire flames crackled and danced, Dhruv and Shin clinked their canteens, and Gwen smiled and sang among friends. It had been a long, complicated week, but it was ending well. Lex looked around him and thought that life on Marjol was very good indeed.

CHAPTER 18

The colony's Monday morning meeting began later than Leigh expected—interesting how drinking songs made people sleep late, even when all they were drinking was water. Like most meetings, this one was longer than necessary. There was ample give-and-take between the leaders and the other colonists as different issues were discussed. That was nice to see, but Leigh felt her shoulder muscles tensing as the meeting dragged. Each new topic delayed the work she considered most urgent: searching for additional signs of a wrecked shuttle.

Once the meeting ended, the pace of things did not improve. Instead of starting the search, everyone in Maps meandered to the newfound cavern. Leigh was happy to show off their discovery, but much of the time was wasted with gossip. A few people asked Leigh about her upcoming interviews, which Ada had announced at the meeting. But the biggest gossip related to a different announcement: new activities three days a week, first thing in the morning—rotations of yoga, tai chi, and swimming on Tuesdays, Thursdays, and Saturdays. A four-week trial period would start the next morning.

Judging from the chatter, people were enthusiastic about the plan, or at least willing to try. Why not? Compared to everything else, a few mornings of yoga, tai chi, and swimming were no problem at all. But couldn't everyone wait and talk about it at dinner?

Eventually, the gossip died down, and they left the cavern. Leigh curbed her impatience as Maps returned to their usual meeting place—the shady spot on Sunrise Beach. There, Rose divided them into three groups: two to search along the coasts for more metal debris and one to work inland.

Shane led the inland group, which was tasked with the long-term project of clearing a path to the Crooked Teeth, the mountain range running from one side of the island to the other. João was in charge of those looking for shuttle pieces along the sunset coast, and Rose kept the cave-mapping group with her on the sunrise side. Well, most of the cave-mapping group.

"Ada's not coming today?" asked Eliana as she, Cliff, and Leigh followed Rose down the beach.

"Not today," said Rose.

Five colonists were too sick to work, so the leaders were taking turns staying at Homesite. Today was Ada's turn. No problem; they'd make do without her.

The four of them walked along Sunrise Beach in the opposite direction from the cavern. This beach was backed by sloping hills instead of cliffs and rocks. It was narrower, but with less vegetation.

"First time I've walked this way," said Cliff.

"None of us have been more than a kilometer this direction," said Rose, "not by foot."

"Really?" said Eliana.

"You'll see," said Rose. "It gets tricky. We've mostly stuck to going inland, trying to find a way over the Crooked Teeth."

"Didn't the video say the other end of the island is inaccessible?" asked Eliana.

"What do they know?" answered Rose. "They're not the ones living here."

"Amen to that."

As they walked, Leigh scanned the shore for glimmers of metal. She assumed the other three were doing the same, though Cliff seemed preoccupied with the conversation.

"Anyone tried taking a raft along this coastline?" he asked.

"Once," said Rose. "Months ago. Michele, Olu, and Lex."

"How far did they get?"

"Near the Crooked Teeth, but not past them. See the mountains at this end of the range?" She pointed in the distance. "We call those the Twisted Peaks."

"Good name," said Cliff.

The Twisted Peaks looked as if a giant hand had reached down and pulled the mountains like taffy, swirling them into unnatural shapes that peered simultaneously at the ocean and the land. The tops of the two mountains were devoid of vegetation, and ridges in the rockface created deep haunting shadows.

"As soon as we built the first raft," continued Rose, "Michele, Olu, and Lex paddled it that way. They were gone a few days, and they all returned in one piece. But the winds and the currents by the Twisted Peaks gave them a lot of trouble. They never got past the mountains.

"By then, we'd figured out the calmest water was over by the plateau on the sunset coast. So they moved the Boats work over there."

"No one's tried paddling past the Crooked Teeth along that side?" asked Eliana.

"The island gets much, much wider on the sunset side," said Rose. "Michele says there's a spot up that coast where hundreds of rocks jut out all over the ocean, like at the tip of the island, only worse. Literally impossible."

"So we've got to find a way by land," said Eliana.

"Don't count out Michele. She'd like to have another go at the Twisted Peaks on this side. Been wanting to for a while now. Says the rafts are better, and she's better at controlling them. But Olu always argues against it, and nothing happens."

"Do those two ever agree?" asked Cliff.

"It's a long story."

"We've got all day."

"Not my story to tell."

Leigh too was curious to hear the story, but she liked Rose all the better for not telling it. Time for a change in topic.

"Have any of you done tai chi before?" asked Leigh.

"No," said all three in unison.

"Me neither," she laughed. "I guess we'll learn together."

"Cliff and I are in the Thursday group," said Eliana.

"Saturday tai chi for me," said Rose.

"Tuesday," added Leigh. "Okay, maybe not all together, but you know what I mean!" She was laughing as they rounded the first bend in the shoreline.

"Now starts the hard part," said Rose.

Leigh stopped laughing. This shoreline was wholly dissimilar from the soft, sandy beach they'd been walking on. Looking at the landscape, she was flooded with memories of a family trip taken the summer she was eight years old, the only time she'd ever visited Maine. Explorations along that coastline had meant clambering over rocks, watching snails and crabs in the tidepools, and slipping on seaweed-covered ledges. They'd never gone far. The rocky crags and inlets had made it impossible to cover much distance, even for an active eight-year-old and her parents. Leigh had never seen another shoreline like it.

Until now.

"We can do this," said Rose, jarring Leigh from her memories. "Take your time and stay near each other. We'll branch off here and there to be sure we're thorough, but I don't want anyone falling in the water."

"What's our goal?" asked Cliff.

"Go slow. See if you find anything," said Rose.

"For how far?"

"However far we get."

"Let's get started." Eliana sprinted up the rocky ledges with the footing of a mountain goat.

"Hey," shouted Cliff, "Rose said go slow."

"Last one to the top is a rotten egg," said Leigh.

"What're you, five?" said Cliff, but he leaped up the nearest ledge as he said it.

Leigh managed her way along the rocks, slipping once halfway up. She neared the top, the last to make it, and expected to be met with joking braggadocio from the others.

She was met with silence.

Her companions stood at one end of a horseshoe-shaped inlet and stared at the other side, where a man-made object had been swept in from the sea. From this distance, it looked like a giant test tube. But they all knew what it was: part of a cryosleep pod, identical to the ones that had brought them from Earth.

* * *

It was afternoon by the time they'd dragged the broken pod across the rocky ledges, back around the bend, and onto the beginnings of Sunrise Beach.

"Let's take a break," said Rose.

Sweat dripping from their faces, the four of them flopped down on the sand. Leigh held on to the rope wrapped around the one spiky protrusion in the otherwise smooth surface of the broken pod. She didn't want to risk an errant wave whisking the pod out to sea.

"Maybe we should move away from the water," said Cliff.

"Should be fine," said Eliana. "We can take turns holding the rope."

"The pod probably floats," said Rose. "I'm hoping we can float it back along the shoreline once we get farther down the beach."

"Might work in the calmer water," agreed Cliff.

"Worth a try," said Eliana.

Leigh was skeptical. As they'd discovered the hard way, the pod was heavier than it looked.

"I still can't believe we found it," said Cliff.

"I know," said Eliana. "I thought we'd be out here for days and find nothing."

"Are you always so pessimistic?"

"You California boys have a strange definition of pessimistic," she replied. "I was hoping *not* to find pieces of a wrecked shuttle."

"Sorry, that hope is over."

Cliff was right. But they still didn't know what it meant.

Leigh handed him the rope and ventured into the waves. Standing in the water felt good after hours of climbing over rocky ledges. She splashed water on her face and tucked a few loose strands of hair under her baseball cap.

"Phew!" Rose heaved an exaggerated sigh. "Didn't know what I got into when the three of you joined Maps. First, the cavern. Now this."

"Must be my lucky hat," said Leigh.

"You and your hat," teased Rose. "I almost don't recognize you when you're not wearing it."

"Hilarious." Leigh grinned. She made a show of ever so carefully rearranging the faded hat as if situating a diamond tiara. They laughed.

The merriment faded as they noticed a figure sprinting down the beach in their direction. It was Sammi. She was shouting something, but they couldn't hear her over the waves and the wind.

"Lorelei, come with me," said Rose, and the two of them jogged in Sammi's direction.

The curly-haired girl was flushed with exertion and struggling for breath. The rash on her arm was bright red.

"Slow down," said Rose. "Why're you out in the sun?"

"For Lorelei," gasped Sammi. "And Cliff. It's Shin. Really sick. Zalfaa needs 'em."

"Stay here and catch your breath," said Rose. "Lorelei, go. We'll bring your bag."

"Tell Cliff," said Leigh, as she raced off down the beach.

By the time she reached the path to Homesite, Cliff had caught up.

"Sick how?" Leigh asked him.

"She didn't say," he replied.

They scrabbled up the hillside path, and Leigh put aside thinking about the cryosleep pod. It could wait. Shin could not.

CHAPTER 19

When Leigh and Cliff reached Homesite, Ada was waiting for them. She stood in front of Q-cabin like a sentry posted at the drawbridge of a castle.

"Shin's inside?" Leigh asked.

"Zalfaa's with him," replied Ada. "Lex too. He got here a few minutes ago. Let me tell you what I told Lex and then we'll go in."

"Shin's here, not at our cabin?" said Cliff.

Leigh turned to Cliff and put a hand on his arm. "Shin may need the space," she said. Unlike Cliff, she'd heard the words Ada had not spoken. There'd been no "everything's fine but …" or "Shin's doing all right but …" or any of the other things people said when there was an emergency but it wasn't life or death.

No wonder Sammi had been running.

"This morning," said Ada, "Shin complained of feeling a lot worse. He was running a fever of 39.5 Celsius, so no wonder. Zalfaa examined him, found a swollen lymph node under his left arm pit and red edges around a lot of his burns. She says it's all signs of infection. We gave Shin antibiotics and some ibuprofen. I hoped that would be the end of it …" she shook her head.

"He's no better?" asked Cliff.

"Worse," said Ada. "His heart rate's too fast, breathing too shallow, fever too high. Zalfaa says the infection is aggressive, the kind where his body tries to shut itself down. He needs to be in a hospital," said Ada in frustration, "but ..." She gestured at the surroundings, which looked even more rudimentary given the comparison with Ada's imagined high-tech medical center.

"Show us how we can help." Leigh tried to sound positive even though the news was grim. She didn't understand the physiology of such diseases, but she knew they could be fatal, even in the finest hospitals and care centers back on Earth.

"Follow me," said Ada, and she led them to the bunkroom in the back of the cabin.

When they walked in, Zalfaa looked up expectantly, her relief at their arrival evident in her half-smile.

Lex said, "The gang's all here," and Leigh felt her pessimism fade.

Until she looked at Shin. The change in his burns was noticeable, the ragged edges swollen and deep red. He lay on a mattress on the floor, not speaking, not moving except for his eyes, which tracked their progress across the room.

"Striving for more attention, I see," joked Cliff.

Shin managed a weak smile, and Leigh once again pushed her pessimism aside.

* * *

Hours later, Leigh longed to see Shin smile again. Instead, as afternoon turned into evening and then into night, Shin became less and less responsive. It became a challenge to dose him with cephalosporin and ibuprofen, to get him to take anything by mouth.

The four caregivers—Zalfaa, Cliff, Lex, and Leigh—experimented. After more elegant attempts failed, they discovered a solution. If one person propped Shin into a slumped but near-sitting position and another provided small sips with encouraging words, their patient would swallow what was given to him. Awkward at best, but they were desperate. With no IVs, it was the only way to keep Shin hydrated.

Late that night, they were coaxing him to drink some Foobrew when Ada and Olu stopped in. By keeping a watch on those who were watching Shin, they could see the obvious: the caregivers had grown more efficient but also more tired. They mandated shifts: Zalfaa and

Cliff in one shift, Leigh and Lex in the other. The pair "off duty" slept only a heartbeat away, in the other Q-cabin bunkroom, in case they were needed.

In the early hours of the morning, before the stars retreated behind Rán's bright rays, Leigh and Lex began one of their shifts. Shin was asleep. Leigh sat down next to his injured side, and Lex sat across the sickbed from her, his messy hair and disheveled clothes at odds with how he conducted himself as a caregiver, acting like a mother bear tending her newborn cubs.

Leigh was trying to live up to the same standard. She pulled a washcloth out of a bucket of cool water, squeezed out the excess, and wiped Shin's face with the damp cloth. "Let's check his pulse," she suggested.

"Okay," said Lex.

She placed two fingers along Shin's neck, felt the blood thumping, and nodded at Lex. On her signal, he began a slow, quiet count of seconds. "One thousand one, one thousand two, one thousand three …"

When he reached "one thousand twenty," Leigh stopped counting.

"Damn," she whispered.

"How bad?" asked Lex.

"Thirty-seven times three is one hundred eleven," she said softly.

"No change," said Lex. "At least it's not worse."

She shrugged.

Lex held out a canteen.

"Let's wait," she said. "Let him sleep."

"For you."

"Oh." She looked at Shin's canteen on the ground next to her. "Duh."

"Ada warned us to take care of ourselves."

"Words of wisdom as usual," admitted Leigh. She took a drink, as did Lex when she passed the canteen back to him.

Forcing herself to stop staring at Shin—leaning over him while he slept wouldn't make him any better—she scooted away from the mattress. Lying down on the cabin floor, she could see through the room's one window. No moons were visible in that particular rectangle of the sky, but the stars helped remind her there was a world outside the sickroom.

Lex moved over and lay down beside her, not touching, but only a few centimeters away. She could smell the brine on his skin and realized they'd both been working and sweating when Zalfaa had sent for them.

"Next time we get a break," said Leigh, "I'm going to wash up a little."

"That a hint?" said Lex.

"No," she laughed softly. She pulled her hat off her head and wiped the sweat from her face.

"You like that baseball cap," said Lex.

"My family's lucky hat," she replied, not meaning to say the words aloud.

"For a long time?" he asked.

"Since before I was born. The L is for Louisville, the University of Louisville, where my mom went to college."

"Ha," said Lex, "I thought it was for Lorelei."

She paused. For a moment, she'd been expecting him to say Leigh. That should have made her change the topic, but instead she elaborated, talking readily about one of the things she had vowed not to talk about.

"My mom got the baseball cap while she was in school. My dad rarely wore a hat, but one day—so the story goes—he needed a hat while working outside, and Mom loaned him the Louisville cap. Dad was an artist, and that was the day the gallery called to offer him a show, the one where he received his first big commission. My mom claimed it was the luck of the hat, and they traded that hat back and forth when I was a kid."

"Did you wear it too? As a kid?"

She stared out the windows at the glistening stars and smiled, happy to have a good memory to share. "When I turned eleven, they gave it to me as a gift. Said it was my turn to have the luck."

"Good gift."

He didn't know the half of it. All three items she'd brought from Earth had been gifts that day. "It was the best birthday," she said. "The same day Grampy gave me the multi-tool." She didn't mention the embroidered handkerchief, not wanting to reveal too much, to slip up and talk about why the Texas bluebonnets were so important.

"Were you surprised to see what you'd brought?" asked Lex. "When you first opened your bag, were you surprised?"

"The hat surprised me a little," she admitted. Not having her necklace had surprised her more, but this conversation had already gone dangerous places without bringing up something guaranteed to make her cry. "My mom must have regifted it to me before I left."

"Huh?"

"A few years after that birthday, I gave the baseball cap back to my mom. At the time, I thought she needed it more than I did. Last I remember, she still had it. But sometime, in my lost memories, she must have given it back."

"For this trip."

"Maybe." Leigh turned her head his direction.

Lex rolled over on his side and looked at her. "I don't remember how I got one of my objects either," he confided, his voice a whisper.

She rolled toward him, her head a little closer, able to hear him better. "Your Swiss Army knife?"

"Nah, that's the first thing I ever bought with my own money. Been taking it everywhere for years, no surprise there."

She waited. He hadn't pushed her into saying anything she didn't want to. The least she could do was offer him the same kindness. But she found herself holding her breath, hoping he would share his thoughts.

"It's a photo," he said hesitantly. "A hard copy photo of me and my dad. Covered in thick laminate. I have no idea where it came from."

"The photo?"

"I remember the picture. I was nine. My dad and I had hiked a long trail that day, one I'd been bugging him to do. It poured rain, absolutely poured. My mom had worried about us going, but we still hiked the whole way." He smiled, the first time since they'd started this conversation. "At the trailhead, before heading home, we snapped a quick photo. Both of us covered, absolutely covered in mud.

I thought my mom might be mad, but she loved it, called the photo 'My Muddy Men', even printed out copies and framed one."

He rubbed his eyes. "I hadn't seen that photo in forever, never seen one laminated. Don't know why I brought it."

Leigh stared at him. "We all should've brought photos."

"I'm guessing we did, just can't get to 'em till we get the techs to work."

"Do you have a laminated photo of your mom with you too?"

"Nope." He did not elaborate.

She reached out her hand and placed it carefully on his bare arm. His skin was warm and dry, crusty with dirt and salt, not sweaty like hers. "Lex, if you close your eyes, I'm sure you can see her. We don't need photos to remember people. But I'm glad to know you have the one, the Muddy Men."

He started to say something, then paused and scooted a little closer. She waited.

"I think we should check on Shin," he said.

"Yeah, right." She stood up and walked over to resume her bedside spot. Part of her wondered what Lex had been about to say, and part of her was relieved to have the conversation end. If it had gone on any longer, she might have told him everything.

CHAPTER 20

ventually, the stars faded, Rán rose in the sky, and a new day began. All day long, the caregiver shifts continued, and Lex searched Shin's face for signs of improvement whenever he and Lorelei took their turn. He found nothing.

Now it was Tuesday evening, and Shin's condition was unchanged. Lex was frustrated with the situation and frustrated with himself. This was what happened when you let your guard down, when you forgot to keep your eyes open for whatever trouble was coming next. He'd been worried about more fistfights; this was so much worse.

Zalfaa took another look at the meds and added the sulfa drug to Shin's treatment, but he remained feverish, uncomfortable, and short of breath. Olu and Ada advocated for more caregiving teams. Lex wasn't sure how he felt about that. On the one hand, he agreed with Zalfaa's desire to stick with those who knew the most about Shin's condition. On the other hand, he could see the bruise-colored smudges under Lorelei's eyes and feel the tension in his own neck; they would soon need a break.

It wasn't just the hours of lost sleep or the claustrophobia from staying inside. It was the nearness of death, the not knowing whether this new friend would take his last breath as they sat and watched, helpless spectators to a life-or-death struggle they could not control.

Things were quiet, but the situation was desperate.

It helped Lex understand why the people most affected by the epidemic had been the caregivers, even those whose patients had survived. The height of the epidemic must have been traumatizing. At the time, Lex had been too ill to know. He hadn't been there when Ada and Olu watched Michele almost die. He'd been too feverish to notice when Dhruv and Shane spent a long night with João. Lex had always appreciated their efforts, but only now did he understand their suffering.

He thought about the unique friendship between Ada and Marko. They too had sat at a sickbed together, taking care of a patient, wondering if the person would live until morning. That person had been Lex.

He would give them each an extra-big hug next time he saw them.

Lorelei pulled off her baseball cap and slid the hairband from her ponytail. Her long hair spilled over her shoulders as she ran her hands through it.

"Why don't you take a quick catnap on one of the beds," he suggested. "I'll wake you up if I need you."

"No thanks. I'm fine." Lorelei refastened her ponytail and slipped it through the back of the hat. Beneath the baseball cap, her face looked wan, but otherwise she seemed ready for anything.

He was surprised she'd been willing to tell him about the hat, to talk about her parents, about her past. Of course, she'd left out some major details. But still, she'd told him more than he would've expected.

He wondered what the third object was that she'd brought from Earth. In the quiet of the early morning hours, he'd almost asked her, almost revealed his own: a faded homemade bookmark. Like the Muddy Men photo, it was something impractical, but unlike the photo, it was not a surprise. He'd made the bookmark for his mom when he was five. She'd had a fascination with actual books, hardback and paperback.

On the day his mom died, Lex's aunt found the handmade bookmark on his mom's bedside table, slotted between pages of a favorite chapter of *Lonesome Dove*. When forced back to Minnesota, the only thing of his mom's that Lex took with him was the bookmark. No, he was not surprised he'd packed it.

He was surprised he'd almost told Lorelei about it. And even more surprised he'd told her about the photo of him and his dad.

At the time, it had felt right. She had listened quietly, had let him talk without interrupting, without judging. It'd seemed natural to talk of such things, lying on the floor of the cabin and looking at her face in the starlight. It'd seemed natural to tell her the story of the photo even though he'd never told that story to anyone else.

He watched her wipe Shin's face with a damp cloth, her calm and caring presence a balm to his soul. But it wasn't enough for Shin.

His skin remained hot to the touch, despite the ibuprofen and cool towels. If the antibiotics were going to help, they should be doing so by now. Lex pictured the infection at war with Shin's body, the two antibiotics standing by Shin's side to give him strength. He placed a hand on Shin's right arm, the one with no injury. "We're here too," he said. "You don't have to fight this alone."

Shin lay there, his shallow, rapid breaths punctuating the otherwise silent bunkroom.

***

A little later in the evening, the stillness in the sickroom was interrupted by a welcome noise: the entry of Ada and Zalfaa.

The two girls kneeled next to Lorelei and inspected the burned side of Shin's body.

"No change," said Lex.

Zalfaa moved closer for a more thorough examination. Eventually, she sat down cross-legged and raised her eyes to the others.

"Anything?" Ada asked her.

"No," replied Zalfaa. "I thought adding the sulfa drug might create some synergy, but apparently not."

"Maybe it needs more time," said Lorelei.

"I wish I knew."

Lorelei put an arm around the smaller girl. "We're all doing the best we can."

"What if that's not good enough?"

"Your best is better than any of ours."

"But Shin could die," Zalfaa whispered.

"Yes, he could," Lorelei said quietly. "And he might not. The fact that he has a chance is because of you."

"Don't give up," said Lex.

Zalfaa tried to smile even as a few tears ran down her face.

"We saved you both some fish," said Ada, "and we updated everyone during dinner."

Dinner? In the sickroom, Lex had lost track of the day's normal rhythms. He eagerly accepted the bowl Ada handed him.

"We need your advice," she said. "Eliana asked permission to come say a prayer, and Myrah did too. Shane and Declan are writing out an Irish blessing.

"Olu and I don't want to turn anyone away, but we don't want to risk making Shin worse. And we don't want to offend him. We don't even know what Shin's faith is. The Japanese have a long history of nature-based religion, but I don't know anything specific. Do you?"

"Shin's from Pittsburgh," said Lorelei.

Lex almost choked on his food. He couldn't help but grin. Lorelei had a way of saying things others didn't want to hear.

The door to the room opened; Olu and Cliff walked in.

"How is he?" asked Olu.

"No change," said Zalfaa. "I never should have let him go to the beach, even with the bandages."

"Hey," said Lex.

"Joint decision," said Olu.

"I encouraged it," said Cliff.

Lorelei gave Zalfaa another hug but said nothing.

"Time for more cephalosporin," said Zalfaa, "plus we've got to keep him hydrated."

"Lex and I can do that," said Lorelei, "while the rest of you sort out everything else. I'll get the meds."

Ada, Olu, and Cliff moved to the other side of the cabin. When Lorelei returned with the medicine, she said to Zalfaa, "I'll support whatever you think is best as far as visitors go."

"Same here," said Lex.

Zalfaa looked as if she might shed more tears, then her face regained its normal composure. She nodded her thanks, stood up, and joined the others on the far side of the room.

Lex and Lorelei propped Shin in a sitting position and began the routine. In no time at all, Shin's back had been washed, and he'd swallowed the medicine, some water, and even a few sips of Foobrew. At one point during their ministrations, he opened his eyes and become confused, but Lorelei's voice and a cool towel on his face calmed him down. By the time they settled Shin into a more comfortable position on the bed, he was fast asleep.

"I'll watch him," she said. "You go join the others."

"I thought we were partners," said Lex.

"You're also one of the leaders."

It was oddly gratifying to hear her acknowledge that. But Olu and Ada didn't need him. They'd been juggling Shin's infection with a growing pile of shuttle debris, three new morning activities, and who knew what else. They were handling everything fine without him.

Shin began shivering.

"Chills," said Lex.

Lorelei grabbed a blanket off one of the bunks and covered Shin with the extra layer. Her movements drew the attention of the others in the room, and they walked over.

"Chills," Lex repeated.

"That's new," said Zalfaa.

"Ada," said Olu, "go organize however you wish. Cliff, please help her. I'm staying here, in this room. And Zalfaa, you're in charge. Any time you think we're doing more harm than good, give me the signal, and I'll take care of it."

With that said, Olu started rearranging the furniture. Time for the sickroom to become a visiting area. Time to try a different type of cure.

CHAPTER 21

Well-meaning prayers freely offered should never be turned away. That was the general consensus. Lex agreed. He helped move the nearby bunk beds to the far end of the room, then set up a half dozen chairs beside Shin. One was for Zalfaa, and the others were for visitors, who were allowed to come in groups of five or less.

He returned to his spot on the floor next to Shin's undamaged side, and Lorelei sat beside him, cooling Shin's brow with a wet towel when needed, helping Lex monitor pulse, breathing, and temperature. They had gotten Shin's chills under control, but he seemed less aware than before.

Zalfaa sat across from them. Perched on the edge of her chair, she watched Shin closely, looking for certain symptoms, engaged in a kind of prayer herself.

Olu stood quietly against the wall, his arms crossed over his chest, his brow tightened in a scowl—a silent bulwark against tumult and trouble. Even Death should think twice about entering the room and causing problems.

The first visitors were three girls from Shin's landing party. Eliana held the cross on her necklace while she prayed; the other two sat silently, heads bowed, eyes closed. Eliana's voice was pure and sweet, with an intonation that bespoke many previous moments of prayer.

Most of it was in Portuguese, so Lex didn't recognize the words. But by the time the girls left, the room felt peaceful and serene.

Though the serenity did not last, the sense of community did. Some visitors sat and talked to Shin and wished him well or told a story. More than a few chanted in languages Lex didn't know. Declan and Shane brought a written Irish blessing, read it aloud, then left it by the door. Others brought leaves from a fragrant plant and crushed them near the bed, leaving a crisp lemony scent lingering in the air.

Cliff ushered colonists in and out, standing quietly near the door during each visit. The order of visitors was anything but haphazard. Pairs of people came interspersed with larger groups, and there were never the same type of prayers back to back; those who were crying stayed for shorter periods of time. Ada's organizational skills were on full display.

Ada herself didn't appear until near the end when she came with Marko. As they entered, Lex rose to give them each a big hug. Though surprised, they readily returned the gesture.

Lorelei gave Lex a smile as he sat back down. She, at least, understood.

During all the visits, Shin never opened his eyes. He grew less restless, but he lay on the bed as pale as distant starlight, and there was no way to know how much he understood what was happening.

Eventually, Cliff ushered out the final visitors and departed himself, hoping to coerce others into singing outside, one last way to show Shin they were thinking about him. Every gesture counted—for Shin, for all of them. When someone was in trouble, the hardest part was having nothing to do to help.

When visiting time was over, Olu and Zalfaa moved the chairs away from the bed. Lorelei stretched her arms over her head, and Lex pressed his palms on his lower back. They'd been sitting for too long.

"We'll be back in a minute," said Olu. "Then it'll be time for you two to take a break."

"No rush," said Lex.

Outside Q-cabin, a few slow, low notes sounded from Eliana's harmonica.

Lorelei once again put two fingers on Shin's neck. That was Lex's signal to start counting, but before he could, she removed her hand.

He caught his breath, fearing the worst. The hopefulness in her eyes told him otherwise.

"Lex," she said, "I think his pulse is slower."

"Let's find out." He spoke calmly, but inwardly he could feel his own heart rate escalate.

She once again found the carotid artery with her fingers. Lex ignored the music outside and began his own cadence: "One thousand one, one thousand two, one thousand three ..." When he reached "one thousand twenty," Lorelei removed her fingers.

"Twenty-six times three is seventy-eight," she said, putting a hand on Lex's shoulder. "We'll do it again in a few minutes to be sure."

He knew she was right: they had to double-check. But it was good news. No, it was great news. Lex could feel it.

"Maybe the antibiotics are working," he said, "or maybe the prayers."

"Lex," she said softly, "why can't it be both?"

He stared at her, his tired body infused with hope and doubt and belief all at once, like an electric shock that brought both clarity and confusion. He'd grown up going to church because that's what his parents did. As a kid, he'd never thought about it, and after his mom died, he'd stopped going. It'd been one more way to thwart his father.

Lorelei looked away from him, but she kept her hand on his shoulder. Lex watched the red hues of the planet's twilight creep through the window. A gust of air blew across the room as Rán's warmth started to fade.

Homesite had been inundated with ... something. Lex couldn't define it, but he could feel it. What was it? The presence of God—a spirit who watched over them no matter where they were? Or the love of everyone in the colony—people who'd chosen togetherness no matter what.

Lorelei's words echoed in his head: *Lex, why can't it be both?*

He listened to the sound of Cliff's voice and Eliana's harmonica and heard other voices join in. He felt the warm pressure of Lorelei's hand on his shoulder. Despite his exhaustion, despite his questions, Lex closed his eyes and prayed.

CHAPTER 22

"Lorelei, Lorelei," a voice spoke to Leigh from outside the fog of dreams. "Lorelei."

She was momentarily awash in the scents of Lex—salt, sand, and a slightly spicy odor all his own. Why was Lex shaking her?

"Shin!" said Leigh, sitting up abruptly and hitting her head on the top bunk.

Lex reached in a hand and gently rubbed her head. She'd been sleeping in her lucky hat. "Careful," he said. "It's all good news."

"Fever gone? Heart rate? Breathing?"

"All good. Even better—Shin's talking."

Swinging her legs over the edge of the bed, Leigh fought against her fatigue. It was dark outside, but Lex had brought a lantern. She took off her baseball cap and combed her fingers through her hair. Like the rest of her, it was covered in a layer of sandy grime.

Lex held out the sweatshirt and pants she'd dropped on the floor before collapsing into the Q-cabin bunk a few hours ago. "Thanks," said Leigh, as she slipped them on. Her mind had cleared enough to notice it didn't feel strange to be dressing in front of him. Perhaps a day and a half of life and death made you stop caring about everything else.

"Our shift?" she asked.

"Not sure. Olu woke me up, said Shin was talking and wanted to see us."

Leigh redid her ponytail and stuffed the hat back on her head.

"You okay?" asked Lex, holding out a Foobrew.

"Is it breakfast time?"

"It is for you."

She was too tired to argue. Leigh gulped the Foobrew and said, "Let's go."

They walked into a welcome scene. Two lanterns lit the far side of the room where Shin lay. Zalfaa, Olu, and Ada sat nearby.

Shin was in the same spot, but he was sitting up, propped by a handful of pillows and holding his own canteen. His skin was an odd palette of colors: sallow where not burned; pink where the burns were mildest; red, raw, and inflamed over his left shoulder, arm, and chest. The burnt skin glistened in the lamplight from a fresh coat of aloe.

"My friends," said Shin in a tremulous voice. His smile was weak, but it reached his eyes.

"You're looking good," said Lex, kneeling down and clasping a hand gently on Shin's undamaged shoulder. Leigh feared if she spoke it'd come out in a sob of joy. She sat down next to Lex and managed nothing more than a ridiculous, tearful grin.

That seemed to be enough for Shin, who said simply, "Thanks. All of you."

Through a mix of euphoria and exhaustion, she tried to pay attention as Zalfaa updated them. Shin had been awake for a while now. He was able to drink water and Foobrew on his own. He needed sleep and rest but had insisted on thanking his caregivers before going back to sleep.

Zalfaa cautioned that Shin would take weeks to recover and that he still needed round-the-clock care for a few days, just in case. Shin and Lex shared a slight eye roll over Zalfaa's protectiveness. The normalcy of the moment made Leigh want to weep with relief.

It was clear that Zalfaa thought the danger was over. She'd already sent Cliff back to his own cabin and was doing the same to Leigh and Lex. Even more telling, Zalfaa herself had agreed to leave as soon as Eliana came to take her place.

Shin was going to be all right.

It was time to leave Q-cabin.

As they walked outside into the moonlight, Lex turned off the lantern. Leigh rearranged her baseball cap and wiped away dirt from under the brim. She pulled her ponytail tighter, then slipped on her shoes.

"I don't know how you walk around barefoot," she said. "My feet would rebel."

"I'd walk around naked every night if they'd let me," said Lex.

"Is that what people do in Minnesota?" she teased.

"Only at the lake."

Leigh spoke before she could think: "Want to do that at the beach?"

Lex paused. "What're you asking?"

"I don't think I can sleep until I get clean. Come with me to Sunset Beach for a quick swim." *What?* What was she saying? It was as if some other person—a mix of Michele and Gwen—were talking.

She saw Lex hesitate. She wondered what internal voices of caution and abandon were warring in his head. She wondered where her own caution had disappeared to.

Lex switched the lantern back on and said, "Let's go."

CHAPTER 23

Less than an hour later, the two delinquents were deliciously clean. They sat against the boulder that marked Lex's favorite spot on the planet. The lantern was off so they could better see the stars.

Once he'd recovered from the shock of Lorelei's suggestion and assured himself he could toe the line, Lex had relaxed and enjoyed the adventure. The skinny-dipping had been less awkward than he'd anticipated. The past day and a half had ripped away most of the protective layers between him and Lorelei. A layer of clothing seemed insubstantial in comparison.

They'd kept their distance from each other in the water, staying close enough for safety, but not too close, leaving the water at different times so that each had the illusion of privacy. Lex had promised himself to keep his hands off her, and she had given no hint of wanting him to do otherwise.

He felt more in danger of breaking that promise now, sitting on the plateau, fully dressed, shoulder to shoulder against the rock. She smelled like the ocean itself—salty and wild. Sitting with her arms wrapped around her knees, wet hair dampening her sweatshirt, eyes gazing at the moonlit waves, Lorelei looked like a natural part of the planet.

"It's a world of possibilities," he said.

"What?"

"Marjol, this planet. It's a world of possibilities."

"Don't need to convince me."

"You're not skeptical?"

"I want to know the truth about how and why we got here," she said. "That doesn't mean I'm skeptical. I'm curious. Two different things."

She leaned a little harder against him and seemed content to stare at the stars. Lex thought he'd better keep the conversation going.

"Did you hear what else Maps found?" he asked.

"Cliff told me. Five more shuttle pieces. You know, there might be survivors from that crash."

"I knew you were an optimist."

"Not usually." She unfolded her legs, stretched, and yawned. "But Shin's alive. Seems anything's possible."

"Marjol's an interesting place to call home."

"Home, I don't know," she said. "My home is over ten light-years away. I don't even know if my mom's alive, but it's still home."

"My Grams told me home was people, not a place. With the right people, anywhere could be home."

"You believe that?"

"The older I get," said Lex, "the more I realize how smart my grandparents are. Or were. It's strange to think they might not be around anymore."

"Stranger to think we may never know. Even stranger that we traveled for thirteen years to get here, and yet almost twenty-two years have passed by on Earth."

"Physics," said Lex. "I can do the math, but it still seems weird." He tilted his head farther back against the rock so he could look straight up at the night sky. The largest moon was a sliver; the canopy of stars, dizzying.

Or maybe it was the company. Lex was aware of the warmth in his right arm from leaning next to Lorelei's left. He resisted the urge to hold her hand.

"I know what your grandmother meant," she said, "about home … and people. But I think places matter. Look at you—you seem partial to this rock."

"True enough."

Lorelei picked up her hat. She bent her knees and wrapped her legs in her arms, holding the baseball cap in her hands and swinging it while staring at the ocean.

"I think," she said, "you like this spot because it looks over the water. I had a spot like that back on Earth."

"You did?"

"Overlooking a pond. It was our getaway spot, for long weekends and stuff. Until my dad died. Then Mom and I moved there full time. I used to go out on the back porch and sit in this old yellow puffy chair. It was massive and ugly, but I loved it. Even on the worst days, I could curl up in my puffy yellow chair, watch the pond, and decide I was going to be okay."

"I'm sorry about your dad."

"You know what it's like."

"Yeah, it sucks."

His comment raised a smile as she turned away from the night sky and looked at him. He returned her gaze but wasn't sure what to read in her face. She was right there, centimeters away, and yet part of her seemed more distant than ever.

"You all right?" he asked.

"Thinking about too many things. I'm worn out but not ready to go to sleep. Know what I mean?"

"Yes," he said, "yes, I do."

She returned to gazing skyward, so Lex did the same. He thought she'd walked to the precipice of telling him who she was, then stepped back from the edge. He wasn't going to push her; he wanted her to jump.

"We should name some constellations," she said.

He struggled to adjust to the change in topic.

"You call that mess of stars the Jellyfish," she said. "Why not have real constellations?"

"Make them up?"

"Sure."

Stars were a good distraction. "I remember learning constellations," said Lex, "when I was young, seven I think. My favorite was the Great

Bear, Ursa Major. My friends would say, 'There's the Big Dipper,' and I'd say, 'No, that's part of a giant bear.' I was a goofy little kid."

"I never learned much about the stars … the science or the myths."

"Really?" said Lex. "I dreamed about traveling to see the Southern Cross."

"I take it you didn't get to go?"

"Nope."

"Well," she said, "now you have a whole new sky of stars to look at."

"Uh-huh."

"And you can make up your own constellations," she said. "Go ahead. Pick one."

"Right now?"

"Why not?"

Why not? Lorelei's words echoed in his head for the second time that night. "What stars stand out?" he asked.

"See the six bright ones over there. They kind of stairstep, there's a pair, and then go left and down, there's three, and then left and down a little more, there's another bright one."

Childhood memories flooded back. Lex followed her finger and studied the upper right quadrant of the sky.

"It's almost like a head," she said, "and then the back of an animal or something."

"I see it," he marveled.

"What does it look like? A duck?" She laughed. "Don't make it a duck. That's too boring for a constellation."

"It's not a duck," he said. "It's a loon."

"What's that?"

"You don't know what a loon is?"

"Not a clue."

"Obviously, you're not from Minnesota."

"Obviously."

"A loon is a water bird, shaped like a duck, only bigger, and better. They're majestic."

"A majestic duck?"

"Duck-shaped. But like I said, bigger. And heavier. Loons are expert swimmers—they can stay underwater more than two minutes."

"Impressive."

"You sure you've never seen a loon?" he asked. "They're black and white, with a checkerboard pattern on their wings, this glossy dark-green ring around the bottom of their necks, incredible red eyes."

"Sounds spectacular enough for a constellation."

Lex looked at the six stars. Was it his imagination, or was one of the background stars in the loon's head red like the bird's eye? Now that Lorelei had pointed it out, he had no trouble seeing a loon in the stars.

"Birds," she said. "I miss birds. I miss seeing them ... hearing them. There's an emptiness in the sky. Strange how the absence of something creates its own presence."

Lex had at least a dozen responses to that statement; he decided to stick with the loons.

"In northern Minnesota," he said, "in the spring, when the ice on the lake goes out, the loons come back. You hear 'em before you see 'em. Loons have distinct calls—yodels, wails, hoots. To hear a loon call of an evening across a peaceful lake, well, that's about as good as it gets."

"You miss it," she said. "Minnesota. You miss it."

"I don't know. That kind of life in Minnesota, the kind where you hear the loons, it was gone for me long before I left."

"Do you miss anything from Earth?"

"I miss ..." Lex hesitated. His chest felt like a weight was on it, but he spoke anyway. "I miss a possibility." He hesitated again, the heaviness growing, but the need to speak growing more. "Shortly before my mom died, she told me that if she could wish for one thing, it'd be that my dad and I became a team again, that we'd reconcile.

"She asked me to promise I'd try." He paused, searching for the right words. "Of course, I promised ... but then, well ... I didn't try, not really, but I always thought I *would*. I always believed I'd keep that promise."

"You miss the lost chance."

"True enough," said Lex, "but I've learned to live with that regret."

"Maybe you shouldn't have to," she said. "Maybe your dad's support of you being a colonist was that reconciliation."

"I'll never know."

"I think you do."

"Don't push it."

"That's why you brought the photo," she said. "The Muddy Men. So you'd know you'd kept your promise to your mom, that you'd repaired things with your dad. At least enough for him to give you the photo ... and for you to bring it with you."

The heaviness in his chest burst into sharp pain as if a firecracker had gone off inside him. Lorelei was voicing things he hoped were true, but they were too much to deal with out here in the open. They didn't belong on this plateau, under these stars. He'd left all that behind.

"Thanks for telling me," she said, and reached out and grabbed his hand. Her fingers were ice cold.

Lex squeezed back. He wanted to wrap his arms around her and not let go. To hold on to her until his heartbeat returned to normal. To stay with her in this spot until Rán's morning light forced them to leave.

But all he did was squeeze her hand more tightly.

She looked at him, the starlight reflected in her eyes. He thought about the scar on her back that he'd glimpsed in the moonlight, and he wondered if this quixotic girl would ever tell him all her secrets in return.

He would wait.

"Let's go back," said Lex, letting go of her hand, forcing himself to breathe normally.

They stood up, dusted off the sand, turned on the lantern, and headed back to Homesite. She didn't reach for his hand again, and he didn't reach for hers. But he was aware of its presence every step of the way.

CHAPTER 24

In the morning, full daylight spilled through the window as Lex hauled himself out of bed. It was a good day. Shin had survived, and Lex was filled with memories of a beautiful midnight swim.

Even so, his body ached as he pulled on fresh clothes, and he found himself longing for a return to normalcy—days of getting up and working in Boats until dinner, days where no one got sick, no one talked about difficult things, and nothing strange washed up on shore.

He grabbed a morning Foobrew, checked on Shin, then met up with Olu and Ada. The three leaders headed to Sunrise Beach, where Rose waited for them next to the pile of recent discoveries.

Lorelei had been right about what had been recovered. In addition to the broken cryosleep pod, Maps had found five other pieces of flotsam. Four were fashioned out of lightweight black metal. Two of those were small, able to fit inside a person's hand; another was the size of a hockey stick, and the fourth was almost as big as Lex himself. No telling what the metal compound was, but all four were the same.

The fifth object was the length of a person's arm and had been cylindrical before being smashed on one side. It was a smaller version of the big cylinder—with smooth white coating on the unsmashed side, irregular dark-silver metal on the other, and a few sheared wires sticking out of one end.

Lex picked it up. Ada watched as he examined the object. It was sturdy and hefty—a larger version of the wedge-shaped chunk that had started all this, the one Lorelei had tossed at him and Olu.

Rotating the cylinder, Lex ran his hand over the uneven side.

"What do you think?" asked Ada.

"Not sure," he said. "Can't tell if it broke off or if some of the metal was made this way."

"No," said Ada. "I mean, big picture. What do you think?"

He looked at her and stated the obvious. "I think a shuttle crashed in the ocean and pieces of it are washing up on shore."

"Hard to believe it could be anything else, but we have to keep an open mind."

"Is anyone still searching on the sunset side?"

"No," said Ada. "After two days without finding anything new over there, Rose and I moved the search to this side. You think that's a mistake?"

"I'm not second-guessing you," said Lex.

"But the first two pieces were found over there."

"If the wreck happened far enough away, debris could easily end up on both sides."

"That's what Michele said."

"And the deep, U-shaped inlets over here, they'd be more likely to trap anything that washed ashore."

"Michele said that too."

"Then you don't need to hear it from me," said Lex.

"I'm not trying to start an argument."

Rose walked over. "Who's arguing?"

"No one," said Ada.

Lex put down the piece he was holding and took a sideways glance at the two girls. He'd been so focused on the debris from the doomed shuttle—and really, what else could it be?—he'd failed to notice the people.

For the past several days, Lex had been immersed in caring for Shin, his world a small bubble of life and death. During that time, Olu had stayed at Homesite, dealing with the needs of the other injured colonists. Ada had juggled everything, helping with the sick and injured while maintaining a sense of normalcy for the colony. She'd even organized the first groups of tai chi, yoga, and swimming on Tuesday morning, trying to start up that routine.

Meanwhile, Rose had kept Maps productive. Half of them were clearing a path to the Crooked Teeth while the rest scoured the coastlines, unearthing discoveries that brought more and more questions, all with no good answers. A lot had been going on outside the sickroom, and Rose and Ada had been handling it. It was time for Lex to share the burden.

"Has all this been found around the corner?" he asked. "In that first horseshoe of rocky coastline?"

"No," said Rose. "The cryosleep pod—"

"If that's what it is," interjected Ada.

"The broken pod," continued Rose, "and the smallest piece, we found those two there, in the area you're talking about, washed up on the rocks, not far from the water. Everything else, we found around the second bend, in the narrow inlet, you know where I mean?"

"Yep," said Lex.

"And today we're searching the one beyond, the wider one with the bit of beach, the last one we can get to."

Lex bent down to check out the smallest piece of debris and ran his hand over the smooth material. It was understandable that Ada sought an alternate explanation. No one wanted to believe a shuttle dropped off the third landing party and then crashed. If that were true, it might mean the end to landing parties. It might mean no one else was coming.

Cradling the lightweight piece of debris in his palm, Lex stood up and looked at Rose, but her attention was on Olu—ten meters down the beach, kneeling on the sand and examining the broken pod.

"Anything else?" Lex asked Rose.

She furrowed her brow and turned back to address him face-to-face. "It's odd," Rose said. "The four pieces we found in the narrow inlet, they were high up in the rocks, as if a giant wave had lifted them out of the sea and put them down all at once, all in the same spot. Strange, huh?"

"It's a puzzle," Lex replied.

One he and Olu had already confronted. A few days ago, they'd talked about this very thing when they'd stood on the other side of the island and stared at the big cylinder. It, too, looked as if it'd been planted by a giant wave. If so, then the wrecked shuttle was not the one that had brought the third landing party but a shuttle that had crashed earlier.

Five days before the third landing party's arrival, a bad storm—brief but fierce—had battered the island. If shuttle pieces had been floating in the ocean at the time, that storm could've been the culprit. Those waves would have been big enough to throw debris up on the shore, to toss a hunk of metal onto a rock as easily as someone might toss a beanbag at a cornhole board.

But wreckage of an *earlier* shuttle would lead to even more questions. Where had this one been going? When and why? Were there other colonies? How many shuttles were there?

Either way, it made Lex wonder. Did they have enough people for a colony? Were there teenagers held in cryosleep who might never be thawed?

He walked over to Olu, who was still kneeling on the sand and studying the broken cryosleep pod.

"Take a look," said Olu. "The edge looks like the pod was cut open. It doesn't look like a break; it looks purposeful."

Lex bent down to examine the transparent material. He ran his hand gently across the edge. "Could be," he agreed. "See this scoring. Like someone used a fine-toothed saw blade."

"Which makes no sense," said Olu.

Lex started to ask the girls to come over and look, but someone else was already calling to them. João was shouting as he ran down the beach with several other Maps members, Lorelei among them. Her feet were racing, but her face showed interest, not panic. Lex opted to hope for good news.

"Catch your breath," said Ada when João and the others arrived. "Whatever it is can wait one more minute."

João's wide-eyed look indicated he did not agree. He pulled a dark-blue bag off his back and held it out for inspection. The bag was intact, despite looking like it'd been thrown off a cliff and churned in a whirlpool.

"We found this," said João. "It's not empty."

"And not one of ours?" said Rose.

"No."

"Have you opened it?" asked Olu.

João teased the drawstring apart and pulled out three objects. He handed them to Olu one at a time: a knotted cord of blue and white rope, a soggy yellow tennis ball, and a rectangular piece of dark engraved metal. Olu passed the objects to Ada, who shared them among the others.

"Anyone know what this is?" she held up the metal rectangle.

Everyone shook their heads.

"It was important to someone," said Lorelei.

Ada passed Lex the metal object. It was heavy but small, only about fifteen centimeters long, a little box with a hole at each end and a three-pronged symbol on one side. He had no clue what it was, and yet he knew exactly what it meant: this wreckage was from a shuttle that had never landed, a shuttle full of colonists who'd never had the chance to unpack their bags.

He handed the object to Rose. Though no words passed between them, he knew she'd reached the same conclusion.

"We also found these," said Eliana as she held up two Foobrew vials. The vials were empty but intact, including the screw-on tops.

Ada gasped.

Everyone else grew silent.

Lex reached out a hand, and Eliana dropped a vial into his palm. He could see a few droplets of Foobrew inside. Someone had drunk the rest and screwed the cap back on.

"The ocean couldn't do that," he said, reluctant to verbalize the rest. These containers were not for the post-cryosleep rehydration meals. Those bottles were larger. The vial in his hand was like the ones they used every day. It was like the ones they'd been instructed to grab a few minutes before landing.

He remembered it well. Grab the vials, grab the bag, strap in for landing. The odds of someone drinking one of those vials before a crash were slim indeed. More than one? No chance.

Lex looked at Olu, hoping to hear him speak, but it was Lorelei who voiced the words in his head: "There may be survivors."

And it was Rose who asked, "What do we do now?"

* * *

That evening, Lex had no appetite for dinner. The day had been filled with endless arguments, pointless conversations, and no decisions. He stood on the edge of Homesite and rubbed his pounding temples.

The leadership was split. Olu was focused on the fifty-nine people he could see and talk to. Anyone else who arrived would be welcomed into the colony, but he saw no reason to risk lives hunting for unlikely survivors, especially since it meant sending a raft to the Twisted Peaks. Last week, everyone in Boats had agreed it made no sense to undertake that voyage until they had a better raft, one with a reliable sail. In Olu's opinion, a blue bag and a couple of empty vials were no reason to change the plan.

Ada disagreed. She saw it as their duty to look for survivors. They'd run out of space to search on land; the next logical step was by sea. Taking a raft would be safe so long as they stayed close to shore.

Lex's head ached because he understood both positions. Olu and Ada were worried about protecting people, but they were going about it differently. If he'd been able to keep things calm, the leadership could've found a compromise. Instead, everything had spiraled out of control.

He should've insisted the three of them stay on Sunrise Beach and hash things out. Instead, they'd gone off to their work groups and shared the discoveries with the rest of the colony. As soon as Lex had told Boats the news, Michele championed the idea of searching for survivors. She told everyone who'd listen about how well things had gone when she, Lex, and Noah had taken out the newest raft for a test run on Friday. When someone asked if the same three people would be searching for survivors, she'd answered, "Probably, I haven't thought about it, and four people might be best."

Michele had spoken off the cuff, but her words were quickly repeated. Who was going on the journey became one more point of contention. Olu grew angry because Michele was planning a crew when the journey itself hadn't been agreed upon. Ada supported the journey, but not Michele's crew. She thought Lex should stay behind, the three leaders guiding the colony from home.

They were all mishandling the situation.

It was the leadership's biggest mess yet.

And he didn't know how to fix it.

No one seemed to notice Lex hadn't expressed an opinion. Both sides assumed his support. It was hard not to resent those assumptions.

He tried to focus on the positive, on the afternoon's one small success: Olu and Ada had agreed to invite the work group leaders—Dhruv, Michele, and Rose—to tonight's leadership meeting. It'd be six equal seats at the table, and they'd meet until a decision was reached. Tomorrow, the colony could move forward one way or another.

For now, the chaotic workday was over, and colonists were beginning to congregate for dinner. That meant Lex had an hour until the meeting began. He slipped away and headed downhill to the spring.

As he'd hoped, the dinnertime water had already been gathered; the spring was deserted. He took off his shirt and sat in a small nook on the rocky side of the pool. Above him grew sweet, fragrant plants that drooped over the edge of the spring. He spared a few minutes to breathe in the scent and watch the reflection of the branches in the still water. Already, his headache was fading.

Lex grabbed a bucket and filled it halfway. Sitting back from the edge of the spring, he slowly poured the cool, fresh water over his head. It always amazed him how good it felt to rinse off the salty brine. He closed his eyes and indulged in the moment—clean, quiet, alone.

"Nice double standard," said a familiar voice.

Lex opened his eyes to find Marko standing nearby.

"Just cleaning up." Lex grinned.

"No one else is allowed to wander alone," said Marko in a teasing voice.

But he was right. What good was a leader who didn't follow the rules?

"Sorry," said Lex.

"Hey, I'm kidding you."

"Doesn't mean you're wrong."

"You all right?" asked Marko.

"Fine."

"Seriously?"

"Seriously, I'm fine."

"Well," said Marko with feigned relief, "that's one out of fifty-nine. I guess the other fifty-eight of us will be fine eventually."

Lex laughed.

"Actually," said Marko, "I'm fine too. And so is Milo by the way—his face is much better."

Lex nodded his understanding. *Focus on the good things. Focus on what you can control.* He and Marko had talked about it more than once.

"Have you looked at all the debris that's been found?" asked Lex.

"Hasn't everyone?"

"True enough." Lex stood up. He moved out of the shade and into the sunshine. "Did you notice anything strange about the cryosleep pod?"

"You mean the scoring along the edges."

Lex laughed again. "So I'm not crazy?"

"Not about that."

"Thanks."

"Looks like someone took a saw and sliced open the pod," said Marko.

"Then broke off the last part?"

"More like the person inside pushed out and broke it off."

"Thought so too," agreed Lex. "But that makes no sense."

Marko shrugged. "That's what it looks like."

Lex rubbed his hands through his hair and shook out the excess water. It felt good to stand in the sunshine, water dripping down his back.

"I assume you know," said Marko, "that Dhruv's going to support Olu."

"That's the rumor," said Lex.

"Dhruv's had a rough few days."

"Haven't we all."

"It's not easy to run Food with a broken arm."

"He hasn't complained."

"Exactly," said Marko.

"Hmm."

"Our work group is the dumping ground for injured people, and now Dhruv is injured himself."

Lex had meant to talk to Dhruv about that very thing, but he'd dropped the ball. Marko was right to remind him.

"Is it a problem?" asked Lex. "Something we need to fix?"

"Not yet, but I'll tell you if it gets that way."

"Good to know." Lex wiped the remaining water droplets off his arms. He put the empty bucket back in its spot and grabbed his shirt off the ground.

"Want a towel?" asked Marko.

"Nah, thanks. I'm going back to the cabin for a fresh shirt anyway."

"I'll walk up with you."

"I'm gonna go check on Shin," said Lex. "Wanna come?"

"Can't," said Marko. "Like I said, we're shorthanded. I'm on serving duty and clean-up."

"Sorry."

"Better than what you've got coming tonight."

"It'll be fine."

"Won't be easy," said Marko, "but, in fairness, easy's not really your style."

Lex laughed and gave Marko a soft punch in the shoulder. "Thanks for your support."

"Anytime, Lex."

The two boys headed back to Homesite. Underneath the flippancy, Marko's words had a bone-deep truth. Lex would go see Shin, and then he'd go to the meeting. He would try to be the leader Marko thought he was.

CHAPTER 25

As Zalfaa coaxed Shin into eating a few bites of fish, Leigh settled herself in a familiar spot—on the floor on the far side of Shin's bed. Cliff entered the cabin a few minutes later and sat next to her.

"Learn anything?" she asked him.

"Nothing new."

"Same."

"Other than the mezuzah," said Cliff.

"You know what I mean."

"Yeah, nothing new."

"What's a mezuzah?" asked Shin.

"A mezuzah," said Leigh, "is the metal thing we found in the washed-up bag. Something Jewish people hang by their doorways."

"To guard the house?" asked Shin.

"I think so."

"And as a welcome," said Cliff, "but it's more complicated than that. The box is supposed to have a rolled-up piece of paper in it, but we didn't find one."

Zalfaa gave up on getting Shin to eat solid food, handed him a Foobrew, and took a seat opposite the others. She picked up her notebook and jotted a few lines at the bottom of the page.

"Seriously?" asked Shin. "You're writing down what I eat."

"Ignore him," said Leigh to Zalfaa. Turning to Shin, she added, "Don't worry. None of the rest of us can read it anyway."

Shin gave a low laugh. His voice was tired, and a purplish tinge encircled his eyes; other than that, he appeared relatively comfortable. It seemed forever ago since she and Lex had sat at his bedside and feared the worst. In reality, it'd only been a day.

What a day. Her muscles felt as if they'd been through a shredder, and her voice sounded hoarse. She needed sleep, but first, she needed resolution.

They'd agreed the best approach was to talk to Lex. A sound decision, but one that meant Leigh was trying hard not to think about their middle-of-the-night ocean swim. She was trying not to remember how warm his body had felt leaning against hers. She was trying not to remember what it had been like when he'd held her hand.

She was forcing herself to remember what it had been like when he'd let go.

"I think," said Zalfaa, "it's time Shin got some rest."

"And we need to get going," said Cliff. "Time to find Lex." He and Leigh started to stand when Lex walked into the room.

"You guys headed out?" he asked them.

"Uh, no," said Cliff as he sat back down. Leigh did the same. Lex's puzzled look shifted into a big grin as soon as he turned toward the sick bed.

"My man," said Lex, "you look good!"

"Feeling better all the time," replied Shin. "Tired, but much better."

"If this is too much company," Lex replied, "I can go."

"Oh, no," said Zalfaa. "Stay. Please."

Lex situated himself on the floor next to Zalfaa, her open notebook between them. On the other side of Shin's bed, Cliff put a calming hand on Leigh's arm. *Wait*, the gesture said. *Don't rush*. It was good advice.

"These your notes?" Lex asked Zalfaa. "Fancy shorthand of some kind?"

"Hardly," she said. "It's a mix of Arabic and English."

"Beautiful handwriting."

"It's like a secret code," joked Leigh.

"Very funny," said Zalfaa, squirming a little under all the attention. "I grew up in Abu Dhabi. Well, I was born in Qatar, but we moved to the Emirates when I was two. I always spoke Arabic and English, but I grew up writing only Arabic. They made us handwrite for years and years."

"Then what happened?" asked Lex.

"When I was eleven," Zalfaa continued, "my mother and I moved to Wichita, in Kansas. I could speak and read English no problem, and I learned to handwrite enough to satisfy my teachers, but you know how it is. There's not much need. My mother insisted I keep up my Arabic. I always thought that meant we'd go back."

She shook her head slightly, as if shaking off the memory. It was the most Leigh had ever heard her bunkmate talk about the past.

"And now you're a Marjolian," said Lex, "like the rest of us."

"You're right," Zalfaa replied. "It doesn't matter where we came from."

"It *does* matter," said Shin. "It matters a lot. But it matters *more* where you are now."

"Hmm," said Lex, in a slightly teasing manner, "someone's gotten philosophical."

"I'm trying to get on her good side," said Shin. "Maybe she'll tell me what all those notes say."

Lex picked up the notebook and faked translating the words: "Shin is the world's most difficult patient. Now that he's awake, he won't quit talking. Of course, if I make a list of all the problem people, I have to start with Cliff and Lorelei."

"Very funny," said Cliff.

"Seriously," said Lex, "your names are listed." He turned the notebook around so everyone could see, but Zalfaa grabbed it from him.

"That's a list of everyone who's offered to take a night shift," she said.

"Oh," said Lex, "you can add me."

Leigh's hopes fell. Maybe the decision had already been made.

The room grew quiet. It was now or never. But she hesitated, and Lex spoke first into the silence.

"What?" he asked.

Leigh's stomach clenched. They were about to put him in an impossible position.

"What?" repeated Lex.

"We thought you'd be going on the rescue mission," she said.

Lex wiped his hands across his face and did not reply.

"Are you canceling it?" asked Cliff.

"Honestly," Lex said, "I don't know. That's why we're having the meeting tonight. And that's why we're including the work group leaders. It's time to decide. Do we look for survivors or not?"

Lex furrowed his brow. His hair was wet, and tidier than usual, plus he was wearing a fresh shirt, one not cut off at the sleeves. Leigh suspected the external order masked some internal dishevelment.

"Tell him," said Shin.

"You should be resting," Zalfaa insisted. She made a move as if to help Shin rearrange the bedding.

"Tell him," repeated Shin. "Everyone's been in here complaining. You all agreed to tell him. Then I'll rest."

Zalfaa adjusted the pillow under Shin's left arm. Leigh tried to organize her thoughts, and once again Lex spoke first.

"Complaining about what?" he asked.

"About not knowing what's going on," said Leigh. "About being confused. Not having a say."

"From what I can tell," said Lex, "everyone's been having their say all day long."

"Not to us."

"Us?"

"Our landing party."

"You were there," he said. "You were on the beach this morning."

"I found the bag," Leigh replied. "And Eliana found the first empty vial. But it has been out of our hands since." She stopped, at a loss for how to explain.

"Late this morning," said Cliff, "we heard that you, Noah, and Michele were going to take a raft and look for survivors. Made sense. But then Rose came to see if Lorelei and I would be willing to go instead of Noah."

"Rose asked you this?" said Lex.

"Yes."

"She wanted to send two from Maps," said Leigh.

"We're two of her best swimmers," added Cliff.

"So we came to talk to Shin," said Leigh. "To see if it was okay if we left. Especially since you were leaving too."

"I told them not to worry," said Shin.

"The point," continued Leigh, "is that Cliff and I told Rose we'd do it. But when we talked to Noah, we got a different story. He was all excited about going on the rescue mission. Later, Rose came back and told us never mind; no one was going. We didn't know what to believe."

"And we still don't," said Cliff. "The current rumor is there are two options—either you, Noah, and Michele are going to search for survivors, or no one is going."

"Which is why," said Zalfaa, "I put Cliff and Lorelei's names on this list but not yours." She held up the notebook for Lex to see, but he wasn't looking. He was staring at Shin's blanket, avoiding eye contact with all of them.

His body language was difficult to read. He sat in a relaxed position, but the muscles in his forearms were taut, and his lips were pressed in a thin line. The closeness Leigh had felt to him over the past few days had still been there when he'd walked in. Now she wasn't sure. And the rest of the conversation wasn't going to help.

"Only one thing is for sure," she said to him. "Nobody knows your opinion."

To her surprise, his mouth twitched into a half-smile.

"Have you decided?" she asked. "Have you decided how you'll vote tonight?"

"No," said Lex. "I haven't ... I ... there's been no decision. That's why we're meeting."

"And none of us will be there." Leigh matched his forced calmness with her own. "When the six of you meet, no one from the third landing party will be there."

He blinked. "You want a voice at the table ... and you think you don't have one."

"Well, we don't."

He started to respond, then paused. Eventually, Lex said, "Do you have someone in mind?"

"We were hoping you'd do it."

"Me?" He sat up straight. "Why would I speak for your landing party? How would I even know all twenty of you want the same thing?" His eyes widened, and a rueful smile spread across his face.

"I see," said Lex, nodding. "I should've seen it earlier."

He didn't make eye contact with her. Instead, he spoke directly to Shin. "That's why Zalfaa's worried about you getting more rest. All day, they've been coming in here and visiting and talking and saying what they didn't feel comfortable saying to one of us. Your landing party's been having its own conversation, right here in this room, and I didn't even realize it."

"Yes," said Shin, his eyes tired, but his voice strong. "We all agree. If we have a chance to save another life, we need to go."

CHAPTER 26

When he woke up the next morning, Lex kept his eyes shut. The previous day, he'd awakened tired but imbued with a sense of hopefulness, his mind filled with memories of a glorious midnight swim. Twenty-five hours later, all he felt was tired.

But reality was waiting, and there was no use ignoring it. He opened his eyes, rolled out of bed, and gave Marko a time-to-wake-up shake.

"Morning, Lex," Marko whispered. "What's today?"

"Thursday."

"Let's make it a good one."

"Always."

The routine exchange felt good. Not everything had been altered by yesterday's events.

The leadership meeting had been relatively short. Olu and Dhruv had voted not to search for survivors until an adequate sailing raft was built and tested. Ada and Michele had countered by voting to send a raft as soon as possible. Rose agreed to back them, on one condition: Maps members had to be part of the crew. Given how readily Michele agreed, Lex suspected the real negotiations had taken place earlier.

The vote sitting at three to two, all eyes had turned to him. Much to everyone's surprise, Lex had voiced the opinion and concerns of the third landing party, which put him squarely opposed to Olu and

Dhruv. He'd looked at the two of them as he talked, but that'd only made things more awkward.

He'd then backed Rose's initiative to include members from Maps, and he'd added a caveat of his own—that they put a cap of a week on the length of the trip, four days out and four days back.

No one had left the meeting completely happy, but the decision had been made: two from Boats, Michele and Lex, and two from Maps, Cliff and Lorelei, would be taking the voyage. Together they would look for survivors and map the coastline.

Outwardly, Lex told everyone it'd be "a grand adventure." Inwardly, he was unsettled by how things had played out. He didn't like being at odds with Olu, and Dhruv wasn't too happy with him either. Even Ada was miffed, believing that Lex should've begged off going on the voyage.

Nonetheless, a plan was a plan, and there was a lot to do. They canceled the morning's yoga, swimming, and tai chi and got to work. The first order of business was to portage the raft across the island. It took half the colony and half the morning to get the raft to its launch point on Sunrise Beach. Lex wished fewer people had used the portage time as a forum for rehashing old arguments, but at least the raft was where it needed to be.

At midday, he downed a Foobrew and reached into his pocket, ready to prepare the raft for the journey. He sighed; his pocket was empty. No Swiss Army knife.

He grabbed Noah to go with him to fetch it from Homesite, knowing he'd be flayed alive if he went anywhere alone. Today, even a quick solo jog to his cabin and back would bring the wrath of several people down upon his neck.

"You all right, mate?" asked Noah as they entered the cabin.

"All good," said Lex.

"You must be the only one," said Noah. "It's a dog's breakfast around here."

"I'm good *enough*. That more accurate?"

"Reckon it's the best we can hope for right now."

Lex rummaged through his bedding and found the Swiss Army knife. Homesite was deserted. Noah leaned against a nearby bunk, in no rush to return. A bit of peace and quiet was worth taking while they could get it.

Lex climbed onto Marko's bed, the bunk above his own, and sat with his legs dangling over the side. "I'm sorry," he said to Noah. "I know you volunteered to go. I was at the meeting last night, and I'm still not sure why I'm going on the raft instead of you."

"No worries, mate. Plenty to do here, and you're not likely to find survivors anyway."

"Thought you were in favor of us going?"

"Definitely," said Noah. "If I were stranded out there, I'd want you to find me. The way I see it, the raft is sturdy, and the trip shouldn't take long. Might as well have a go."

"I agree."

"But let's face it: you're a lot more likely to find wreckage or a dead body. Odds are … no one survived."

Lex thought of Shin. He thought of the empty vials. Long odds didn't mean impossible. But before he could reply, they heard voices outside.

"Shhh," said Noah.

The voices drew closer and stopped in front of Floraville, the cabin next door.

"I thought Noah was going," said Lorelei's voice.

"I changed my mind," replied Michele.

"Because Olu told you to?"

"Don't insult me. Get the canteens, and let's go."

There was a pause in the girls' conversation. Noah and Lex sat still. In a few seconds, the talk resumed.

"I'm sorry," said Lorelei, "I hate to see you upset."

"I'm not the one who's upset," said Michele.

"You know what I mean."

"No worries. It'll be nice to have two of you from Maps along to check out the coastline."

"As long as you're sure."

"The Māori have a saying—"

"Big surprise."

"Don't be rude," said Michele, but the two girls chuckled. "The saying is, *He manako te koura I kore ai.* 'There are no crayfish as you set your heart on them.'"

"Noah's a crayfish?"

Lex looked away from Noah to keep from laughing.

"It's like the chicken saying," replied Michele, "don't put your eggs all in one basket."

Again, there was a pause in the conversation. Lex spared a moment to marvel at the easy camaraderie that'd already developed between the two girls. He supposed that was the benefit of bunking a new landing party in with an old one.

"Here's the thing," said Michele. "Noah's in charge of getting us ready to sail."

"I thought that was weeks away."

"For long distances, probably," she admitted. "But for a basic working sail, we're close, really close."

"That's amazing."

"We made the sail smaller, easier to handle. The problem now is tying the cloth to the mast and the boom. Too much wind, and those spots start to rip. But Noah thinks he's found a solution. He tore open his blanket and found a thin layer of material inside—no idea what it is, other than ugly and orange, but it's also thin and strong."

"The liner inside the duvet," said Leigh. "Makes sense. It's probably why water doesn't soak through our blankets."

"That's our guess," said Michele. "We're reinforcing the edges of the sail with the orange material, then we'll give it a try. I need Noah to stay behind and run those tests on the sailing raft while we take the other one."

"Is that what you told him?"

"I did."

"And he was okay with that?"

"No," said Michele, "but he'll stay and do it."

After that, the boys could no longer hear the conversation, but they heard laughter as the girls walked away, past Q-cabin and toward Sunrise Beach.

"They knew we were up here," whispered Noah as soon as the girls were out of earshot. "They saw us leave the beach."

"No way they meant for us to hear that."

"Don't apply logic to girls," said Noah.

Lex smiled. Noah attracted a lot of female attention. It was nice to know he was baffled by them too.

"Besides," said Noah, "I'm not stupid. I know why I'm not goin'."

"Really?"

"Sure, Olu thinks I'm after his girl."

"His girl?"

"Michele."

"She hasn't been 'his girl' for a long time."

"Well, I reckon she wouldn't like the possessive."

Lex laughed.

"But it's true," said Noah. "Olu doesn't want me hangin' with Michele."

"No," said Lex. "It's complicated, but that's over. Trust me, I've been here for all of it."

"Whatever you say, mate." Noah shrugged. "But you're wrong. And seriously, I'm not makin' moves on Michele."

"Not my place to care."

"Maybe your place to tell the boss man to stop worryin' about it?"

Lex hopped down from the top bunk. "Right now, Olu isn't listening to anything I say. But when he does, I'll see what I can do."

"Thanks. I admire the hell out of Michele, but believe me, when I set my sights on a girl, she'll be a simple one, not someone complicated like her."

"Simple is good," said Lex.

Noah burst out laughing.

"What's so funny?"

"You, mate." He clapped Lex on the back. "No offense, but I think you're fallin' for the most complicated girl on the planet."

"Umm."

"No worries, your secret's safe with me!" Noah stepped back and said more seriously, "But watch yourself. Always plannin' somethin', that one. You can tell."

Lex stared. He was desperate to redirect the conversation but couldn't think of a thing to say.

Noah grinned, his normal carefree manner returning. "For myself, I'm hoping for a sweet simple soul. One who'll help me make a surfboard, then sneak off to have a naughty every now and again."

"Do you really need the surfboard?" said Lex.

"Good point." Noah laughed. "Let's head back. Lots to do."

"True enough."

The two boys walked outside and headed back toward Sunrise Beach. Lex was unnerved. Noah was way more observant than he appeared.

"Are people really sneaking off?" asked Lex.

"It's not happenin' at your cabin?"

"Not that I know of."

"That'd be easier to take," said Noah, "since I'm not one of the lucky ones doin' the sneakin' off."

Lex laughed. He found himself sorry Noah wasn't part of the upcoming adventure. Cliff was more than capable, but nobody put things in perspective quite like Noah.

* * *

The rest of the workday went surprisingly well. Everyone's mood improved while occupied and busy. Dinnertime, however, was another matter. The launch would be first thing in the morning, and the reality of the enterprise had sunk in.

Lex watched Michele and Olu have a tense conversation on the edge of Homesite. It was too quiet to be overheard, but their body language spoke volumes. After a few minutes, Ada joined them—further proof that Ada was braver than he was.

As everyone cleaned up from the evening meal, Olu approached Lex. The exchange did not begin well. Olu continued to argue against taking unnecessary risks, while Lex argued that not going would be a death sentence for any survivors. This was old ground, but if it helped Olu to retread it, then Lex was willing to go along.

Unfortunately, the conversation took an ugly turn. Olu blamed Lex for "taking sides" with "the girls." Even more infuriating was his accusation that the third landing party had been a bad influence.

"Things have been harder since they arrived," said Lex. "That doesn't mean those twenty people shouldn't have a say."

"You're missing my point," Olu retorted. "They haven't been here long enough to make this kind of decision. They don't know Marjol as well as we do. When you gave them your vote, you took yours away. And you *have* been here long enough to know better."

"Everyone needed a say."

"Yes," said Olu, "and then the leaders needed to put their personal feelings aside and do what was right for the colony. Being a leader doesn't mean doing what's popular; it means doing what's right." Olu stepped closer. "People are counting on us to do that, Lex. They're counting on *you* to do that."

"Fine." Lex crossed his arms and looked Olu straight in the eyes. "If you don't think I deserve to be a leader, I'm happy to give the job to someone else."

"You know that's not my point."

Yeah, he knew. And he knew this wasn't about ego; it wasn't about Olu not getting his way. His friend was worried. He truly believed they shouldn't be going.

"I know you're angry," said Lex. "But your anger with the third landing party is misplaced. Save your anger for those of us who've been here just as long as you have."

"That's why you and I are having this conversation."

"What about Michele?"

Olu's jaw tightened. "She's being stupid."

"Michele is many things, but rarely stupid."

"She's ignoring her own advice. A few days ago, she said it'd be smart to wait on the Twisted Peaks until we could sail."

"Things changed," said Lex.

"Not enough to merit being stupid."

"We'll be fine."

"You and Michele," Olu shook his head. "It's like you've forgotten all the lessons we learned the hard way. You've forgotten how dangerous those waters are, how quickly storms can arise, how little we know. You've forgotten ..."

"What?"

"You've forgotten what it's like to have one of us die."

It felt like Olu had thrown him to the ground and stomped on his chest. Actually, that would've been preferable. For a moment, Lex couldn't speak. He grabbed Olu's shoulders and looked him in the eyes. "You know," he finally said, "you *know* that's not true. I will *never* forget."

Lex let go of Olu. The two stood silently while dusk arrived at the end of a long day.

Olu shifted his feet and said, "I'm sorry."

"Have you considered," said Lex, "that Rina's death is one of the things compelling us to go? That the thought of another person dying when we might have saved them is too much to bear?"

"Realistically, if you find someone, it will be too late."

"Maybe," said Lex. "But this way we'll know. We'll *know* we did the best we could."

Olu lowered his voice. "We can't afford to lose any of you."

"The raft is sturdy—"

"And half of your crew has no experience with the raft," said Olu, "much less the Twisted Peaks. You and I, we know what it's like out there."

That's when Lex understood why he was going instead of Noah. "Our first raft was a twig compared to what we have now," he said.

Olu bowed his head a long moment. When he raised it, he looked weary but calmer. "There's no way," he said, "Michele will let me on the raft."

Lex stayed quiet; he hadn't known Olu coming on the journey had ever been an option.

Olu continued. "I'm counting on you to be the voice of reason, to avoid unnecessary risks."

"To make sure we all return," said Lex, finally understanding the point of the conversation.

"Yes."

"To turn us around if it gets too dangerous."

"Yes."

"Because you don't trust Michele to do that."

"No," said Olu, "because I trust you *to* do it. That's not the same."

Lex wanted to say that it was impossible to guarantee anyone's safety, that it was impossible to protect everyone from everything. Instead, he said, "You can count on me."

Olu reached out as if to shake hands, but Lex wasn't having it. He grabbed his best friend in a bear hug and pounded him on the back before letting go.

"I'm still pissed at you," said Olu.

"I know," said Lex. "I know."

CHAPTER 27

The explorers left at daybreak. Olu had cast a pall over the endeavor. He was, however, one of the half dozen colonists on the beach to see them off. Leigh gave him credit for that.

Once they were on the ocean, the land-based tensions lessened. It helped that there was work to do. Leigh and Cliff were unfamiliar with the nuances of how to use the paddles, but they were eager to learn. Michele and Lex switched off at the rudder.

Midmorning, they tested the raft's new tether system. The goal was to have those who were paddling tethered to the raft because they were most in danger of going overboard. Lex looped a rope over his foot and around his ankle and dove into the water.

At the most basic level, the test worked: the tether didn't break, and Lex returned safely to the raft. However, his ankle was rubbed raw, plus it took both Cliff and Leigh hauling hard on the rope to get him back—and that was in calm seas. The tether system needed some work, but it was better than nothing.

The rest of the morning, they kept the raft close to shore and stopped to investigate every inlet, every possible place where someone or something might have washed ashore.

"At the rate we're going," quipped Lex, "I could swim faster."

"No reason to do this if we're not going to be thorough," said Michele.

Leigh agreed, but she understood Lex's impatience. With each passing hour, the odds of finding survivors diminished. And the odds hadn't been that good to begin with.

She and Cliff took turns documenting what they saw, jotting notes and making sketches of the coastline. Lex and Michele educated them about the currents, and Leigh wrote down those observations too.

She'd brought a fresh notebook and a handful of pens. When they weren't using the notebook, she wrapped it in a rain jacket and stuffed it into her bag. By wearing the bag on her back, she hoped to keep the notebook dry. The other three personal bags were stashed in the storage area, along with medical supplies, Foobrew, and filled canteens.

Optimism got the better of them around midday, and they beached the raft. Cliff had spotted dark ledges and a possible cave. Michele stayed with the raft while the other three scrambled up the rocks. They found not one cave but two, both disappointing: no survivors, no shuttle debris, no sign of human life.

When Leigh, Cliff, and Lex climbed back down the rocks, they discovered Michele had been busy in their absence. She'd slung the shoulder strap of one of the canteens across her body, rearranged the storage area, and pulled out four Foobrews for them to drink.

"No luck?" she asked.

"Two caves," said Lex. "Both small, both empty."

"Have a Foobrew before we leave."

"A whole one?" asked Cliff.

"Nothin' but the best for my crew."

"Easy to get dehydrated out here," explained Lex. "Everyone drink some water too."

They sat down on the sandy shore.

"Can I borrow your Swiss Army knife?" asked Michele.

"Sure," said Lex. "It's in my bag."

He stood up to grab it, but Leigh pulled her multi-tool out of her pocket and handed it to Michele. "Will this work?"

"Should do the trick. Need to smooth out a spot on the rudder."

"Good idea," said Lex. "I've already pulled two splinters out of my hand."

In only a few minutes, Michele had fixed the rudder while the rest of them drank Foobrews, took bathroom breaks in the vegetation, and prepared to head back out on the ocean. Leigh flexed her hands, surprised how stiff they were after less than a day of paddling.

"Thanks," said Michele, handing back the multi-tool.

"No problem." Leigh stuffed it in her bag under the jacket-wrapped notebook.

"Trust me," said Cliff, "she never goes anywhere without that."

"You've borrowed it often enough."

"Not complaining." He grinned. "Just observing."

"He's not wrong," said Michele.

"I left my lucky hat behind," said Leigh. "Had to bring some kind of good luck charm."

"You and your luck get over here. I'll teach you how to use the rudder."

"That'd be great."

"They made me bring you Maps people … you might as well be useful."

"Nice try, Michele," laughed Lex. "You got exactly what you wanted."

Michele smiled broadly.

Lex laughed again. "Get on," he said. "I'll launch us."

⁎

The following afternoon, Leigh's arms ached from what felt like constant paddling. In truth, it wasn't constant, not even close. They'd beached the raft overnight and taken numerous breaks both days. But it'd been a lot of paddling. And a lot of finding nothing.

Even so, she hadn't given up hope. Not yet.

The exploration was proving to be its own reward. This second day on the water, Leigh kept staring at the Crooked Teeth, the mountain range she'd previously seen only from a distance. The individual mountains had become more distinct, sharp lines against the backdrop of the light-blue sky. As they approached the jagged heights of the Twisted Peaks, the two mountains towered above them, their name all the more apt when seen up close.

The rocky outcroppings extended far into the sea, and Michele had to quadruple the raft's distance from shore. The waves grew choppier. The wind blew harder against them, and the muscles in Leigh's back ached. She felt the force of the wind, heard the splashing of the waves, and was reminded of Rose's words about seeing things as yet unseen.

They rounded the last of the rocks and headed toward shore, hoping the inflowing tide would help them find a landing spot. Leigh kept paddling, but she couldn't stop staring at the shoreline. The terrain was similar to what they were used to, with one big exception: the trees. So many trees. An entire forest stretched all the way past the Crooked Teeth into a deep valley and up into the next range of smaller mountains.

"I don't know what I expected," said Lex, "but it wasn't this."

"Lorelei," said Michele, "take a break. Make a sketch before we land."

Leigh pulled the bag off her back, grabbed her notebook, and got to work. Her hands were cramped from holding the paddle, and drawing was tricky with the rough seas, but she could sketch enough to jog her memory for a more precise drawing later.

Michele worked the rudder while Lex and Cliff paddled, one on each side near the front of the raft, eyes alert for rocks as the waves and the tide brought them closer to shore. Cliff voiced a few observations about the coastline, and Leigh wrote those on a separate page.

"You want to draw anything?" she asked him.

"No, but be sure to show where the forest ends … up the side of those mountains. It's an odd tree line."

"Good point."

"Don't take too long," said Michele. "Time to land. We could all use a break."

"Got to admit," said Cliff, "my arms are sore."

"I'd think you were slacking if they weren't," joked Michele.

"Lorelei," said Lex, "finish up."

"Your arms sore too?" teased Michele.

"I don't like those clouds."

Near the island, the sky was clear; however, a wall of dark clouds loomed in the distance. Leigh had been so intrigued by the landscape, she hadn't even noticed.

"I suggest," said Lex, "you put away the notebook and grab your paddle."

"Agreed," said Michele, and she turned the rudder so as to head directly toward shore.

The tone of their voices worried Leigh more than their words. She quickly wrapped the notebook in her jacket, stuffed it in the bag, looped the bag over her shoulders, and picked up her paddle.

"Switch to starboard," said Michele, and Leigh saw the wisdom in it. There was a beach not too far up the coast.

They paddled toward shore, using the tide and the swells to their advantage. Leigh clutched her paddle and drove it hard in coordination with Michele's commands. As the storm drew nearer, she couldn't stop herself from looking at it. The clouds were a deep purple, almost black. The upper half of the cloud wall was smooth and layered; the underside was a mass of turbulence.

Less than a hundred meters from their goal, the raft stopped moving forward. Rip currents were pushing them away from shore. Cliff cussed. Lex lifted his paddle and motioned toward a spot up the coast. Michele shifted the rudder, and soon they were angling toward the coastline. The storm's approach seemed to speed up whenever Leigh glanced that direction.

She stopped looking.

The waves grew rougher, the sky grew darker, and the paddling grew harder. For the first time, she realized they might not make it to land before the storm hit.

"Lorelei," shouted Michele, "come take the rudder."

They swapped places. Leigh struggled to stay upright. She hadn't anticipated the amount of pressure being exerted on the rudder compared to when she'd used it before. Her arms shook, but she held on.

"Use your whole body," said Lex, "not just your arms."

"Keep angling," said Michele.

Leigh strained her muscles to keep the rudder where they wanted it. She knew the other three were stronger paddlers, and it looked like they'd need every ounce of strength to get to shore. Working the rudder was the most helpful thing she could do.

A large wave crested the raft. They were soaked, but no one and nothing fell off. The good news—they'd closed the distance to land down to less than fifty meters. The bad news—they'd been pushed past the beach. Nothing but sheer cliffs along the shore in front of them.

Leigh ignored the pain in her shoulder and the dark clouds racing toward them. She concentrated on holding the rudder steady.

"Up there." Lex pointed.

Ahead, the higher rocks turned darker—the same color as where Leigh had found the big cavern, the same color as where they'd found the small caves the day before.

"I see it," she said.

"See what?" asked Michele.

"Ledges," said Lex. "Cave if we're lucky."

They were five raft-lengths from the coast with possible shelter ahead, but nowhere to put in safely.

"Look!" cried Cliff. "Waterspout!"

The raft lurched as a wave engulfed them. Leigh hung on to the rudder, no longer steering, simply trying not to drown. The raft righted itself with all four of them somehow still aboard. The storm had stripped Cliff's paddle from his hands, but Michele and Lex still had theirs. Leigh pulled hard on the rudder and the two of them dug their paddles into the ocean. Cliff pointed and once again yelled, "Waterspout!"

Leigh tightened her grip. Some of the clouds had dropped low, reaching down as if to touch the sea. On the far edge of the storm, one of the tendrils had connected, and a waterspout whirled in a frenzy of twisting motion.

"Not heading this way," said Lex.

The waterspout would miss them. But it was small comfort. The other half of the storm would be a direct hit. They could see the wall of rain headed straight for the raft.

Another huge wave washed over them, and for a long moment Leigh held her breath, wondering if they would tip. They didn't; instead, the wave pushed them dangerously close to the rocky coast. Lex struggled with his paddle, working to keep the raft from crashing into the rocks in front of them.

"Trade!" Michele yelled at Leigh as she grabbed the helm and thrust a paddle into Leigh's hands. She tried to join the boys near the front of the raft, but the waves knocked her off her feet. Cliff threw her a tether rope.

"No," cried Michele. "Get ready to swim for it."

The front line of the dark clouds moved in, and the rain began. Cliff took off his tether.

Leigh crouched low on the raft, feeling useless. It was all she could do not to go overboard.

Although going overboard was apparently what Michele had in mind.

"We can't leave the raft," yelled Lex.

Another wave swamped them, and Leigh felt a jarring slam as the storm shoved them into an outcropping of rock. The water tore the paddle from one hand as she held on to the raft with the other. The raft righted itself, but not without mishap. A fourth of it broke off and smashed into shore.

In front of them was the spot Michele was aiming for—ledges, tiers of rocks instead of sheer rockface. It was their best chance.

Lex took off his tether.

"Swim for it," shouted Michele.

"All of us!" said Lex.

"I'm the captain. Do what I say!"

Michele pulled hard on the rudder and swung them around. They were only a few meters from their goal.

"Jump!" yelled Michele, and Leigh did. The ocean ripped off her shoes and sucked her down. She spun wildly and opened her eyes in a desperate attempt to get her bearings. Seeing foam to her left, Leigh swam for it, breaking the surface to find the ledge right in front of her. Cliff was already there, climbing out of the water.

From nowhere, part of the raft came pounding into shore, just missing Leigh's head. It smashed into Cliff's right leg before he could get out of the way. A wave crashed over them, forcing Leigh back underwater. When she resurfaced, Cliff was lying on the rocks.

A dozen arm strokes took her to the ledge. Skin tore from her hands as she pulled herself out of the water, but in seconds, she was next to Cliff.

"I'm okay," he said.

Michele and Lex were not.

About twenty meters away, they clung to what was left of the raft—two logs strapped together with the ends snapped off. Leigh could barely see through the pummeling rain, but it looked as if Lex and Michele were trying to kick the logs toward shore ... and not making much progress.

"Another waterspout!" Cliff shouted. "Hurry up! Waterspout!"

He was right. Another waterspout had formed, and this one was coming their way.

Cliff sat up, holding his leg.

"I don't think they can hear you!" Leigh shouted.

"Waterspout!" he yelled again.

"You're bleeding."

"It's not bad," said Cliff. "Waterspout!"

Lex and Michele shoved the logs away and made for shore. Michele beelined for Leigh and Cliff. Though it seemed to take forever, in less than a minute, she was safely on the ledge beside them.

Lex was not so fortunate. He headed off course toward a crevice about fifteen meters away. A broken log from the raft had come to rest there. The crevice was deep, big enough to provide shelter. But it offered no way of getting to higher ground.

Lex pulled himself out of the water. He yanked the errant log farther into the crevice and wedged it tightly. The gale roared around them. The waterspout drew nearer, and the tide was coming in. Lex would never survive if he stayed where he was.

"Waterspout!" yelled Cliff.

"Get to higher ground," Michele said to Leigh and Cliff.

"What about Lex?" asked Leigh.

"Go!"

"Lex!"

"I got him. You take Cliff."

"I'm fine," said Cliff. He climbed the craggy wall and disappeared over a ledge, the blood from his wound dripping down the rocks until the rain washed it away.

"Cave!" Cliff called back down.

"Up!" yelled Michele, but Leigh wasn't going anywhere.

She and Michele watched as Lex ripped off his shirt and jumped into the water. He swam toward them with slow, powerful strokes, maximizing being underwater between breaths. He made steady progress until nearing the edge, where the waves knocked him back.

"Waterspout!" Cliff yelled from above.

Leigh and Michele reached out their arms as Lex resurfaced, but he was several body lengths away. He looked at them, then ducked under the water.

"What's he doing?" cried Michele.

The winds grew stronger, and the girls flattened themselves on the ground. A wave crashed over them and onto the rocks. Leigh swallowed a mouthful of water and slid toward the edge as the wave receded. *No!* She clutched at the rock face, but her battered hands found nothing to grip. She plummeted toward the water and flailed her arms as if clinging to the air might help.

But it was not the air that saved her—it was Michele. Her hands grabbed Leigh's leg and dug into her skin, pulling her roughly onto the rocky ledge.

She gasped for air, unable to say thanks, out of breath from the exertion, dizzy from the pain slicing through her back.

"There!" shouted Michele.

Lex had resurfaced. He'd pulled off his pants and was attempting to swim holding them bundled in one hand. It was a futile effort, and he let the clothing sink. Less encumbered, he was able to make it to the edge and grab on. Michele hauled him onto the ledge. The tempest howled around them. Leigh ignored the pain in her back and managed to stand.

They spared half a second to look for the waterspout.

"Up!" said Michele, and they scrambled up the rocks.

"One more!" shouted Cliff from above, and as they landed on the third ledge, they saw him at the entrance to a cave.

"Follow me!" said Cliff, and they raced inside.

CHAPTER 28

Leigh awoke in utter darkness. Her back hurt, and she was cold and damp.

The raft. The storm. The wreck.

She could see absolutely nothing, but she could hear the distant sound of pounding surf. She could feel the rock wall behind her and warm bodies next to her on both sides.

The cave.

"Lorelei," whispered Lex. He had an arm wrapped around one of hers, with his hand clasping her wrist.

Lex.

He tightened his grip and whispered again, "Lorelei."

"Yes," she said quietly.

"You okay?"

"Fine. You?"

"Fine. A little cold."

"We're in a cave."

"Thanks for pointing that out," he whispered, and Leigh would have sworn she could hear the smile accompanying his words.

"How're Michele and Cliff?" she asked.

"Can't tell."

"You sound worried."

"I think Michele's fine."

"She feels warmer than me."

"What about Cliff? His leg?"

"Can't tell. He's on the other side of Michele."

"We need to move," said Lex. "We're soaking wet. It's too cold to stay here."

She didn't feel like moving, but his suggestion made sense. Leigh thought back to her first night on the planet. Maybe there were more reasons to worry about Cliff than his injured leg.

"Lorelei, you there?" asked Lex.

"Thinking."

"Think out loud, please."

"We should check Cliff's leg."

"I agree."

Leigh nudged the others awake. A sharp pain shot through her back. She ignored it. This was no time for old wounds to create new problems.

＊

Hours later, Leigh sat on the ledge in front of the cave and stared at the stars. The Jellyfish had long since passed its zenith and was heading toward the horizon. She stretched her arms overhead. The acute pain from earlier was gone, replaced by a dull ache under her shoulder blade. Nothing to worry about.

Ten meters behind her, inside the mouth of the cave, the others slept close together. Unlike the cavern near the tip of the island, this cave had a big, wide opening that narrowed into the tunnel where they'd waited out the storm.

Leigh debated getting up and checking on Cliff's leg. Strips of material from his shirt had stanched the bleeding, but they hadn't changed the bandage all night. He'd need a fresh one soon.

No need to wake him though, not yet. She stayed seated and unstuck her shirt from her back, letting the breeze blow through the material. The next shirt bandage wouldn't be clean, but at least it could be dry.

She was more than willing to give up her shirt even though it would expose the scar on her back. Time for her vanity, and her paranoia, to take a back seat. How much did it matter if someone recognized her? What might change if they knew her story?

She looked at Lex, sleeping in his boxer shorts and underneath her jacket, then redirected her attention to the shoreline. She was sitting at the top of a series of three ledges, her lower legs hanging over the edge, toes only about ten centimeters from the middle one. The bottom ledge, the one they'd first landed upon, was two or three meters farther down. It looked barely above the current sea level, but it was hard to tell for certain.

The rain had stopped a few hours ago; a warm breeze stirred the few remaining clouds. All three moons had emerged. Even with the moonlight, it was difficult to assess how easily they might climb back down to the water. It looked slippery ... difficult for Cliff with his bad leg but manageable with some help.

Then what?

They were stranded with only a few supplies: Michele's canteen, the soggy contents of Leigh's bag, and the clothes they'd been wearing minus Lex's shirt and pants. None of their shoes had survived the storm, and there was no sign of the raft except for the lone broken log Lex had wedged into the nearby crevice.

The solution was clear. Someone would have to take the log and swim for help. On a calm day, even the Twisted Peaks could be managed now that they better knew the currents. Once past the mountain range, traveling close to shore, it shouldn't take more than a couple of days of swimming. Long days. But it could be done.

Leigh looked out over the ocean: turbulent hours ago, now placid. She was half-tempted to jump in the water, grab the log, and swim off herself. But she wasn't that stupid. Or maybe she wasn't that brave. Either way, she'd wait and work it out with the others when everyone was awake.

Glancing back at the cave, she was surprised to see Lex sitting up, watching her.

"Still my shift," she whispered. "Go back to sleep."

Lex ignored the command and joined her on the ledge, sitting right next to her, his legs dangling beside hers. He handed over her jacket. Leigh took it but didn't put it on. She wasn't going to wear two layers of clothing while he was practically naked.

"Weather's finally cleared," he said.

How was it possible that with nothing on but boxer shorts, his body temperature felt so much warmer than her own?

"You sure you don't want the jacket?" offered Leigh.

"I'm not cold."

She needed to talk about something other than Lex's body heat and lack of clothing. "Have you named any more constellations?"

"Nope, just the loon."

He reached over and gently grabbed one of her hands, raising it skyward and outlining the loon constellation. Their hands stalled in midair as he pointed to the sixth and final star. He lowered her hand but did not let go.

"Your hand is cold," said Lex. He reached for her other hand and sandwiched both of them in between his. Her palms were tender from being injured on the rocks, but Lex's hands were worse—torn and bloody from his battle with the remnants of the raft. Even so, his hands felt soothing wrapped around her own.

"Full moon," said Lex. "Lucky night."

"Lucky?"

He laughed softly. "We're alive. I'd call that lucky."

He wasn't wrong.

The full moon glowed yellow-orange, outshining its larger neighbors that were thin crescents in the sky. A crisscross of reflected light danced across the dark water, but night was ending, and the moonlight would soon be hidden from view.

"Morning soon," she said.

"True enough."

They sat facing the sky, his hands encircling hers. She stared at the stars and wondered where Earth's sun might be. They could be looking at it and not even know.

She leaned against Lex's shoulder. She could hear his breathing, feel his hair next to her cheek. Everything but Lex faded into the background. "Not exactly the 'grand adventure' you expected," she said.

"Not exactly."

"Too many surprises."

"Seems to be true whenever you're involved," he said.

She sat up straight.

Lex held on to her hands. "No offense. Actually, I meant the opposite."

She waited for him to elaborate, but he grew quiet. Leigh considered putting her head back on his shoulder. She thought he would welcome it, but his comments were enigmatic; maybe he was just being nice. She settled for feeling the warmth of his hands wrapped around hers.

They sat, unspeaking, as a new day emerged—the ocean shifting its colors to greet the dawn. The orangeness of Epsilon Eridani was on full display. As the star broke the horizon, it coated the water in a fiery glow.

"This is my favorite time of day," said Lex, his voice barely above a whisper.

"Sunrise?"

"Marjol sunrise. The orange-red glow that colors everything—land, sea, and sky."

She leaned closer.

"The rest of the day," he said, "Rán looks much like the Sun. But first light is different. With the one-color sunrise, I remember … I remember I'm seeing things most people have never seen, will never see."

"True."

"It's a good reminder not to waste this chance." He tightened his grip on her hands. "It's a good reminder that we don't know what the day will bring."

"Doesn't it scare you?" she whispered.

"Every day," he said. "Every. Day."

They watched in silence as the morning light grew brighter. Soon they were bathed in a deep orange-red. It was as if a child dipped a paintbrush in a favorite color and slathered it over a sunrise. Only they were sitting in the middle of the painting.

"Vermilion," whispered Leigh.

"What?"

"This color," she said, "it's vermilion."

Lex squeezed her hands. She squeezed back and did not let go. The flaming ball of gas that was Rán rose higher in the sky before either of them spoke again.

"Light-years away," whispered Lex, "yet I keep hearing my grandfather's voice." He turned to look at her. His face was shaded

s gleamed. "Gramps, he's still reaching out to me across the
Joes that sound crazy?"

't know. What does he say?"

it life should be an adventure." Lex drew nearer, and his voice
ven softer. "I can hear him word for word. 'Alexius,' says Gramps,
: adventures are taken with your feet, and others with your mind.
he greatest adventures ... those are taken with your heart.'"

he couldn't take her eyes off him.

He leaned slowly closer.

"*Taniwha!*" cried Michele. "*Taniwha!*"

Lex's hands parted from Leigh's as they whipped around to look at Michele.

"What?" said Lex, as they clambered to their feet.

"What is it?" Cliff struggled to sit up.

"Come look!" said Michele, slightly calmer and speaking once again in English. "Have a look!"

The sunrise lit up the entrance to the cave. Along the wall were markings, detailed markings scratched into the rock.

"Someone left a message," said Lex.

"Not in any language I know," replied Leigh. She was dizzy. Her hands felt cold again.

Cliff scooted over toward the markings but did not attempt to stand.

"Here are the rocks they used." Michele picked up two stones with sharp edges and handed them to Cliff. Each rock had a point worn to a white shade, the same color as the message carved into the wall.

The white marks stood out against the dark rock. Had they been made by survivors from the wrecked shuttle? How long ago? What did they say?

There was no way to tell. Cliff thought the writing was Korean. But really it was all guesswork.

Only one thing was certain: they weren't alone.

CHAPTER 29

A few hours later, Lex sat by himself on the ledge in front of the cave. The raucous sunrise was long gone, replaced by light-blue skies and bright sunshine. The ocean sparkled in the sunlight, and the water remained blessedly calm.

The scene's beauty did not reflect his mood.

The group's decision was a good one. He had no second thoughts. It'd been the right choice to send Lorelei and Michele for help. They were the best endurance swimmers. If any two could get back safely, it was them.

Lex had wanted to be the hero, to go for help and make a glorious return rescuing the others. Girls still wanted that from a guy—the knight in shining armor, the cowboy riding in on his horse to save the day—except when they didn't want it, except when it would've been stupid.

He couldn't get the moment of parting out of his head. At the time, Lex thought he'd handled it well. Now he wasn't sure. Michele was the bravest person he'd ever met. He wished he'd told her that.

And Lorelei, well, he had tried to tell her how he felt. Early that morning, he'd tried to say he knew she was Leigh Crawford. He'd wanted to tell her it didn't matter.

He'd wanted to shed his own secrets.

He'd wanted to kiss her.

But then the world turned upside down with Michele's discovery, and he'd put all that aside. He'd gone back to focusing on survival.

They had cleaned Cliff's leg and quickly settled on a plan. The girls had taken off their shirts, leaving them behind for use as bandages. Lex had tried not to stare, but it'd been impossible not to notice the bumpy light-pink scar running from Lorelei's left shoulder to the middle of her back. He'd instinctively reached out to touch it and been saved from the misstep by Michele, who grabbed his arm.

He'd nodded his thanks, then asked Lorelei about the scar, simply wanting to know if it hurt. She'd assured him it was old and not worth worrying about. Under any other circumstance, he could imagine an entire conversation about that scar.

But these were not any other circumstances.

When the girls were ready to leave, he'd given each of them a big hug and said awkwardly, "Good luck. You won't need it, but ... good luck anyway."

Michele had nodded, jumped in the water, and swum over to grab the log. Lorelei had turned to him and clutched his arm. "Lex," she'd said, "I promise ... I *promise* I will not abandon you."

Then she too had jumped in the water.

He had stood, speechless, and watched them swim away.

Hours later, in the bright light of midmorning, he stared at the sun-speckled waves and wished he'd said more.

But what? What words would've been enough? Maybe there were no words for how he felt about these people: Lorelei and Michele. Olu, Marko, Ada, Rose. They were his family now. Of course, he was loyal to everyone on the planet, but ... wait.

Not everyone. There were others here. Not just the fifty-nine of them, but others.

Earlier that morning, Lex had stood in the cave and traced the white markings with his fingers. Carving that deeply into the dark rock would be much harder than the work he and Marko were doing to the outside of their cabin. Whoever had carved into the cave wall had put in a lot of time and a lot of effort to leave a message no one might ever see.

Who were they? Where were they? What message had they left?

Lex heard movement and turned to see Cliff limping over to join him.

"You look better," said Lex.

"Feels good to be up." Cliff settled himself gingerly on the ledge. "Your bandage is leaking."

"Not much."

"We should wash that leg again."

Cliff sighed. "Give me a few minutes."

"No rush."

The two boys watched the waves hit the rocks below. For a long while, they sat and talked—about anything other than the injury to Cliff's leg, the girls who'd gone for help, and the markings in the cave behind them.

***

Two mornings later, Lex sat in the same spot and watched Rán crest the horizon. He felt no sense of wonder when the light first stretched across the ocean, no awe at the vermilion glow that bespoke the dawn. That's when he realized the extent of their distress: when daybreak barely registered.

Cliff was in bad shape. Whether from the splinters in the wound or something else, his leg was worsening. The bleeding had stopped, but the leg was swollen, reddish-purple, and oozing yellow-green pus.

Dehydration was an even bigger worry. They were both light-headed; Cliff was feverish and confused. Finding fresh water was the day's main priority. There was not a drop left in the canteen and not a cloud in the sky. Lex would have to go searching.

But first, he needed to address the second priority. He stood up, feet stiffening as he walked back to the cave and gently shook Cliff awake.

"I'm sorry," said Lex, "we need to get you down to the water and clean this leg."

"You sure?"

"I'd rather do it now than when it's hotter."

Cliff nodded.

The task was easier said than done. Halfway down the rocks, Lex felt a searing pain shoot through his left thigh. His leg shook, but it held long enough to support Cliff's weight and to keep them from tumbling into the ocean. Cliff braced his good leg against the rocks, leaped onto the lower ledge, and cried out in pain.

"You all right?" yelled Lex as he hung on to the rockface and waited for his leg to stop shaking.

"Fine," said Cliff. "What can I do?"

"I'm good," said Lex. "Probably just a cramp." But he knew that was a lie, and he imagined Cliff knew it too. "Maybe a pulled muscle or something."

"Take it slow," said Cliff.

Lex heeded his advice. Gingerly pushing his injured left leg flush against the rocks, he felt the spasms subside. Stretching his other leg as far down as he could, Lex put all his body weight on his arms and carefully maneuvered himself the rest of the way, the toes of his good leg finally reaching solid ground. Collapsing on the ledge, he heaved a sigh of relief. Somehow, they'd made it to the water's edge. The tide was going out; they had plenty of room.

He scooted over to Cliff, who said, "Not sure we'll be doing that again."

Lex unwrapped Cliff's wound. The redness had spread, and the yellow-green pus was a darker color than it had been the day before.

"I'm going to lie down so I don't have to look at it," said Cliff. "Do whatever you need to do."

"I need to clean it," said Lex, "like the last two mornings."

"And evenings."

"Then I'm going to take out more splinters. A few are closer to the surface."

"That's good, right?"

"Yep."

"Do what you need to do."

Lex took him at his word and thoroughly washed the injury while ignoring the string of cusswords Cliff loosed into the air. He could only imagine what the salt water felt like on his friend's leg. It was bad enough with the cuts on his own hands—stinging sharply at first, as if hot wax had been dripped into his open sores—then settling into a dull throbbing burn that was hard to ignore. They could only hope the salt was doing some healing along with the pain.

Once the wound was clean, or at least as clean as he could get it, Lex began to work on the splinters. Two mornings ago, before the girls had left, they'd pulled out over a dozen slivers of wood. Now more pieces had migrated to the surface. Lex did what he could, working as quickly as possible. Cliff gritted his teeth, barely even swearing during this part of the procedure.

"Almost done," said Lex. "Only two more."

"What're you using?" gasped Cliff. "Feels like knives."

"Tweezers."

"Thought you lost everything."

"I did, but Lorelei didn't." He held up the multi-tool.

Cliff made eye contact. "Good," he said, and then closed his eyes again. "That's good."

Lex took advantage of the moment and yanked hard at the stubborn splinter. He tried not to think about anything beyond the task at hand.

* * *

In the darkness that night, Lex sat propped against the edge of the cave. Cliff was sleeping next to him, his injured leg awkwardly positioned on a few rocks to keep it out of the grit. They had used the last piece of Lorelei's shirt as a bandage, and Lex had draped her jacket over Cliff's bare chest.

The injured teenager lay on the ground, one hand clutching the edge of the jacket, eyes closed in a fitful sleep. It'd been hours since he'd last spoken.

Lex had spent much of the day climbing around the rocky coastline, searching for fresh water. His left thigh still hurt, and his feet throbbed from those efforts, but it'd been worth it. Inside a small, deep fissure in one of the higher rocks, he'd found some stale rainwater. It wasn't much, but it wasn't nothing. Lex had drunk a little on the spot and collected the rest. Filling less than a third of the canteen, it had tasted stale and acidy, but Cliff had drunk it.

Lex had felt a modicum of optimism after that, until Cliff started talking. "Lex," he'd said, "if I don't make it, do me a favor."

"Don't talk like that."

"I need you to do this."

"What?"

"Two messages," said Cliff. "Number one: tell Eliana the two rocks are hers."

"Two rocks?"

"Just tell her."

"Okay."

"Second."

"Yes?"

"Tell Lorelei it's not your fault."

"Her fault?"

"No, your fault."

"My fault?"

"*Not* your fault," said Cliff. "Don't want her to blame you. If I don't make it."

"I don't think anyone tells Lorelei what to do," said Lex, "so you'd better plan on making it."

He had waited for a reply, but it never came. Cliff had been sleeping ever since.

Lex gazed out over the ocean. Three nights ago, he had woken up in the exact same spot. Three nights ago, Lorelei had been sitting on the ledge. She'd looked luminous, a vision amid the backdrop of the galaxy. He had thought how well suited she was for this world, one full of possibilities, a world only sixty of them had ever seen.

Turned out, others had seen it too. Were they nearby?

Were they even human?

He had scoured the cave for additional hints but found only a few black rocks. Nothing more.

Lorelei and Michele had been gone three full days.

They were strong swimmers. The water had been calm. They must be home by now. They were fine.

They'd be back. They'd be back, and Cliff would be fine.

Then Lex could stop all this worrying.

CHAPTER 30

Lex felt someone's hand on his shoulder. His swollen eyes opened, and Michele's face appeared—blurry, but definitely Michele. He blinked a few times to clear the fog. Her normally serene visage wore a crease along her forehead.

"Good to see you, my friend," she said.

The morning light streamed into the cave. Lex lifted his head and looked around. Olu and Noah were kneeling next to Cliff, who was prostrate on the ground.

Lex tried to speak, but only a dry croaking sound came out.

"Shh," said Michele. "Cliff's alive. They're patching up his leg. You did great. Let us do the work now."

Lex closed his eyes. He started to roll on his side, but his leg hurt. He put his hands over his face to block Rán's morning rays and felt the rawness of his palms against his sunburned skin. But Cliff was alive.

He tried again to speak, to ask about Lorelei, about what had happened on their swim, but all he did was cough. And the coughing made him dizzy.

As if from the end of a long tunnel, he heard Michele say, "He's all right. Weak, though. We need to get him in the shade. He needs water."

When Lex reopened his eyes, Olu stood over him, casting a cool shadow.

"Time to sit up," Olu commanded. Slowly, slowly, he helped Lex move deeper into the cave ... sit against the wall ... put on a shirt ... and drink some water. Lex's hands shook as he took the proffered canteen. Though he was able to take a gulp, most of it missed his mouth. Olu sat next to him, helped hold the canteen, and made sure the rest of the water went inside Lex instead of down his chest.

His mouth hurt. It felt like someone had fished his Swiss Army knife off the bottom of the ocean and carved little ridges in his lips ... deep ones. His throat was swollen. He hadn't realized how thirsty he was. Olu stayed by his side, allowing Lex only sips, ensuring he did not throw up or pass out.

The worry in Olu's normally staid face made it clear that Lex looked bad, but Olu said nothing about it. They sat in the cave, and Olu told Lex what he needed to know: "Lorelei is fine." He reaffirmed what Lex needed to hear again: "Cliff will be fine." Lex nodded. The boys did not talk about how Olu had feared such a disastrous end to this undertaking; they did not talk about the writing on the wall behind them. They sat, and Lex sipped from the canteen.

Eventually, Olu handed him some fresh boxer shorts and a pair of pants. Lex stood up, leaning on his friend for support. His left leg shook, and his damaged feet pulsed with pain. He assured Olu they looked worse than they felt.

Olu refrained from commenting as he helped Lex put on the clothes and hobble over to the others. They watched as Noah wrapped Cliff's leg with an actual bandage, not a shirt fragment.

Without preamble, Michele reported on Cliff's condition: "The leg looks infected. I don't think it's broken. He's weak and feverish, but he drank some water."

"Can he walk?" asked Olu.

"Yes," said Cliff, "and he can talk."

Lex grinned. His sunburnt lips cracked with the motion, but it felt good to smile.

"Let me rephrase that," said Olu. "Can you walk?"

"Yes," said Cliff.

"It'll be tough gettin' you down these rocks," said Noah, as he finished neatly bandaging Cliff's leg. "But we can do it."

"Better than staying here."

"No worries," Noah said. "Gettin' you home today."

"Good," said Cliff, "no more time alone in a cave with Lex."

As Noah and Michele laughed, Lex felt a warmth unrelated to his sunburn. Cliff looked terrible, but his spirits were intact.

Michele directed her attention to Olu. "Let me give Cliff an antibiotic," she said, "and then we'll move farther into the cave; should be cooler. I'd like to see if we can get a Foobrew down these guys before we head back."

"And look at the writing," said Olu, "if that's what it is."

"That's what it is," said Cliff, his eyes closed.

Michele studied his face, then turned to Lex. "You might want this." She handed him a tube of aloe.

"Thanks," Lex replied, his voice still raw.

"Lorelei sent it," said Michele. "We had quite a swim, Lor and I … two full days and two long nights. Found enough places to rest and plenty of rainwater in the rocks. We did all right. Lor's fine. She's got terrible blisters though. We wouldn't let her make the trip back.

"I don't know why the two of you got so sunburned out here. You've never burned like that before."

Lex agreed it was a mystery, but he didn't care. Her words had soothed his worries, the water had soothed his throat, and now the aloe was soothing his skin. Life was good.

"Incredible," said Olu from deeper in the cave.

"Definitely Korean writing," said Noah.

"Thought so," said Cliff.

Lex laughed. It hurt.

He laughed anyway. Life was good. But it was also complicated.

*　*　*

Sunrise. Two islands. Tall tree.

That was Noah's translation. Five simple words inscribed in the rock.

What did they mean?

Who had written them?

And where were those people now?

Everyone else wanted to debate and discuss. But Lex breathed a sigh of relief. In his dehydrated state, he'd begun to imagine some other life form, something not human, had carved the markings on the wall. Now that worry was gone.

Maybe his concern had been ridiculous, but though he didn't voice it to the others, he felt truly thankful there were no aliens ... or rather, aliens who could write. The entire planet was alien—from the grasses to the glitterblobs—and that was proving to be challenge enough.

He drank his Foobrew, rested in the shade, and contributed nothing to the conversation going on around him. The pulled muscle in his leg convulsed with pain, and his feet throbbed as if they'd been tasked with keeping the beat for a second-rate band. Last night, he'd barely noticed. Now it was as if his pain receptors had been revived. He smiled anyway; soon they'd be going home.

It took them a while to prepare to leave and for Lex and Cliff to make it down the rocks one last time. They loaded onto the rescue raft, and Olu pushed them away from the ledge with one hand, no Herculean effort needed amid the calm seas and clear skies.

As they moved away from the rocks, Lex was once again reminded why Noah was part of the rescue mission. One reason was his gift with languages. Fluent in three and proficient in several more, including Korean, Noah had been an obvious choice. Even more so for another reason: they were sailing.

Noah worked the sail, Michele held the rudder, and Olu paddled when needed.

They were *sailing*.

Sitting upright on the raft, Lex watched the shoreline—first sheer rockface, then the beach that'd been an unattainable goal in the storm. As they shifted direction, allowing the sail to grasp more of the wind, their speed increased. Lex braced himself against the logs. The raft crested a small wave, and the ocean caressed his face with a gentle spray, nature's way of saying, "Now you're doing it right."

The waves became rougher, and the sailing became trickier when they approached the Twisted Peaks. The crew handled it well, each of the three in step with the other, the harmony of their movements a testament to how quickly they'd learned to work together.

"Head out farther!" called Michele.

"Same as before?" asked Olu.

"More."

Noah pulled on the sail and adjusted the rope. Lex admired the sail's orange edges. Handsewn in irregular patterns, they strained against the wind, holding up under the increasing pressure. Water splashed over the logs, Noah adjusted the sail as needed, and the raft took them out farther.

And farther.

Still farther.

It was a vantage point they'd never before achieved. Lex could see the full length of the island. All of it spread before him ...

There was so much they had never seen.

So. Much.

Oh, they'd done the math. Logistically, he'd known it was true, but seeing the whole island in front of him made it real.

"Good work," said Michele. "Let's get closer to shore."

Noah said something to Olu, who struck at the water with his paddle while the sail shifted. Michele moved the rudder, Noah pulled on something, and the sail once again caught the wind. The raft turned toward the coastline, moving even faster than before.

Olu had been right.

Lex had been wrong.

Sailing made all the difference. They should have waited.

He lay down on the raft. He rolled on his side and watched as Noah taught Olu how to use the sail. Before drifting off to sleep, Lex's last thought was how worried they'd been about Noah when he'd first arrived.

Lex had been wrong about so many things. But sometimes ... sometimes ... it was good to be wrong.

***

Sunrise Beach was empty when they first sighted it, but it was astir with friends by the time the travelers made it to shore. Ada greeted them and helped Lex off the raft.

"Should you be walking on those feet?" she asked.

"Good to see you too," said Lex.

Marko handed him a Foobrew. He grabbed Lex's shoulder and brought him in for a hug.

"Thanks," said Lex.

Marko stepped back.

Lex stumbled. "Sea legs," he said. "I need to stretch." He walked a few steps. His injured leg hurt, but he could do it.

"We brought chairs," said Ada. She gestured up the beach where several colonists were placing Cliff on a chair. They lifted him in unison and started up the path to Homesite, carrying him up the hill.

"Good idea," said Lex.

"For you too."

"No."

"Lex, be reasonable."

"I need to stretch," he repeated.

Olu approached.

"Want a canteen?" asked Marko.

Lex nodded, and Marko ran off.

"Ready?" asked Olu.

"We brought him a chair," said Ada.

Olu shrugged. "His choice."

Lex knew his feet would suffer if he climbed the hill. He knew he was being stubborn. And that he didn't deserve Olu's support for yet another stupid decision.

But it wasn't just Ada and Olu watching. It was Marko and Mia and Shane and others. And he needed to show them he was all right.

Marko returned with a fresh canteen, which Lex slung over his shoulder. He gave Ada a sunburnt smile and started hobbling toward home.

It was slow going.

As he made his way up the winding path, Marko ran on ahead, but Olu stuck by his side. People came to see them, to talk to Lex, to welcome him home. Lex tried to maintain a steady, albeit slow, pace. He tried to say hello to all who approached. But as the throbbing in his feet radiated up into his hips, he had no energy for conversation.

He plodded upward.

And he grew silent. Olu stayed beside him and carried the burden of answering everyone's questions.

As they neared the edge of Homesite, Lex felt his legs grow weaker, but then he saw the person he'd been looking for. Lorelei was there on the trail. She had her hair in a ponytail and stuffed through the back of her hat. Her face had started to peel from the sunburn, and there was a raw spot on her cheek. When she smiled, her eyes showed an unhidden joy at his return.

She was beautiful.

He approached her; Olu stepped up beside him.

"Lex," she said, "glad you're back."

His thoughts swam in dizziness and his left leg shook with exhaustion, but he was grinning like an idiot. "Thanks," he managed.

"I've filled some buckets of water for you by the spring," she said. "They've been warming in the sun. I know cold water will feel good on that sunburn, but Zalfaa said you'd probably have a fever and would be better off not getting chilled."

"Thanks." It was the only word he seemed capable of uttering.

"Olu," said Lorelei.

"Don't worry," said Olu, "I'm not leaving him alone."

"Good."

"Can you help me?" Olu asked her.

"Of course."

She reached out and held Lex's hands in her own. "I promised you," she said. "I *promised* I would never abandon you."

He squeezed her hands and couldn't even manage to say thanks.

***

Before dawn the next day, Lex lay in his bunk. His body hurt … well, everywhere. But it hurt less lying in his own bed.

That was Marko's doing. Only Marko's assurance that he'd watch over Lex had kept him out of Q-cabin. Add that to the long list of thank-yous Lex needed to say out loud to people today.

Later though. Right now, Marko was asleep like everyone else. Lex should roll over, close his eyes, and join them. But morning was certain to bring fresh worries, and lying in his own bed was a nice respite from trouble. Even if he couldn't stop thinking about the homecoming ...

Yesterday's bath had been worth it. Lorelei had done more than set out buckets of water to warm in the sun. She'd brought aloe and other medical supplies, soap, a fresh set of clothing, and several towels. She and Olu had been right not to leave him alone, which was good. And they'd been serious about Lorelei staying to help, which was weird. As they got Lex clean and doctored, Olu had never acted like Lorelei's presence was unusual, and Lex had been too tired to question it.

Eventually, she'd cleaned up the supplies and left the boys alone. Olu had filled a few empty canteens and slung them over his shoulder.

That was when finally ...

Finally.

Lex had found the words. "I'm sorry," he'd said. "You were right. We never should have gone."

"No," Olu had replied, "you shouldn't have. But now that all of you are safe, I can only be thankful." And he'd reached out a hand and helped Lex stand up.

Sometimes a few words made all the difference.

Lex rolled over onto his back. Ah, that hurt. He turned on his side and stretched his legs. That hurt too. He drew his knees up, which relaxed the muscles in his legs and did absolutely nothing for the feverish pulsing in his feet or the heat radiating from his baked skin.

But his friends were alive. His friendships were intact. He closed his eyes and went back to sleep.

* * *

When Lex finally emerged that morning, he was surprised to see Homesite deserted. Then he realized it was Wednesday, and Rán was far above the horizon. Everyone was working.

Or maybe not. Chipping noises came from the side of the cabin, and Lex went to investigate.

"Good to see you up," said Marko.

"Good to be up."

Lex studied Marko's new pattern—a double spiral, looping around on itself like a Mobius strip. "You've been busy."

"I could use some help."

"Lost my Swiss Army knife."

"I heard." Marko held up a tool in each hand. "Thought we could share."

"Not sure my hands are up to it yet." Lex displayed his cut and blistered palms. They looked worse than he remembered.

"Can I get you something for those?" asked Marko.

"I need to go see Cliff."

"He's still in Q-cabin."

"Thanks."

"You okay?"

"Sure."

"I'll go with you."

Marko wiped off his tools and stuffed them in his bag. "Want some help with those feet?" he asked.

"I just rewrapped 'em."

"Hmm. Maybe ask for help next time?"

"Good advice," laughed Lex.

"Your face hurt?"

"How bad does it look?"

"Truth?"

"Always."

"Worse than your hands."

"That's how it feels," said Lex. "But don't tell anyone. I don't want to be put in Q-cabin."

"Got your back."

Lex walked slowly with Marko at his side. His feet throbbed so hard he thought they might fall off. He stumbled. Marko caught him under the shoulder and didn't let go until Lex was steady again. They walked on toward Q-cabin.

It was great to be home.

CHAPTER 31

That evening, Leigh hunched over a piece of paper and tried to draw the sweep of land between the Twisted Peaks and the next mountain range. Although her notebook had not survived the storm, she was determined to preserve the knowledge they'd gained.

When the others had sailed off to save Lex and Cliff, Leigh had distracted herself by writing copious amounts of feverish notes—no logical order to them, but she'd gotten her thoughts on paper. It made her realize she'd been trying to hide her past not only from the others but also from herself. No more. Lessons learned from previous trauma were proving helpful. She had once scoffed at the advice of her old therapist, Dr. Tracy. Now Leigh was putting it to good use. Writing everything down had helped her process the storm, had helped her see she'd done the best she could at the time.

Today, Leigh had spoken to everyone else who'd made the journey, gathering detailed recollections from those who'd been stranded at the cave and snippets of observations from those who'd gone to rescue them. The result: scraps of paper filled with information were scattered around the table where she sat in the Q-cabin common room. It was up to her to organize them, to put the pieces together, to make the voyage mean something.

"That does it for me," said Ada, the room's only other occupant. She closed the notebook she'd been writing in and placed it in the top cabinet. The table at which she'd been working was empty except for a lantern.

"Obviously," said Leigh, "you're more organized than I am."

"Different kind of work."

"More organized kind."

"Perhaps," admitted Ada. "But I'm not trying to draw anything." She sat down next to Leigh and pulled close a small stack of completed drawings. Ada fanned them out on the table: the Twisted Peaks as seen from the raft; the cave where they'd found shelter; a view of the ledges from down below; and a close-up of the writing on the cave wall. "Are they hard to draw?"

"I haven't sketched for a while," Leigh conceded, "but it's coming back to me."

"No," Ada said quietly, "I mean, after all you went through. Is it hard?"

"It's therapeutic. Good to get the images out of my head and on the paper." Ada didn't appear convinced, so Leigh added, "It feels good to make something useful out of the disaster."

"It *was* a disaster. Wasn't it?"

"Not … entirely. Look at what we learned." Leigh ticked off four items on her fingers. "First, there are more colonists out there; we're not alone. Second, those colonists are trying to communicate with us. Third, we've learned how to sail. And fourth, there's an enormous forest on the other side of the Twisted Peaks … resources galore."

"You forgot lesson number five," said Ada.

"What's that?"

"We're a step away from death every day."

"We already knew that," said Leigh.

Ada shrugged. "Maybe Olu's right. Maybe I'd forgotten."

"Guilt will get you nowhere."

"True," she conceded. "But every time I see the beach cabins, and I think of you out in that storm …" Ada shook her head.

Everyone—not just those on the raft—had been unnerved by the storm. Damage to Homesite was minimal, a few uprooted plants and whatnot. But the beach cabins were hit hard. One cabin sustained damage along the front wall, and another lost its roof. The third cabin was demolished, nothing left but a pile of rubble where the building had once stood.

No one had been in there; no one was hurt. But until now, the colonists had thought of the buildings as indestructible, a safe harbor. The storm was a nasty reminder that safety was never guaranteed.

"No use worrying about what could've happened," said Leigh.

"It's important to learn from our mistakes."

"Not sure it was a mistake. We got unlucky. It doesn't mean we made the wrong decision. It means we got unlucky." She almost laughed. How Dr. Tracy would love to hear Leigh parroting her words!

"You may be right," said Ada, "but I'm not eager to send anyone out on a raft again, not anytime soon, not even with a sail. We have a lot of healing to do." She restacked Leigh's finished sketches, placing the drawing of the cave on top and giving it one last glance. "I'm going to sleep," said Ada. "You want me to leave both lanterns?"

"I only need one."

Ada stood up, pushed her chair in, and picked up the lantern from the other table. She moved slowly, as if weighted down, but her voice regained its normal briskness. "Don't stay up late. Tomorrow's Thursday, and we're back on track with morning groups, if you're up to it."

"That's yoga for me," said Leigh. "I'll be there."

"Good."

"I won't be much longer."

"Good," repeated Ada, and she closed the door.

* * *

A short time later, Leigh took a break to stand and stretch. The two-day swim had further aggravated her old back injury, and sitting in a chair wasn't doing it any favors. Even when up and moving, her back was stiff. She stretched carefully—no bouncing—with long, slow movements to remind her muscles how it was done.

Now that Ada had left, the room felt empty, even a little spooky—a silly feeling, especially since she wasn't the only one in the cabin. Despite his improvement, Cliff was spending a second night in a

Q-cabin bunkroom. The official story was that he couldn't sleep well and didn't want to disturb his cabinmates.

It had not escaped Leigh's notice, however, that six people had joined Cliff for an evening visit and only five had left. Eliana was apparently "taking the night shift." Hmm. Sooner or later the no sex rule would change. For now, everyone just looked the other way.

Other changes were official, though, and Maps had been given the common area of Q-cabin as a place to make them happen. The record-keeping would be more organized and more extensive, with Rose in charge of the maps and Ada in charge of the recorded history. As part of that, Leigh was to start her interviews on Monday.

She stretched once more, sat back down, and returned to work on the drawing. As she sketched the forest, Leigh mulled over her conversation with Ada. It was the only time she'd ever seen the other girl show weakness or doubt. *Doubt isn't weakness*, Leigh could hear Dr. Tracy saying. *Not if it helps you make a decision and move forward.*

Ada was already using doubt that way. She feared a storm would one day destroy part of Homesite, but instead of fretting about it, she and Olu had taken action. They'd divided medical supplies among the five cabins instead of leaving them all in one. They'd collected a stash of medicine, blankets, and canteens and stored them in the large cavern near the tip of the island.

Ada wanted to put copies of their most important documents in the cavern as well, and plenty of colonists had volunteered to help write those copies. The problem was figuring out what was important enough to merit the effort.

Leigh stopped drawing and wrote two reminders to herself: *talk to Rose about adding rock color on coastal maps*; *talk to Michele about ocean currents.* She returned to her sketch and finished shading the tree line. That was a good place to stop. She gathered her piles of papers and started to put a small rock on each stack.

The silence of the workspace was interrupted by a soft knock, and Lex walked in. The fresh, verdant scent of aloe entered the room with him. He was wearing long sleeves and long pants, and his feet were wrapped in a clever bandage-towel combination. His sunburned face was healing faster than hers, but it looked more painful.

"Michele told me you were here," said Lex. "I came by to return this." He handed over her multi-tool. "It may have saved Cliff's leg."

"You may have saved Cliff's life."

"Took a lot of people to do that," he said. "You included."

Leigh turned over the multi-tool in her palm. "I'm sorry you lost your Swiss Army knife."

"Could've been worse."

"True, but Lex—"

"Yes?"

"You're welcome to borrow this anytime."

"Thanks."

"Seriously," said Leigh. "To work with Marko, or in Boats, or whatever."

"Thanks," repeated Lex. "Do you need help? With all these papers?"

"Not tonight."

He looked at the table as if in disbelief.

"Really," said Leigh, "I'm finishing up. And you need to sleep."

"I suppose." He walked around the table, idly looking at the piles of loose papers, stopping at the drawing of the cave where he and Cliff had been stranded for three days. As he studied it, his body listed to one side. Her suspicions were correct—he'd injured his left leg.

Leigh wanted to ask him about it but couldn't think how to phrase the question. Couldn't find the words for anything she wanted to say. She put the multi-tool in her pocket so she'd stop fiddling with it.

"Do you want to sit down?" she asked.

"Uh, for a minute."

He slid into the chair next to her, not even bothering to turn it around first. She tried to look him in the eye, but his attention was on her drawings. He'd spread them out on the table, much the same way Ada had done a little while ago.

"These are good," he said, "really good."

"Thanks."

"You like to draw?"

"Yes," said Leigh, surprised to hear herself say it. "I do."

"You should keep it up. I mean, after you finish these. Draw what you want."

"I need to do the useful ones first."

Lex shrugged. "Art is useful by being art."

Leigh smiled. It was something her father would have said.

Lex finally looked at her. "It was a hell of a trip!"

She laughed at the unexpected remark, then covered her mouth. "Shhh. People are sleeping in the back."

"You're the one who laughed," said Lex. He smiled for the first time since entering the cabin. "And it *was* a hell of a trip."

"Ada called it a disaster."

"Yeah, it was that too." He picked up her drawings and stacked them neatly. "I met with Olu and Ada three times today. Had a long conversation with Dhruv. A short one with Michele. A really good one with Rose." Lex pushed his hair away from his face. "We won't be doing another trip again for a while, even with the sailing, no matter what washes up on shore."

"You should make that public," she suggested. "Be sure everyone knows we're not going anywhere."

"Olu agrees. We're gathering the colony after morning groups tomorrow. Going to make an announcement."

"Might want to do it first thing, before morning groups. Less gossip."

"Good advice." Lex stretched his legs and slouched in the chair. "Speaking of gossip, does everyone know what the Korean writing says?"

"Mia confirmed Noah's translation: 'Daybreak. Two islands. Tall tree.'"

"Noah used the word 'sunrise' instead of 'daybreak,' but I think it amounts to the same thing."

"What does it mean?" she asked.

"Best guess, it's directions: go toward sunrise to the second island with the tall tree."

"Hmm. Then why didn't they say that?"

"Yeah," said Lex, "good question. Although ..."

"Although what?"

"They may have been injured, too weak to do more."

"What makes you say that?"

"We found what looked like old blood. Took a couple of lanterns into the tunnel. In the dirt, even on the dark rock, you could see it. Looked like rust."

"That was probably from Cliff's leg."

"No," said Lex. "You could see that too. This was farther back. Looked like someone had moved a handful of rocks out of the way, piled them in a corner, and rested in the cleared spot."

"And been wounded."

"That's what it looked like," said Lex, "but I was pretty light-headed at that point, so you should ask the others."

"You think it was survivors from the shuttle crash?"

"I don't know," said Lex. "Doesn't make sense they'd make it to our island then leave for another one."

"Or know where another island was."

"Exactly."

"So," she said, "what now?"

"Not sure, but I know what we're not doing. We're not heading across the ocean looking for a tall tree on a mysterious island that's who knows how far away."

"We could," she whispered.

Lex started to reply but paused. He looked down at his bandaged feet.

"We could," he admitted. "But we shouldn't. We need to regroup. We need to take care of our injuries." He raised his head. "It's only a little over nine weeks until the fourth landing party arrives. It'd be nice to be ready for them."

"I'll help any way I can."

She waited for one of his warm smiles that often showed up right when she needed it, but the smile didn't come. Instead, he leaned over and gave her a gentle hug. Her heart was pounding, but there was no romance in the gesture, just kindness … familiarity.

She hugged him back, hoping she wasn't hurting his sunburn, wondering whether his feelings were half as jumbled as hers. After a long moment, Lex let go, stood up, and walked toward the door.

"Don't stay up too late," he said.

"First Ada, now you."

"Well," he paused. "A lot of people care about you."

"And I care about them."

"See you in the morning." He closed the cabin door.

Leigh put her head in her hands. She didn't know what to make of at least half the conversation. At the heart of it all, Ada and Lex were telling her the same thing: it's been chaos since your landing party arrived; please help us find some stability.

It made sense. Leigh had been on the planet nineteen days, and there hadn't been a stable thing about any of them. Everyone was exhausted. She'd have no trouble supporting the leadership's desire to establish a routine and keep things structured, even on a world that was anything but.

Ada and Lex wanted to regroup, to put the past few weeks behind them. Leigh understood. Really, she did.

But she was beginning to realize there was danger in ignoring the past, danger in putting it completely, 100 percent behind you. The trick was to embrace it, to let the past be part of you—to let it be part of you while not letting it break you.

She shuffled some of her papers and looked at the sketch Lex had left on top of the pile: the Twisted Peaks, looming like monstrous, craggy guardians over their portion of the sea. In the picture, the tallest mountain shaded the others, the way it'd looked when they'd paddled past it on the raft. She'd drawn it that way instead of with the long dark shadow from when she and Michele had swum by the following day. They'd had to venture far from shore, and the mountain's shadow had made it the coldest part of the trip.

Leigh rubbed her eyes and pushed the drawings away, carefully placing two rocks on top of the pile.

She turned off the lantern.

Moonlight shone through the room's one window. For a long time, she sat in the darkness, unmoving, a lone figure watching the three alien moons create a shimmering slice of light on the barren cabin floor.

CHAPTER 32

Nothing about living in a distant solar system became routine. Nonetheless, over the next two months, life in the colony settled into a regular rhythm.

The morning rotations of yoga, tai chi, and swimming were a success. Leigh was entertained by the silly rivalries that evolved, each group vying to be labeled "the best" from week to week.

The morning groups were especially good for the leaders—the leaders of Marjol because they could, for once, be regular participants, and the leaders of the morning groups, all of whom had risen to the challenge. Marko and Noah led the swimming, Gwen and Mia the yoga, and Shane and Declan the tai chi.

Leigh enjoyed all three, but the latter was her favorite: Irish-led tai chi on the beach. It was a widely held belief that only Shane had known much tai chi before leaving Earth. However, no one could question Declan's enthusiasm. His unbridled energy was part of what made it fun … and why they'd had to move tai chi farther down the beach. Yoga on the plateau and tai chi down below had been a calamitous combination.

Leigh still laughed thinking of the confrontation from the third week of morning groups, when Gwen had endured one disruption too many. She'd marched down from yoga just as Declan had called to Matt, "Whoa, bud, your leg's goin' arseways there!"

"Watch it, mate," joked Matt, "or my leg'll be finding your arse."
"If you don't quiet down," yelled Gwen, "I'll kick both your asses!"
Leigh had smothered a giggle, and Lex had laughed out loud.

"We're trying to focus," said Gwen. "I don't know what the hell is going on down here!"

"Why don't you join us," offered Declan. "We're havin' a whale of a time."

Gwen glared at him. Declan, who at least had the courtesy to blush a brilliant red, smiled in return. Leigh continued to hold back laughter. Lex took a more productive route.

"How 'bout we move this party down the beach," he said.

Declan and Shane started to protest, but Lex held up a hand. "Come on, guys. We can meet near the beach cabins. For easy water breaks at the spring."

Shane and Declan hadn't liked being pushed around by Gwen, but they'd agreed to the move. It wasn't in their nature to court real trouble. And, Leigh had noticed, people tended to go along with whatever Lex suggested.

"Thanks," said Gwen.

"Ah," replied Declan, "go way outta that." Leigh had no idea what the phrase meant, and she doubted Gwen did either, but it didn't stop the other girl from giving Declan a flirtatious smile in response.

"Let's go," said Lex.

And so tai chi had moved down the beach.

That'd been the same day Dhruv first attempted tai chi. Even with his broken arm, he had done what he could while it healed. These days, Dhruv was back to a hundred percent, as were Sammi and Gwen. When the next landing party arrived, no one would ever know the three of them had been injured.

The same could not be said for Milo, Cliff, or Shin. Though Milo otherwise recovered from the rash, his left eye did not. His vision in that eye was blurry, and bright sunlight triggered painful headaches. Noah and Lex had made him a "pirate patch," which he wore with pride over the damaged eye.

That sort of positive approach had helped Cliff's recovery as well. Though he still walked with a slight limp, Cliff insisted his leg looked worse than it felt, and it didn't stop him from participating in everything.

Shin's wounds were more extensive. His chest, arm, and hand had scarred; his range of motion was hampered. During his recovery, Shin had not been allowed to expose his skin to the sun. On Marjol, that could've been isolating, but some of the boys had started early morning, sunshine-free swimming sessions with Shin almost every day. Lex, Noah, and Marko were the regulars. João and Matt went frequently, as did Olu. Recently, Cliff had started showing up, and even Nick and Raj, who both prized their sleep, got up at dawn for the early-morning swim outings from time to time.

Leigh and Michele had offered to join them but were quickly rebuffed. "No girls," said Noah.

"Seriously?" Michele replied. "We swim as well as any of you."

"Better," said Lex. "Your swimming saved my life. Skill has nothing to do with it. Trust me, you don't want to be there."

"Maybe I do."

"Michele," interjected Leigh, "let's have our own club. Girls only."

Lex gave her a wink, but she wasn't being diplomatic for his sake.

"Perfect," said Michele. "That'll be more fun anyway."

And so began the girls-only early-morning swims, which gave Leigh time to enjoy the ocean without the distraction of a certain male. It also gave her the chance to help Ada and Rose, who were terrible swimmers despite being chosen to colonize a waterworld.

The girls went twice a week: Fridays and Freedays. The four of them—Leigh, Michele, Ada, and Rose—would wake before dawn and walk the path to Sunrise Beach. Together, they'd watch Rán emerge from the horizon; afterward, they'd stroll to a nearby cove with water placid enough to teach hesitant swimmers.

Today was one such morning. It was Friday, and the instruction portion of the morning was over. As was typical, the other three girls sat on the beach while Leigh floated in the ocean a few more moments, treasuring the luxury of morning sunshine. It made her appreciate what the boys gave up by swimming on the island's other side, where the cliff shaded the water until midday.

Floating on her back, Leigh closed her eyes and listened to the water sloshing around her. During the past three months, she'd learned to keep a close hold on her thoughts—to stay busy during the day so as not to think about the enormity of it all, and to be tired enough to fall asleep at night. But these early-morning swims were an exception; she allowed her mind to wander.

It was a little over nine weeks, seventy-four days to be exact—but who was counting—since the night Lex had hugged her in Q-cabin. Leigh had not had another private conversation with him in all that time. Sure, she talked with him every evening—they hung out during morning group, and they bodysurfed together on Freedays—but the two of them were never alone.

It required effort to be alone with someone who was neither in your cabin nor your work group. She had not made such an effort with Lex. Nor he with her.

Whenever she watched Rán's vermilion light announce a new day, she thought of him. And late at night, she often found herself gazing at the loon constellation, looking skyward and remembering other nights under the stars. She didn't know whether Lex noticed his loon anymore; she never asked.

Her interviews had begun as planned on Monday, Virgil 25. Workdays were busy, and Freedays were saved for fun, but she managed six interviews per week—one each evening, Monday through Saturday. On Sunday evenings, she met with the three leaders and reported on what she'd learned that week. Ada asked the bulk of the questions; Lex asked the fewest. Olu gave her another reason to be impressed. Despite originally disliking the enterprise, he embraced it once the interviews began.

During her second meeting with the leadership, Leigh had come clean with Olu and Ada about her reasons for conducting the interviews—her hopes of figuring out why they'd left Earth and how they'd been selected as colonists. She wondered aloud whether their colony was the only one. Were the people who wrote on the cave wall supposed to join them? What about the person whose unopened bag had washed ashore? Were these colonists who should be with them right now? Or was there another colony out there past the horizon, on an island with a tall tree?

Two months of interviews, and she'd failed to answer any of those questions. Last week, another piece of lightweight black metal had washed up on Sunrise Beach, an unwelcome reminder of all the things they didn't know.

Floating on her back in the cove, Leigh watched a fluffy cloud pass overhead, then she sank down under the water and listened. The soft, steady gurgling of the sea mixed with the sound of shifting sands on the ocean floor. In the distance, she could hear her three friends' voices. Though she couldn't make out the words, it was easy to tell who was talking, almost like listening to birdsong. The chirpy canary was Ada, the cooing dove was Rose, and the melodious owl was Michele.

Leigh blew bubbles into the water, laughing at herself for the fanciful thoughts. She floated back up to the surface, wiped her hair out of her face, and waved at the three girls.

"We're ready when you are," called Rose.

"Five more minutes," said Leigh.

"That works!"

Leigh turned onto her stomach and leisurely kicked closer to shore. In the calm, clear water, she scanned the cove for the tiny silver creatures they called darters. Scaly but without fins, the darters flicked their tails and slid through the water. Some mornings, shoals of them shimmered in the sun-kissed waves.

Though no darters appeared, her search turned up a gorgeous black rock with bright blue speckles. A slug-like creature sheltered underneath, so she left the rock where it was and swam away, laughing again into the water, spreading bubbles across the sand. Because, in truth, her interviews were much the same—worthwhile in ways she'd never anticipated. The process uncovered little details she'd never gone searching for: Zalfaa's Batman LEGO keychain had been a gift from her ParaemergencyMed instructor at the halfway point of the course; Mia had lived in an igloo when she was eight years old; Milo had once stolen from an orchard and still felt guilty about it. Those were not the facts Leigh shared with the leadership. But they were the stories that colored her world, the ones that had helped her get to know everyone in the colony.

With only fifty-nine people, it might seem like knowing everyone would be easy. But she spent seven out of eight days a week with Maps. And learning everyone's name was not the same as knowing who they were.

Sometimes, the interviews made Leigh question even more why she'd been selected as a colonist. She had no specialized training or scientific knowledge. No exceptional talents. And she was one of the few who didn't speak at least two languages.

Maybe she'd learn more when the next landing party arrived. Only four days to go. Of course, it'd be another week until they really met, when the quarantine was over.

"Lorelei!" called Michele from the beach. "Lor! Let's go."

"Come back in," said Leigh, treading water. "Just for a few more minutes. It's so perfect this morning!"

She was pleasantly surprised when Michele, Ada, and Rose took her up on the offer. Usually, they were ready to leave by now. But truly, it was perfect in the cove.

The sunlight glimmered off the smooth dark-blue water. On shore, the tall purple grass was flecked with water droplets. When the breeze blew, the droplets scattered over the dark sand like confetti.

"Look at the shoreline," Leigh said as the girls swam near. "Isn't it—"

The other three pounced and dunked her, splashing mercilessly whenever she came up for air. When the ambush stopped, Leigh couldn't keep the smile from her face. These were the mornings she wished would never end.

CHAPTER 33

The following night, Leigh interviewed Michele. She pulled out a notebook and pen, no longer needing a question list. After conducting fifty-four interviews, Leigh could recite the important questions in her sleep.

She already knew that Michele had been raised from a young age by her maternal grandparents, whom she called Nana and Kākā. Both embraced their Māori heritage, which explained Michele's penchant for Māori sayings. What Leigh hadn't known was the reason Nana and Kākā had raised her: her parents had been killed in the record-breaking earthquake that hit when baby Michele was only eight months old. Her mom and dad had taken a weekend away to celebrate their third anniversary. The earthquake hit, and they never returned.

"Oh, Michele," said Leigh, "I'm so sorry."

"I don't think that's the way real interviewers talk," she replied with a grin.

The way Michele told the story, she'd experienced a lovely childhood. She retained no memories before living with her grandparents, and so, according to her, the hardship part felt like someone else's tale. Leigh found herself hoping that was true, but it didn't make her heart ache any less for her friend.

Nana and Kākā had provided boundless amounts of love, a bond with nature, and a safe place to grow up. They lived on the island of

Te Waipounamu, the largest island of Aotearoa, the Māori name for New Zealand. Michele had grown up loving the mountains, the lakes, and the ocean, never wanting to leave.

"So were you surprised," said Leigh, "to discover you'd volunteered to colonize this planet?"

"Surprised is putting it mildly. However, the Māori have a saying, *Kaua e mate wheke mate ururoa.* 'Don't die like an octopus; die like a hammerhead shark.' I kept that in mind."

"You're going to have to explain that one."

"Have you ever caught an octopus?"

"Uh, no."

"Octopus are tricky to find, but they don't fight back much when you capture them. An octopus gives up too easily."

"I assume the point of the saying is that a hammerhead shark does not."

"Lor," said Michele, "you could be part Māori."

"Very funny."

"A hammerhead shark will not give up no matter what. If you catch one and chop off its tail, the tail will still fight at you on its own."

"You did this?"

"No! It's just a saying."

"Okay," said Leigh, "so you were surprised to find yourself on Marjol but determined to be like a hammerhead shark and not an octopus."

"If you want to put it that way," said Michele.

"You're the one who put it that way."

"Do you talk this way to all the people you interview?"

"Only the ones who answer me with Māori sayings."

"Cute."

"Talking about your grandparents," said Leigh, "do you think they supported your decision to become a colonist?"

"Oh yes."

"Why do you think they would've wanted you to be a colonist?"

"I don't think they would have," said Michele. "But I do think they would've *supported* my choice. Whatever my choice was."

"I guess the question is why do you think it was your choice?"

"No idea," laughed Michele. "I asked myself that same question during the first month here. On Earth, I read a lot about space travel—both real stories and science fiction—but I never wanted to do something like this myself. I never even wanted to leave Aotearoa. I've told you how magical it is ..."

"Yes," said Leigh, smiling, "I believe you've mentioned it once or twice or a hundred times."

"Ah, my friend, your interview technique is interesting. But no, I have no idea why I wanted to come to this planet. Most of us don't. Have you found any clues?"

"Not really," Leigh admitted. "Observations, but nothing that gets me any closer to an answer."

"Like what? What observations?"

"Like ... the cryosleep kills those over twenty, and yet none of us arrived older than seventeen. Where are the eighteen- and nineteen-year-olds?"

"Olu."

"Olu?"

"Last memory he has from Earth was only a few weeks before his eighteenth birthday. So he was definitely eighteen by the time we arrived."

"Hmm."

"What else? Any similarities among all of us?"

"Nothing," said Leigh. "Other than tragedy."

"What do you mean?" Michele leaned forward and rested her forearms on the table.

"It's sad ... everyone suffered some horrible loss. A lot of us had a parent die, or leave, or both. Or their grandparents were killed in a terrible accident that they watched happen, or a sibling died. Something awful. Every single one of us. It's as if they recruited people who grew up defined by tragedy and trauma."

"That's depressing."

"I know," said Leigh, "but it's too consistent to be a coincidence."

"Resilience."

"Huh?"

"They recruited people who'd shown resilience."

"I don't know."

"Think about it." Michele leaned harder on the table. "You said we were 'defined by tragedy and trauma,' but were we? Or were we defined by how we chose to deal with it? Did we have people, like Nana and Kākā, who helped us through it? Look at us. We've been here almost nine months. It hasn't been easy, but I'm proud of how we've done. We're resilient."

"You may have a point." Leigh wrote some more notes. "I hadn't thought about it like that."

Michele smiled broadly. "You should talk to me about this stuff more often. I had to wait forever just to be interviewed."

"Ada creates the interview schedule," said Leigh, unruffled by Michele's friendly ribbing. "Okay, here's another question: What's your last memory of being on Earth?"

"Ah, that's an easy one. My last memory is standing at the edge of a lake and skipping stones with Kākā."

"Your grandfather."

"Yes." She removed her arms from the table and leaned back in the chair. Michele always looked relaxed when she talked about her grandparents. "My grandfather looks kind of like a parrot—a parrot looking for trouble, as Nana says—so as a little kid, I called him Kākā, Māori for parrot. The name stuck. You would like him."

"Yeah, I'm sure I would."

"Kākā and Nana usually made everyone help with dinner. Even if I had friends over, part of the meal was preparing it in the kitchen together. But every once in a while, Nana would take over the kitchen all by herself and make what she called her 'special surprises.' Kākā and I would walk to the lake and skip stones, and he would tell me stories. And that's what we were doing in my last memory from Earth."

"That's a nice memory."

"Most of my Earth memories are nice."

Leigh sighed. So many others couldn't say the same.

"Most of my Marjol memories are nice too," Michele added.

"Really?"

"You don't believe me?"

"I believe you. It's just, I was there when the raft wrecked, remember. And when it took us two days and two very long nights to swim back."

"We made it," said Michele.

"We did."

"See ... that's a good memory."

Leigh persisted. "A lot of people have said you almost died, though they don't give details. And, uh, you don't want me to ask about Olu, right?"

"It's your interview."

"Technically, this interview is about your life on Earth."

"Like I said, it's your interview."

"Do you want to tell me the story?"

"It's no secret," said Michele. "I mean, everyone in the first landing party knows it, and everyone in the second, for that matter. I'm surprised you haven't heard the gossip. Or that you haven't asked me about it before."

"About what?"

"About me and Olu trying to have a baby."

"What?" Leigh stopped taking notes.

Michele continued to lounge in her chair.

"Those first months here," said Michele, "there were only twenty of us. It was scarier than it is now. But there was Olu. And he and I decided we were going to have the first baby, the first little native of this new world."

"Uh, I assume this was before the rule about not having sex."

"Tell me that wasn't a real question."

"Sorry," said Leigh, "trying to process."

"That rule came after the epidemic."

"Yeah, sorry," said Leigh, "I know. Go on. You were saying something about you and Olu having sex."

"I swear," said Michele, "and people think you're so nice."

"Well, you know me better than most."

Michele laughed, then she grew contemplative again.

"Sorry," repeated Leigh, realizing her friend had wanted to share this story for a while. "Tell me about Olu, back when there were only twenty of you. I guess it was different."

"Very different. We were a small bunch. Literally the first humans to ever set foot on the planet—as far as we know, anyway. And no techs! We were, honestly, crushed by that at first. But the twenty of us managed. And, well, there was Olu."

"You don't have to explain."

"It seems so naïve." Michele shook her head. "But I was in love with him, and we were excited about being parents, about having that first baby. I didn't have any signs of being pregnant yet, but we figured it would happen. I'd never had my period since landing, and others hadn't either, so who knew. Our only worry was that the cryosleep might have affected our ability to get pregnant."

Leigh could understand. There were plenty of so-called feminine supplies in the cabins, but they were almost never used. She, Eliana, and Zalfaa had talked about it too.

"And then we got sick," said Michele. "You've heard the story. Some of us got a lot sicker than the rest. No rhyme or reason. Lex was one of the sickest of all. Marko ran a fever for less than a day. Rina didn't seem that sick, and then she died. It made no sense. It still makes no sense."

"I heard," said Leigh, "that Olu and Ada watched you almost die."

"And that's the heart of it." She paused but never looked away. "Olu thinks I almost died because I had a miscarriage."

"I'm," Leigh paused. "I ... I am so sorry."

"It is what it is, my friend. And Ada disagrees. She thinks it was hemorrhaging having nothing to do with a baby. I hadn't thought I was pregnant before I got sick. Olu and I had just been hopeful. And sometimes hope changes how you think about things.

"During the epidemic, I was in a terrible way, 'crook' as we say— throwing up constantly, running a high fever for days. Dehydrated, but couldn't keep anything down. I was so out of balance. Separated from *whakapapa* and *whenua*, from my ancestors and my land, by light-years of space. No wonder my body was a disaster. The sudden bleeding was one more thing."

"What do you think happened?" asked Leigh. "You agree with Olu or Ada?"

Michele laced her fingers together.

"I'm sorry," said Leigh. "I shouldn't have asked."

"Stop apologizing. The story is part of my life, part of who I am. It's a hard part, but hey ... we all have hard parts."

For a moment, Leigh felt compelled to tell her own story, hard parts and all. She took a deep breath and let the compulsion fade.

"You all right?" asked Michele.

"I wish I were as strong as you."

"Oh, my friend, you are! You just don't know it yet." Michele reached out a hand and laid it on Leigh's arm. "In answer to your question, I decided I didn't have to know. It didn't matter. It was desperately sad either way."

"Because," said Leigh, "Olu banned everyone from even thinking about having a baby after that."

"It wasn't just Olu. We all agreed. The epidemic was the first time any of us had been sick. And Rina *died*.

"It sounds dumb, but we hadn't thought about how little we knew about taking care of each other, much less a baby. And yes, either way, the chance for a baby with Olu was gone. This idealized image I had of us with our new little Marjolian, that was what I mourned."

"And that's why no one talks about having kids."

"A conversation that needs to start up again at some point," said Michele. "I mean, they put a bunch of teenagers on a planet with no condoms. What do you think is going to happen?"

Leigh laughed. "You think we should get rid of the no-sex rule."

"I think plenty of people are already breaking the rule."

"Really?"

"Yes," laughed Michele. "Maybe you should add that to your interview questions."

"Very funny."

"Or pay more attention to what happens in the middle of the night."

"Are you serious?"

"Are you that clueless?" said Michele, and she laughed again. "But honestly, the usefulness of the rule is ending. Other rules have already shifted—people talk about their life on Earth, and it's fine. Things are changing.

"The no-intimacy-of-any-kind rule was always excessive, an overreaction. No one can share a kiss because someone might get carried away and end up with a baby? That's crazy! But we were scared." Her voice lowered. "Really, really scared. People deal better with hard-line rules than judgment calls when they're afraid."

"I can see that," said Leigh. "And tell me if I'm wrong, but I think the rule's not just about health. All the rules encourage unity—loyalty to the group more than to any individual. The rules apply to everyone, not just people who might have a baby."

"See," said Michele, her smile returning, "you're smart. You don't even need to ask half these questions. You already know the answers."

"Hardly!" said Leigh. "But yes, I've learned a lot after fifty-something interviews."

"Better you than me. And you're right. Everything we've done since the epidemic has been about keeping the colony together. Sometimes a desperate attempt at unity."

"Olu's single-minded that way."

"Admirably so," said Michele. "Nowadays, there's less fear and more people. We're growing. Three more days, and we'll have a new landing party and be up to seventy-nine colonists. We have Zalfaa and her medical training, and others are learning. She's instructing, what, six people right now?"

"Yes, two from each work group. Then they'll teach others."

"Good," said Michele. "And who knows what skills people may come with when they arrive next week, or three months after that. I think we're going to need additional work groups later. One for taking care of kids, maybe one for building some homes that aren't big cabins. More people are coming. Change will come with them."

"And you and Olu?"

"Ah, it is hard to explain."

"You don't have to."

"But I will try even so." Michele leaned her arms once more on the table. "Back on Earth, did you ever drop a plate or a vase or something and have it break?"

"Is this another Māori saying?"

"No! This is me trying to explain."

"Okay, sorry," said Leigh, but both girls were smiling.

"Sometimes," said Michele, "you drop a plate, and it cracks in two. Other times it shatters into lots of little pieces."

"Done both."

"When it breaks in two, you can glue the pieces together, and it won't be the same, but it'll be whole. You can use it again."

"Uh-huh."

"The plate that shatters," said Michele, "that's different. You can find as many pieces as possible and try to glue them all together, but the plate is never whole, not really.

"Olu and I, we lost the chance at having the baby we dreamed about. My heart broke in two, but I've repaired it. It's not the same, but I'm whole again."

"And Olu is not?"

"During the epidemic, his heart shattered into lots and lots of little pieces. My story is only part of why, though I fear it is a big part. I'm not sure whether Olu's heart will ever be glued back together or not, and I don't think it will ever be quite whole. I wanted to help him with that, but he has shut me out."

"Ah," said Leigh, finally understanding. "He blames himself for you almost dying."

"Which is stupid!"

"He thinks he's protecting you."

"From what? *Life?* You can't protect people from life," said Michele. "You can watch out for them, but only if you let them watch out for you too. With Olumayokun, it's all one-sided."

"Do you know what an arroyo is?" asked Leigh.

"Arroyo? Another word for idiot boy?"

"No," Leigh laughed. "An arroyo is a mostly empty creek bed. We had one near where I used to live. A deep cut in the land with a trickle of water. Except when it rained. After a storm, the arroyo would flood with raging water.

"My grandmother used to tell me that the arroyo was like problems, and that I was always trying to cross the arroyo after a rain instead of waiting for the water to become a trickle."

"She was trying to teach you patience," said Michele.

"I'm just saying," replied Leigh, "that maybe Olu needs more time. Maybe, eventually, Olu will learn how to let others watch out for him, like he watches out for them."

"Yes, and maybe we'll walk down to the beach tomorrow and discover the ocean has turned a brilliant shade of pink. That seems more likely."

Leigh smiled, but she wasn't fooled by her friend's attempt at humor. She reached out and put a hand on Michele's arm.

"Thanks," said Leigh, "for telling me."

"Lor, my friend, our stories make us who we are. I have no secrets from you."

Leigh wished she could say the same. But that was the thing about secrets … the longer you held on to them, the harder they were to get rid of.

CHAPTER 34

Sunday evening, Lex leaned over the back of his chair and listened to Lorelei summarize the week's interviews. It did not escape his notice that she talked more about the other five than about Michele's.

He looked forward to these weekly reports on the interviews. Lorelei had a gift for learning information without making people feel pressured to share it, and she'd uncovered an array of talents among the colonists. Who knew that five of them spoke Chinese? That Raj, Eliana, and Peigi wrote their own music? Lex hadn't even known how Peigi spelled her name. Focusing on survival, he'd lost sight of everything else.

He rested his chin on his hands and listened as Lorelei brought up Michele's thoughts about resilience. Olu and Ada asked a few questions and shared a few observations. Lex didn't have anything to add, especially since Michele had already talked to him about it. The interview had pushed her trickiest emotions to the surface, and she'd been eager to confide. Lex would certainly not be sharing any of *that* conversation at this meeting.

At least he knew where Michele stood on things. Lorelei remained an enigma. Over two months had passed since their skinny-dipping adventure, and she'd never alluded to it. Not once had she mentioned the sunrise they'd shared in front of the cave. Not once. Did she think about those moments? Did she watch for the loon in the night sky?

"What do you think?" asked Ada.

"Think?" said Lex.

"See, I told you he wasn't paying attention."

"Yes, I am," said Lex. "You want my opinion on resilience. Obviously, we all have it, or we wouldn't be alive."

The three of them laughed, and he thought he was off the hook. Until he realized they were, indeed, laughing at him and not with him.

"Two topics behind," said Lorelei.

"One's a topic we've discussed before," explained Ada, "how so many of us don't have siblings. The other is something new."

"New," said Olu, "and not too important."

"Now I'm doubly interested," said Lex.

"I was saying," said Lorelei, "I've interviewed over ninety percent of us, and as far as I can tell, there's no one from Canada."

"Eh?" quipped Lex.

"Seriously," she replied, "don't you find that surprising?"

"Even if it is," said Lex, "does it matter?"

"Exactly," said Olu.

"It seems strange," said Lorelei.

"Strange how?" asked Ada.

"Canada's a big country, and they speak English, most of them. Almost half our colony is from the US, with Canada right next door. Don't any of you find it odd?"

"Not especially," said Ada.

Lex grinned. He loved when Lorelei got worked up about the little stuff. She was usually so painfully calm.

"Think about it," she said. "As you know, we have lots of colonists from the United States. The others are from Australia, Aotearoa, Singapore, India, Pakistan, Botswana, South Africa, Ghana, Croatia, Germany, Denmark, England—"

"France," said Ada.

"Obviously," said Lorelei. "Also, Ireland, Scotland—oh wait, I almost forgot Portugal. Barbados, El Salvador, Mexico, and Brazil.

Hmm, think I missed one, but you get the idea. All of those, but not Canada. Isn't that odd?"

"Proof no one wants to leave Canada," said Lex.

"Maybe you'll be surprised," said Olu, "and find a Canadian this week. You still have a few interviews to go. You haven't interviewed me yet."

"No way you're from Canada," she said.

"Nigeria."

She laughed. "You're proving my point."

"Maybe," teased Lex, "there's a whole landing party of Canadians arriving on Monday. All twenty will walk off the shuttle saying 'eh' and talking about hockey."

"Right," said Lorelei, "and the pilot will be waving a Maple Leaf flag as they disembark."

"Pilot?" said Ada.

"The pilot of the shuttle."

"There's no pilot," said Olu.

"I saw her," said Lorelei. "She talked to me."

And just like that, the tenor of the meeting changed.

***

As they peppered Lorelei with questions, it was clear she knew little more than the fact of the pilot's existence—a startling enough revelation. Lex, like everyone else, had always assumed their travel had been automated.

But then, they knew almost nothing about the spaceship's journey, only bare bones from the shuttle's video with promises to learn more details on the surface, promises broken thanks to the malfunctioning techs. It'd been a while since Lex mourned the loss of the electronics, but here they were again, wishing for more knowledge and no way to get it.

They *did* know the trip had been in stages. The teenagers had been put into cryosleep before launching from Moon Base II, a process that affected their memories so that everyone's last memory was from Earth, not the Moon.

The spaceship had traveled from the Moon to the Epsilon Eridani system using solar sails, which enabled them to travel at around 80 percent of light speed. The flight was somehow enhanced with lasers, a breakthrough that allowed the solar sails to operate across vast amounts of space.

Lex had no idea how the solar sails or the lasers worked, but it made sense that a different system was needed for the final leg of the journey. Solar sails were enormous, so at some point, they were folded in, and short-range propulsion was used to get the ship to the space station orbiting Marjol. Given such a voyage, it was reasonable to think that pilots would be needed for the final stage—to dock at the space station and fly shuttle runs to the planet's surface and back. It was reasonable to think that … now they knew there was a pilot. He wished Lorelei had mentioned it earlier.

But she hadn't, and wishing wouldn't make it any different.

How many pilots were there? How old were they? Lorelei thought the pilot looked to be in her twenties, but that couldn't be right. Any pilots would have to be teenagers to survive the cryosleep. Would they join the colony on the surface once their work was done? Or would they reenter cryo for the trip back to Earth, returning to a planet almost fifty years in the future from when they'd left?

What were they doing up there? Why hadn't they helped fix the techs? Had Lorelei's pilot died in the wrecked shuttle? Once again, the colony was faced with enough information to stir up theories but no way to discern the truth.

* * *

Twenty-five hours later, Lex sat on the floor of Little Italy's common room and pulled out a fresh crate of Foobrews. It was Freeday night, Saul 32. He'd been on the planet for exactly nine months.

They had a solid plan in place for the fourth landing party's quarantine. The beach cabins were full of notes and instructions, and the entire Boats work group would be on the plateau for the shuttle's arrival. Hopefully, it'd be more of a welcome and less of a "What in the name of heaven and hell is happening to us?"—Lorelei's description of her arrival three months ago. She'd been mollified upon learning the beachfront quarantine had been a last-minute idea, but all the more reason to do a better job this time around.

Lex was tired of worrying about the upcoming quarantine and tired of listening to theories about shuttle pilots. He was ready for the fourth landing party to arrive. Ada was worried about the newcomers' reaction to the destroyed beach cabin, but there was nothing to be done about that. They'd fixed the other two cabins as best they could. It was what it was.

He pulled out Foobrews and started lining them up in rows of ten each. The only part of the plan that worried him was Marko. His task was to contact the pilot, in person if possible, otherwise by leaving a letter.

Lex dropped ten Foobrews into a dark-blue bag. They took up more room than he'd expected. He rolled his shoulders to release some tension, then began carefully adding more vials in groups of five.

The stupid letter. A handful of people had worked on it, and everyone had signed it. The letter recounted the significant events of the past nine months. It also asked for help with the broken techs.

The plan was for Marko to climb the ladder and board the shuttle as soon as the door opened, dash past those exiting, and seek out the pilot. If he couldn't find her quickly, then he'd leave the letter as near to the front of the shuttle as he could. Theoretically, Marko would be off by the time the twentieth person disembarked, then spend a few days by himself in Q-cabin.

Lex had argued, perhaps obnoxiously, that Marko could simply toss the letter into the ship. That would eliminate the risk of his being trapped and minimize his potential exposure to disease. But Lex had lost the argument. Supposedly, the advantages of a face-to-face encounter outweighed the risks, which was why he was currently packing vials of Foobrew into a bag.

Eighty vials turned out to be a tight fit, but with a bit of finagling, Lex stuffed in three more. He pulled the drawstring tight. Eighty-three vials. Not bad. If Marko got trapped on the shuttle, he could be stuck at the space station until it was time for the next landing party. He could be stuck for ninety-six days. Assuming there were pilots on the station, there would have to be water, but who knew about extra food supplies. With eighty-three vials of Foobrew, Marko might get even skinnier than he was now, but he'd survive.

Lex had been lured into relaxing his guard the past month or two, but in the end it all came back to survival.

* * *

At sunrise, those greeting the fourth landing party stood on the plateau. Marko wore the Foobrew-stuffed bag on his back and a canteen slung across his right shoulder. Ada's brow was furrowed, and her lips were pursed, but her hands were steady as she helped Marko adjust both the canteen and the bag so that they were secure.

Lex put a comforting hand on Ada's shoulder as the three of them situated themselves behind boulders on the edge of the plateau. Olu stood near them, while Michele and the rest of Boats congregated farther back in the tall grass. They knew it was likely to be an hour or so before the shuttle's arrival.

They waited.

And waited.

The first two landing parties had arrived well before midday, but as Rán rose to her highest point, the shuttle still had not appeared. The third landing party had arrived late in the afternoon, and it looked like this would be a repeat.

As they waited, and waited even longer, the mood changed from anticipation to boredom.

People grew antsy; frustration set in. Too many people had been sitting around for too long. Eventually, they'd had enough, and Michele took her group to get some work done.

Lex was the only one from Boats who didn't leave. He stayed with Olu, Ada, and Marko, all of them ready to put their plan into action.

They waited.

They watched the sky, but all they saw was Rán slipping toward the horizon.

Still they waited.

But when dusk came, no shuttle had arrived.

The four of them remained on the plateau. Dhruv and Shin brought some dinner; Michele and Noah carried out lanterns and blankets. Later,

Rose and Lorelei brought pillows and fresh canteens. Each pair stayed a while to visit, but soon enough it was once again only Lex, Olu, Ada, and Marko, scanning the night sky, hoping to see a fiery glow.

At the others' urging, Marko shed the canteen and the bag and got some sleep. Ostensibly, the leaders took shifts that night, but Lex suspected Ada and Olu slept as little as he did.

In the morning, Michele and Boats returned to the plateau. Everyone took up the same places they'd occupied twenty-five hours earlier. Maybe they'd counted wrong, or maybe there'd been a one-day delay.

A sense of optimism returned.

But still no shuttle.

They waited.

By midmorning, Boats went to work per usual, and a new plan was put in place. For the next three days, everyone in the colony took turns sitting near the plateau with Marko, waiting for the fourth landing party's arrival.

Waiting.

And waiting …

On Thursday, nightfall arrived, and they were forced to face reality: no one was coming.

CHAPTER 35

When the colony returned to a normal schedule on Friday, after four days of watching for a shuttle that never arrived, Lex hoped the omnipresent worry would start to dissipate. Instead, it got worse. By Sunday night, a wave of depression had washed over them, one that felt as if it might never recede.

Even so, Lex began Freeday with renewed optimism. It was one of those crystal-clear mornings with low humidity and not a cloud to be seen. Surely, a good Freeday would help the mood.

But no—it did the opposite. Without work to keep people busy, the gossip floodgates opened. Freeday became a speculative slog.

Lex wasn't immune to the colony's mood. Midday, he sat glumly on the sand in front of the beach cabins with Lorelei and Michele; the three of them watched Noah in the waves. On a typical Freeday, they and a handful of others would've been out in the ocean with him, but no one seemed to have the energy for anything other than complaining.

"You'd think Noah would give up," said Michele.

"Too damn stubborn," said Lorelei.

"No kidding."

Lorelei and Michele calling someone else stubborn would normally have elicited a wisecrack from Lex, but it wasn't worth it. He stayed quiet and watched Noah battle the surf.

The two girls were right; it was a miracle Noah didn't give up. He was trying to use an ill-suited piece of driftwood as a surfboard, and he was failing miserably. It was vintage Noah—willing to try one hundred approaches that didn't work in order to find the one that did.

Michele and Lorelei usually admired such tenacity. Today, they watched and complained.

"I have an idea," said Lex.

The girls sat there.

"Let's grab Noah," he suggested, "walk across the island, and swim on the other side."

"Why?" said Lorelei.

"Why not? Maybe the waves are better at Sunrise Beach. Or we can go swim in the cove."

"And stop looking at the empty plateau," said Michele.

"Exactly," said Lex.

"I'll get Noah," she offered.

"I'll see if Cliff and Eliana want to come," said Lorelei.

"Marko too," said Michele. "And Shane and Declan."

Just like that, both girls were off and moving.

Lex grinned for the first time in hours. Maybe Freeday could be saved after all.

* * *

In the end, a full dozen of them traipsed over to Sunrise Beach to see if a change in view could help a change in attitude. The mood remained different from normal, but the whining stopped.

After an hour in the waves at Sunrise Beach, Noah finally admitted defeat. He went roaming farther up the coast, hoping to find a better piece of driftwood. Marko went with him. The rules had loosened up, but no one wandered alone.

Everyone else swam into shore and headed down the beach the other direction, with plans to indulge in the placid waters of the cove. Only Lex and Lorelei remained. He bobbed in the light waves past the break point, and she floated on her back nearby.

Lex scanned the sky.

How stupid! It was his first time alone with her in over two months, and he was wasting it looking for a shuttle that wasn't coming. He stopped staring skyward and tapped Lorelei on the foot.

She righted herself to bob alongside him. "What's up?"

"Just checking to be sure you're alive," said Lex. "You haven't moved in a while."

"It's nice out here."

"True enough."

"Good plan coming over here, by the way."

"Thanks."

A wave pushed them toward shore. Lex ducked underwater to get the hair out of his eyes. When he resurfaced, Lorelei was watching him.

"I can't stop thinking about the fourth landing party," she said.

"Same," he admitted. "Though I hate to waste a Freeday worrying."

"Worry isn't always a waste."

"It's a waste to worry about things out of our control."

"Maybe, but ... never mind."

"What?" Lex waited.

Finally, she said, "What if two shuttles have crashed."

"Two?"

"The bag, the sliced pod, the writing on the cave wall. I know some people think they're from a shuttle that tried to land before yours, that you weren't the first to arrive, weren't originally going to be the first landing party on the island. But I don't think so. I've always assumed those discoveries mean there's another colony on Marjol, and it was their shuttle that crashed."

"I agree."

"It couldn't have been our shuttle that crashed ... the shuttle that brought my landing party. We saw it take off and disappear. The bag alone proves it wasn't ours."

"Uh-huh."

"But what if ... more than one shuttle crashed?"

"What?" Lex stopped treading water for a second. This was an idea he'd never considered.

"What if ours did crash?" she said. "If the pieces my landing party found during quarantine weren't from the same shuttle as the rest of the debris."

It was true that all the other debris had been found on the sunrise side, the same side as the writing on the cave wall. But still.

"It's not likely there'd be two crashes," said Lex.

"It's not likely I'd volunteer to colonize a planet, but here I am."

A wave broke right in front of them. Lex wiped the salty spray off his face. Lorelei stared at the sky, her eyes focused on something he couldn't see.

"Lex," she said, "what if there's no Earth anymore? Not like we remember. What if we came here because of some catastrophe, some reason people had to leave? Or something we feared would happen, and now it has?" She looked at him. "What if there are no more shuttles? Maybe the ship has already gone home. Maybe the shuttle crashes, the broken techs ... they've given up."

Another wave crashed in front of them. Lex swam a few strokes away from shore, hoping for calmer water.

Lorelei followed. "Lex," she said, "what if no one else *ever* comes?"

"I'm not willing to jump to conclusions until we know more."

"We may never know more."

A wave crested slightly past them and rushed toward shore. Lorelei spread her arms wider, gently treading water. Lex considered what to say and caught himself unconsciously scanning the sky, light blue with scattered clouds ... and no shuttle.

"Your idea about two shuttles may be right," he conceded. "But it's much more likely something happened to only one, and somehow, that means we got no landing party. I won't be surprised if three months from now, on the first of Danny, a shuttle arrives, a fourth landing party arrives, and we can stop worrying."

"And if three months pass and no one comes?"

"Then," said Lex, "I guess we'll have to hurry up and populate the planet."

Lorelei's laugh came simultaneously with a wave and left her sputtering. As she finished coughing, Lex had time to rue the remark. He'd been trying to lighten the tone, not make a pass at her. But his attempt at humor had perhaps revealed his thinking more than he would've liked.

She didn't seem to hold it against him. Despite coughing up sea water, Lorelei was grinning.

"You okay?" he asked.

"Fine," she said, "but I think I've swallowed enough ocean for one day."

"Let's swim in."

They waited for a big wave and rode it to shallow water. The two of them waded into shore together and plopped down on a big towel. Lex scanned the beach and wondered how long until the others returned. Lorelei lay flat on her back and closed her eyes. The doom and gloom she'd expressed while in the water was gone, but her fists were clenched, and her body radiated tension.

"Can I tell you something?" she asked.

"Sure."

"No, I mean be totally honest about something you may not want to hear?"

"Anytime," he said carefully, "about anything."

"I think," she said, then paused.

He waited.

"I think we should go look for them," she said. "I think we should go."

It was not what he'd expected. He stared at her, but she hadn't moved and hadn't opened her eyes. "Go?" he asked.

"Yes. Take one of your spiffy new sailing rafts and go."

"Where?"

"Toward sunrise." She propped herself up on her elbows and looked at him, her eyes wide and searching, but for what he wasn't sure. "Toward sunrise," she repeated. "To the second island with the tall tree."

"We have no idea how far away that is," he said. "Or who wrote the Korean on the wall."

"I know." She sat up and leaned toward him, wet hair framing her face, her skin glistening with droplets of salt water.

"We have no idea what else might be out there in the ocean," he said.

"I know," she said. "We have questions piled upon questions piled upon more questions."

"Exactly."

"What do you say, Lex? I think it's time to get some answers."

He feared she was right.

And he wanted to go.

**

That evening, Lex stood on the plateau with Olu and Ada. The three of them had paid a visit to Rina's grave. Although the boys had shared a favorite Rina story at the gravesite, Ada had remained quiet. And none of them had spoken a word since walking the path back to the plateau.

It was the end of a long day at the end of a very long week. It'd be important to make an appearance at the Freeday bonfire, but they delayed returning to Homesite, giving themselves a few more minutes alone.

All three leaders agreed with Lorelei—they were tired of waiting around. Until the past week, their job had been to keep the colony intact as more people arrived. But the goalpost had shifted. The fifty-nine of them might be it, at least on this island.

They had no idea who else might be on the planet, but it was time to find out.

The leaders had made a brief announcement to the entire colony, with a guarantee that tomorrow's Monday morning meeting would provide plenty of time for discussion. But that would be a formality. The short, seemingly innocuous questions they'd each field at tonight's bonfire would be the key. Perhaps that's what was compelling them to dawdle. Ada, especially, seemed in no rush to get back.

She stood between Lex and Olu as they watched Rán begin her slow descent into the horizon, the ball of fire seeming to ooze into flaming liquid as it sank into the ocean.

"I have no second thoughts about the trip," said Ada. "But I don't …" she paused and cleared her throat. "I don't want to bury either of you up on the hillside next to Rina."

"We'll be careful," said Lex. Realistically, if something went wrong, they'd be buried at sea, but he kept that thought to himself.

"It's not for sure I'm going," said Olu.

Ada put a hand on Olu's arm. "But you should. If you think that's where you can help the most, then you should go."

"I've offered, but ultimately, it's up to Michele."

"You sure?"

"She's the captain," said Olu. "Anyone Michele doesn't want shouldn't go, and that includes me."

"You tell her that?"

"I did."

Ada nodded.

Lex began to understand why Michele was leaning toward including Olu. "Speaking of Michele," he said, "she thinks we can be ready to leave in a day or two."

"That's too soon," said Ada. "The three of us may be in agreement, but others will have questions. We're doing all right. Some people won't see any need to leave the island."

"We're isolated, completely isolated. Everyone will understand."

"Once they have a chance to think about it, yes. But give them a chance to think about it, Lex."

"Besides," said Olu, "rushing will make everyone think we're worried."

"I get it," said Lex. "We rushed it last time, and we all know how that turned out."

"Different circumstances." Olu reached over Ada's head and clasped Lex on the shoulder. "Let's give it a week."

"Good plan," said Ada.

"And," said Lex, "that's enough time for us to convince Raj to lead Boats while we're gone."

"Noah's definitely going?" asked Ada.

"Yes," said Lex. "Michele, me, Noah, Lorelei, and Marko."

"And possibly Olu."

"I'd give that a fifty-fifty chance."

"Assuming Lex and I are both leaving," Olu said to Ada, "a full week is plenty of time to appoint someone to help you."

"No," she replied, "no one's replacing either of you. I'll have the work group leaders. It'll be fine. Really."

Olu and Lex stepped closer to her, putting their arms around each other so that the three of them stood side by side, staring at the sunset. Ada seemed even smaller than usual, sandwiched between them. It was hard to imagine how they'd managed without her for the first three months.

"Don't get too used to running everything on your own," Lex teased her. "We'll be back before you know it. All for one and one for all."

Ada smiled. "That's French, you know."

"*Oui*," said Lex. "The Three Musketeers."

"*Tous pour un, un pour tous*," echoed Olu. "Exactly right."

CHAPTER 36

One week later, it was almost time for the journey to begin. Leigh lay in bed, her eyes closed, her mind open. She thought of her last trip on a raft: the crash against the rocks … the long swim with Michele … the way the ocean had stretched out before them. She thought of her parents: the wreck that killed her father … her family's ranch … the way the dry fields had stretched into the distance. Her mind raced with memories of long ago and memories of the past few months.

She'd finished the last of the interviews and compiled lists of the most important observations. In the end, nothing she'd written came close to reflecting all she'd learned.

She'd drawn sketches in a futile attempt to fill the gaps: the bodysurfers on a Freeday. Olu and Ada up front at a Monday morning meeting. Milo making a perfect catch with his pirate eyepatch. Shane and Declan leading tai chi. Zalfaa laughing with Shin during his recovery. Rose learning to swim. Cliff and Eliana sitting on the beach. Lex leaning against the boulder on a moonlit night. The pasts they'd shared with her during the interviews had made them the people she knew today.

She would leave tomorrow with five of those people: Michele, Lex, Marko, Noah, and Olu. She'd been the one to say, "I think we should go," but when she'd said it, she hadn't thought about how going in search of one thing meant leaving something else behind. She still thought they should go. But it was harder to leave than she'd imagined. And there was one more thing to do before she left.

Leigh pulled back her duvet and slid softly to the floor.

"You good?" whispered Zalfaa.

"Yep. Back soon."

Leigh made her way outside. The night was relatively dark, but she could see well enough to step next door. She ran her fingers along the side of Little Italy, curious to see what had kept Lex and Marko chipping away during their last waking hours before departure.

At the far end of the wall, she discovered the answer. They'd finished the design. Along the back edge, two names were painstakingly carved into the russet-colored blocks: *Marko. Alexius.* They'd dated it *10.16.1.*

With a lump in her throat, she tiptoed back to the cabin's front, thankful her feet had toughened enough to walk barefoot on the sandy dirt of Homesite. Her next stop was Q-cabin. The door squeaked upon entering, but it didn't matter. Leigh had the cabin to herself.

She turned on a lantern, grabbed an empty notebook, and sat down at her usual table. No more excuses. It was time. She opened to the notebook's first page and began.

> Interviewee: Leigh Anabelle Crawford
> Interviewer: same
> Interview date: Freeday, Linus 16, Year I
>
> Dear Friends,
> I am not writing a typical interview sheet, but here is my story. You know me as Lorelei. On Earth, I was Leigh Anabelle Crawford. Some of you may know my family's story (or at least the parts that made the news) from hearing my name. Others will remember news stories when I tell you my mother is the former governor of Texas who went to jail. But I am getting ahead of myself.
> I was born in Austin, Texas, not far from New Braunfels, the town where my parents grew up. My parents knew each other during high school, though they were not friends at the time. After high school, my mother wanted to see another part of the country and

went off to the University of Louisville, in Kentucky, for her college years. When she graduated, she wanted to see another part of the world, so she traveled in southern Europe for three months before deciding it was time to either return home or earn some money. She took a job in Seville, Spain, rented a room, and began working on a long-term plan to stay awhile. A month later, a message came that her mother had died. No warning. My grandmother was walking in the park with a friend, had a stroke, and died before ever reaching the hospital.

My mother returned to New Braunfels for the funeral, realized Texas was home, and never left. A few weeks after the funeral, she saw her future husband, my father, at a local coffee shop. The way my dad always told the story, they sat down to share a cup of coffee, and by the time that cup was gone, he knew he wanted to share coffee with her every morning the rest of his life. Apparently, my mother felt the same because six months later they were married.

They moved a little bit north to Austin so my mother could go to law school. My father, an artist, worked at a local museum and used their studio apartment as an actual studio. My parents originally planned to move back to New Braunfels after three years, but it never happened. My father showed his paintings in a gallery, and they began to sell. He was recruited by an agent to be a children's book illustrator. He moved his studio out of the apartment, sharing a building with an art therapist and a psychiatrist, who both became close family friends. My mother took a job at an Austin law firm, but it was clear her future was in politics. She made all the right connections and took all the right clients. Soon she was working at the capitol building, and it was clear that was only the beginning.

Then I showed up. As kids, we don't really understand our parents' lives. It must have been difficult for my parents to juggle their responsibilities, but all I remember are happy times, evenings in the park, and painting wildflowers with my dad on the walls of my bedroom.

My mother ran for governor when I was nine years old. I knew she wanted to win, but for me it meant she wasn't home as much. My father cut back his hours in the studio, but he was home less too. I saw a lot more of my grandparents on my dad's side, who came to stay often, liked my friends, and took me swimming almost every day.

My mother became governor. We moved into the governor's mansion, which was fine. We bought a small ranch with a little fishing pond, a few horses, and a herd of real Texas Longhorns, which was great. The folks who worked the ranch treated me like I was a kid, not the governor's daughter, which was even better. We spent many weekends and vacations there. The ranch was the place where politics didn't reach us.

I was a fairly normal kid in school. I had friends. I got good grades. I played water polo. I rode horses. Looking back, I can see that my parents made a big effort to let me have a normal life even though we lived in the governor's house.

Then came the scandal, and everything changed. During my mother's third year in office, charges were brought against her for embezzlement. The Justice Department accused her of having accepted gifts from several businesses in return for using her power to help them. The way it was explained to me by my parents, my mother got caught in the middle of some business deals and ended up being the scapegoat. My father called her a naive idealist. I never knew the whole story. But instead of running for a second term as governor, my mother was sentenced to a two-year jail term, with a chance for early parole in eighteen months.

My dad and I moved to a small apartment, and my mother went to jail. We sold half the ranch and rarely visited the half we still owned. We got lots of intense media attention. I never had a day at school without someone making a hurtful remark. I stopped having friends.

It was a two-hour trip to the prison. The Texloop gets you close, but then it's forty-five minutes by car. My father worked Mondays, Tuesdays, Thursdays, and Fridays. On Saturdays, he took a break, though sometimes the two of us would spend the day in his studio, each making our own art. On Wednesdays and Sundays, my father visited my mother in jail, and on the Sunday visits, I was expected to go with him. For fourteen months, I rode with my father every Sunday to visit my mother in prison. Until one weekend, the one

Sunday I didn't go. A new girl had moved into the apartment building and invited me to a sleepover on Saturday night. Thrilled that I was willing to make a friend, my father allowed me to change our normal routine and promised me my mother would understand. Because I wasn't going, he set an earlier alarm.

That early Sunday morning is when the accident happened. Some idiot out for a joyride in an old-fashioned, human-driven car smashed into my dad. Officially, they said the driver was so erratic that Dad's car didn't have a chance. Unofficially, I know the public transport cars at that Texloop stop are poorly maintained. No one uses them except those headed to the prison. The nearby solar farm has its own private fleet.

Whatever the cause of the accident, my father was killed. The media couldn't get enough of the story, of the photos of my father's ruined car side by side with a photo of my mother being led away in handcuffs.

My parents' friends packed up everything in our apartment and moved me to our ranch, where my grandparents stayed with me until my mother was released from jail. I hated people figuring out who I was and looking at me. I chopped off most of my hair, dyed it strawberry blonde, and wore glasses to try to be invisible. My father's psychiatrist and art therapy friends came to visit, then gave me appointments with colleagues. I talked, but I refused to draw.

My name stayed mostly out of the news until about a month after my mother's release. Old friends from the town near our ranch invited me to a slumber party. I thought they were trying to be nice. In spite of everything that had happened, I was still a naive fourteen-year-old. The twin girls who invited a handful of us to their home offered me my first beer. Which led to a second one. I thought I was being welcomed into a circle of friends. I thought other people liked me even while I was hating myself.

But it was all a setup. As we partied in their backyard, the twins let several girls take photos from an upstairs window. The one of me holding a beer, sopping wet from standing under the fake waterfall in their backyard, was the one that went viral first. Some photos of children are illegal, but a photo of me acting like I was partying away in a wet T-shirt contest was apparently fine and showed up everywhere. Now I was making the news as much as my parents. The ex-governor's daughter gone wild with her father fresh in the grave and her mother just released from prison. I will never forgive those who paired that image with an image of me standing at my father's gravesite—another moment that was supposed to be private.

I didn't deal well. I had three months of behavior I'd rather not spell out though it was accurately reported. Fortunately, I survived and came out clean. My mother sees it as a miracle. My grandfather says I was too stubborn to die. Mostly, I think it was luck. That and the love of a few people who refused to give up on me.

My mother offered to send me to a boarding school, though she really didn't want to let me out of her sight. I didn't want to leave her either. We hunkered down together out on the ranch for a year of homeschooling. The first four months went well. But then there was an accident, a stupid bike accident on my part, though the press tried to make it into more. It wasn't a suicide attempt, it wasn't because of a relapse, and it wasn't part of a conspiracy against my family. It was just an accident. But it was a bad accident. I ended up in a Houston hospital, and my family ended up back in the news.

My mother and I decided it didn't make sense to hide out. She said we were stronger than that; she said my father wouldn't have wanted it. And she was right.

You can see the scars on my back from the bike accident, but they've healed now. When they were still bright red and swollen, I returned to the ranch. A few weeks later, I started going to the local school. My mother started meeting with people who wanted to hire her as a consultant. She began sleeping regularly again, and I tried to do the same. And that's how things were until I ended up here.

I asked all of you what was your last memory from Earth, so I think it's only fair to share mine. It's of me and my mother planting flowers. My father is buried in New Braunfels. However, my mother created a stone monument to him on the ranch. It's hard to explain, but it's beautiful and rugged, just like Dad.

Mom and I decided to put flowers around his monument—his favorite wildflowers and flowering cacti. My last memory is the two of us planting, working together in the red-brown soil. I remember thinking how much I loved both my parents, and then feeling sad, angry, guilty ... all those emotions that too easily take control. I hugged my mom but ran for the safety of the house. That's the last thing I remember.

When our landing party arrived, I wanted to be someone else, someone better. Lorelei was my grandmother's name, my maternal grandmother, the one I never met, the one who died while my mother was in Spain. I had planned to use her maiden name too, but when I realized everyone here went by first names, it made my deception even easier.

I wanted to be Lorelei, colonist of a new planet, instead of Leigh Crawford, who came with all this baggage. I thought it would make me a better person. But if I have become a better person, it is because of the people I've made my home with these past few months. It is because of all of you. I'm sorry now that I didn't tell you the truth right away. I'm sorry that as you told me your stories, I did not tell you mine. I hope you can forgive me.

Lorelei Leigh Crawford

She started to review the words, as she would've done for a normal entry, but stopped. She'd said what needed to be said. Her hands shook a little as she closed the notebook and searched for a loose scrap of paper. On it, she wrote:

Ada and Rose,
I'm off to see what's not yet been seen.
Please read this while I'm gone. And share it with everyone.
– Lorelei

She left the message on top of the notebook, weighted down by a small rock, then turned off the lantern and walked back to her cabin in the dark.

CHAPTER 37

arly the next morning, fifty-three colonists stood on Sunrise Beach and watched the other six set sail toward daybreak. As the figures on the beach grew smaller, Lex tried not to worry about everyone they'd left behind.

He glanced around the raft at his companions: Michele, Lorelei, Olu, Marko, and Noah. The raft could've held two more, but no one else had volunteered. Lex had no misgivings. Having six people aboard instead of eight made the raft less crowded, and he couldn't have picked better shipmates.

The raft was well stocked. With two storage areas, they had enough space for over a dozen canteens, plus a bucket for collecting rainwater. In addition to medical supplies, they carried a stash of water purification tablets, dried seaweed, and some fishing gear.

They'd packed plenty of Foobrew vials, both full and empty. Noah had suggested using bunches of empty vials as floats, and other Boats members had perfected the design. The crew had two floats that could be tied around a person's chest in case someone had to go into dangerous waters. It looked ridiculous, but it worked.

Eventually, they could no longer see the island. Nothing but sea and sky in all directions. It was the biggest raft they'd ever built, and with the sail in the middle, it was the sturdiest too. Lex gripped his paddle a little more tightly. Looking at all that water made the raft feel tiny.

The first day was uneventful except for one mishap. Noah tested the tether and float system, and the equipment worked fine, but he sliced his foot climbing back on the raft. It was a deep, clean cut. Not terrible, but not nothing.

Lorelei claimed Noah's injury was a good omen; they were bound to have one piece of bad luck, and now it was over. Michele's approach was more practical: she told Noah to keep his foot out of the water. On Earth, blood attracted sharks. Who knew what sea creatures might be attracted to blood on Marjol?

Nightfall arrived, and it was Lex's turn at the sail. The six of them spent the first hour of darkness double-checking the ropes and reviewing navigation. The cluster of stars they called the Jellyfish could guide them fairly well, especially with triangulation the second half of the night. Besides, heading "toward daybreak" wasn't exactly a precise set of directions. No reason to get worried about slight deviations along the way.

A few hours later, it was Lex's turn to sleep. The ocean was calm. He was tired, and his blanket was warm. But his sleep was fitful. The floor moved underneath, the universe spread out above, and the ocean extended in all directions.

He'd never felt so small.

* * *

It was easier to sleep during daylight without the Milky Way staring at you. Lex managed a few hours of rest early the next morning, until Marko nudged him awake. A small storm was approaching, one they couldn't avoid.

Michele reminded them to tether up as she and Noah rolled up the sail and tied it down, and Olu double-checked the storage compartments. Lorelei took off her lucky hat and stashed it in a bag, assuring everyone the hat's luck would still work. They were as ready for bad weather as they could get.

When the storm hit, Lex was surprised at its ferocity. He wondered if both girls were thinking the same as he—this was nothing compared to the storm that'd hit them months ago, and they were still at its mercy. Michele issued orders periodically, but in truth, the six of them were simply holding on and waiting for the storm to pass.

After about twenty tiring minutes, the wind and the rain lessened. "Wave!'" shouted Olu, and Lex saw it too.

"Hang on!" yelled Michele as the giant wave swamped them.

Half the crew was swept overboard: Olu, Marko, and Noah all went in the water.

But the tethers held. Noah was closest to the raft and managed to pull himself back using the rope. With help from Michele, he climbed aboard. The process reopened the wound on his foot, but Noah shrugged it off, saying, "Get them first."

"His tether broke!" cried Lorelei. She pointed at Olu, who was floating farther away.

A quick look at Marko's rope showed it was fraying too. The ocean swells lessened, but the rain and wind increased.

Michele took off her tether and began tying it to the spare rope. "Grab a float!" she said to Lex. "Tie it on me!" His fingers worked as quickly as possible.

"Noah," said Michele. "Get ready. I need you to pull me in when I get to Olu."

"Finished," said Lex as the float was secured.

"Get Marko!" Michele shouted at Lex. "You and Lor, get Marko!" With no further words, she dove in the water, the extended rope tied roughly around her ankle.

Lorelei was already pulling at Marko's tether, and Lex joined her. It was a race to haul him in before the rope snapped under the tension. They could see Marko's head bobbing in the waves; little by little he came closer. Lex kept his attention on the task, smoothly pulling at the rope, trying not to think about what was happening on the other side of the raft.

"She's got him!" Noah called.

"Hurry," Lex said to Lorelei.

With a final heave, they managed to get Marko a body length away. A wave crashed over them, but they held firmly to the rope, and Marko remained nearby. He swam over and grabbed the side of the raft.

"Go," gasped Marko.

"I got him," said Lorelei.

The winds flattened Lex when he tried to stand, so he crawled across the raft, slowly making his way to where Noah strained at the remaining tether. Out amid the choppy waves, Michele had Olu in a rescue hold, but she struggled to keep their heads above water.

In his periphery, Lex saw Lorelei help Marko onto the raft, where he leaned over the edge and promptly threw up. Lex had to trust she would take care of him.

The raft was holding together, but Lex's hands and knees scraped against the rough wood as he finally made it to the other side, then grabbed the rope to help Noah. Michele's tether remained intact, all the hastily tied knots secure for now, but the ocean was pulling hard against them. He and Noah hauled on the rope, and it barely moved. Michele and Olu remained seven or eight body lengths away.

The wind grew calmer, but hail began to fall.

"Less wind!" shouted Noah.

Lex nodded. They continued to pull on the rope hand over hand, bit by bit as little pellets of ice fell from the sky. He wanted to say, *What next?*, but there was no time for talk as the hail stung their skin.

He could barely see Michele and Olu through the ice and rain.

On the other side of the raft, Marko threw up again.

"He's okay!" yelled Lorelei over the hailstorm.

A wave swallowed Michele and Olu. "Hold tight!" yelled Noah, and Lex strained against the ocean as it tried to pull the lifeline from their hands. His arms shook, but the rope held, and his friends once again appeared bobbing in the waves.

"Now!" said Noah, and slowly—ever so slowly—the rope moved under their hands, closer and closer, finally bringing Michele and Olu to the edge of the raft.

"Help him," said Michele as Lex and Noah hauled them in. The hail slowed. A few last chunks of ice fell from the sky and then stopped.

Olu's eyes were half-closed, his face ashen, as if the ocean had drained the richer colors from his skin. His ragged breathing could be heard over the waves, and his fingers gripped the raft the way a sick baby clings to his mother. But Olu was alive.

The rain fell lightly, and the waves subsided. The storm was disappearing as quickly as it had arrived.

Michele coughed up water but was breathing fine. More worrisome was her ankle, rubbed raw with a deep cut from the hastily tied rope.

Noah's foot was worse. There was a lot of blood and no time to dig out bandages. Lex took off his shirt and wrapped it around the gushing wound while Noah bent over Olu, thumping lightly on his back and talking in words too soft for anyone else to hear.

Olu convulsed and threw up. Unlike the others, he had no control over his actions; the spasms wracked his body. On that part of the raft, it was an awful mix of Olu's vomit and Noah's blood.

Fortunately, Olu's desperate movements lasted briefly. He stopped throwing up; his breathing became more regular.

"She'll be right, mate," said Noah, clasping Olu on the shoulder and visibly heaving a sigh of relief.

"What can I do?" Lex asked Michele.

"The ropes," she shook her head, "they couldn't take the extra pressure."

"Don't worry," said Lex. "Everyone's all right." He helped her untie the float from her body.

Lorelei sat holding Marko, whose eyes were bloodshot but otherwise looked fine. Noah helped Olu move to another section of the raft, over by Michele, away from the blood and vomit.

Lex grabbed the bucket, full of ocean water and rain, and washed the disgusting mess off the raft. A few more bucketfuls and the raft was clean.

The clouds passed and Rán appeared. It seemed almost farcical that a few minutes ago they'd almost drowned. Olu stuck his head over the side of the raft and dunked it. He spat out salt water, then rolled over and lay there.

Lex was shell-shocked, his muscles tense. It had all happened so fast. "We need to treat that foot," he said to Noah.

"I reckon it can wait a few minutes." The shirt-wrap bandage had turned a nasty purple-brown and was dripping blood. Noah gently swung the injured foot over the edge of the raft and into the salt water.

"You don't want to attract sharks," said Michele. "Or whatever the hell on this planet acts like sharks."

"No worries," he said. "Give it a sec. Everyone catch their breath." Noah kept his foot in the water and gingerly unwrapped the bloody shirt.

Olu leaned back over the edge of the raft, dunked his face in the water again, and ran his hands over his wet hair. When he sat up, he was right next to Michele.

"Thank you," Olu said to her. "Thank you." He touched a hand to Michele's ankle where the rope had injured it. "Don't ever, ever do that again."

"It's not your job to tell me what to do."

"You're right," said Olu. "I'm sorry. You're the captain. You're—"

Michele interrupted him with a kiss.

Olu held Michele's face. He touched his nose and forehead to hers for a long moment, and then he kissed her back.

Lex sat in stunned silence. Marko gave him a subtle thumbs up, and Lorelei cracked a smile, as the three of them tried to be as unobtrusive as possible while sharing a small raft.

But Noah was having none of that attitude. He let out a whoop loud enough to chase away any shark-like creature or lingering storm clouds.

Michele laughed, then leaned closer to Olu and kissed him again.

"About damn time, mates!" said Noah. "It's about damn time."

CHAPTER 38

Two evenings later, the convivial atmosphere on the raft continued, albeit in a more subdued manner. Noah's foot and Michele's ankle were healing, and no more storms had crossed their path.

The six travelers had settled into a routine. Two people would sleep while two others worked the sail and rudder. The remaining two would scan the ocean for danger, paddle when needed, and take care of other chores. This evening, it was Lex and Noah. With less than an hour of daylight left, the two of them were squinting into the distance, hoping for a sign of land.

"See anything?" asked Michele from her spot at the helm.

"Heaps and heaps of water," said Noah.

"How helpful."

"You asked."

"Anything else?"

"Reckon you'd be the first to know," said Noah with a grin.

"Nah," said Lex, "if you see anything, don't tell Michele."

"All right, all right," she laughed. "I deserved that."

Lex and Noah resumed staring at what appeared to be an endless body of water. They were not necessarily the best combination of people for the task—the other four had more patience—but Michele kept the pairs shifting so that everyone worked with everyone else.

After four days and three nights on the raft, they could've easily gotten on one another's nerves. But none of that happened. Michele kept them united.

Olu deserved some of the credit too. From the first moment of the voyage, he'd made it clear Michele was the captain. On land, Olu had been their leader since day one. It was different out here on the ocean: Michele was the boss.

Lex was still getting used to their renewed relationship. Olu and Michele had seemed meant for each other since their first days on the planet. But Lex had watched circumstances rip them apart.

It'd been a very public, very dramatic breakup. Most people placed the blame on Olu. But Lex knew it wasn't that simple. He too had struggled with Michele's Pollyanna attitude after the epidemic. Michele had a faith in the cosmos that life would work out as it was supposed to, and such faith changed the way she grieved. It prevented her from understanding Olu's self-blame or helping Olu get past it. It prevented her from understanding that Olu could never again be the same person he was before. And it prevented Olu from understanding that Michele could be.

At least, that'd been true six months ago. Somehow, they'd both found a way to understand the other. Somehow, they'd both found a way to forgive.

Lex had not seen it coming, and he knew them as well as anyone.

"Noah," said Michele. "Why don't you take a break and double-check the storage areas. If we have enough empty Foobrew vials, go ahead and make another float."

"Aye, aye, captain," said Noah, complete with a mock salute.

"And me?" asked Lex.

"Keep looking for land," she said. "I want a sharp lookout until dark."

Lex resumed peering at the waves, training his eye along the horizon, hoping the horizon would change.

***

Despite his best attempts at squinting into the distance, no island—with or without a tall tree—appeared. Four days and no sign of land.

However, as dusk settled over the raft, a wondrous but monstrous sight appeared: a glitterblob. Even with the fading light, its skin glowed with shifting, luminous colors.

Michele and Lorelei were at the sail and rudder; they expertly maneuvered to within two raft-lengths of the creature and paralleled its course. Lex woke up Olu and Marko so that no one would miss it. But when the glitterblob shifted direction, Lex realized they'd have a companion for a while. It was heading the same way they were.

Oddly, no one else seemed worried about their proximity to the monster—and monster it was. The glitterblob's body extended far below the surface, making it easily the size of two hundred humans, twice as large as they'd previously guessed. Or maybe this glitterblob was particularly huge.

It didn't have a head or tail. They could discern no eyes or nose or even a mouth. Those features might be below the surface. Or perhaps it did not see or breathe in ways they could understand.

Without a discernable difference between the two ends of the glitterblob, they found themselves using the labels front and back based on the direction it was moving. Lorelei was the first to point out that fallacy.

"Maybe it always moves backwards," she said.

"Then the back is the front anyway," said Marko.

"It may not have a back or a front at all," said Noah.

Lex rubbed his forehead. The philosophy could wait. "Don't get too close to the tentacles," he said.

"What do you think they're for?" asked Lorelei.

The tentacles were arranged in circular patterns on the creature's sides; thin and translucent, they extended at least a meter. Whatever the tentacles' purpose, Lex wished they were farther away.

"Propulsion?" said Michele.

"Eating?" suggested Marko.

"Herbivore or carnivore?" asked Noah.

"Whatever it is," said Olu, "it's magnificent."

"You're only a raft length away," said Lex.

Michele and Lorelei swung the raft out to three times that distance. The glitterblob didn't change course or respond in any way. Lex couldn't help but think about the potential disaster if the mysterious creature came up under their raft. It would not need to intend harm to do so.

"That's better," said Marko. "We don't want to hurt it."

Lex almost scoffed at the remark, but the earnestness in Marko's voice held him back. The others must have heard it too, because no one replied.

Eventually, Marko added, "I worry about what we're doing here. Us showing up on this planet. Are we damaging things … hurting these creatures or ones we don't know about? I mean, we put tablets in the water to be sure we can drink it, but maybe that's poisoning it for something else. What if humans don't belong here?"

Lex wanted to say it was too late for those questions, but he knew the observation—true though it may be—would not assuage Marko's worries.

Fortunately, Michele had a more useful perspective. "I think we're all connected," she said. "All of us in this big, crazy universe."

"Really?" asked Marko.

"Sure. Take this beautiful creature." Michele gestured toward the glitterblob. "It's not a whale, but it could definitely be related to *Takaroa*, the god of the oceans."

"Makes sense," said Lorelei, "that a god of the oceans could be for all oceans in the galaxy."

"In *te reo*—" started Michele.

"The Māori language," interrupted Lorelei.

"Yes, my friend," Michele replied with a smile. "In *te reo*, the word for whale is *tohora*. They're the direct descendants of *Takaroa*, the ocean god. It is said the greatest Māori sailors each had a special *tohora*—one who was their guardian spirit and kept them safe while at sea."

"That explains it," said Lorelei. "This glitterblob is your guardian spirit, Michele."

"You're calling her one of the greatest Māori sailors?" asked Noah.

"No doubt about that!"

"Indisputable," said Olu.

"I don't know," teased Noah, "anyone here know *another* Māori sailor?"

"One is enough!" said Lorelei.

"Also indisputable," said Olu.

Michele laughed, but she looked pleased.

"Got to admit," said Lorelei to Michele, "you did make it across the arroyo."

"Even though there was still some flooding," replied Michele.

What?

Both girls laughed.

Noah called them to task. "No inside jokes."

"Sorry," said Lorelei. But as they settled back into their normal routine, neither girl appeared the least repentant.

Their banter had lightened Marko's mood. He was still contemplating the glitterblob, but his expression was one of admiration, not concern.

Dusk turned into darkness. For the first hour of nightfall, the glitterblob continued alongside them, or they continued alongside it. Lex wasn't sure which was more accurate. And then, with no warning and no visible movement, the creature dove into the ocean depths and vanished from view. Guardian spirit or not, Lex was glad to see it go. The six of them were out here on their own. Best to remember that.

***

Morning brought new wonders and new worries. They'd been looking for an island. They found an archipelago.

Bits of land stretched in front of them as far to the left and right as Lex could see. The island directly ahead looked smaller than their own island, but even from a distance, he could tell others were larger. And dozens were tiny, the kind you could explore in less than a day.

The sight was dizzying. Welcome, certainly, but in an overpowering way, as if his senses had forgotten what it felt like to have a horizon filled by more than water.

"Lex," said Michele, "your turn at the sail; I'm taking the helm. Noah and Olu, you're on break."

"Not sure anyone needs to sleep right now," said Noah.

"Depends on where we're going." Michele grabbed the rudder from him. "Do we land on the island in front of us? Do we sail down the archipelago and look for a tall tree? Thoughts?"

"Sunrise. Two islands. Tall trees," said Marko, looking far to the right of the island in front of them.

"Exactly," said Noah, staring the same direction. "We got it wrong."

"Got what wrong?" asked Michele.

"The translation," said Noah. "Two islands, not the second island. Trees not tree."

"Two islands," echoed Michele.

"I see them," said Lorelei.

"I guess we know where to go," said Olu.

Lex had been busy situating himself to control the sail, but now he looked into the distance. It took him a moment to understand what the others had seen: a pair of islands with giant forests. Two islands with tall trees.

"Change of plans," said Michele. "Olu, Lor, Noah, all of you try to nap. I want us rested when we land, and it'll take us a while to get there. Lex and I will manage the raft. Marko can be our extra set of eyes."

Michele gave the command to turn starboard, and Lex adjusted the sail. Half the crew was already following captain's orders to get some sleep.

Lex was glad not to be one of them. He looked over at Marko, whose face couldn't quite hide his excitement. Michele wasn't even trying to hide hers.

"Ready," said Lex, a wide smile breaking across his face.

They tacked. The sail caught the wind. And the two forested islands drew nearer.

* * *

It was past midday by the time they reached the first island. Brief consideration was given to passing it by, but if the Korean directions were designed to send them to a pair of islands, those who left the message could be on either one.

Besides, they were all more than ready to get off the raft.

Michele had divided up tasks and given instructions long before they got close to shore. No talking. Eyes and ears open for danger.

Approaching the island was like entering a different world. The towering trees looked to be a mixture of palm, pine, and moss; they were like nothing Lex had ever seen. The island itself was relatively flat with long, sloping sandy beaches, few rocks, and shallow water extending off the coast.

As they left deeper water behind, Noah and Michele rolled up the sail and fastened it down. Lex and Marko stood on the front two corners of the raft and paddled. The water was calm. They neared the island with slow, decisive strokes.

Soon they were close to shore. Marko lifted his paddle out of the water and silently set it down beside him. Lex did the same. He heard Lorelei and Olu slide into the waist-deep water to push them into shore. The rest of them focused their attention on scanning the shoreline. The trees were magnificent, but the forest was dense. If anyone wanted to hide, Lex doubted he'd see them until they left the forest for the beach.

A scream pierced the air. It took him a second to realize the scream came from behind.

"Help!" cried Lorelei again, as Noah hauled her onto the raft. Olu shoved the raft onto the beach and ran out of the water, pulling off his pants and frantically but methodically brushing at his legs.

Noah was doing the same to Lorelei's legs as she ripped off her shirt and began swiping at her torso.

"Get the gloves!" yelled Noah.

"And the antihist," said Olu.

Tiny square jellyfish-like things were clinging to Olu and Lorelei and were scattered around the raft. Marko dug out the first aid supplies and handed Noah some gloves. He threw a pair to Michele as well.

"Get off the raft." Michele pulled on the gloves and leapt to help Olu.

As Lex waited for Marko to find the antihist, he helped Lorelei try to stand.

"Legs won't work," she said in a garbled voice.

Lex grabbed her and carried her to the beach. She had hives erupting all over her body, and her face was pink. Noah's hands were swelling. He gave up on the gloves as he and Lex tried to remove the slippery little beasts. The creatures didn't look like much, but each touch stung worse than a hornet.

"Lie down," Noah said to her. "Stay still. If there's venom, we don't want it to travel quickly."

"I think that's all of 'em," said Lex.

"Here." Marko laid down a towel. "Put her on this." He held out an antihist tablet. "Take this," he said to Lorelei.

Unable to grip the medicine with her swollen fingers, she opened her mouth for the tablet as Lex and Noah moved her to the towel and checked for any tiny clear creatures they'd missed.

Marko looked at the boys' swollen hands and gave them each an antihist as well. He ran over to Olu.

"I'm all right," said Olu.

"Take it," said Michele.

Olu agreed to their ministrations, but only after he walked over and sat down next to Lorelei. "How is she?" he asked.

Lex shook his head, a fearful pressure building in his chest. "Give her another pill," he said to Marko.

Marko tried the same approach as before, but Lorelei's lips and face were swelling. Michele ran to the raft and grabbed a Foobrew. "Thanks," said Marko, crushing two of the tablets and mixing them in a vial.

Lex held one of Lorelei's swollen hands in his own. He propped her against his chest, holding her upright so Marko could get some of the antihistamine-laced Foobrew down her throat. It worked.

However, one glance at Olu made it clear Lorelei was much worse off. Olu's legs were covered in small red dots, but the rest of him looked normal. In contrast, Lorelei's entire body had erupted with large red welts, her hands were swollen almost beyond recognition, and her face was puffy.

"Keep talking," said Lex, forcing his voice to be calm.

"Can't. Bre ..." was all she managed.

"Hang in there, my friend," said Michele, kneeling right beside her. "The antihistamine should help any minute now."

Lorelei closed her eyes.

"You promised!" said Lex.

Her eyes opened, but she didn't speak.

"Don't abandon me," he whispered.

He felt her swollen hand clench his own. She moved her lips, but no words came out. He could see the swelling around her mouth taking on a blueish tinge.

"Ah hell!" Noah leapt up and raced for the raft.

A second later, he shouted, "Marko, catch."

"Epineph-injector," said Marko. "It might hurt." And he jammed a long needle into Lorelei's thigh. Her leg jumped; Lex held her.

"Come on, Lor," said Michele, "we're all here. We all love you. We all need you. Breathe. Please. Breathe."

As if on command, Lorelei gasped for air.

"It's all right," said Michele. "Slow breaths, that's it, slow breaths. Relax. It's all right." Michele looked at Lex, and he was unashamed of the tears sliding down his face. "Lex, why don't you lie our girl down on the towel so she can rest."

He did as Michele bid him but kept ahold of Lorelei's hand. His own hand hurt, so he couldn't imagine how hers felt, but it wasn't in him to let go. He'd been worried about the big monsters—the glitterblobs, the ones he could see. But the little unseen monsters had turned out to be more dangerous. He should've known.

"I'll get her some fresh clothes," said Michele. She leaned on Lex's shoulder, squeezed it hard, then pushed herself upright.

Lex nodded, his attention on Lorelei.

In less than half a minute, her face was returning to normal and her breathing, though a bit wheezy, was otherwise regular. Noah's quick thinking had saved her life.

Marko remained on the sand next to her, his hand tightly gripped around the empty epineph-injector.

"You did it," Lex said to him.

Marko stared at him, color slowly returning to his face.

"Uh, mates!" called Noah from the beached raft. "We've got company."

Lorelei lay on the towel while the rest of them turned in Noah's direction. A wiry brown-skinned girl walked toward them. Her mouth was set in a hard line. A steely glare gave her a look of ferocity, accentuated by two distinctive marks: a jagged red scar down one arm and a black birthmark covering half her face. She looked Indian, not Korean.

She had a bag over her shoulder, well-worn but recognizable, the same type of dark-blue bag they'd all been issued. Her feet were bare; she wore a ripped shirt that might once have been yellow and a pair of faded blue-striped boxer shorts.

The unknown girl walked closer. She held out her right hand in a fist as if to challenge them. Noah stepped off the raft to intercept her; Michele stood by him.

"Here," said the girl, opening her hand to reveal an epineph-injector. "It often takes two doses."

CHAPTER 39

Only a few stars peeked through the canopy of trees. Even the moonlight was kept at bay by the closely packed foliage. All was not dark, however, as a few rocks glowed nearby.

Leigh vaguely remembered the girl from the beach, Kala, explaining about the rocks, but the details were a blur. Min-seo, the island's only other inhabitant, had put one of the glowing rocks in Leigh's hand. It weighed almost nothing; that was all she could remember.

Leigh rubbed her eyes and sat up slowly. For the first time since being stung, she wasn't dizzy. Her body felt like it'd been attacked by a giant sea monster instead of flimsy squares the size of her thumbnail. But she could breathe, and she could move, and now she could see.

They were in a natural alcove of dirt and stone surrounded by forest. The air smelled like wet soil and moss with a hint of pine. A trickle of water ran over the far side of the rocky outcropping and dripped down into a pool. Leigh thought it was a natural spring, but perhaps the rainwater gathered there as well. It was too dark to be sure.

Nearby, a small campfire encircled with stones had burned down to glowing embers. Lying near the fire, Olu was the only one awake. Leigh felt silly waving to him, but he acknowledged her silent greeting with a wave in her direction. His back rested flush against Michele's.

The others slept surrounding Leigh—Lex and Marko on either side, Noah on the ground near her feet. She stared at Lex. His face was hidden in the darkness, but she could see the gentle rise and fall of his chest as he slept. He had shouted at her not to abandon him, carried her into the forest, and stayed next to her ever since.

She didn't have the energy to think about it.

Her gaze shifted to the two girls who lived on the island, both of them curled up on the forest floor. Leigh had caught only snatches of the evening's conversation, but she remembered the basics of Kala and Min-seo's story. They were fugitives, having escaped a colony out of Leigh's worst nightmares.

Elsewhere in the archipelago, there was, indeed, another colony of teenagers. Kala, Min-seo, and eighteen others had been in the second landing party. Upon arrival, they'd been met by the seventeen surviving members of the first one, including the colony's leader, Terence. He was a bully. Members of his landing party said Terence had been power hungry since day one, then grown progressively harsher, especially after the techs stopped working and one of the colonists drowned.

When the second landing party arrived, they were initiated into Terence's regime. Everyone coped one way or another. Some joined Terence's inner circle, and one became his girlfriend. The rest survived.

Kala befriended Jack, one of the older boys among the initial colonists, the one most opposed to Terence. Kala and Jack had something in common: they saw escape as the only option. And Jack had the knowledge to make it happen. He and two others, Jenny and Ping, had been skilled with the techs before they stopped working. They'd done what was commanded but kept some research to themselves—including the precise locations of the other four colonies on the planet.

When Jack shared this intel with Kala, she began planning a way to leave. The colony had built a handful of small "boats"—two big logs tied together. These were often unattended, simply pulled up on shore and left there. Terence kept the carefully carved paddles in his cabin, not realizing there was a chance of escape using paddles less perfect than those. So Kala took advantage of the error. She hoarded paddle-sized flat pieces of wood and stashed them in a secret spot.

Min-seo began to take an active role in the escape plan too. The rebels wanted a secret way to communicate, one that Terence and his followers wouldn't understand. That's why Min-seo began teaching Korean to her cohorts—rudimentary knowledge, enough to write a few words and pass along basic information. They didn't know if it would be useful, but it gave them something productive to do instead of feeling helpless.

They lived one day at a time. Kala and Jack urged everyone to get ready to make a run for it, but people were scared. Things were bad, but bad enough to take such a risk?

Little by little, things got worse. They gathered more wood and learned more Korean. And little by little, plans for an escape gained momentum.

Then tragedy occurred. A plague infected the group. Two girls died, and several other colonists came close.

Terence tightened his grip. Fearful that the dwindling number of females meant they'd have difficulty populating the colony, he began preaching to the girls about their duty to produce babies. He threatened to force the issue if necessary.

According to Kala, it was the insistence on reproduction that produced clear battle lines. Either you were with Terence or against him. No more space for a middle ground. The colonists who had opposed Terence had been moved to a well-guarded prison cabin and forced to do most of the work.

Leigh must have slept through the girls' story at that point. She couldn't remember how long they'd been prisoners or what that existence had been like. She vaguely remembered something about the water supply in connection to pregnancy, but she didn't know what. She did remember one thing that was obvious: Min-seo was now six months pregnant.

She also remembered the girls talking about people's change of heart once they became prisoners. They had a new goal: wait for the twenty members of the third landing party and have them help take down Terence's gang by whatever means necessary.

That plan had sustained them ... until it fell apart. The third landing party never arrived.

Hope was replaced by despair, which gave way to desperation. They tried to escape, and it was a disaster. Only six out of fifteen even made it from the prison cabin to the shore.

Those six split up into three pairs, each twosome grabbing one of the small two-log boats. Jack and Ping were captured, but Kala and Min-seo escaped, along with the other pair, Sahir and Grace. The four escapees found their way to open water and turned left, paddling with the strong current that flows alongside the archipelago. Eventually, they took refuge on the forested island.

For three days and three nights, they kept a lookout for others. But neither friends nor enemies arrived.

Despite their fear of leaving the archipelago, the four fugitives were determined to find another colony, maybe even get help for their friends. The next morning, they left the forested island and paddled out onto the open ocean. But once again, disaster struck. Stormy weather separated the two pairs that first night. Tossed by wind and waves, Kala and Min-seo hung on to their boat and to each other. They weren't sure how, but somehow, they survived.

The storm passed, they climbed back onto the logs, and the two girls thanked the heavens their boat remained intact. They huddled together, anxiously awaiting the dawn.

In the morning light, there was no sign of Sahir or Grace.

Emotionally numb from all that had happened, Kala and Min-seo faced a grim reality—their paddles had been lost to the storm, and they'd been blown back near the forested island. There was nothing to do but return and regroup.

Their bad luck continued: Min-seo fell ill. By the time she recovered, the two girls were well established on the island. They'd also deduced that Min-seo was pregnant. They stayed a bit longer. And the longer they stayed, the harder it was to decide to leave.

The two girls had been alone on the forested island for 117 days. For 116 of those days, they'd seen no one. Then came day 117, and they'd heard Leigh's scream.

Seeing her plight, Kala had offered medical supplies without hesitation.

That was worth remembering.

Leigh stretched her arms over her head and ran her fingertips across the moss-covered ledge. Her muscles rebelled, but move she must. Bodily necessities prompted her to seek a private place in the woods.

She hadn't taken more than five steps before Olu stirred. Five more steps, and he was beside her.

"I'm going to pee," she whispered.

"I'm coming with you."

"Really?"

"Yes."

Olu stayed closer than she would've liked but farther away than he would've preferred. When Leigh walked back in his direction, she noticed he was holding one of the glowing rocks.

"What's up with those?" she asked.

"The glows?"

"Yeah," said Leigh. "Must've slept through that."

"You want to sit?"

"Yeah. Thanks."

They sat at the foot of two large tree trunks that had grown together. Looking around the forest, Leigh noticed similar trees with braided trunks. She'd have to inspect them more closely in the daylight. Rose would want to know the details.

"How long till morning?" Leigh asked.

"Not sure," said Olu. "Hard to tell in here. I'm guessing a couple more hours. How're you feeling?"

"Much less dizzy."

"My legs hurt. Can't imagine what yours feel like."

"Can't complain." Leigh leaned against the tree. "Especially after hearing what Kala and Min-seo have been through."

"You were awake?"

"Some," she said. "I still don't understand why they were looking for us. Heading for our colony."

"Kala says we're the closest one. The other three colonies are much farther away."

"On the continent?"

"Two are on the continent. One is on an island not far off the continent's coast. All three are near each other but far away from us.

Turns out we're in the northern hemisphere. The other three colonies are all south, if words like north and south even mean anything here."

"The other three …"

"I know."

"So many of us."

"Not really," said Olu. "Not if no more landing parties are showing up."

"You think they won't?"

"I worry they won't."

Leigh worried the same thing. She stretched her legs and immediately regretted the movement. Everything hurt.

"Who left the message in the cave?" she asked.

"It must've been their friends, Sahir and Grace. Or at least one of them. Who else could it be?"

"Didn't Sahir and Grace drown?"

"They thought so. Until yesterday."

"Hmm." No telling how long Sahir and Grace had been in the cave. No way to know if they were still alive. "It's like you told me the first day," she said. "There's no reassurance about anything."

"You and Lex always throw that back in my face."

Leigh tried to smile, but even her face hurt. "Doesn't mean you weren't right," she conceded.

"Now I know you don't feel well," said Olu.

She did smile at that. "Tell me about the glowing rocks," said Leigh.

"Kala and Min-seo call them glows." He handed her one. "They're from the lanterns."

She examined the glow. It wasn't a rock at all. Lightweight, egg-shaped, and coated with what felt like little grains of sand on an otherwise smooth surface, the glow was aptly named. Its texture reminded her of the chairs in the cabins.

"From the lanterns?" she asked.

"I'll show you when everyone's awake. It's simple when you know how. There are five glows in each lantern. The glows themselves are solar powered. Leave them out in the sun during the day, and they light up all night. The darker it is, the brighter they shine. Or you can put them in a lantern so that you have an on/off switch."

"But we never keep the lanterns in the sun."

"No need, the glows charge automatically when they're left in a lantern."

"Ah," said Leigh. "How did Kala and Min-seo figure it out?"

"Same way they knew where we were," said Olu. "Same way they knew about the forested islands. From the database."

"How long did their techs work?"

"About a week."

Leigh handed the glow back to Olu, and he placed it on the ground between them. "What else don't we know that they do?"

"I imagine there's a lot," admitted Olu. "So far, the lanterns, the maps, and the water treatment are the biggest ones we've learned."

"The water treatment?"

"Thought you were awake for that."

"Guess not."

"It's a little disturbing."

"Disturbing?"

"A bad assumption on our part. The water treatment we've been using is one of two kinds. I assumed they were all the same. You've seen the tablets?"

"Yeah," said Leigh, "they come in those white canisters."

"There's a bunch that come in blue canisters too, sitting in rows behind the white ones. We never knew they were different."

"Why would they be?"

"Because the blue canister tablets do two things—they purify the water and protect from sunburn."

"Ah," said Leigh. "And the white tablets?"

"Same two things, but also one more—birth control."

"You're kidding."

"Would I make that up?"

Leigh rubbed her forehead with the palms of her hands.

"You ready to go back to sleep?" he asked.

"No."

"Kala said it could take a week or two to get over the jellbox stings."

"I know."

"Water?" Olu offered his canteen.

"Thanks."

"Drink as much as you want. That's a spring we're sleeping next to."

"Probably not treated with white or blue tablets."

"I imagine not."

The cool water tasted wonderful even though it hurt to swallow. "I hate to think about what else we don't know."

"Don't think about it. You should sleep."

"In a minute," said Leigh. "Tell me two more things."

"Sure."

"How long since they escaped?"

"Almost four months."

She looked over at the campsite where Kala and Min-seo were sleeping, the two girls shadowy lumps on the ground. What would it have been like to land on a strange planet and be met by someone like Terence instead of Olu? What would it be like to know your friends were still there?

She listened to the sounds of the forest—the water dripping over the rocky alcove into the pond below, the breeze moving the smaller branches in the trees. Kala had talked of lizard-like creatures and insects so large they made good eating, but Leigh heard no animal sounds in the dark woods.

"Haven't seen you do that for months," said Olu.

"Do what?" asked Leigh. But she knew. Her fingers were up near her throat.

She put them in her lap. "It's a reflex. A necklace I used to wear on Earth."

He said nothing, so she kept talking. "My dad made it. A chain with a rock from our favorite spot. Near the cactus that bloomed bright pink. I wore that necklace a lot." She risked looking at him. "And I'd worn it every day since Dad died."

"But you didn't bring it with you."

"No."

"Hmm."

She put her hand back on her chest, thumb and forefinger under her collarbone where the necklace used to rest.

"Maybe," said Olu, "they wouldn't let you take it off-planet because it was organic material. Or maybe you thought someone else needed it more."

She nodded, though she'd never before considered either option.

"What's your second question?" asked Olu.

"Huh?"

"You said you had two questions."

"The second one can wait till morning." She was too worn out from telling him about the necklace to deal with anything else.

"Nine," said Olu.

"Nine?"

"How many people did they leave behind in the prison cabin? I'm guessing that was your other question."

"Not exactly."

"It's nine," said Olu. "Eleven if Jack and Ping are there."

"Jack and Ping ... the boys who were caught?"

"Yes."

"Kala and Min-seo are afraid they're dead," said Leigh. "I remember that part."

"Yes," said Olu. "And after almost four months, who knows what's happened? Who knows if we'd be able to help at all?"

"Ah, you're answering my other question—what's our plan?"

Olu had been staring into the darkness of the treetops, but now he turned to look at her. "We argued about that last night. Be glad you slept through it."

"What'd you decide?"

"Nothing."

He picked up the glow and passed it back and forth between his hands. Never before had she seen Olu fidget. Not once.

"I asked to come on this journey," said Olu. "Do you know why?"

She shook her head.

"Michele didn't want me along," said Olu, "not really, and Lex worried it was unfair to leave Ada by herself. I knew that. But ..."

"You didn't listen to them."

"I was taught to do good and to be useful. I believed I could do more good here."

Leigh thought back to her interview with Olu. Both of his parents had died doing good and being useful—doctors battling one of the terrifying epidemics that had hit West Africa during the drought. Olu felt a compulsion to honor their memory by prizing the same two qualities, a compulsion so strong he had gone against both Lex and Michele in order to be here.

He continued. "I thought I could be more useful on this trip than back at Homesite."

"You thought you could keep us out of trouble."

"I admit, I was wrong."

"About what?"

"Everything. I'm the one who put others most at risk during the storm. Now I'm the one advocating we rescue people we don't even know. And yet, the more I think about it, the more I think we should."

Leigh tried to keep the surprise off her face.

"See what you slept through?" said Olu.

"Must have been an interesting argument."

"No one agrees with me."

"They're *against* a rescue?"

"No one is firmly against it," said Olu, "but no one else feels compelled to go. Kala and Min-seo say it's our call. Michele and Marko have reservations, but they're undecided."

"Lex and Noah?"

"Lex," said Olu, "is worried about you."

"I'll be fine."

"And Noah thinks we should spend a day or two resting here and prioritize getting Kala and Min-seo to safety. Rescue those we know we can rescue."

"Noah said that? It sounds like something you would say."

"Tell me about it," Olu said ruefully. "I understand his point of view."

"But you disagree?"

Olu quit fiddling with the glow and put it on the ground beside him. It lit up the intricate twisted trunk of the tree.

"The lack of landing parties concerns me. What if our worst fears came true back on Earth?"

"You're worried about numbers."

"I'm worried about … I don't know what to call it. But if we are humanity's last hope, I want us to be worthy of it. … I don't know how to explain it."

But Leigh understood. Olu wanted to create a society worth believing in. He'd always fought for that. He'd always pushed them that direction.

Her dizziness had returned, and her throat hurt. She was too tired for further conversation, but one thing couldn't wait.

"Olu," said Leigh. "I need to tell you … I need to say … thank you."

"For what?"

"For being the person who welcomed me to the planet."

Olu stood up, then offered her a hand in assistance.

"You're welcome," he said.

CHAPTER 40

Hours later, Leigh felt much better. It was early afternoon. Floating in fresh water, she ran her fingers through her wet hair and marveled at the lack of tangles.

Kala and Min-seo had shown them where to dig up roots for bathing. The lather created by the roots was far superior to the all-purpose soap they'd been using, soap the colony used to wash skin, hair, bowls, clothes, and everything else. Each root was a dull gray lump, on its surface not a plant to inspire admiration. But its appearance belied the silky-smooth feel the roots gave Leigh's hair, not to mention the fresh scent—like spring rain on prairie grass or newly washed cotton sheets hung out to dry.

Even better than the root-based lather was the location for their bathing: a freshwater river. After months of washing in the salty ocean or with half a pail of spring water, submersion in the river felt like visiting a spa at the world's most sumptuous resort.

No, the river was better.

About fifteen meters wide, it flowed between banks of dirt and moss, both sides lined by trees whose trunks intertwined with one another. The water near the banks was shaded, but the rest of the river sparkled in full sunlight, a dramatic change from the dark forest.

Leaving the lumpy roots behind on a spot of dry moss, Leigh swam back to the sunshine-covered water. Min-seo and Kala had led them to a small oxbow in the river, and the four boys were on the other side. Even with thick forest between them, Leigh could hear Noah whooping and hollering in joy. She felt equally happy, but an aching body left her expressing that happiness in less voluble ways.

She stole a look at Kala, the only one who'd exited the river, dried off, and put on fresh clothes. A shirt Marko had brought with him was a decent fit, and a pair of Leigh's pants completed the outfit. Kala rolled up the cuffs and sat under a tree on the nearby mossy bank. Min-seo and Michele floated slightly downstream.

"You look better, Lor," called Michele. "How do you feel?"

"Could be worse."

"Could be dead," said Kala from her spot on the bank.

Min-seo laughed, a lovely, trickling sound like water running through musical pipes.

"It's true," said Leigh.

"I know." Min-seo swam toward her. "But there's no need to dwell on it. Kala, as you may have guessed, is a worst-case scenario type."

"Understandable," said Michele as she too swam closer. "Most of what you've been through has been worst case."

"Could've been worse," said Kala.

Leigh laughed. Maybe Kala was mocking her, or maybe she and Leigh were more alike than they knew. Either way, it was funny.

"It feels good to hear you laugh, my friend," said Michele. "As the Māori would say, *Ahakoa he iti he pounamu.* 'Although it is small, it is a treasure.'"

"You're Māori?" asked Kala.

"Yes."

"Michele doesn't sound Māori."

"You're right, it's not," she said to the girl on the riverbank. They regarded each other for a moment before Michele continued. "My parents chose my name. My father wasn't Māori. But my mother had a lot of Māori in her, though she chose to ignore it. I don't know why. My parents died when I was a baby. My grandparents—my mother's parents—adopted me, and they raised me Māori. But they mourned their daughter and honored her by using the name she'd chosen for me, her only child."

"So you're only part Māori," said Kala.

Michele swam over to the edge of the river, climbed out, and dried off. No one said a word as she slowly put on clothes and sat down.

"When I was four years old," said Michele, "my grandparents explained the story of my parents to me. They told me that my name meant 'gift from God' and that I was the greatest gift they'd ever received. Are my genetics one hundred percent Māori? No, probably not even half. Doesn't matter. My soul is Māori. And I don't know why you would question who I am. I mean, who are you?"

The two girls stared at each other.

Leigh was begrudgingly impressed. When Michele used that imperious tone, people tended to back down. Kala didn't budge.

Min-seo swam closer to shore, and Leigh followed her.

"I understand you, Michele," Kala eventually replied. "You're like the plants that grow on the riverbank." She looked down and ran her hand over the soft groundcover.

"Really?"

"If you look closely," said Kala, "there are two layers of plants. The underlayer is thick and dark. It's purple, but so dark as to look almost black. There's a thin layer of growth on top. See … it's not the same plant at all; it's not even moss. It's lighter colored, with tiny leaves like a clover, though it does not bloom."

With a brusque motion, Kala grabbed a chunk of the vegetation and tossed it into the river. Only a barren patch of dirt remained.

"Here's the interesting part," she said, her voice calm and steady. "When the plants grow back, the small tiny-leafed plant grows first, then the dark moss grows behind it. For a while, the new groundcover is like most people: the fragile, beautiful exterior put on display with only a hint of the thicker, mossier layer underneath.

"But, Michele, you are different. You know exactly who you are, and you are not afraid to show yourself. You are like the riverbank when everything has grown back."

Neither girl spoke while Michele studied the plants and Kala studied Michele. Finally, Michele raised her head.

"I'm going to take that as a compliment," she said.

Kala nodded.

"And you, my new friend?" asked Michele. "What are you like?"
"The riverbank never shows who I am, for I have no glossy covering at all." Kala placed a hand over the lower side of her face, leaving exposed the large black birthmark that extended from her left cheek to her right eye. The darker pigmentation was smooth except for a bumpy ridge near her hairline.

"Don't worry," said Michele. "I still see you."

Kala removed her hand from her face and turned toward the two swimmers still in the river. She called, "Min-seo, you ready?"

Min-seo swam for shore. "Give me a minute. This baby's already making me less graceful."

The self-deprecating statement was clearly an attempt to lighten the mood. Min-seo moved with that rare feline agility reserved for dancers; six months of pregnancy wasn't affecting her gracefulness at all. Leigh shared a pointed look with Michele and tried to convey her puzzlement at Kala's behavior, but Michele shrugged it off.

"I'll go tell the boys to get ready," she said and headed into the woods. Leigh swam to shore and climbed the embankment. The welts on her body had reddened, and she gently patted them dry.

"You tired?" asked Min-seo.

"Yes," admitted Leigh, "but it's not bad."

"You must nap," said Kala. "The jellbox poison takes at least a week to leave your system. If you want to make a full recovery, you'll have to rest. Same with Olu."

"Thanks for the advice. I'll see what Michele thinks."

"Oh, Michele will agree with me." She laughed—a raspy laugh, but not unfriendly. "And listen to your body. It'll tell you too."

Leigh wasn't sure what to think of Kala. She'd offered medical help, provided shelter, and taken them to a favorite swimming hole. If actions spoke louder than words, then she'd been welcoming. But Kala was testing them. And Leigh had no idea what might count as "passing" the test.

CHAPTER 41

True to Kala's prediction, Leigh and Olu both needed sleep. As they settled into their blankets, Michele tasked Noah with watching over them while the rest of the group went looking for lizards. Noah chaffed at being left behind, but Michele insisted. The deep cut on his foot was festering; the wound needed time to heal.

"It's better than yesterday," insisted Noah.

"Not much," said Michele.

"You don't want your foot to end up looking like this," said Kala, drawing a finger down the rough, uneven scar that ran the length of her arm. "You don't want to be so marked."

"I wouldn't mind the scar," Noah replied.

He and Kala exchanged a long, uncomfortable look before Michele interrupted. "You'll mind if you can't walk, Noah, and you'll really mind if you get on my bad side."

Noah responded with one of his most charming roguish grins. Not that such an approach worked on Michele, nor apparently Kala, but at least it avoided an argument. In the end, five people went hunting lizards, Leigh and Olu slept, and Noah contented himself with sketching plans for improving the raft.

Hours later, the mood was once again congenial. All eight of them sat around the small stone-circled fire pit and ate roasted lizards and bugs. The lizards were about as much like Earth lizards as Marjol's fish were like Earth fish—barely close enough to earn the name. The roasted lizard was palatable, however, and though the inevitable "tastes like chicken" jokes occurred, there was truth in the assertion. Leigh preferred the bugs, which were crunchier and saltier. They actually resembled bugs from Earth, only larger, like giant dragonflies with bodies the size of a human hand.

"I'd like to see some of these bugs when they're flying around," said Leigh. "What do you call them?"

"*Jag-eun yong*," said Min-seo, "little dragon."

"Even though they don't look anything like dragons," said Kala.

"You call them *yong*," laughed Min-seo. "Dragon. I don't think you're one to talk."

"*Yong*," said Leigh, "that works for me too."

Min-seo offered a small smile.

Everyone was being friendly but also on their guard. Kala and Min-seo sat next to each other. Leigh was flanked by Lex and Michele. No one was as relaxed as they appeared.

"You're right," said Lex. It took her a moment to remember they'd been discussing the bugs. "You'd enjoy watching something fly again, even if it's a bug-dragon."

"In one spot," said Marko, "I saw a *jag-eun yong* eating from those squished pinecone-like things. It was hovering like a hummingbird. So beautiful, I didn't even try to catch it."

"Why don't we see them around here?" Leigh asked.

"They tend to stay near the treetops," said Min-seo. "You don't notice them as much in here where the trees are tall."

"Well," said Leigh, "I hope to join you tomorrow."

"Maybe in two days," said Kala.

"Tomorrow we could all go dig for the big purple roots," suggested Min-seo. "That's less tiring."

"Those roots taste like wax," said Kala.

"They're not *that* bad."

"Let's see how I feel tomorrow," said Leigh.

"How do you feel now?" asked Michele.

"Good," she replied, ignoring the pain in her legs and the fever creeping its way back.

"You'll sleep better if you take an ibuprofen," said Kala.

"That's one thing we have a lot of," added Min-seo.

"Thanks." Leigh tried to sound grateful. The two girls' medicinal horde was a sore point. When the fifteen prisoners had tried to escape, they'd failed to divide resources evenly. For that reason, Kala and Min-seo had a lot of medical supplies, one canteen, a scant amount of clothing, and nothing else.

Last night, Min-seo had cried when they'd offered each of the girls a blanket. Even Kala's face had shown emotion when they'd pulled out fresh clothing. She'd recovered quickly, joking about her relief that Min-seo wouldn't have to go naked when her pregnant belly outgrew her current clothes. But Leigh understood using humor to mask despair.

When everyone finished eating, Olu and Lex exchanged a look—the one Leigh recognized as, *Let's get to it*. She settled into the most comfortable position she could find. This was the third conversation about their plans. Last night, she'd slept through it, and this morning, she'd done the same. Tonight, she was determined to stay awake.

"Kala," said Leigh, "I think you're right about that ibuprofen. I'll take one."

In unison, Lex and Michele asked, "You all right?"

"All good." She almost laughed at the looks her five raftmates gave her. They knew she wasn't feeling well, but they didn't say anything.

There was an undercurrent of unity among the six of them, even though they didn't agree on what to do next. Leigh felt sorry for Min-seo and Kala—alone for almost four months and still outsiders.

Kala handed her the medicine and sat back down between Min-seo and Marko.

"Can we talk about what everyone's avoiding talkin' about?" asked Noah.

"Talk all you want," said Kala. "As we've said before, Min-seo and I are at your mercy. We set off to find a new colony to join—your colony—and we'd still like to do that. We left friends behind. I don't know if they're still there.

"Do I want to go get them? Absolutely. But I don't want to risk Min-seo and her baby. I don't know if it's fair to ask you to help. Terence and his gang have knives. They've made spears and clubs.

They won't hesitate to kill any of you. I've said all this already. Twice. I don't know what else you want from me."

"So," said Noah, "you'd be willin' to go back to our island and leave your friends behind."

Whoa.

"I'd be willing," said Kala, "to get Min-seo and all you injured people safely to your home. It sounds like that four-day trip will be difficult enough. After that, I'll start making plans to come back for a rescue."

"All of us injured people are fine," said Noah.

"Enough," interrupted Olu. "I don't know why you two are arguing. I thought you were on the same side."

"Reckon I don't enjoy bein' treated like an invalid," said Noah.

"There are no *sides*," said Michele. "And Noah, don't be stupid."

The others remained quiet as Olu, Michele, Noah, and Kala continued to debate options. Leigh wished she'd had a chance to talk to Lex, to figure out why he was reluctant to enact a rescue. A few months ago, Olu and Lex had been on opposite sides of the same argument. What had changed?

Everything.

Everything had changed.

They'd met Kala and Min-seo. They'd learned about the other colonies. And they had reason to think no one else was coming to help. They were alone, and what happened on this planet was up to them.

That's what Olu had been trying to say to her. She understood but didn't know how to explain it to anyone else. Her head pounded; her thoughts were jumbled. Leigh put her face in her hands and rubbed her eyes.

"The odds," said Olu, "seem to be against expecting more landing parties. I worked through the calendar, and I think the spaceship wreckage we found on our island came from the one that had your third landing party. It should've arrived before ours."

"Then why would that affect our fourth landing party?" asked Noah. "Makes no sense."

"It does if there's only one shuttle."

"It's not about that," said Leigh, raising her head. "It's not about any of that."

No one responded. She could hear the low hiss of the flames in the fire pit and the brushing of branches as the wind moved through the tops of the trees.

"It doesn't matter," said Leigh, "whether anyone else is coming. Whether the pilot who helped me can't help us anymore. And we can't save her." She shook her head to clear it, but it only ached more. She kept talking. "It could be that something terrible has happened on Earth, or that we've been abandoned, some kind of failed experiment … or it could be that more colonists will show up in a few months or years or decades. There's no way to know. But we're here. Together. That's our one and only certainty. No matter what, we have each other."

Michele put an arm around her. "Oh Lor," she said, placing the back of her hand on Leigh's forehead, "you're burning up."

Without a word, Kala handed her a second ibuprofen, and Lex gave her a canteen.

Leigh swallowed the medicine. Her throat hurt, but she wasn't done. "Ever since I landed on this planet, part of me has felt like I'm looking around from inside someone else's life. Who am I to be here? Why would they choose me? How can I do it?

"But this *is* my life. *Our* life. And we *can* do it. We get to decide who we want to be."

She scooted back a little from the fire. It was so hot. The trees rustled, and the slow drip of water trickling over the ledge echoed in the darkness. "We decide," Leigh repeated.

Everyone stared at the fire. Min-seo pulled out some glows and set them on the ground.

"Lex," said Olu. "What do you think?"

"Lorelei's right. We decide. Together. The eight of us."

The eight of us. Yes, exactly.

"Marko," said Lex, "your thoughts?"

Marko looked across the fire at Lex. "We can't decide based on fear." He looked down at his hands, then raised his head. "We don't agree on what to do because we're all afraid of different things. But fear is no way to decide."

"Focus on the good," said Lex quietly.

"On what we can control," replied Marko.

Lex gave Marko a nod, and Leigh could feel the silent communication between them.

Marko tossed another log on the fire. A few sparks crackled in the night air.

"A couple of nights ago," said Lex, "we talked about whether humans should even be on this planet. About how much harm we might do without even trying."

"What does that have to do with this?" asked Michele.

"I'm not sure," admitted Lex. "Except that we are here. And since we are, it's up to us to do it right."

Leigh glanced at Olu, who was nodding. In one sentence, Lex had summed up everything Olu had tried to say to Leigh the night before, everything she had tried to express tonight.

"We all want to rescue the prisoners," said Lex. "The question is whether the eight of us should try now, or whether we should go home, regroup, and come up with a better plan.

"You're right, Marko. I am afraid. I'm afraid because we're a ragtag group. Lorelei and Olu are recovering from the jellboxes. Noah's foot has a cut so deep it's making him grumpy, and Noah's never grumpy. Michele, even if you won't admit it, the rope burn on your leg is showing signs of infection. And let's not forget, Marko, that you and Olu almost drowned a few days ago.

"Kala. Min-seo. I don't claim to understand what you've been through, but it's *a lot*, and let's face it, your earlier plans against Terence didn't go so well. Add to that, one of you is expecting a baby, and I'm pretty sure the other one hasn't eaten well for four months to ensure her pregnant friend did."

Kala glared, but she did not deny it.

"I'm worried about all of you," said Lex. "I want to take you home and get you well."

"You're not our caretaker," said Kala.

"Yeah, you're right. Feel free to call me overprotective. I've been called worse. Olu asked my opinion. I'm just being honest."

No one spoke. Leigh stared at Lex's hands. His voice was calm, but his hands were balled up, his fingers pushing so hard on his thumbs that his knuckles were discolored.

"And if I'm honest," continued Lex, "then I have to tell you that the trip from our island to this archipelago is not easy. It's risky. If we go home now, it may be a long time before anyone comes back. People may die because we did not try to save them now." He looked at Olu. "So maybe we should try."

"Sometimes," said Olu, "inaction is wise. But sometimes, it's important to try."

Leigh noticed Lex's hands relax, palms open on his legs. He leaned forward, as if eager to share the rest of his thoughts.

"I believe that we can do this," continued Lex. "But we'd need everyone to agree, and we'd need to be smart about it. Let people heal. Plan carefully. Work *together*." He gestured toward Kala and Min-seo. "If we're going to save your friends, we need to know as much about Terence and his island and your experience as you can tell us, even the parts you don't want to talk about. Especially the parts you don't want to talk about. Otherwise, I don't think we should go."

Kala and Min-seo gave each other a long look. After so much time together, the two girls didn't need words to communicate, but it was unclear what they were deciding.

Leigh turned toward Lex. "Ruthless," she whispered, because it was true, and because she could see how much it cost him. She resisted the impulse to grab his hand.

Eventually, Noah broke the silence around the fire. "I'll go," he said to Kala. "I'll help save your friends. Tell us what you know, and I'll go."

"Same," said Marko.

"Min-seo, Kala, what do you think?" asked Michele. "Could you do that? Could you tell us everything you know?"

"It's been a hundred and twenty-three days since we were there," said Kala. "We'd be dealing with a lot of uncertainties."

"One thing I've learned," said Olu, "is that there are always uncertainties."

Michele reached over and clasped his hand.

"Min-seo?" Kala asked.

"You know what I think."

"Then it's decided," said Kala. "We're in."

CHAPTER 42

Four nights later, they were on Terence's island. The early stages of the plan went smoothly. Lex and Min-seo stole one of the two-log boats and set the others adrift. Upon discovering a small sailing raft, Lex grabbed that too.

When they returned to the inlet where the others were hiding, Lex handed over the stolen raft to Noah, who mocked its inferiority but agreed to take charge of the smaller vessel.

Towing the raft behind him, Noah moved into position with Michele, who remained in charge of their own raft, and Min-seo, who held the stolen two-log boat. The three of them stood knee-deep in the water toward the back of the inlet. They would stay behind and organize the departure.

Lex, Marko, and Lorelei stood on the inlet's pebble-strewn shore waiting for Olu and Kala to return from scouting. It'd been 127 days since Kala and Min-seo had escaped. No telling how much had changed. He hoped Kala wasn't finding too many surprises.

Lex strained his senses. There was nothing to hear but the ocean and nothing to see but the shoreline. Min-seo had talked about hills in the distance, but there were none nearby. Like other islands in the archipelago, this one was relatively flat. Lex missed the cliffs and the mountains on the island he called home.

In the moonlight, he could see that the vegetation was sparse—
tall grass and bushes with an occasional clump of short trees. The
island looked exactly like Kala and Min-seo had described. Still, it
was unfamiliar terrain. No amount of hand-drawn maps or discussion
could make up for lack of personal experience.

They were counting on stealth, not strength, to free the prisoners.
Weapons weren't needed. Even so, Lex wished his Swiss Army knife
were in his hand, or at least his pocket, instead of at the bottom of the
ocean. The largest moon was near full, and nighttime vision was easy,
but should they have waited for a night that wasn't so bright?

Lorelei reached over and placed her hand firmly on his wrist. Only
then did Lex realize how tightly he was balling his fists. He stretched
out his fingers and took a deep breath. She removed her hand and
resumed waiting.

A few minutes later, Olu and Kala came jogging along the shoreline.
Michele walked up from the water's edge to hear the scouting report.

"Mostly no surprises," said Olu in a low voice. "The prisoners
haven't moved cabins, but their ankles are tied at night. It'll take extra
time to free them."

"Wish I had a knife," said Marko.

Lorelei reached into her pocket and handed him her multi-tool.

"Thanks."

"How many guards?" Lex asked.

"Two," said Olu. "One awake and one asleep. Kala and I will
take them."

"How many prisoners?" asked Lorelei.

"Only six."

"I'm sorry."

Kala nodded in Lorelei's direction, but she spoke directly to
Michele: "Tell Min-seo I didn't see Jack or Ping. Natalya is pregnant.
That's all I know."

"I'll tell her."

"Anything else?" asked Lex.

"No," said Kala.

"Let's get busy," said Olu. "You know what to do."

"See you soon," said Michele.

"Soon." Olu gestured for Kala to lead the way.

* * *

Fifteen minutes later, the five would-be rescuers stood in a copse of thin trees and giant fern-like plants. They were not far from the edge of Terence's homesite and could see the back of the prison cabin.

Olu and Kala crept up to the building and disappeared around the corner. Lex silently counted to thirty. Then he, Lorelei, and Marko followed.

Two guards were slumped on the ground. One was breathing and one was not. Marko stepped over them and entered the building. Lex and Lorelei remained outside. Everything was quiet. Even the air seemed to sit still.

In less than a minute, Olu emerged with two of the prisoners, and they walked back to the hiding spot in the giant ferns.

Four to go.

Two more emerged. Lorelei escorted them away, and Lex kept watch.

Kala came out of the cabin and whispered, "Complication."

"What?" asked Lex.

"Ping is alive."

"Ping and Jack?"

"Only Ping," said Kala. "He's in another cabin."

"Which one?"

"Not here. Down near the beach."

"Go tell Olu," said Lex, and Kala disappeared into the shadows.

Lex grabbed the body of the dead guard and dragged him inside. The cabin looked similar to his own, but it smelled different, like moldy bread and dirty socks.

"Last one," whispered Marko, tugging at a girl's ropes. Another girl crouched beside him. In the light of Marko's glow, Lex could see her face—eyes wide, mouth set in a thin line of determination. Given the girl's pregnant belly, Lex assumed she was Natalya.

As soon as the girl on the floor was free to move, she stood up. Marko whispered something Lex couldn't hear, and the two girls nodded. One of them held the door open while Marko and Lex stepped outside and picked up the unconscious guard. Everyone kept a careful eye on the boy as they moved him. Lex didn't want to do more damage than needed, but he'd do what was necessary.

Fortunately, the guard was out cold. Once he was stowed inside, Lex, Marko, and the final two prisoners ran to join the others.

"All quiet," said Lex as they arrived at the ferns.

"You heard?" asked Olu.

"Ping."

"I'm going after him," said Kala.

"No," said Olu. "You *and* Lex."

"Me too," said Lorelei.

"Go," Olu agreed. "Marko and I will take these six."

"Have the rafts ready to leave," said Lex. "Up at the mouth of the inlet."

Marko nodded.

"We'll be ready," said Olu. "You be careful."

"Let's go," said Kala.

Lex and Lorelei followed her into the brush.

There was no way they'd rescue six and leave one behind. Lex knew all too well how guys like Terence operated. If Ping wasn't rescued tonight, he'd be blamed for the escape. They had no choice but to go get him.

* * *

The beach cabin setup was familiar. Three in a row.

"No one stayed here before," said Kala.

"Doesn't look like anyone's here now," whispered Lorelei.

Lex agreed. The place looked deserted.

The only light in the encampment came from the moons in the sky, and there was no sign of life, not even an extinguished campfire. Just sand and rocks and cabins that looked empty.

"I'm going to go scout," said Kala, and before Lex could respond, she was gone.

He watched as she crept around in the shadows, circling back behind each of the three buildings. It smelled better down here, with the scents of sand and water, but the emptiness was eerie. Lex could hear nothing but the breeze.

When Kala returned, he could tell by the pace of her steps that she'd found someone.

"Third cabin," she said.

"How many guards?" he asked.

"One. He's asleep."

"And Ping?"

"There's someone small sleeping on the far side of the room, but his back was to me."

"You think it's Ping."

"Ping's size, and he was sleeping on the floor."

"Which bunkroom?" asked Lorelei.

"Neither. They're both up front. One's asleep on a mattress near the window. Gordon. I could see him. Ping's on the floor across the room."

"You think," said Lex.

"I'm going even if you aren't," said Kala.

Lorelei grabbed the other girl's arm. "That's not how we work."

"She's right," said Lex. "We're doing this together."

"I can take care of Gordon," said Kala.

"No. I got the guard. Ping needs to see a familiar face."

"And me?" asked Lorelei.

"Stand watch," he replied.

"Follow me," said Kala, and once again they did.

Lex felt better now that they had a plan. He left Lorelei at the cabin door and crept over to the guard sleeping by the window. As Kala had said, the boy named Gordon was sound asleep. Lex stood near the bed, ready to attack if the guard stirred but hoping to avoid any interaction.

He kept his eyes on Gordon while his ears tracked Kala and Ping's movements. At least he assumed it was Ping, given that Kala was untying ropes and helping the boy to his feet.

It took them a while to get across the floor. Lex didn't look away from the sleeping guard; even so, it was obvious Ping was having trouble walking.

Finally, they made it out the door. Lex left the sleeping Gordon behind and joined the others outside. Ping was leaning on Kala for support. He was gaunt and smelled like he hadn't bathed in weeks. His left leg hung uselessly at an awkward angle.

No wonder there was only one guard.

Lex pointed around the corner of the cabin, and they walked that direction.

Slowly.

Ping hadn't spoken. Either Kala had allayed his fears, or the boy figured it couldn't get any worse.

"Ping?" asked Lex.

The boy nodded.

"I'm Lex. I'm going to carry you. Sit down so I can get a good grip."

"Thanks," he whispered.

Lex put one arm under Ping's knees and the other around his back. He started to stand up.

"Lex!" screamed Lorelei.

"Gordon!" yelled a female voice.

There was a loud thunk.

"Shit!" said Kala.

Holding Ping, Lex stood up and whipped around to see what was happening. A girl lay on the ground, holding a spear in one hand and a knife in the other. Her head had been smashed by a rock, and blood was oozing from her temple. Lorelei stood nearby, holding out her hands as if they belonged to someone else.

The cabin door slammed open. Gordon stepped out and saw the body on the ground.

"Ellie!" he screamed.

"Run!" shouted Kala. She grabbed Lorelei's arm and pulled her toward the beach.

The two girls took off. Lex held on to Ping and ran after them, faster than he would've thought possible with someone in his arms. Fortunately, Ping was even lighter than he appeared. It was like carrying a small child.

Kala led them straight down the beach toward the inlet. In minutes, Lex could see Olu and the rest in the distance, silhouettes in the moonlight, people and rafts waiting.

Cries rang out from inland. Gordon was no longer the only one who knew about the escape.

Lex doubled his efforts. Far down the beach, the stolen raft headed out to sea, loaded with people and towing the two-log boat behind it. Noah was at the helm giving directions. Their paddling was slow, but they were moving.

Only one raft remained on shore, waiting.

Lorelei and Kala were farther ahead now. Lex angled along the beach, away from the water, hoping to find sand that was packed more tightly. It was no good. His feet sank with each stride, and the cries from Terence's gang grew louder.

The two girls in front of him were almost to the raft when he saw Lorelei go sprawling. Kala helped her up. As they looked back, Lex thought desperately, *Run!* He had no extra breath to shout it, but the girls followed his wishes all the same. They jogged to the raft, Lorelei favoring her right leg, Kala slowing her pace so that they reached the raft together.

Ping had not uttered a word the whole time, so when he said, "Behind you," Lex knew the pursuers were getting close. He sprinted for the raft as he watched Michele ready the sail and prepare to launch. Marko and Olu stood in the water, holding the raft offshore.

Waiting.

Lex's muscles screamed to slow down, but his heart was pumping. The yelling behind him grew louder. Sand sprayed beneath his feet. He focused on the raft and the people on it and the need to get them home.

He heard Michele shout and could see Marko and Olu turn the raft into the wind, but it was as if those things were happening at the far end of a tunnel he was trying to enter. His friends were out on the water, and he was still on land.

It was now or never. He ran into the waves, the water slowing his pace as he waded in a direct line to those waiting for him. Everyone on the raft urged him onward. All that mattered was one foot in front of the other. All that mattered was not giving up.

He was close.

He was closer.

He was there.

He lunged onto the raft, spilling himself and Ping in a heap. Lex gasped for breath, his left leg shaking, his arms aching, his heart pounding. Cries rose up behind them as the sail caught the wind, the paddles caught the water, and they escaped to the freedom of the open ocean.

CHAPTER 43

ith Lex and Ping safely aboard, Leigh grabbed her knee with both hands, bracing it to lessen the pain. Focusing on the injury kept her from dwelling on the rock she'd thrown ... on the girl she'd killed.

She was still panting from the run down the beach, and she was sweating all over. For the first time in days, the dizziness had returned. She lay on her side, clutching her knee, and watched the angry people on the shore get smaller. Several of Terence's crowd waded into the water; two of them dove into the waves and started swimming. Not a problem. No swimmer could catch the raft. They were safe.

She started to close her eyes, but an unfamiliar voice began shouting.

"Yes!" called Ping, his voice surprisingly strong. "Get them! Yes!"

Leigh blinked. What she was seeing made no sense. The two members of Terence's crew who'd started to swim weren't heading toward them at all. They were aiming for the other raft, which shouldn't have been a problem ... except Noah had turned the stolen raft back toward shore, as if to meet the swimmers halfway.

"You can do it!" Ping yelled to the swimmers.

"What the hell?" asked Kala.

"They saved my life," said Ping.

"Looks more like they beat the crap out of you."

"No." Ping shook his head. "Not Carlo. Not Ray."

Leigh sat up, determined to watch the drama in the water. One of the two swimmers was laboring, but both had made it past the break point in the surf. Ping continued to shout encouragement.

Noah had folded up the sail, and everyone on his raft was paddling—some with paddles, some with sticks, others with their hands. It was a unified effort. But they were fighting against the tide, and the progress was slow.

On the far side of their own raft, Michele gave orders to relax the sail and stop paddling. They were downwind. No way to reach Noah quickly. All they could do was watch; all they could do was hope the other raft reached the two swimmers before they drowned.

Clearly, there had been a change in Terence's colony: some of the guards had been helping the prisoners. And now, two of those guards were seeking refuge. It seemed crazy. But Ping was malnourished, with arms covered in bruises and a leg that didn't work. If he thought Carlo and Ray deserved another chance, that was enough for Leigh.

Things did not look promising, however. One of the two had stopped swimming and was floating on his back. The other one stayed with him, a noble but dangerous decision. The tableau worsened when three more people left the beach and dove into the waves. The swimmers were being pursued.

"Suppose we should rescue those three as well?" said Kala.

"Oh, no," replied Ping.

Kala's face softened.

Ping yelled again. This time Kala joined him.

Across the waves, Noah exhorted his crew to paddle harder.

Leigh felt helpless. She was almost as dizzy as she'd been the first few hours after the jellbox stings. Fearful of throwing up, she scooted closer to the edge of the raft.

Kala grabbed her arm. "Where are you going?"

"Dizzy," said Leigh.

"Lie down," Kala commanded.

Leigh wanted to tell her that she didn't like being bossed around. She wanted to explain why it was important to rescue the two swimmers; that having thrown that rock, having killed that girl, it was even more important to save as many others as possible. But she was too dizzy to talk.

"Lie down," Kala repeated. "I'll tell you what happens."

Leigh lay down. She kept watching. Even so, she appreciated Kala's narration.

Kala said she could see Min-seo shouting as she paddled. Noah repositioned people on the raft. And the raft started moving faster, slipping through the water more like a canoe than a clunky raft. Kala thought they'd caught a lucky current, but Leigh wondered if it was another example of Noah's ingenuity. Either way, the raft's speed encouraged the two swimmers, who redoubled their efforts.

The pursuers hit the break point and misjudged the waves. The ocean held them back, only for a moment, but a moment was enough. The raft swooped in and the two swimmers were plucked from the water.

In a heartbeat, Noah's crew began paddling the other direction. Heading away from shore with the tide, the raft soon escaped to safety. Noah raised his sail, and Michele gave the orders to ready hers. Soon both rafts were headed back down the side of the archipelago, the three swimmers who'd given chase left bobbing in the water. Those on shore receded into specks in the distance.

The fugitives were safe.

Leigh gently stretched out her injured leg. Her knee was swollen, but she could move it.

Lex crawled across the raft to see her.

"You okay?" he asked.

She nodded but otherwise did not reply. This was pain she wasn't ready to handle.

He reached out to touch her arm. She flinched involuntarily and could taste the blood on her lip from where she'd bitten it. Too much had happened. She couldn't process any more.

"You saved my life," Lex said to her.

"Please," she whispered, "don't talk about it."

She closed her eyes and curled into a ball, unable to explain. The dizziness was back.

"I'll take care of her," she heard Kala say to Lex.

Michele called, "Lex, I need you to take the sail."

Leigh sent silent thanks to the two girls and a silent apology to Lex. She gripped her knee, ignored the world, and let the cadence of the raft lull her to sleep.

CHAPTER 44

By morning, they were back at the forested island. Lex wished they could stay and recuperate before heading home, but that would be asking for trouble. No doubt Terence would be heading their way. The loss of prisoners was one thing; Carlo and Ray's betrayal was a whole other level.

At Michele's behest, Lex and Marko took the stolen two-log boat and paddled offshore, keeping a lookout while everyone else prepared the two rafts for the journey home. The water was calm, and the air was clear. They could see all the way up past the next two islands in the chain. Nobody was headed their way.

Not yet.

He and Marko patrolled for an hour, and then Michele signaled the group was ready to go. As they paddled to shore, Marko said, "Did Min-seo tell you? Back home, there's another archipelago off the tip of our island."

"I thought the other colonies were far away."

"No colony. A string of uninhabited islands, grouped close together like this one."

"How far from us?"

"Not sure, but Olu thinks they're worth exploring."

"Let's worry about getting home first."

"We'll get there."

As the boys approached the beach, they watched for jellboxes. There hadn't been any when they'd paddled out, but this was no time to let their guard down.

"You think Ping will be okay?" asked Lex.

"Yes," said Marko slowly. "I don't know if Ping will walk again, but he'll be okay."

"I hope you're right."

"Lex."

"Yeah."

"Don't ever question saving him."

"Why would I?"

"Lorelei."

"It's all good," said Lex. They slid the log boat onto the shore, Lex clapped the younger boy on the shoulder, and the two of them walked over to join the rest of the group.

Lorelei's hair was wet from a dip in the ocean. She was back on the raft, her knee had a fresh bandage, and she was sitting up, talking to Kala and Noah.

"Glad to see you feeling better." Lex sat down next to her.

"She's still feverish," said Noah. "Too stubborn to lie down."

"Nothing wrong with a little stubbornness." Lex smiled, but he received no smile in return. "I wanted—"

"No," said Lorelei. "Don't talk about it."

"—wanted to thank you for saving my life."

"Lex," she pleaded, "don't thank me for murder."

Lex stared at her, nausea rising in his throat. He didn't mean to upset her. He didn't know what to say next.

Kala jumped into their conversation. "Ellie would've killed him," she said to Lorelei. "If you hadn't stopped her, Ellie would've killed him. Ask the others if you don't believe me. Maybe Carlo changed. Maybe Ray. But not Ellie. No question. You did right."

"My friends," interrupted Michele, "time to get moving. Lor, no offense, but you and that bungled knee of yours aren't going to be much use the next few days. Get some rest. Sleep when you can.

"Kala," continued Michele, "be sure her fever stays in check. The rescue wore her out."

"She's still recovering from the jellboxes," said Kala. "I told you it was too soon."

Lorelei lay down without another look at any of them. Lex realized that Marko had tried to warn him: she was very much not okay.

"Lex," said Michele, holding out a hand to force him to his feet. "I told Noah the two of you are in charge of the other raft. We've altered the sail and tightened the bindings, but I'm not sure how that'll go. Here, let me show you."

He followed Michele to the stolen raft, and Noah explained what had been done. The raft looked functional, not great, but if they positioned people correctly, it should be able to get them home. They wouldn't know, of course, until they were out on the ocean, once again at the mercy of the sea.

"Michele," said Lex, "please ..." His voice faded, unsure how to put into words all he wanted to ask of her.

"Don't worry," she replied. "We'll take care of Lor. It's not only Kala who'll be looking out for her."

"She's sick."

"And sick at heart," agreed Michele. "Lor doesn't realize how tough she is, but she'll figure it out. Give her time."

"Michele?"

"Yes."

"Never mind." He raked his fingers through his hair.

"Give the girl some time, Lex. She needs space. And look around you. I need your help. We have a long way to go. Both rafts have more people on them than I'd like. I need you at your best."

"You know you can count on me."

"Yes, I do." She poked a finger at his chest. "Same for me."

He nodded. Michele and Olu. If he didn't trust them to take care of someone, who did he trust?

Meanwhile, they were counting on Lex to do his part. They were counting on him to be a leader. He turned his attention to the stolen raft and to the task of getting home.

* * *

For three days and three nights, Lex focused on coaxing the inadequate raft across the ocean. The sail was an odd shape and made entirely of the orange material; it held up better than expected. The raft itself needed an overhaul. Each afternoon, he and Noah spent an hour in the water, tightening ropes and trying to ensure the logs didn't come apart. That hour was break time for everyone else. With the sail stowed and Marko on the reinforced tiller, the raft could be kept steady enough for Lex and Noah to do the necessary work.

Michele's raft always took a break alongside them; it was the only time they tied the two together. People took turns tethering up and getting in the water. A few even changed clothes. He saw Kala help Lorelei, and he noticed them watching as he and Noah worked on the raft. But they never looked his way when the rafts were sailing.

Michele, however, checked on them regularly, the hand gestures back and forth a language of their own after three days and three nights of keeping the rafts near each other in the middle of the sea.

Before dawn of the fourth day, Michele indicated they needed to turn starboard. That made sense. Her original plan to head at a 45-degree angle had been thwarted by the wind. They'd been heading in a relatively straight line, so a 90-degree turn was to be expected.

As he and Noah readied the necessary changes in the sail, Lex thought he could see land in the distance, far off to the port side. It could be the archipelago Marko had mentioned. It could be tired eyes playing tricks in the darkness. Either way, home lay in the other direction, so they adjusted the sail and turned starboard.

Once again, the wind was at their backs. Most people slept. Lex did not. He'd had so little sleep for the past seventy-five hours, he'd almost forgotten what it was. But the wind helped, and he was awake enough to hold the rudder.

It turned out he was awake enough to notice an arm waving his direction from the other raft—Lorelei, seeking his attention for the first time in over three days. She pointed at the sky, and Lex looked up, following the direction of her finger. He saw it immediately—the loon made of stars. Watching over them, guiding them home.

His eyes were moist, but that happened in the sea spray. He looked back at her. She was still pointing at the loon. Lex waved, a gesture to show he'd seen it, a gesture that couldn't possibly show everything he wanted to say. She waved back, then lay down, her eyes either closed or fixed on the stars, he couldn't tell.

His hands focused on holding the rudder steady, but his gaze returned to the loon. When Lorelei had almost died from the jellboxes, he'd promised himself to get everything out in the open upon their return. He'd promised himself he'd tell her everything.

A few days ago, he'd promised Michele he'd give Lorelei some space.

With the wind in his face and the stars in the sky, the plan ahead seemed obvious. First, get home. Then, keep his promise to Michele. He could do that. He could give Lorelei as much space as she needed for as long as she needed. After that, he'd keep his promise to himself.

CHAPTER 45

Leigh rolled from her back to her side, bending her knees as she did so. Under a cloudless sky, the heavens stretched out before her. It was the third night of the return journey, but it was the first night she'd felt well enough to appreciate the view.

The rest of the trip, she'd been ravaged by a high fever. Her legs had been covered by hives, smaller than those from the original jellbox stings, but she suspected Kala was right: the venom from the flimsy little creatures had punished her body one last time.

Now the fever and hives were gone. Only the injury to her knee remained. And the heartache. She could still feel the heft of the rock before she'd thrown it. She could see the girl's bloody face in her nightmares. But she was working on it. One day at a time. She was healing.

That's why she'd waved at Lex and pointed to the loon. She wasn't ready to talk about what had happened, but she wanted him to know it wasn't because of him. If she'd learned anything, it was that she could heal from trauma only if she let it seep into her soul for a while. It had to stir around inside before she could talk about it with anyone else.

Lex was different. He wanted to tackle it head on. She hoped he would understand why, for her, that conversation needed to wait.

Leigh sighed. There were other things she and Lex needed to discuss that couldn't wait. Her name. Her past. She'd left her story behind for people to read. Soon that would include everyone on the two rafts. No more secrets.

And if there were to be no more secrets, then she needed to share the suspicions that had crept into her head over the past few days and nights of fever and pain and memories. Her body had been overwhelmed, but that had freed her mind—it had allowed her mind to go where it'd been unwilling to go before. The first feverish night, she'd stared out at the stars, unable to see familiar sights—no three moons, no Jellyfish, no loon constellation. Instead, she'd seen her mother's face, over and over. Her final Earth memory had replayed itself on an endless loop against the backdrop of the night sky.

That's when she'd realized her mother had known. She had known those images would be her daughter's last memory from Earth.

The more Leigh pictured it, the more she was sure. She saw the widening of her mother's eyes, the tears welling in a face that rarely cried, the tremble of her lip lasting one brief moment. Her mom's hands had reached out for an instant, and then she'd pulled them back, forced her hands to her sides, and smiled.

How had her mother known the cryosleep would erase Leigh's memories right up until that moment? A niggling suspicion had occurred, then grown as she'd had plenty of time on the raft to think.

Most colonists' final memories were good ones: Michele had skipped rocks with her grandfather, Eliana had gone surfing with her aunt, Rose had sat on the couch surrounded by family with her dog on her lap ... the list went on and on. Leigh had thought it was something about the nature of recollection that had given everyone such a poignant final memory. Now she suspected it was something else, something darker, something unbelievable.

A few colonists had final Earth memories that were awful. Lex's altercation with his father had always made her sad. Now it made her suspicious. What were the odds that such a confrontation would be Lex's final memory from Earth?

The odds were small.

Leigh's mom had talked for weeks about planting cacti and wildflowers around her dad's memorial. What were the odds they'd done it on the morning that happened to be Leigh's last memory?

The odds were small.

After all the interviews and all the notes, it'd taken a feverish night in the middle of the ocean for her to see it. To reset her assumptions. To ask the scariest of questions.

Not a single colonist knew why they'd volunteered to come here. Could that be because they had not? Could it be that their parents and guardians had volunteered them?

She couldn't say for sure. But it would explain a lot, including, perhaps, why their last memories all happened before they'd turned eighteen.

It horrified her.

She hoped, desperately, that she was wrong.

No more secrets though. When they got back, she'd share her suspicions. She'd tell Lex everything.

Her head ached from too much thinking. Her heart ached from too much worrying. She adjusted her injured leg to a more comfortable position and listened to the sound of the raft as it cut through the waves. A single cloud drifted overhead. The reassuring presence of all three moons lit up the night. The stars dotted the sky all the way down to the horizon, their reflections dripping into the sea like glistening raindrops into a giant puddle.

It was a beautiful sight in a beautiful world, a world that held a great many questions and very few answers, a world full of as much joy and as much pain as could be imagined. A world that was hers no matter how she'd gotten here.

* * *

Late in the morning, they spotted land, and by early afternoon, they pulled the rafts ashore on Sunrise Beach. Tears pricked Leigh's eyes as she stepped onto the sand. They were home.

She made a point to walk over to Lex, to have a chance to say something before he was busy with everyone and everything else.

"We made it," he said. "How do you feel?"

"Much better."

"Good."

Michele yelled to Lex, "Can you give me a hand?"

"In a minute!" he called back.

"Lex," said Leigh, and she paused.

He waited.

Noah said, "Here they come!" and people ran down the beach to greet them.

"What is it?" Lex asked her.

"It can wait."

Before he could respond, they were swallowed by a welcoming tide of friends. Stories were told, introductions made, and hugs given freely. Though her injured knee made Leigh a bit wobbly, she was able to walk on her own. One by one, she soaked up the joy of familiar faces. It'd been only thirteen days since she'd last seen them, but it felt like years.

Cliff grabbed her in a bear hug and swung her around as Eliana said, "Careful! Can't you see she's hurt?"

"Really?" Cliff put her down gently.

Leigh's knee buckled a little, and he helped steady her.

"Landed wrong on my knee a few days ago," said Leigh, "nothing major. Hey, *your* leg must be doing better!"

"Still looks terrible," said Cliff, "but much stronger."

"He hasn't needed a cane for the past four days," said Eliana.

"Fantastic!" said Leigh.

Eliana stepped closer and said, "We all read the notebook. You know, you didn't have to tell us anything."

"I think I did."

Eliana gave her a hug.

"Are people mad?" asked Leigh.

"Mad?" said Eliana. "Why would they be?"

"Really," said Cliff. "None of us thought it was a big deal."

"Cliff!" said Eliana.

"You know what I mean."

She did. And had no idea how to thank him.

"A few people wondered whether you'd want us to start calling you Leigh," said Eliana.

"No," she said, "definitely not!"

They laughed.

"All right, *Lorelei*," replied Cliff. "Whatever you say."

Leigh laughed again, relieved at Eliana and Cliff's reaction. Maybe Lex would feel the same.

CHAPTER 46

That evening, Lex paced back and forth in front of Q-cabin. It had not been the homecoming he'd hoped for.

Mere hours after their return, he'd had an unexpected and unwelcome conversation with Ping. Then, before he could decide what to do about it, Olu had come to see him, holding a notebook that revealed Lorelei was Leigh Crawford. It was a gut punch. Lex had been guarding her secret since she arrived. Turned out, she'd seen fit to tell everyone but him.

Olu had remained calm.

Lex had turned over a chair.

But Olu hadn't been hiding her secret, and Olu didn't know Ping's secret either, the one Lex had promised not to talk about until tomorrow. It was all too much.

Lex had stomped over to the plateau, wandered one place and another, circled the boulder a gazillion times, and found himself back at Homesite in front of Q-cabin. It was obvious he was too wound up to talk with Lorelei. Or was she going to start calling herself Leigh?

He knocked on the door to Q-cabin and opened it.

"Bloody hell, Lex!" said Rose. "No need to bang the door down."

"Sorry, it's been a long day."

"Exciting though," said Rose. "Your return. All our new friends."

"Where's Lorelei?"

"In the back bunkroom with Min-seo and some of the others. We're helping them settle in."

Rose had put eleven bags on the table in front of her and was making eleven piles, each with soap, a towel, clothes, a notepad, and a pen.

"Do you think you could get her for me?" asked Lex.

Rose stopped what she was doing. "Any reason you can't go back there?"

"I'd appreciate it if you'd get her."

"Can it wait till morning?"

"Not really."

She narrowed her eyes and stared critically at Lex, as if to see further into his head. "I heard about the poisonous stings, the jellboxes—"

"Yes," said Lex.

"—the injury to her knee."

"Yes."

"I heard Lor ran a bad fever most of the way back."

He nodded.

"She saved your life."

"She doesn't want to talk about that."

"I'm worried about her," said Rose.

That almost stopped him. He almost turned around.

Almost.

"Can you please get her?" he begged. "Rose, please."

They stared at each other, the shared experiences of the past year an invisible bond between them.

"Don't make me regret this," said Rose.

* * *

As Lex and Lorelei reached the plateau, he began to have second thoughts. He was tired, she was silent, and nightfall wasn't far away. Perhaps he should've taken Rose's advice and waited until morning. Olu had advised the same. He didn't want to think about what Michele would say.

"Is this where we're going?" Lorelei asked. "Your rock?" She pointed at the familiar boulder on the plateau.

"No, but it isn't much farther."

He led her to a spot in the tall grass where they could barely make out a narrow path. Strong gusts whipped the grass back and forth across the trail.

"I've never been through here," she said.

"We'll have to go single file, but it's not far."

The path headed parallel to shore for about two hundred meters, then turned inland. That part became rockier, but it was lined by tall shrubs, and the wind didn't buffet them as roughly.

When they arrived, Lex was flush with agitation—not the way he'd hoped to start the conversation. But no turning back now.

"Oh," she said, "is it Rina?"

He didn't have to answer. She read the makeshift headstone, not a headstone at all but a few words carved into a heavy piece of wood placed amid the pile of rocks that marked the grave:

Rina
first landing party
died 4-12-1
never forgotten

"Why are we here, Lex?"

"I wanted to tell you a story," he said as the wind blew harder.

"It'll be dark soon. Can you tell me the story on the way back?"

"I'd rather tell it here."

She looked at him with an expression so full of compassion that it almost changed his mind. He almost said, "Let's wait till morning." But he didn't. Instead, he said, "I want to tell you how Rina died."

For some reason, he'd expected her to protest, to say she already knew, or to brush him off. He should've known better.

"All right," she said, "but let's sit by this tree. My knee hurts."

As they sat, he felt bad he hadn't asked about her leg. Hadn't even considered it when marching her up here. Well, too late now.

She pulled a glow from her pocket and set it on the ground. It was already giving off light. "You seem upset." She reached for his hands. "Tell me what's going on."

If he was going to be angry at her for her secrets, he didn't deserve to keep any of his own. Lex held her hands and took a deep breath.

"We don't know why Rina died and everyone else survived," he said. "Part of why we don't know is … no one was with her. She was alone. No one talks about that because they don't want to blame me. But I was the one on duty that night, and I fell asleep.

"We had five in Q-cabin at the time, and everyone seemed okay. Mia, Peigi, and Declan were recovering. Marko and Rina were running fevers, but nothing terrible. When I woke up to check on them, Marko was fine, and …"

"Rina had died."

"Yes."

"Which was not your fault."

"Did she cry out?" said Lex, the words pouring out of him. "Did she ask for help? Did I not hear her? I like to think she went to sleep, and that was it—she didn't wake up. But I'll never know. I will never ever know." He stopped talking because his voice was shaking, filled with emotion from saying aloud the words he'd repeated in his head so many times.

Lorelei didn't respond right away. She looked again at the gravesite, then back at Lex. When she finally spoke, it wasn't what he expected.

"How does Olu fit in the story?"

"What do you mean?" said Lex.

"Why does he feel responsible?"

"He thinks we should've had more than one person on duty and someone awake at all times."

"Ah."

As Lex watched her stare once again at the grave, he could guess she was cataloguing all the times similar tasks had been done that way—always two on duty, always someone awake.

"And after that, you got sick yourself," she said.

"I was too sick to help bury her." Such a simple sentence for something so complex.

"Did you carve the marker?" Lorelei asked.

"Marko."

"Lex, why are you telling me this? Don't get me wrong, I'm glad you brought me here. Glad you told me. But why tonight?"

"Because ... I don't want to hide anything from you. Because ..."

"What?"

"I'm tired of secrets."

She grasped his hands more tightly but did not speak. Twilight was upon them, and the glow burned brighter.

"I promised myself I'd tell you," said Lex. "I wanted all this to mean something, that being here on Marjol would mean something. But I'm not sure anymore. Rina's dead, and no one even knows. No one on Earth cares or ever cared about any of us, or they wouldn't have sent us here, but I thought ..." Words were failing him. In his mind, it was all connected, but he couldn't explain.

"Lex," she said, "we can't worry about the people on Earth. They stopped worrying about us a long time ago."

"Ping told you," he gasped.

"Told me what?"

"About the letters."

"What letters?" She let go of his hands to prop herself more firmly against the tree.

He moved next to her. The wind blew harder, and nighttime drew nearer, but he was going to sit under this tree for as long as it took to have this conversation.

"What letters?" she repeated.

"Ping didn't tell you?"

"Tell me what?"

So she didn't know. He reached out to hold her hands again, but she kept them in her lap and repeated, "Tell me what?"

He hoped Ping would forgive him.

Lex looked her in the eyes and said, "We did not volunteer to come here."

She leaned her head back against the tree. "Damn, I was afraid of that."

"You were afraid of that? You never mentioned it."

"I put it together on our journey home." She shrugged her shoulders. Shrugged! Whatever reaction he'd been expecting, this was not it. "What letters?" she asked. "What did Ping tell you?"

"He told me our parents volunteered us to be colonists. We didn't sign up. There's no big memory loss, not from the cryosleep, not like that." Lex was trying to keep his voice calm, but it wasn't working. "They set us up, Lorelei. Our parents. Set. Us. Up.

"My dad, he signed me up to leave Earth, allowed people into my grandparents' home, where they grabbed me and jabbed me with a needle that made me forget what had happened. Then they stuffed me in cryosleep and shipped me off."

"My mom did the same."

He nodded, too upset to speak but fortunately too angry to cry.

"How does Ping know this?" she asked.

"He hacked the database. Sixth day on the planet. He and Jack. Found info we weren't supposed to get until all the landing parties arrived. There was a letter for each of us."

"From our parents?"

"Yes."

"Did they say why ... " Her voice cracked. "Why they sent us away?"

"Jack's grandfather feared he'd starve; Ping's parents talked about sending him to a life away from poverty and war. But he doesn't know if there's a common reason in most of the letters. He and Jack read their own, then scanned a handful of others. Their shift ended, and they told no one what they'd found ... figured they'd learn more the next day. But that night, the techs stopped working."

"And have been broken ever since."

"Yes."

"Coincidence?"

"Maybe. Maybe not. How would we know?"

She stretched her injured leg out in front of her, then pulled both legs up and wrapped her arms around them. The wind gusted her hair around her face. For the first time since they'd met, Lex could see how fragile she was. "So," said Lorelei, "we'll never know why our parents shipped us off."

"No."

"I wondered why you wanted to talk to me."

"That's not why," he said, incredulous. Anger bubbled inside him, threatening to boil over. He wanted to shout at her, but he didn't want to shout at her. And he didn't want to shout in Rina's graveyard.

Lex stood up, trying to expend some energy by moving.

"Then why?" she asked. "Why did you bring me here?"

"You spent all afternoon avoiding me," he said. "You walked up here without saying a word." He paused, trying not to erupt in a geyser of angry words.

She looked down at her hands, not even having the decency to look him in the eyes. His anger exploded.

"How're you so calm?!" he said. "All your emotions—you hold them in. Would it kill you to let 'em out a little? You suspected our parents dumped us here, and you didn't think to mention it? You didn't think I'd want to know? I'm hiding nothing from you. Nothing! And you've never even told me your real name!"

"I wrote it down." She finally looked at him. "I wanted you to read it."

"How about telling me face-to-face?" demanded Lex.

"I never told anyone face-to-face."

"You're a coward!"

"And a hypocrite," she said. "I'd do it differently if I could go back and do it again."

He raked his hands through his hair. Life was one chance. There were no do-overs, and she knew it.

"But Lex," she said, "I can do better. Starting right now. I'll tell you anything you want to know. Ask me any question. I'll answer it. Anything. You can ask me hundreds and hundreds. I promise I'll answer them. I'll sit here all night if you want, right here in this graveyard, and I'll answer any questions you have. Anything, if it will help you forgive me."

He stopped moving and stood directly in front of her.

"I'm sorry!" she pleaded.

"It's too late."

"Too late for what?"

He didn't respond because he didn't have an answer. He didn't even know why he'd said it. Lorelei stood up. Even in his anger, Lex noticed she used the tree for support.

"Are you all right?" he asked.

"Lex, I was afraid to tell you."

"You were afraid to trust me," he clarified.

"No," she shook her head. "No."

He started to pace again, but the wind was strong. He had to stand right next to her to ensure she could hear him. "You *don't* trust me," he said. "I just told you our parents shipped us away to another solar system without asking us if we wanted to go, and you ... you shrugged. You're not telling me anything! I've told you things I've never told anyone. Not anyone. And yet you made sure everyone in the colony knew your whole life story before I did. You didn't trust me not to care about your past. You didn't trust me to understand your choices." He moved half a step closer; they were centimeters from each other. He lowered his voice because he was close enough not to have to shout over the wind. "The funny thing," he said, "is that I already knew."

"Knew?"

"Knew you were Leigh Crawford. The year I lived with my mom and my aunt, the year I didn't live in Minnesota, guess where I was? Texas. Your family was in the news. Hell, your family was the news. All my friends had your photos."

Her surprise was palpable. She opened her mouth as if to speak, then closed it. He was still simmering with anger, but as he watched her struggle to find some words, he found himself irrationally longing to kiss her. He resisted.

"You never told me," she said.

"I wanted you to trust me. I wanted you to tell me yourself. But you don't want to tell me anything. You feel guilty about saving my life—"

"Not about saving your life," she said, "about killing that girl. That girl who was trying to survive, that girl who could've been me if I'd landed on Terence's island instead of here."

"You could never be that girl."

"You don't know that!"

"I do. You've tried to hide yourself from me, but I know you anyway."

"I'm sorry." She swiped at a few tears. "I've just … I've been so afraid."

She looked down.

His body pulsed with enough energy to hurl a boulder, but he channeled it into one small gentle movement: he put a hand under her chin and brought her face up to look at him.

"I'm afraid too," said Lex. "Don't you get it? We're all afraid. Every day."

Rose and Marko burst into the clearing. Marko was carrying a lantern and had a bag looped over his back. Rose was carrying only rage.

"You bloody idiots!" she yelled.

"Bad storm coming," said Marko.

Lex looked at the sky. Darkness had fallen, and it was cloudy, so there wasn't much to see. But he'd rarely felt wind gusts this strong, and he could hear the ocean pounding in the distance.

Marko turned to Lorelei. "Can you run?"

"More or less," she said, hastily wiping her eyes. "But don't wait for me. I'll meet you at Homesite."

"Not Homesite," said Marko, "the cavern."

"That bad?" asked Lex.

"Quit talking," said Rose, "and start running."

They took off in single file. Marko set a moderate pace, likely one he judged manageable for a tough but exhausted girl with an injured knee. Rose ran behind him, pushing Marko a little faster and regularly glancing over her shoulder at Lorelei, who was third in line.

Lex came last, thankful to be hidden from the others. He felt as if his emotions were flitting across his skin, laid bare for all to see. Anger, fear, loss. Love, hope, forgiveness. All jumbled together in one big mess.

A monstrous clap of thunder rang out, and Lex tucked his emotions back inside. Once again, it was time to focus on survival.

CHAPTER 47

Keeping a steady pace, the four of them ran straight through Homesite, with Rose adamant they not stop for anything. The wind roared, and the air smelled like rain.

Leigh's knee buckled twice. The first time, she caught herself. The second time, she fell.

Lex helped her up.

She kept running.

They crested the ridge and headed downhill toward Sunrise Beach. A flash of lightning lit the sky. Leigh gasped. The storm was a monster, its clouds darker than the night. A second bolt revealed a waterspout— no, two waterspouts on the front edge of the storm. Who knew how many more were hidden in the recesses of the clouds?

She stumbled, kept running, and stopped looking at the storm. Rain began, lightly at first, then pelting their skin. When they reached the beach, Marko picked up the pace. Adrenaline helped Leigh keep going, but the sand was tough on her injured knee. Marko and Rose drew farther away, then slowed and waited for her to catch up.

Leigh glanced behind her. Lex was right there.

Upon reaching the rocky area, the four of them waded up to their waists, the shallow water teaming with whitecaps. Marko slowed and waded hand in hand with Rose, her newfound swimming skills not enough to give her confidence in the choppy waves. They exited the water, waited for Leigh and Lex to do the same, then resumed running.

"Almost there!" Rose called over her shoulder, and Leigh told herself the worst was over.

She was wrong.

Halfway to the cave's entrance, her knee gave out, and she went down hard.

"You got this," said Lex, picking her up from the wet sand. Pain shot through her leg. She tried to stand but collapsed back onto the ground.

Rose and Marko turned.

Lex waved them on ahead. The rain poured harder as he bent down to feel her swollen knee, then helped her stand, more slowly this time.

She put some weight on the injured leg; her knee throbbed, but her leg held steady. Wind roared off the sea and threatened to topple her. Lightning crackled and lit up the waves.

Lex kept one hand on her arm. For the first time since Rose had commanded them to run, Leigh looked at his face. He was staring at the storm, his jaw set in grim realization, but as he turned toward her, his eyes flashed with other emotions—hope, determination. She felt herself standing taller.

"I can carry you," said Lex, "or I can let you run." He stood there waiting, giving her the choice. There were so many reasons she loved him. Why hadn't she told him *that* back at Rina's grave?

A clap of thunder reverberated nearby.

"Let's go," she said and took off down the beach the best she could. Lex was exhausted. She would not make him carry her unless there was no other choice.

She ran.

With each staggered stride, she felt pain pierce her leg, but she could do it. Lex stayed nearby, neither racing ahead nor shoving her from behind.

She ran harder.

As they drew near, she could see Marko and Rose waiting at the cave's entrance, waving to be sure they didn't miss it. She sensed the colonists stuffed into the cavern—her colony, her people.

"Up," said Lex.

They climbed the rocks and followed Marko and Rose through the short entry passage and into the giant cavern. As Lex stepped into the cavern behind her, Leigh grabbed his arm.

"Thanks," she gasped.

Before he could reply, Olu turned him away from her.

"Don't start," she heard Lex say.

"Glad you made it," said Olu.

"Come on," Rose said to Leigh, "we're over this way."

***

In a short amount of time, Leigh was dry and sitting on a blanket. Eliana rewrapped her knee, João brought her a canteen, and Cliff unearthed a pair of acetaminophen tablets.

Lanterns and glows were here and there on the floor and in the rocky crags, so a soft light permeated the cavern. It felt smaller with seventy people in it, but they had plenty of room.

Ada, Olu, and Lex stood near the entrance. The rest of the colonists had sorted themselves based on work groups. Leigh sat on one side of the cave, surrounded by the rest of Maps. The other groups ran together, loosely organized along the opposite wall. Those they'd rescued were near the front, by the leaders. Boats was in the back. Between them and the newcomers sat everyone from Food.

Leigh needed to thank Rose and Marko; she needed to talk to Lex. Instead, she sat there—her leg throbbing—and watched the crowd. Dhruv had handed Marko some fresh clothes, and now a dry Marko was sitting where Food and Boats overlapped. He stood up when Lex walked over to talk to him.

No one had given dry clothes to Lex. He stripped off his wet shirt and stood in soaking wet pants, hair dripping down his bare back. Leigh chose not to watch the boys' conversation.

She wondered if Marko knew about the letters.

Looking toward the rear of the cavern, she hoped to catch Michele's eye, but her friend was busy. She scanned back along the wall, found Zalfaa, and waved hello. In return, Zalfaa held up a bag, reached in, and pulled out two items—Leigh's baseball cap and her handkerchief.

Leigh almost burst into tears. Her chest heaved, but the last thing this night needed was more drama. She took a deep breath and put her hand over her heart, trying to convey gratitude across the distance. Zalfaa replied with a nod and a smile, then tucked the treasured belongings back in the bag.

Leigh hoped someone had done the same for Lex.

She lay down and repositioned her sore leg. As the winds outside roared louder, the colonists quieted. People settled into spots and stayed there; conversation grew sparse.

When the storm raged at its wildest, no one in the cavern made a sound. The surf pounded in loud, irregular beats, and the wind blasted against the rocks. She refused to think about what might have happened if they'd delayed their return one more day, if they'd been on the rafts when the storm hit.

If.

Life was full of *ifs*.

She listened to the wind and tried not to think.

Eventually, the worst of the storm was over. Rain and wind could be heard, but at more normal decibels. The colonists turned off the lanterns. Scattered glows kept full darkness at bay. The bulk of the colony tried to sleep.

At the front of the cavern, Ada lay down next to the newcomers. Only two shapes sat upright: Olu and Lex. Leigh watched them, but neither of the boys looked her way. She gave up, curled into her blanket, and closed her eyes.

She'd wasted so much time worrying, so much energy hiding. The only person who'd cared about her life as Leigh Crawford was the one person who'd known it all along. And the only reason he cared was because she'd kept it a secret.

Of course, Lex had kept his own secrets. But it'd be foolish to hold that against him.

She rolled over, tucked a sweatshirt under her head, and pulled the blanket up to her chin. Sleep came more quickly than she expected.

* * *

Leigh awakened with a start, heart racing as if from a bad dream, though she didn't remember having one. She stared up into the darkness of the roof of the cavern. Her hands and feet were cold.

She had killed that girl. Had picked up a rock and aimed it right at her head. Her hand hurt with the memory. She stopped staring at the darkness above her and rolled onto her stomach.

Light from the glows seeped from crevices in the walls and gaps between sleeping people. After everything that had happened, the colony slept peacefully on the cold, hard rock—some physically next to each other for warmth or comfort, others wrapped tightly in their own blankets.

Her mom had *sent* her here, without asking. They'd all been abandoned, shipped off into the unknown. With almost nothing.

Nothing except each other.

Olu had been right. When they'd rescued the prisoners, they'd made a choice about what type of society they wanted to be. But Olu had been wrong too. He'd been wrong about when that choice had happened.

It'd been made when twenty teenagers landed on the island, woke up every morning, and made plans together—choosing to look out for one another after being marooned ten light-years from home. Each decisive moment since then had been shaped by those initial weeks, reinforced by shared joys and shared tragedies alike.

How had the first few weeks gone on Terence's island? Was it the first days on the planet that had shaped his colony so differently? By what chance had Leigh landed among people who would treat her like family? By what chance had others not been so lucky?

She looked toward the cave's entrance at those they'd rescued. Carlo and Ray were in the mix of sleeping bodies. They'd lived a different kind of nightmare, taken a different kind of risk. Kala was on the edge of the group, away from the two former guards, still adjusting to that reality.

Sitting next to her was Ada. Wide awake, she occupied the spot Olu had held earlier. Lex's spot was empty. Only one other soul in the whole cavern was awake: Marko. He sat huddled in a blanket. A glow lay nestled in a nearby crevice, close enough that she could see his face. She waved at him, and he nodded her direction. She found herself near tears at the silent exchange.

Leigh shed her blanket. She looked for her hat and remembered Zalfaa had it. She searched for her shoes but found only one. Unwilling to disturb those sleeping nearby, Leigh gave up, ran her fingers through her hair, and tied it in a knot. She stepped carefully with her bare feet and headed toward the front of the cavern.

When she got there, Ada gave her a hug. Leigh's eyes teared up again. Unbelievable. Lex had accused her of holding in emotions. This morning, she could use a little holding in.

"You need a break?" Leigh whispered to Ada.

"No," she said. "I'm good. Want some fresh air? Rain's stopped. Olu and Noah are outside if you want to join them."

"Thanks."

"Lorelei?"

"Yes."

"You saved a lot of lives."

She knew Ada meant well. She knew the math seemed simple: one cruel person had lost her life, eleven others had been saved. And Lex was alive. But life was rarely simple. Could they have rescued Ping without taking a life? Could she have saved Lex without a killing blow? Were there other ways the story could have had a happy ending?

Those questions could never be answered. She would have to find a way to live with the uncertainty.

As Olu had said, there were always uncertainties.

"We can talk about it," said Ada, "when you're ready."

"I'd like that," said Leigh, surprised to find she meant it. She wiped her eyes, closer to tears than ever, and headed outside.

The warm night air was a welcome change from the damp chill of the cavern. The fresh, salty breeze kissed her face, and she inhaled the familiar scents of sand and water. The wind gusted in brief spurts, and the waves were rough. But the clouds were gone, and Aegir had already disappeared. Morning couldn't be too far off.

A little way down the coast, Olu and Noah sat on a ledge. Leigh's sore knee compelled her to choose the easier path, even though it was longer—to climb down the rocks, walk along the beach, then up to where the boys sat.

The storm had thrown seaweed, driftwood, and a few boulders up on the sand. Stepping around the debris, her feet made footprints, the trajectory of those sand grains slightly altered forever, each of her steps making a tiny impact.

She climbed the slippery rocks up to the two boys. "Good morning!" she called.

"Morning," said Olu, scooting over to make room.

"You're up early," said Noah.

"You're up late," she replied.

"No worries. Napping is an Aussie specialty."

"According to you," said Leigh, "everything is an Aussie specialty."

"Everything worthwhile."

She laughed. Noah's goofy bravado and Olu's quiet presence were reassuring. Things had changed—they always did—but some things remained the same.

The three of them slipped into easy conversation, speculating about whether Homesite might have been damaged or destroyed. They'd go back and find out when all seventy of them could face the news together, whatever that news may be.

Questions of what lay in the future were left alone. Conversation focused on immediate concerns, such as the best spot for a permanent lookout and how to care for the new arrivals, especially the injured Ping and the two pregnant girls, Min-seo and Natalya.

The stars began to fade. A soft glow ebbed along the horizon. No sign yet of Rán, but her arrival was imminent.

"Red sky rising," said Olu. "Lorelei, you good to stand watch while we get everyone organized?"

"Sure."

"Sorry to desert you," said Noah. "Won't be long."

"No worries," she replied.

Noah and Olu retraced her footsteps down to the beach, across the sand, and up the rocks. When they entered the cavern, Leigh was left alone—truly alone—for the first time since her second night on

Marjol. The night her wanderings had led to a pair of boys leaning against a boulder.

What a long time ago that was.

She peered at the beginnings of sunrise and was reminded of another sunrise in front of a smaller cave farther up the coast. That morning, three months ago, she'd looked at the stars and been overwhelmed by how far away from home she was. Now she felt how far away the stars were because her home was here.

Sunrise erupted in full. She closed her eyes and let the warmth of first morning light envelop her. In her mind's eye, Leigh could see herself on the ledge, awash in the fiery rays of sunrise on this watery planet, spinning around a glorious orange star, in the midst of the Milky Way in a universe of stars upon stars.

When she reopened her eyes, the sight of three moons in the clear morning sky was before her, but something in the periphery drew her attention—someone stepping out of the cavern.

Lex.

He did not descend to the beach, but instead picked his way across the rocks to reach her. She watched as he drew near, forcing herself to sit and wait. Perhaps there would always be moments on this planet when she felt compelled to hold her breath.

He was wearing fresh, dry clothes, though the pants were a size too big and the shirt a size too small. The wind blew his unkempt hair in all directions. He pulled it back, containing most of it with a band like Marko used. A few loose strands blew across his face.

"Can I sit?" he asked.

Leigh stood up. "You just missed sunrise."

"Didn't come out here for sunrise."

They looked at each other, a safe distance between them. Lex's face was shadowed, backlit by the early morning light. Judging from the puffiness around his eyes, he'd not been awake long.

"How's your knee?" he asked.

"Better, thanks."

"I had a whole speech planned."

"No. We're too tired—"

"Listen. Please."

She took a step toward him and waited.

"I have something for you." He reached into the pocket of his pants and pulled out a woven cord. Tied in the middle of it was a small rock, darker than those that surrounded them—deep black with a streak of shiny blue through the middle. "Olu told me about your necklace. The one your dad made for you."

She gasped, though it sounded more like a sob.

"I found this rock up the coast, in the cave, not long after you and Michele swam out of sight. Brought it back with me, just ... well, just because." He shrugged. "And then, Olu told me about your necklace, and I knew ... I knew why I'd kept the rock."

He held out the homemade necklace, one hand on either end of the cord. "Marko helped me hollow the rock. It's tied on tight. It won't come off."

Her eyes welled with tears.

"Want to wear it?" he asked.

She closed the remaining distance between them and bent her head so he could tie the cord around her neck. She felt his fingers brush her hairline as he fastened the two ends together.

"You're all set," said Lex.

She lifted her head, and the weight of the rock rested against her skin.

Leigh reached up and clutched it, feeling the contours of the small rock dig into her hand. After a moment, she let go, and the rock once again settled against her chest, its presence a reminder of all she'd lost. And all she'd gained.

She was afraid to speak.

"I had this whole speech," said Lex. "I spun it around in my head half the night. All the things that might happen, all the things we don't know. But this morning, I realized most of it doesn't matter ... whether Homesite has been destroyed or is perfectly fine, whether Terence comes after us or leaves us alone, how we got here, why we got here.

"When it comes to you and me, none of that matters." He paused, glancing at the ocean. "Yesterday, you offered to answer however many questions I had, and ... to be fair, yesterday, I had a lot." He smiled hesitantly. "But now ... well, the truth is ... I have only one."

They stood there, looking at each other in the morning sunshine. In a world of uncertainties, Leigh knew one sure thing: she would answer any question he asked.

"Months ago," said Lex, "you made me a promise. My question is … do you still want to keep it?"

Tears ran down her cheeks. *This* was his question?

"I promise," he said, "that I will never, ever abandon you. No matter what. Do you feel the same? Because if you do, all the rest doesn't matter."

"Oh yes," she whispered, "I promise."

He kissed her.

They stood on a rocky ledge of a small island over ten light-years away from where they'd been born. Two tiny specs in an enormous universe.

She held on to Lex as if nothing else in the universe existed. He kissed her; she kissed him. And he was right. All the rest didn't matter.

ACKNOWLEDGMENTS

Thank you to my husband, Allan, who's supported my writing efforts even when I questioned them myself. Thank you to our sons, Austin and Luke, whose encouragement and insight kept me going throughout the process. There are no words to adequately say thanks. Without the three of you, this book would literally not exist. Thanks for brainstorming with me about anything and everything—from astrophysics to survival skills—and for always being there when I need you most.

I was lucky to grow up in a family of readers. My parents, Marty and Don, are no longer here, but their influence shows throughout these pages. Thank you, Mom and Dad, and to my brother, Christopher, for sharing your love of stories, watching the original *Star Trek* with me, and embracing chaotic dinnertime conversations over many years. The desire to tell a story germinates somewhere; for me, it was around that small round table in our dining room.

Thank you to Mindy Kuhn and the team at Warren Publishing, including Amy Ashby and Melissa Long, for your belief in this story, your patience with my many questions, and your talents in turning my manuscript into a "real book." Thank you to Lacey Cope for helping me figure out the marketing side of publishing while still embracing the creative aspect.

Thank you to my editors: Melisa Graham, who helped me frame the parameters of this world in ways easier to understand; and Gail Marlene Schwartz, who understood my teenage characters and helped me find better ways to tell their story.

The publishing industry is full of dedicated people who work long hours. Thank you to all who run contests and offer feedback to first-time writers. A special thank you to these six individuals: editors Julia A. Weber and Michelle Rascon; agents Peter Knapp and John M. Cusick; and authors Nancy Werlin and Laurie Dennison. Each of you offered feedback that was instrumental in guiding me toward needed revisions.

Thank you to the following people who answered my questions on a variety of topics: Yvette Cendes (astronomy); Martha Edwards (medicine); Lauren Keenan and Lilly Brice (Māori language and culture); Megan Pollitt (chemistry); Charlie Miracle, Kim Marinus, and Jaeho Youn (Korean language and writing). Your expertise helped shape this novel, and the responsibility for any errors is my own.

Thank you to my first alpha reader, Austin, and my second alpha reader, Luke. Common wisdom says not to give drafts to family members if you're seeking useful critique. Thanks always, Austin and Luke, for being uncommon.

Thank you to my beta readers Martha Edwards, David Miller, Jean Stillman, and Maggie Towne. As a YA author, I was fortunate to receive feedback from people who not only know the intricacies of storytelling but also have decades of experience working with teenagers. Your insights were invaluable.

Thank you to Sarah Shartzer and Lisa Stringfellow for help with technology, with the "What now?" questions about having a book out in the world, and with a myriad of odds and ends in the past, present, and (I'm sure!) future.

Thank you to all my former eighth-grade, tenth-grade, and twelfth-grade students. You introduced me to new authors, new books, and new ways of thinking about literature. Teaching you was fun!

An extra shoutout to the seniors who took my Origins of Science Fiction elective; those lively discussions encouraged me to consider writing some science fiction of my own. And thank you to my former student and advisee, Lilly Brice, whose college honors thesis on Māori healing practices helped inspire the character of Michele.

Thank you to the faculty and staff at Kentucky Country Day School, who supported numerous collaborative projects during the years I taught there. One such project was a middle school book club. As part of that, I read a novel with a group of sixth-grade girls. The students expressed repeated dismay at a character's failure to question the world she lived in. Those girls were unafraid to ask the big questions, and they wanted a character who did the same. Many years later, when I began writing Leigh's story, that character trait was my starting point.

Speaking of starting points … I find myself back at the beginning. Thank you again to Allan, Austin, and Luke. This book is about adventures, and our family is my favorite adventure of all. Thanks for being you.